DAY·OF·
ATONEMENT

DAY·OF· ATONEMENT

A Novel of the Maccabean Revolt

David A. deSilva

Day of Atonement: A Novel of the Maccabean Revolt
© 2015 by David A. deSilva

Published by Kregel Publications, a division of Kregel, Inc., 2450 Oak Industrial Dr. NE, Grand Rapids, MI 49505.

Map (p. 8) adapted from Bill T. Arnold and Richard S. Hess, eds., *Ancient Israel's History: An Introduction to Issues and Sources*, Baker Academic, a division of Baker Publishing Group, 2014. Used by permission.

Quotations of Old Testament Scripture have been adapted by the author from existing English translations.

Library of Congress Cataloging-in-Publication Data
DeSilva, David Arthur
  Day of atonement : a novel of the Maccabean revolt / David A. deSilva.
  pages ; cm
1. Judas, Maccabeus, -161 B.C.—Fiction. 2. Jews—History—586 B.C.-70 A.D.—Fiction. 3. Bible. Old Testament—History of Biblical events—Fiction. 4. Maccabees—Fiction. 5. Seleucids—Fiction. 6. Jewish fiction. I. Title.
PS3604.E75755D39   2015   813'.6--dc23   2015000416

ISBN 978-0-8254-2471-7

Printed in the United States of America

15 16 17 18 19 20 21 22 23 24 / 7 6 5 4 3 2 1

To Donna Jean,
in honor of our twenty-fifth wedding anniversary

CONTENTS

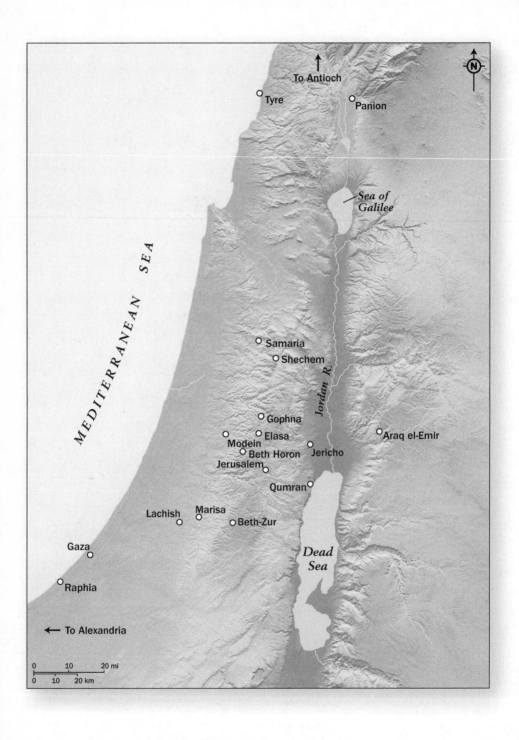

AUTHOR'S·NOTE

Judah had lived under foreign domination since Nebuchadnezzar's initial conquest in 597 BCE, made more real for Judah's inhabitants by the king's return in 587 to destroy Jerusalem and its Temple. Throughout this period of domination, first by Babylon and then by Persia, Jews lived in tension. On the one hand, assimilation to their overlords' way of life promised greater acceptance, security, and even prosperity within their new political realities. On the other hand, commitment to remain true to their ancestral way of life promised the preservation of their identity as the people of Israel's God and the enjoyment of that relationship.

That tension was never greater than after Alexander the Great conquered the Persian empire in 331 BCE, uniting the people as far west as Macedonia, as far south as Egypt, and as far east as the edge of India under his rule. Alexander was unlike previous conquerors and emperors, actively seeking to blend local elites into the Greek and Macedonian ruling class, inviting the conquered to become partners with the conquerors. After his death in 323 BCE, his empire was divided among his generals, Ptolemy taking control of Egypt and Palestine, Seleucus eventually taking Syria and Babylonia, others seizing Greece, Macedonia, and Asia Minor. While each regularly sought to expand his territory at the other's expense, they nevertheless continued Alexander's policies of extending not only Greek domination, but also Greek language, Greek learning, Greek culture, and

9

Greek citizenship. The dominated elites often welcomed the chance to raise their status by becoming partners with the dominators.

Thus "some renegades went out even from Israel and led many astray, saying, 'Let us make a covenant with the Gentiles around us, for since we set ourselves apart from them many evils have overtaken us'" (1 Macc 1:11) . . .

BOOK · 1

The High Priest

In the 137th year of the kingdom of the Greeks (175 BCE) . . .

1

The first glow of dawn appeared over the horizon. In an hour it would be beautiful, an ocean of fire setting the thin veils of clouds ablaze. But for now, it was still that pale green that appeared almost sickly, especially to the man who had already been staring at the sky for most of an hour. Jason slouched in a large alabaster chair upon the terrace outside his bedchamber. A cushion below him took off the chill of the stone seat. A wool blanket made of the finest weave shielded him from the bite of the morning air. He had seen far too many sunrises of late. How long had it been since the sun last woke him up rather than the reverse?

Jason pulled the blanket up closer around his neck. If he could not have the enjoyment of sleep, the gift of God that made the poor and the rich equal, he took some measure of satisfaction in that he could enjoy awake what few indeed in all of Judea would ever experience. He glanced briefly at the slender marble pillars and the decorative work that made up the railing before him, luminescent in the light of the moon that was still strong above him. Beyond, the Kidron Valley that separated him from the Holy City was dark, like a black sea, on the far shore of which he could see the outline of the city walls and, above them, the Temple Mount itself. No one else in Jerusalem awakened to such a view, the darkness still hovering over the city like a curtain about to rise upon a play that was performed for him, and him alone.

The poor laborers sleep soundly upon their beds, but the rich lie awake anxious for their riches. Jason recalled the face of his old teacher who had first recited to him the sayings of the wise. But it was not anxiety for his wealth that drove

Jason from his bed for his nightly vigil. Money had never been a cause for worry among his family. Other anxieties, other aspirations, other—endless—details to be worked out seized him, exiling him from his bed at that point in the night when most were simply turning over to go back to sleep.

Jason breathed in, closed his eyes, and let himself feel what it was to be the brother of the high priest, the second son of Simon the Just, the most sought-after associate in all Jerusalem. Indeed, his political clout far outstripped that of his brother. Honiah enjoyed the authority of the high priesthood, and all important decisions needed his approval. But it was Jason who was shaping the future of Jerusalem and, with it, all Judea. He breathed in again, imagining that he could feel the wave of destiny impelling him forward toward his vision as he exhaled.

Was this not better than sleep?

Dark crimson fires began to light the sky behind him. The edges of the clouds over the city began to glow orange like scraps of papyrus ignited in the hearth. Any lingering resentment Jason entertained against Morpheus for eluding him began to burn away as well. For his refreshment, his energy for the day ahead, came from this part of the dawn. It was the reflection in nature of what he was striving to bring about in the civil realm. He drank it in, storing its energy for the sake of releasing it into Jerusalem, continuing to drive his city forward out of night into a new day.

The sky grew brighter as crimson heated to orange and spread farther across the city beneath, pushing back the dusky grays. Jason lowered his blanket in anticipation of the warming day, revealing a sleeved tunic sewn in the Greek fashion, its squared neckline enhanced with scarlet embroidery. He had done what he could to remake his own image after the noble Greeks that he frequently encountered, keeping his tight-curled hair cut short and his face clean-shaven, but his pure Semitic features still sat uncomfortably within that stylish Greek frame.

He turned his eyes back toward the city, fixing his eyes upon the Temple Mount, now ablaze with orange-yellow light. Jason smiled with pride and satisfaction at the sight. Many residents of Jerusalem would do the same, but he had his own private reasons. His father had dedicated himself to the expansion and fortification of the Temple during his long term as high priest. Jason had himself inherited Simon's zeal and—even Honiah would have to admit—gift for architecture, and had continued to direct the public building projects in and around the Temple. But unlike Simon or Honiah, Jason invested in the Temple as a means and not an end. He looked to the spaces just west of the southern part of the Temple enclosure, a site that had been at the center of his vision for four years now.

After endless examination of the landscape of the city from every vantage point—from his villa's terrace, the upper floors of the high priest's palace, the walkways atop the fortified walls surrounding the city, and the Temple porticoes themselves—Jason had settled on that location some time ago. It was the most prominent location that would also require the least displacement of existing public works and private citizens. In his mind's eye, he saw the space cleared of its existing structures and, rising in their place, the central organs of the new Jerusalem. He saw the *lyceum*, the center for learning, and the *gymnasium*, with its sprawling courtyard for athletic events, standing proudly alongside the elevated path leading up to the Temple from the west. In the shadow of the Temple would sit the renovated *bouleuterion*, the council chamber where all those educated in the finer arts of rhetoric and civics would deliberate about the future of the reborn city. The new forum would be made complete with the erection of a theater, built in the Greek way, through which the rivers of Greek literary and musical culture would pour into the mainstream of Jerusalem's civic life. The magnificent Temple, renowned in its own right, would become the Acropolis above Jason's own incarnation of Athens. He tried each morning to imagine anew how they would look juxtaposed, hoping they would sit together more comfortably than his own features.

The rustling of the draperies that separated the bedroom from the terrace and the elements interrupted his reverie. He felt the warm touch of his wife's hand upon his shoulder. Looking over his right shoulder to greet her, he saw only the disk of the sun, now cleared of the horizon, the only source of morning warmth since his wife had died giving birth to his stillborn son two seasons ago. *How the early morning hours, how the sleepless nights play tricks on the senses!* But he was married now to his vision and about to give birth to a new Jerusalem, gaining a memory for himself that would outlast generations of sons.

The sun's separation from the horizon was the appointed time for his servants to begin their daily attendance upon him. A young woman entered with a serving tray bearing a round loaf of wheat bread, several kinds of fruit, and a flask of wine. She set the tray on the table beside Jason and unfolded a linen cloth that she draped over the front of his tunic. After pouring the wine, she took his blanket and went back inside the bedroom to lay out his clothes while a male servant entered with a basin of water.

"Nothing too ornate today, Niobe. I'm going to see my brother." *Honiah doesn't understand how to be rich and unashamed of the fact.* Steam escaped from the bread as Jason broke off a piece and began to eat. *No need to antagonize him. Not today, at least.* He alternately took a mouthful of fruit and a drink of wine—new wine, from his own vineyards, still sweet and barely fermented, just enough to be interesting. Jason had spent the third and fourth watches of the night turning around in his mind all the possible permutations of his conversation with Honiah, down to the details of what not to wear. The bulk of that time, however, was given over to the more difficult question: what he would do if—perhaps he should just admit *when*—his brother refused to play along.

Niobe came out to the terrace again. "*Adoni*, my master's friend Agathon is in the atrium."

"Escort him here," Jason instructed her in their native Aramaic. "And bring a second cup."

A moment later, Agathon's voice greeted him in perfectly inflected, if not perfectly pronounced, Greek. "Good morning, Jason. How was your sleep?"

"Do not mock me, old friend," Jason retorted, casting a dark glare before breaking into a warm smile. A middle-aged man in a simple tunic set a chair behind Agathon just in time to anticipate the latter's descent, then retired into the house to resume setting out Jason's toiletries. "You got my message, then?" Jason inquired in somewhat better Greek.

"Yes, I did," Agathon said as Niobe placed a cup of new wine in his waiting hand. "Philostratos arrives with his party today, rather than three days hence as we anticipated. Your messenger arrived late last night."

"An hour or so after he informed me, then." *Whence this night's insomnia.*

"That's good news, isn't it, Jason? Less time to wait and worry?"

"Timing is everything, Agathon. Have you forgotten what day this is and what the delegation will be expecting?"

Agathon looked puzzled for a moment, then drew a deep breath and raised his eyebrows, signaling his comprehension.

"The delegates will be in need of refreshment tonight, not in the mood for formal business, so this part doesn't concern me." *Though Honiah's absence would be conspicuous.* "But they will be impatient to meet with the official representative of the Judean people tomorrow, especially if he is not present tonight. Honiah's lack of enthusiasm for the project would have been evident enough even without putting them off an extra day." Jason shook his head slowly. "Just one day later, and all kinds of issues could have been avoided, as if they weren't issues for anyone at all." *Timing is indeed everything.*

"Honiah might surprise us, Jason. He's not oblivious to political necessities."

"I appreciate your efforts to cheer me up, but Honiah has never surprised me. Perfect piety has made him perfectly predictable." Jason stood up, subtly signaling that the conversation was over. He forced himself to smile as he dismissed

Agathon. "Perhaps if you have leisure today, I could ask you to arrange for the entertainment at tonight's banquet and to make sure our guests are properly welcomed upon their arrival in the city?"

The recipient of so many of Jason's favors, Agathon would never refuse, whatever his plans had been. "Whatever I can do to ease your burdens today. *Chaire, phile.*"

Alone again, Jason walked forward and placed his hands firmly on the cool marble railing of his terrace, taking its strength and the strength of the vision before him into himself. He would need it to persuade Honiah. Feeling sufficiently braced, he turned and entered his house. He approached the basin of water like a priest performing some rite of preparation, his garments like a general being armed for a decisive battle that would be well fought, but impossible to win.

Eleazar rapped gently on the heavy wooden door with the head of his walking stick. The door swung open on its iron hinges to reveal a servant, still holding the flask of oil that he had been using to refill the lamps throughout the main floor of the house.

"Peace be to you, Master Eleazar," the servant said, bowing his head slightly.

"And peace to you," the priest replied. Though nearly sixty, Eleazar had lost none of his stature and very little of his strength. His gray hair flowed out from beneath a round, white linen cap, down over his broad shoulders. His beard, fanning out over his woolen tunic, bore silent witness to his age and dignity.

"Welcome once more to my master's home." The servant took a step back from the door and gestured toward the interior of the house. "May I pour water over your feet?" he asked as he knelt to untie the priest's sandals.

Eleazar smiled. "Thank you, but the fifty paces from my home have not wearied me." The aged priest stepped inside, and the servant shut the door behind him, leaving the room suddenly dark. Even without the light from the single open window beside the door, however, Eleazar could have found his way, so often had he been to this house. In fifteen steps, he successfully navigated the oak furnishings of the living room and dining room and found the small staircase that led to the upper floor and the private spaces of the house. The chatter of people, the clatter of sandals and carts upon the pavement, the occasional objections of animals being led to the Temple, none of these sounds of life rising from the street below betrayed any awareness of the quiet approach of death in the upper room.

Eleazar paused at a bedroom doorway to consider the old man who lay sleeping upon the wooden-framed bed. Layers of woolen blankets beneath him cushioned his bones. Layers above him kept his body as warm as possible, compensating for the now inadequate pumping of blood. Three pillows propped up his head and shoulders, allowing him to take water or thin broth, or to look at his guests when he was permitted periods of consciousness. Eleazar smiled to see Binyamin once again at Yehoshua ben Sira's bedside. *How unlike those who wait beside the beds of the rich, hoping for a last-minute inheritance.*

Binyamin was keeping vigil seated on a low wooden stool. His body had all the firmness of a young man still approaching his prime, but his countenance bore a gravity sufficient for a man twice his age. A year short of twenty, he had already carried the responsibilities of husband, parent, and guardian of the household for the five seasons since his father had been gathered to his fathers, leaving him with the support and care of his mother and brothers. Binyamin was absorbed in reciting psalms that he had committed to memory. He uttered the sacred songs unhurriedly, prayerfully, softly, to ease the old man's mind if he heard them, or at least to sanctify his rest if he did not.

Eleazar waited for the young man to complete the psalm before greeting him.

"Shalom, Binyamin. Has anyone been to see Rabban Yehoshua this morning?"

"Peace to you, Rabbi Eleazar. Elam ben Jacob has been here."

"A good man, a fine scribe who learned his craft from Rabban Yehoshua three decades ago. There will be others in the afternoon, after they have concluded their morning business."

"Somehow, I expected more. How many men in Jerusalem have not been indebted to his wisdom?"

"Few indeed." Though only ten years his junior, Eleazar had always been something of a student of ben Sira throughout the four decades of their acquaintance. How many times had he sought the older man's guidance in the course of his own career as a priest and a scribe? How many hours of how many days did they spend together doing the very thing that the *Shema* enjoined—talking about God's commandments when reclining and rising, when at home or walking beside the road? "Many more people are willing to pay their respects after death than as a man lay dying." *Besides, quite a few of his former students wouldn't dare face their teacher now.*

Eleazar walked past the bed to the small window and let in the morning light. For a moment he looked out at the houses that lined the opposite side of the street, with their second-story bedrooms and their rooftop porches, and then up to the Temple platform, clearly visible over the housetops across the street. Craftsmen, merchants, people from all walks of life making their way to the Temple passed by on the street below, but only the elite lived in such homes in the shadow of the Temple. *But how many still lived under its aegis?* Eleazar wondered. Many members of these households had studied under ben Sira but had since abandoned the principles of their old teacher, walking around like drunken men intoxicated by the new spirit of the Greeks.

The priest abandoned his musings and remembered Binyamin, both because he was in the room and, more importantly, because he was not a cause for such regret. "This room is a place suspended between this world and the next. A strange place to keep finding one so young, who has so much of this world left before him."

"'If you find a discerning man, visit him early; let your foot wear out his doorstep.' Isn't that what Rabban Yehoshua advised?"

"'And do not forsake him when he is old,'" Eleazar finished. Behind the proverb, Eleazar knew another reason for Binyamin's faithfulness. He had brought Binyamin to ben Sira at a vulnerable time in the young man's life, after the initial pangs of grief for his father had given way to an awareness that the loss was even deeper than those first pains intimated. Ben Sira had given Binyamin the guidance, the wisdom, the formation that Zerah, had he lived, would have given. Binyamin understood this need. He understood ben Sira's role in filling that need. And now he returned the favor at a second bedside of a second dying father with filial devotion.

"You've been a good friend to him, too, Binyamin." Eleazar looked at the young man with piercing but kind blue eyes—the color most common among the priestly families. "For years, many of his former students have been sending their own children elsewhere for their training, to the schools established by Jason. Rabban Yehoshua has watched his own influence driven back like a mist before the Greek sun god. Those who have shown interest in his wisdom have been a joy to him."

"A remnant. A faithful remnant," the old man whispered.

"Ah, you're awake, old friend, and listening in on us," Eleazar chided wryly. "And how are you today, Rabban?"

"Keep yourself in good health, Eleazar. Eternal sleep would be better than this endless sickness."

"Rabban Yehoshua," Binyamin offered, "most of my friends feel as I do about the ways of our ancestors. Most of the families who frequent our shop or who live in the streets around us walk in line with the wisdom of Torah. What you have taught me has often been the subject of our conversation."

"How different your estimation of my teachings from the estimation of many priests, many scribes, many even that sit on the council." Ben Sira smiled weakly as he looked at Eleazar. "Perhaps if I had shaved my beard and wrapped myself in a Greek tunic and lectured on Homer instead of the sayings of the wise?"

"What a fine sight that would have made," Eleazar said, his eyes rolling upward in a mock appeal to heaven. "An old rough-hewn Jew trying to recite Greek hexameter. I'm glad to have been spared."

Binyamin cast his eyes down to the floor, suddenly aware of the kind of person ben Sira had been accustomed to teaching. "I fear I've been an imposition, that I've spent your time unwisely. I'm just a craftsman, not a future scribe or sage or statesman."

Yehoshua ben Sira realized his error at once. "God forgive a vain, old man. People will honor the great, the famous, the powerful," he said faintly. He raised his head slightly to look Binyamin squarely in the eyes before finishing his pronouncement: "But none of them is greater than the person who fears the Lord. I have spent much of my time poorly, but not the time I spent with you." Ben Sira thought of the many sons of the elite priestly and lay families that he had taught and how fruitless so much of that labor had become. He thought about his own ambitions—or if he must admit it, his own vanity—that kept him seeking to attract students exclusively from among the rich and powerful families, mistaking the richest soil for the most fertile. "You may not serve among great men or appear before rulers, but you walk in honor before God." Ben Sira allowed his head to rest again on the pillow. "Now go. Get on with your day. You've spent enough time by the bed of an old man."

Binyamin rose, bowed slightly to the dying man, and wished him peace. Stepping away from the bed, he turned to acknowledge Eleazar with the same gesture of respect. He was arrested on his way to the door with ben Sira's voice speaking once again, this time with a hint of urgency.

"Don't ever be ashamed of the Torah, my son; don't ever crave what the ungodly enjoy. Torah is our wisdom. It is our deliverance."

"Yes, Rabban," said Binyamin, looking slightly puzzled by the warning. With a final nod, he quit the room and went down the stairs.

"I think I will not see that young man again, Eleazar," ben Sira said softly, looking off into the vacant doorway. "Keep watch over him. Help him if you can."

"Of course I will, Yehoshua. Zerah was my friend, and until my death I'll be a friend to his family, so I can greet him as a friend again in the world to come."

"'Be like a father to orphans; be a guardian to their mother,'" ben Sira recited, half to himself. "It's not easy, Eleazar, lying here at life's close, seeing how little an impact one has had, how futile were one's efforts to stem the tide. I might as well have spent my life shouting at the seasons to stop changing, or the sun to stop rising and falling."

"And your shouting might well have stopped it," Abigail said as she entered the bedroom. She smiled warmly at her father. "It always stopped us in our tracks."

Ben Sira smiled, no doubt remembering the sight of his two daughters and two sons tearing about the house, a sight now forty years behind him. Abigail set a tray down upon a table next to the bed. She put her arm behind the pillows supporting her father and lifted gently. Taking a pillow from beside the bed, she inserted it behind the others. "Let's see if this helps you drink more comfortably."

"My daughter has become my nurse and my mother," Yehoshua said to Eleazar. "And a good one at that."

"So perhaps the birth of a daughter is not a complete loss after all," Abigail said, smirking playfully at Eleazar. The aged priest could not help chuckling to hear the master's words thrown back at him. *The birth of a daughter is a loss.*

"Will you never let that pass, Abigail? You never brought any of a father's many fears to pass. If every daughter were like you, the birth of a daughter would be a great gain." Ben Sira's voice trailed off as a wave of sorrow washed over his face. "But not every daughter is like you."

No one spoke for half a minute, as if observing a brief silence for the dead, until Abigail's voice rescued the moment from undue discomfort. "Here, Father. I brought you some breakfast." She put a cup to his mouth, and he took a few sips, swallowing with difficulty.

"Do you remember Simon the Just, Eleazar?" There was a new energy in ben Sira's voice as he turned to look at his friend, the energy that comes to old men as they remember earlier, better times. "What a marvel it was to see him officiate in the Temple! How the beauty of holiness adorned all he did during his priesthood!"

"Yes, Yehoshua. I think of him often."

"Those were glorious days, Eleazar." Ben Sira's gaze turned back to the ceiling, the canvas on which his mind painted its memories. "When all Jerusalem, it seemed, cared about the service of God, the keeping of the covenant, the reverence due God's house. When the Temple was rebuilt after the exile, it is said that the elders who remembered Solomon's Temple wept at the sorry replacement. Would they have wept after Simon's renovations? Would they not have had to acknowledge that it was good?" Ben Sira was smiling broadly now, as his chest filled with pride. "And under Simon people cared about wisdom. They sent their children. They sent their young men."

The pride drained from his face as he returned to the present. "Where is that all now?" he asked, as he seemed to sink more deeply into his bed. Abigail took the opportunity to give him another drink and to feed him a spoonful of thin wheat porridge. "Arrogance begins when a man turns away from obeying God to serve himself. The arrogant run through Judea like a pack of dogs, men who increase their wealth by stealing the land from underneath their brothers and the bread from the mouths of their children."

"Yehoshua, it is not as bad as all that," Eleazar said, not quite convinced himself. But he quickly fixed on the one ray of hope he could, wishing to restore ben Sira's mood. "Simon's spirit lives on in his son."

"Blessed be Honiah ben Simon for loving the Lord with all his heart and all his strength! Simon's spirit lives on in his son, but not his sharp and politic eye. I fear for him. He would steer the ship of this city straight, but lacks the charisma to lead the mutinous crew behind him."

Ben Sira turned to look Eleazar directly in the eyes, showing the earnestness—almost the desperation—in his own. "Do not leave your post in this struggle, Eleazar. You are revered as a priest, and as an interpreter of the law, your word carries authority."

"Hardly, Yehoshua. My influence in the council has diminished at the same rate as attendance at your house of instruction."

"You must keep your voice strong, all the more when the priest is weak or disposed to lead the land away from the covenant."

Eleazar began to voice his objection, which ben Sira immediately anticipated with a wave of his hand. "O, not Honiah, to be sure, as well they know—hence their attempts to remove him from his office and install their own puppet. But one day their attempts may succeed, and then, Eleazar, who will speak for God? Who will speak for the covenant?"

Abigail looked beseechingly at Eleazar, who understood at once her meaning.

"I had best take my leave, Yehoshua. You have exerted yourself enough for one day, and it is not even the fourth hour." Eleazar looked upon his old friend and mentor with deep kindness in his eyes. "Peace be with you, Rabban."

As Eleazar passed ben Sira, the old man reached up from his bed and grabbed Eleazar's forearm. He pulled himself up slightly from his pillow and said, "The hope of the people is not with Judah's rulers, but with her faithful ones. Keep feeding them. Keep nurturing faithfulness among them."

Eleazar placed his free hand on his mentor's, trying to give what strength and assurance he had to him. "I will, Yehoshua. I will do all I can."

Ben Sira relaxed his grasp and allowed his head to fall back onto his pillow. Eleazar gently placed his friend's hand back on his bed. "Rest now, Yehoshua. Rest in God." He turned to Abigail and raised his hands slightly in a gesture of blessing. "May God remember the many kindnesses you have shown your father. I shall come after the morrow."

Abigail wished him peace and turned back to her father. As he descended the stairs, Eleazar glanced back to see her tuck Yehoshua's arms beneath the blankets and remove the extra pillow to afford him better rest. He knew his friend was in good hands, and it would have been easy for him to leave save for the conviction he felt that they would not speak again.

Jason stood in the main hall in the west wing of the high priest's palace. He had arrived moments before and had been courteously received and announced to his brother by the steward of the house, as always. In a sense, it was his house as well, and he was welcomed here as such—but as the *junior* son of Simon the Just.

A servant girl appeared with a tray bearing a glass flask filled with a lightly colored liquid, an alabaster cup, and a bunch of large, round grapes. She bent slightly to set it down on a table braced against the inner wall.

Jason walked over to the table and sampled the drink. Water, flavored with the juice from a mango and another fruit he did not immediately recognize. He looked out the large window upon the inner courtyard and was transported back thirty years, chasing playmates around the covered walkway that ran the perimeter of the courtyard, playing with wooden boats as he sat at the rim of the shallow pool at its center, being called in for lessons or for the evening meal. Though his own villa was far more spacious and boasted fine gardens that would be unthinkable in the crowded city, he missed this home from time to time.

"My lord Jason?" The steward's voice recalled him to the present. "My lord Honiah will see you now."

Jason turned around in time to see the oaken doors at the far end of the reception hall swing open. Jason walked toward them to find his brother seated in a wooden chair behind a table with a fine marble inlay. Several scrolls sat in one corner, while official documents and requests from individual petitioners covered the greater part of the desk's periphery. These awaited the high priest's attention, more in his role as premier and official representative of the province than as high priest of the Temple. Behind and slightly above him was a window, the shutters opened so as to allow the morning light to illumine his work. Two cedar cabinets were set against the wall on either side of the window. A series of drawers containing official records and copies of correspondence occupied the middle third of each cabinet. These drawers were flanked by shelves and compartments of various sizes, each pigeonhole containing scrolls, a veritable library of the literature of the Jewish people.

"Peace be with you, Brother," Jason said in Aramaic.

Honiah rose from his chair to greet his brother. His face was as Jason's might be in another decade, but there the fraternal resemblance ended. Honiah kept his hair and beard, the reddish-brown losing the battle for dominance against the gray, neatly trimmed but quite long. He was dressed in a finely woven but simple white tunic bound at the waist with an undecorated linen cord, an austerity of attire that Jason's best efforts to appear understated could never match.

"Peace be with you, Yeshua," Honiah said in Aramaic. "Did you come into town to officiate with me in the afternoon sacrifice?" It was difficult to tell whether it was genuine hope or sarcasm that inflected Honiah's voice.

"Why is it so difficult for you to call me *Jason*?" He regretted the question as soon as it left his mouth, both because he did not want to get into an argument with his brother—at least, not today—and because Honiah usually had a long and somewhat patronizing answer for such questions.

"*Yeshua* was the name our father gave you. It means 'God delivers' and recalls the splendid deeds of the son of Nun who first led our people into the land of promise and dispatched the Gentiles and their idols that had polluted that land too long. *Jason* means God-knows-what and recalls a Greek opportunist who seduced a witch, stole a national treasure, prostituted himself to the princess of Corinth, and ended up an exile running for his life." Honiah paused in an air of triumph. "Can you tell me again why I should call you *Jason*?"

No, thought Jason, *there will be no surprises from Honiah today.*

Honiah had already turned his gaze to the papyri piled up on the right side of his table before he finished speaking, as if he were already calculating the next bit of business to attend to after Jason left. Jason was not particularly offended, for Honiah was always in haste on this day of the week, as he tried to conclude the week's business and foresee the needs of tomorrow.

Jason sat down in one of the two olive-wood chairs in front of Honiah's desk. *A brief change of subject, then, and on to the matter at hand.* "Are things well between you and the new administrator of the market?"

"Merari is a generally agreeable civil servant, but he seems to be infected with the growing tendency to evaluate matters based on the wisdom of the market rather than the wisdom of Torah." Honiah looked sadly at the scrolls to his left, which Jason knew to be the five books of Moses, the only reference works his brother kept on his table at all times. "Just now we were discussing a petition that has come once again from several noble families to allow the meats of unclean animals to be sold in the market place and to allow tanners and craftsmen to work with the hides of such animals within the city walls. They allege that our traditional practice impedes showing proper hospitality toward our Syrian and Greek residents, for whom such restrictions are a mere nuisance rather than an expression of piety." Honiah cocked his head slightly and looked at Jason. "I suspect they would not find you as unsympathetic."

On another day, Jason might have taken that bait. "I have tried not to involve myself in such debates, Honiah. My efforts to improve our youth's educational opportunities have left me with little time to entertain partisan economics."

Jason could see Honiah's defenses relax slightly, and so he decided to pursue more directly the opening that his segue afforded him.

"In fact, that is what brings me here. You may remember that I have been in conversation with Philostratos, the gymnasiarch and director of the lyceum in Antioch, for some time and that we expected him to visit our city early in the new week."

Honiah nodded to signal his recollection.

"Due to a last-minute decision to travel down the coast by sea rather than make the entire trip from Antioch by land, Philostratos is expected to arrive later today." At this, Jason paused, waiting for Honiah to grasp the significance of the statement.

Honiah widened his eyes and tilted his head back slightly, indicating that, if any inferences were to be drawn, Jason would need to be the one to do so explicitly.

"They will be anxious to meet with you," Jason continued.

"I will be most interested to meet with them as well," Honiah said in a tone conveying more suspicion than genuine interest. "I have reservations enough about the private schools you've already established in the shadow of the Temple—schools where our youth read about the exploits of the demons of the Greeks rather than concentrating on the acts of God, and where they are taught to measure the commandments of Torah against the ethics of Aristotle and Zeno."

"It has always been the custom of the sages to study the philosophy, religion, and ethics of other cultures," Jason interjected in self-defense. "Even Rabban Yehoshua spent considerable time abroad studying both Egyptian and Greek authors before establishing his school here. This is what our people need in order to succeed in a Greek world. As our own teacher said, 'A wise magistrate will educate his people.'"

"'In the fear of the Lord,' Yeshua! And you know perfectly well that *that* is what he meant," Honiah retorted.

"Nothing I have done has jeopardized commitment to the fear of the Lord, Honiah. But we have to come to terms as well with the fact that the world around us has changed and that our survival depends on making the Greeks and Syrians feel as 'at home' as possible here. Their caravan routes are quite happy to pass far to the north and south of us, and their merchants are content to raise their families in the Greek coastal cities and the Decapolis. But if we put a few basic institutions in place, we can both equip our own youth for success in the larger world and capture the attention of enterprising Greeks and their wealth. We are threatened with becoming an irrelevant pocket of *barbaroi* if we do not adapt."

"Adapt? They ought to be emulous of us, Yeshua, not we of them! It is written that 'ten men from among the Gentiles will cling to each Jew, holding him by the cloak and saying, "let us follow you, for it is reported that God is with you!"' That is the vision I serve!"

"And that is the future that I strive for as well, but how will they seek us out if our sages don't speak their language?" Jason stopped to take in a breath, hoping the pause would alleviate the tension in the room as well as in his own heart. "I do not wish to bicker with you, Honiah. We have our differences, which some-day you may come to respect when you understand that we both want the same thing for our nation."

"Do we?" Honiah sounded positively peevish. "This gymnasium you want to build—how will it make the nations desire to know the one God? I've looked at your proposal at length, and I know something of what goes on in Greek cities and their gymnasia. Will you teach the Greek children that it is impossible for them to exercise in the nude in the city of God's holy dwelling? Will you teach the Syrians to abandon their idols rather than bring them in to defile the Holy City? Will your gymnasium close during every Sabbath, festival, and daily offering so that the law may be observed and the many youths from the priestly families may be in their proper place—in attendance at the Temple?"

"Honiah, I swear to you that I will satisfy your every concern about the lyceum and gymnasium, and contrary to what any slanderer may have told you, nothing is being taught presently in the schools that leads our people astray from what is essential to our ancestral ways. If anything, it gives them the tools to reinterpret the ancestral faith and keep it living and vibrant in our changing world." Jason could see Honiah's resistance abate slightly. "As for the foreigner, we will need to think carefully how the holiness of the city will be maintained together with the requirements of hospitality. Many on the council are concerned that they be made to feel welcome here."

"Yes, but on God's terms; if that's not good enough, then on the terms of the law of this land," Honiah declared. "'Even the stranger within your gates shall keep my Sabbath.'"

"But Moses also speaks to us this warning: 'You are not to oppress a stranger.'" Jason had been ready for this objection since two hours before dawn. "Is it not oppression to force them to conform to our ways without first converting their hearts to the love of God?"

Honiah's expression softened considerably, and Jason congratulated himself for meeting his brother on the common ground of Torah—if only to disagree.

"Every step shall proceed under your supervision, Honiah." Jason felt a twinge of guilt at having to keep his brother in the dark about how many steps were already in place to follow the present one, which Honiah was finding difficult enough. "But right now I need to ask a favor of you."

Even though he knew very well what Jason would ask, Honiah remained silent. With elbows resting on the arms of his chair, his fingertips touching, Honiah opened his hands slightly toward Jason, inviting him to finish the rest of the request aloud.

"Would you be willing to grant them a brief interview tomorrow?"

"Ha!" Honiah exclaimed in mock surprise, pulling back his forearms as if his fingertips had been singed by the words Jason spouted in their direction. "You're asking me to engage in business on the Sabbath! Or have you simply forgotten what day it is?"

"Honiah, I'm only asking you to meet some guests," Jason protested. "I'm not asking you to give them a tour, to carry their luggage, or to cook for them, for heaven's sake. Just to spend half an hour receiving them graciously."

"Are you even listening to yourself? You're asking the high priest to do work on the Sabbath." Before Jason's open lips could vocalize the objection, Honiah pressed on: "Yes, work, Yeshua. These are not my guests; they are not guests in my house who would be keeping the Sabbath with me. They are your business associates. The meeting for which you ask is in an official capacity, and thus associating with them is work."

"I am asking you, please, to see them tomorrow. I can put them off for today. They expect you to be busy with your priestly duties. But they will not appreciate being put off for a day on which you will be doing nothing."

Jason instantly realized his misstep.

"Doing nothing? I will be honoring the God who created the heavens and the earth by mirroring his rhythms of work and of rest, and honoring the God who redeemed us from slavery by observing the rest that was once forbidden to us in Egypt. Is that now nothing to you?"

"Not to me, Brother," Jason said with an earnestness that was not entirely manufactured. "I understand our laws. Perhaps I could even make Philostratos understand. But others in his party won't be quite so broad-minded. Several wealthy men from Antioch—some from the Jewish community there, to be sure, but some Greeks, as well—are traveling with him. They have taken an interest in our endeavors and are considering helping to finance these public works."

"You will have to make them understand," Honiah countered. "And if they will not, I want nothing to do with them. Our law is divine, our calling to keep what is holy to the Lord inviolable. They must yield to God's demands, not the reverse."

"This is not about yielding," Jason pleaded. "It is about opportunity—one that I have taken great pains to orchestrate. You are the premier, and your support is essential for all public undertakings. These patrons must see that you stand behind me." Jason's tone modulated to that of gentle but forceful reminder. "I stood by your side when Simon ben Iddo, the former chief financial officer of the Temple, challenged your commitment to regulate the market according to our law. I put my voice and the support of my clients behind you when he came to you to demand the office of administrator of the market with considerable support from the nobles." He paused to allow the recollection to sink in and, with any luck, Honiah's sense of indebtedness to rise. "Can you not also give a little when so much is at stake?"

Honiah's eyes dropped momentarily down and to the left, which Jason took to mean that he was actually thinking about it. He pressed his advantage.

"If you do not see them tomorrow, you will cause me no small embarrassment and put at risk all I have been working for. You will show that the administration is less enthusiastic for these educational reforms than I have represented, and will offer an insult to people who wish to expend great sums to benefit our nation."

But Honiah weighed matters from a different vantage point. "Should I rather insult the God upon whose favor our nation has depended from its beginnings?" He drew a deep breath that made his chest and shoulders inflate with an air of indignation. "If you weren't my brother, I might begin to hear you as a false teacher trying to lead the people and their high priest astray from God—trying to lead me into violating one of our most sacred laws."

The threat was stronger than Honiah intended, so he modulated to explanation. "And I *am* less enthusiastic about your lyceum than you represented. Honestly, I don't understand why you should be so enamored of the arcane knowledge of the Greeks." Honiah softened his tone further, which only made him sound more condescending to Jason's ears. "Reflect upon what has been assigned to you, your portion from the Lord. I mean the Torah, the wisdom that God has made to live among us and no other people! Build a school where that is at the center again, and you will have my complete support."

Jason wished he had been born first.

"As for your faction and your guests, remember the words of the psalmist: 'Favored is the man who does not walk in the counsel of the wicked, nor stands in the way of sinners, nor sits in the seats of the scornful, but his delight is in the law of the Lord.' I would advise you to keep better company than the sinners who have your ear and seek to use you to their advantage."

Honiah rose, signaling that their conversation was at an end. Jason stood, never breaking eye contact with his brother, seething at having to listen to ethical lessons from a man who would never read Plato or Aristotle. *You probably couldn't even handle that level of Greek.*

As he turned to leave, Honiah's voice stopped him at the door. "Yeshua, you were right to get behind me in my dispute with Simon. As my brother, that is where you belong in every matter. Honor our father, and be content to follow my lead."

Jason remained still a few seconds longer, feeling Honiah's gaze upon his back. Then he drew in a breath, raised his head, and walked out of the high priest's office into the great hall. He was surprised at how angry he was, especially since he knew from the start that the outcome would not be any different.

Binyamin walked down the crowded street toward his house as if in a dream. The clamor of artisans at their work, the din of voices negotiating trades or exchanging gossip, even the jostling of people brushing past him registered more

as something remembered than experienced. He returned his neighbors' greetings half a beat late, requiring the extra second to process what would have normally been instantaneous. Though he had walked almost a half-mile to get to the
market (his mother had been quite explicit: "Go to the *agora*, not the little veg-
etable stands at the head of our street where everything has been sitting in the
sun for two days") and another to make his way back here, part of him was still
sitting in the little room with ben Sira. He was reluctant to turn his thoughts
away from him, afraid that if he let the old man out of his mind, he would let go
of the lifeline that anchored ben Sira to this world.

He walked through the open door of his father's house, his meditations
ended abruptly by his brother's greeting.

"Ah, *Adoni*, could you spare a few moments to sit beside a poor working
man?" Meir's tone was half accusation and all sarcasm. Binyamin's younger
brother, a strong lad of fifteen years, was sitting on a reed mat and bending over
a perfectly smooth stone block on which lay some thin strips of silver. A leather
apron covered his bare chest, the heat of the day and his frequent trips to the
forge having made him abandon his tunic.

"I know, Meir," Binyamin said, his tone warm with unexpected sympathy. "It's not fair. You feel like you're carrying the load for two men." Binyamin
looked earnestly into his brother's eyes. "Now you know what it feels like to be
me every day of the week!"

The expression on Meir's face showed that he was completely taken off guard,
and Binyamin smiled wryly with a slight snort as he walked away. But he did not
make his escape before he felt the sting of a small ingot of silver Meir had tossed
at his backside.

"Seriously, Binyamin, we're up against a deadline here. A messenger came
this morning to ask if we could have the set ready by this afternoon. Something
about a change in plans. I still have the ornamentation on three cups left to do."

"All right, all right. I'll be right back to give you a hand."

Binyamin was still smiling as he left the front room of the house that had
been used as the workshop since before he was born, passed through the small
family living area, and entered the women's spaces in the back of the house. To
the left was a loom set facing the back door, where Miryam had spent many
hours working while she watched her children playing in the narrow alleyway
between the two rows of adjoining houses, a kind of poor person's courtyard
shared by all the families on the street. To the right was the kitchen, Binyamin's
destination.

"Peace to you, Mother." He set down the burlap sack he had been carrying and began to empty its contents. "Six tilapia, brought in this morning by the smell of them." Binyamin made a show of holding the fish up to his nose. "Ah, such freshness as only the *agora* can provide."

"That's enough, young man. I know where to find quality," Miryam retorted in mock severity. She was sitting on a thick mat woven from cloth remnants, working meal into dough for the bread she would bake for both that evening and the next day. In front of her stood a large stone block on which most of the food preparation—including the kneading of bread—was done. Behind her were two clay ovens over low charcoal fires, ready to transform the lumps into fresh loaves. Later she would use the ovens to broil the fish, after she had marinated it in the vinegar and herbs she had already prepared, anticipating Binyamin's return. Beside the ovens was another hearth with a metal grill above the fire, on which she was stewing some lentils and barley.

She paused her kneading long enough to see what Binyamin had brought home—and to make sure that he had not forgotten anything. He was highly attentive to the details of his own craft, but his mother often accused him of not being as particular about hers. She kept her kitchen well stocked with grains, dried fruits, nuts, olive oil, wine, date honey, lentils, garlic, spices, and whatever else would keep in the covered earthenware jugs and the tightly woven baskets that lined the inside wall of the kitchen. But it was impossible to keep a garden of any decent size in the city, so she relied on almost daily trips to the market for vegetables, fruits, and anything special.

Binyamin continued to empty out the sack and sound out the inventory. "Pomegranates, grapes, and *fresh* figs." He closed the sack and began to turn away.

"Binyamin?" she said with a hint of apprehension in her voice.

He smiled broadly as he turned back to the sack and produced a final item. "And of course, I didn't forget the cucumbers."

She looked at him with amused exasperation as she went back to kneading the dough with renewed energy. "Honestly, Binyamin, you'll do anything to provoke me."

"A small reward for walking over half of Jerusalem to gather only the freshest produce and fish in the city." Binyamin started to leave, when it dawned on him that his mother was working alone. "Where is Ruth?"

"I sent her home to be of use to her own family on the eve of the Sabbath."

"Mother, I pay her to be of use to *you*."

"I am quite capable of cooking a few meals, Binyamin ben Zerah," Miryam scolded before breaking out into a smile at her son's solicitousness. "Besides, should we not be generous to a servant before the Sabbath rest, remembering that we were slaves in Egypt?"

Binyamin could not resist such an argument head-on, so he took a lateral step. "Well at least let me get Ari in here to help you. It's about time he did more around the house anyway." He stepped out the back door into the narrow alley and shouted. "Ari?" No answer as he walked on a few paces. "Ari? Ariyeh ben Zerah!" A head peeked out midway of the third door beyond an intersecting alley.

"What do you want, Binyamin?"

"There you are!" Binyamin waved Ari closer. "Mama could use your help in the kitchen this afternoon. She's alone and has a lot of work to do before sundown." Binyamin leaned over slightly and brought his face nearer to Ari's, both to get his full attention and to lend a modest air of menace that would impress his next words upon his brother's ten-year-old memory. "Do whatever she asks, and don't complain about it. And if she doesn't have anything for you to do, wait with her till she does."

Ari began to shuffle reluctantly toward their house until a playful kick adeptly placed on his buttocks convinced him to scamper well ahead of his brother.

Binyamin passed through the kitchen with a last admonitory glance at Ari—who quickly found a place at the stone table and began to cut up the cucumbers—and went back into the front workshop. He took off his cloak and hung it on a peg driven into the wall, then removed a leather apron from a neighboring peg and sat down beside Meir. He looked for a moment at the embellishment his brother was making to decorate the bottom of the decanter and cups. At the moment he was working silver wire into vine motifs, splitting off little pieces from the wire to press into leaves.

"Very nice work, Meir. You always had the eye for detail." He watched as Meir struggled to keep his pleasure at the compliment from showing. "I'll stamp some more lilacs and pomegranates, then I'll start soldering all this on while you finish those vines." Binyamin moved over to another work bench, selected the die with a small inverse lilac on the bottom, and began to strike it into a thin sheet of silver.

They worked quietly together, save for the sound of the mallet against the die within, and the bustle of their neighbors without. Not half an hour passed before their work was interrupted by a rap on the open door. The brothers looked up to see a Syrian mercenary—probably the bodyguard of some aristocrat, Binyamin guessed—standing in their doorway.

"Peace to you," Binyamin said, rising to meet him. "How may we be of service?"

"I understand that you are metalworkers. Locals say you're about the best for fine work," the mercenary said in rough Aramaic.

"We are honored to have our neighbors' confidence," Binyamin replied matter-of-factly, neither sounding arrogant nor denying the compliment.

The Syrian produced a gold chain and two gold coins. "I got this chain from a merchant, and I'd like to make a present of it to a special woman. Can you make a charm of Astarte to hang on it as a pendant? I've got more gold if it's needed for the work."

Meir leaned forward, clenching his jaws so as not to speak out of turn.

"We have a surplus of work here," Binyamin said evenly, hiding his disgust. "I don't think we could take this on."

Meir could not hold back. "Perhaps if you would be content with a different pendant, I could work it in between jobs. I could make a floret, or a cluster of grapes. I've even learned the Egyptian way of making names in cartouche. Truly an exotic gift for your special lady, and not so complicated as an Astarte." Meir was not lying entirely. While the cartouche would actually be far more complicated from an artistic point of view—especially if the soldier's mistress had some impossible name like Philartemisia—it would be far less complicated from the point of view of living with Binyamin.

"No, I want to give her a charm that will protect her while I'm away on business. She's devoted to Astarte."

"My younger brother hates to disappoint a customer," Binyamin said, casting a sideways glare at Meir, "but we really can't help you. I'm sorry."

Binyamin returned to his work bench as the Syrian, his face a blend of confusion and annoyance, retreated to the street and started off in search of another shop.

Meir's eyes followed his brother and continued to bore into him as Binyamin resumed his work.

"Are you going to finish that cup with your eyes on me and your hands idle?" Binyamin said after he had endured enough.

Meir struggled to keep the frustration out of his voice. "We're busy today, Binyamin, but you know that we don't have much work lined up for after the Sabbath. Are we so rich that we can afford not to have work?"

"Are we so poor that we have to steal?"

"Steal! What are you talking about, steal? The man offered us work!"

"Well, you said we needed the money. Are you ready to steal from others to get more money? Do you want to leave this customer's order for later and go out into the market and cut a few purse strings?" Binyamin continued, as if he were making perfect sense.

"Of course I'm not going to steal, but we're talking about—"

"Breaking the commandments. If you're ready to make graven images of false gods, you should also be ready to steal, kill, and dishonor our parents." Binyamin spoke with unyielding conviction. "We do not make idols, Meir."

"I'm not talking about worshiping idols, Binyamin. I'm talking about doing business with people who do. If we don't take the jobs that the *goyim* offer us just because they happen to involve some image of some god of theirs, they'll find someone else—to whom they will happily ever after take all their other metal work as well."

Binyamin turned back to his task.

"How many Jews came in last week with gold to work? Last month?" Meier asked. "Why, in the past year I think we've had two jobs involving gold. The scraps from those coins plus our fee would have kept us in food for a month." Binyamin kept his attention fully on soldering the lilacs at even intervals onto the cups. Meir shifted his appeal more directly to Binyamin's heart. "And we could have purchased new clothing for Ari, rather than make Mother spend all her evenings at the loom making a larger outfit for him."

Binyamin looked pointedly into Meir's eyes. "How many times do you remember seeing our father casting some idol for a Gentile customer? Hm? How many times did he accept a commission to repair some piece that had graven images on it?"

Meir sighed out the answer, "Never."

Before Meir could object to this line of reasoning, Binyamin continued, "That's right. And I can remember several occasions when he politely but firmly refused such business." Binyamin kept Meir silent with his gaze. "Was our father wrong?"

Meir searched for some way to answer this without dishonoring their father or reneging on his own position but saw no way forward. Binyamin pressed on. "Did our father make bad choices?"

"No, Binyamin. He did what he thought was right."

"Yes, he did. And we will do as he taught us."

ב

Honiah walked up the finely paved road that led from his palace to the sacred spaces of Mount Zion. Four lightly armed Levites escorted him, two in front and two behind. At first, Honiah had felt their presence to be ostentatious, calling undue attention to his movements around the city. But he had made serious enemies in his years in office as high priest and premier, and ever since matters had come to a head with Simon ben Iddo, he had ceased to complain openly about the escort.

The Temple filled his view from the first step outside of the palace doors. The Temple had watched over him from his earliest childhood. It had changed much during his lifetime. His father, Simon the Just, expended vast amounts of energy and public funds on the Temple and its courts. He remembered how, when he was a boy and Yeshua but a baby, Father would tell them stories about the grandeur of the Temple when it was first built by Solomon eight centuries before. He told the story of how the Babylonian king Nebuchadnezzar destroyed the city and the Temple four centuries ago when he punished Solomon's last successor, Zedekiah, for his treachery and took all the noblest families into captivity. He spoke of the return of the Judeans from their exile in Babylon, how they rebuilt the Temple by permission of the Persian king Cyrus, and how those few elders who still remembered Solomon's Temple wept when the work was done, so poor was the replacement, so unworthy of the worship of the God of heaven. Honiah doubted that they would have wept to see it now.

The first thing Simon had done was to build towering retaining walls alongside the Kidron Valley on the east slope of the Temple Mount and more modest retaining walls on the other three sides. Filling these with dirt and rubble, he was able to expand the Temple courtyards considerably, and he finished his work with a two-story-high wall around the expanded enclosure. As a result, the Temple became a far more imposing sight even from afar. But Simon's aim was not merely aesthetic. These improvements also made the Temple more defensible from attack on the north, south, and west sides, and nearly impregnable from the east side. Honiah glanced momentarily to his left, where, immediately to the north of the Temple, he could see the tall towers that his father had built on top of Nehemiah's fortress for a loftier position of defense on the city's weakest side.

Yeshua had taken a keen interest in his father's architectural improvements, and when Honiah became high priest, Yeshua occupied himself with designing and overseeing the construction of columned porticoes around the perimeter of the courtyard, the decorative paving of the expanded courtyard for people of all nations, and finally the beautification of the inner courts with colonnades and other ornaments. Honiah was pleased to entrust this to his brother, both because Yeshua had an agreeable aesthetic sense and because it provided him with a safe outlet for his creative energies. Yeshua might not have shown much interest in serving the Temple in his capacity as priest, but he did serve it in other ways with commendable energy. It was telling, Honiah mused, that Yeshua showed no interest in improving their father's military fortifications. *Yeshua never gives a thought to anything that would help keep Gentiles out of Jerusalem.*

As he turned his thoughts to the sanctuary, he could feel the heaviness across his chest lighten with each breath, with each stride that brought him closer to the house of God. Entering through an arched gate in the western wall, he turned left to walk the long portico that led past the sanctuary and the priests' chambers. Its familiar colonnade had an almost hypnotic effect upon him as he passed column after column, each one distancing him further from his anxieties about Yeshua and the growing strength of the families that were guiding his brother's hand. *One thing have I desired from the Lord. This alone I seek—that I may dwell continually in the Lord's house, to behold the fair beauty of the Lord and to meditate in God's temple.*

Honiah found the walk through the Temple precincts to be a welcome refreshment, and so he decided to prolong it rather than to enter the areas for the priests' preparation by the direct and obvious route, namely through the rear of the inner courts. He had come sufficiently early, and so he strolled along the entire length of the western portico, passing several gates opening onto stairways leading down to the streets below. A number of Levites—the more brawny and formidable among their tribe—stood at their stations as gatekeepers, making sure that those who entered were not carrying anything into the Temple other than what they needed for sacrifice. Honiah would not permit anyone to profane the Temple courts by conducting a little business on the side.

He proceeded to walk the length of the northern portico, passing a number of gates opening onto considerably shallower staircases, since the north side of the city was the most elevated. Honiah turned at last into the eastern portico. He turned his head slightly to the right as he walked, so that he could see the front of the sanctuary appearing and disappearing behind the columns. Adonai *is in his holy Temple; let all the earth keep silence before him*. Honiah's concerns about human affairs receded before the rising awareness of the Holy One in Israel's midst.

Honiah came to the point where he stood opposite the face of the Temple and stopped for a moment to survey the scene. The sun had already descended halfway from its zenith and appeared to hover directly above the sanctuary. The white limestone surfaces of the Holy Places seemed to glow with the reflection of divine glory, signaling to the eye that the *shekinah*—the sheltering, resplendent presence of God among mortals—rested over this place like no other.

The sanctuary towered majestically above the ramparts that separated the various courts from one another. The central section, which contained the Holy Places, rose a full twenty meters above its base. Built against it on both sides were slightly shorter enclosures that ran the entire length of the sanctuary and added to the impression of weightiness, stability, permanence. These were store-rooms mostly, but they also contained the Temple treasuries where the wealth of the Temple, votive offerings, and private deposits were kept. The sanctuary and its storerooms were made from large stones so expertly fitted together and so carefully plastered that, even up close, they seemed to be hewn from a single, massive rock. It was a suitable representation of the mighty character of the One who, though not contained even by the vast expanse of the heavens, somehow dwelt here in a distinctive and immediate way. "'The Lord is my rock and my fortress,'" Honiah pronounced under his breath.

Honiah walked more energetically across the court of all nations, through a chest-high divider past which only full-blooded Israelites could enter, and up several stairs toward another gate that allowed access through the walled enclosure around the inner courts. Several Temple guards—chosen from among the hardiest Levites and trained in the military arts—kept their station here, ready to protect the Holy Places against encroachment by non-Israelites. Honiah emerged in the court that was opened to all Israelites, both men and women. Four chambers were built into the four corners of this enclosure, and elegant columned porches lined the perimeter.

As he passed through the court of Israel, he could see other Levites busy with their divine service. To his right, some brought logs for the altar from the Chamber of Wood, where they had first been meticulously inspected for mildew and infestation. From a chamber to his left, another brought pure wine and olive oil for the sacrifice and for the lamps. Some of the most musically gifted Levite males were clustered ahead of him, retrieving their instruments from a chamber built into the western wall of the courtyard, while others proceeded directly into the next court to gather with the choir that would offer to God the sacrifice of praise throughout the entire service. Men and women from the other tribes began to gather as well, the wives finding a place in this lower court, their husbands proceeding to the upper court. *This is as it should be,* he thought. *People busied with the things of God, attentive wholly to how God requires to be served, to what is worthy of him.*

Honiah climbed the fifteen stone steps on the west side of the court and passed through the great bronze gate through which no woman was permitted. This brought him to the beating heart of the Temple complex, the place where mortals interacted with the Immortal God daily through the offering of gifts and sacrifices. He glanced up toward the two-story system of rooms built into the walls that surrounded these interior spaces, the chambers in which the priests gathered, prepared themselves, and resided during their one-week term of service each year if they were from outside the city. *Where God was all in all.* He looked ahead to the altar, a massive stone block whose top stood four meters above the floor. The cinders in the fire pit on top never cooled, causing the air above the altar to shimmer like the waters of a fountain night and day, a motion made more striking by the solid, immovable surroundings of the place.

Behind the altar was a grand staircase ascending by twelve steps into the Holy Places themselves. Two massive pillars, mainly decorative with ornate capitals and bases, were built into the limestone wall surrounding the entrance into the sanctuary. Its large brass doors stood perpetually open, a thick, woven curtain covering the opening. When the wind caught it, it sighed as if to the rhythms of the breath of God. Honiah stood watching its movement for a few exhalations, releasing his own last anxieties about the machinations of the worldly minded and coming alive again to the presence of Eternity.

Jason sat down on one of several cedar chairs set against the wall of his main dining hall. These were mainly ornamental, but he needed something with a backrest right now, having spent the last hour ranging throughout his villa, giving instructions for the evening menu, selecting which casks of wine would be opened for the evening's festivities (and in what order), and inspecting the rooms that were being prepared for his guests. Ordinarily his steward would have attended to these matters, presenting his plans to Jason for final approval, but the lack of preparation time made him anxious to do the planning himself. He looked out at the three large couches set in the middle of the room, their inner edges making three sides of an open square where food would be served by attendants and where entertainment would be offered. He closed his eyes and envisioned the order in which his guests would be invited to recline, three or four on each one of these couches, heads and hands toward the center. He tried to envision them having a good time and leaving with very positive feelings about affairs in Jerusalem.

He opened his eyes and sought refreshment in contemplating the artwork that filled the room. He had sought to surround himself and his guests with images that suggested—even subtly promoted—cultural rapprochement while alienating neither his more devout Jewish nor his Greek friends and associates. He looked across the room on a fresco of Noah, whom the Greeks could appreciate as their own hero Deucalion, constructing a massive, landlocked ship. The artist made the ark to resemble an oversized trireme as a means of giving a more contemporary—and Greek—interpretation of the ancient myth. The next wall panel, separated from the first by a decorative column, featured Abraham, whose status as the "father of many nations" was made conspicuous by being written out above and below in Greek and Hebrew.

The central panel was set within an arch that raised the ceiling by a meter, making it the focal point of the room. On it was painted a life-size representation of a beautiful, radiant woman dressed—admittedly with less modesty than Honiah would ever countenance—in a white linen tunic with a band of gold under her breasts. As a Judean, Jason would describe her as the figure of Wisdom, but his Greek contacts could identify her as their goddess Athena, while associates from Egypt or other eastern Mediterranean regions would name her Isis. She had proven to be, Jason reflected, an excellent choice for a conversation piece in a room in which people from all three regions were often entertained at the same time—not to mention an attractive female figure for his guests to enjoy.

To the right of the arch, the sequence of shorter panels continued with a depiction of Boaz and Ruth on the threshing floor, a reminder that the nation's grandest era—the reign of David—was made possible only by the intermarriage of Jew and non-Jew. After much debate, Jason decided to have a Greek artist paint this in a style more reminiscent of depictions of the Greek myths, with the result that Ruth had uncovered most of herself rather than Boaz's feet. A final panel portrayed Solomon and the Queen of Sheba, her outstretched hand held by his. This was, for Jason, the crowning image of intellectual and cultural inter-marriage between Jewish and non-Jewish worlds, and notably with the Gentile coming to seek out the wisdom of the Jewish sage. Their story well captured his vision for the educated among his people, who would have so thoroughly pro-cessed their ancestral heritage in light of the wisdom of other lands as to become valued conversation partners for leaders in the Greek kingdoms, intellectual pio-neers in every field of civic life. *Ten Gentiles will cling to one Judean*, Jason mused. *This is indeed how it will come to pass.*

His reveries were interrupted as he became aware of Castor's presence, wait-ing to be acknowledged. "My lord, your guests have been seen leaving the city by the Pool of Siloam and crossing to the foot of the Mount of Olives. They will arrive, no doubt, within half an hour."

Jason rose reluctantly from the chair and found his way to his bedchamber. Servants approached to help him out of the "simple" garments he had chosen to wear to see Honiah, and into something more appropriate for the evening. Niobe had laid out an elegant tunic with elaborately embroidered brocade adorning the collar and running down the center of the garment in front and behind. *This will do nicely*, he thought as they slipped it over his head and fastened the cord about his middle. He walked over to a small chest and put several gold rings on his fingers and a braided gold rope chain around his neck.

Feeling more himself, Jason walked to the reception hall in the front of his villa in time to find Castor coming toward him and announcing the arrival of his guests.

Honiah walked along the narrow court of Israelite males—already crowded with the pious who had come to attend the evening sacrifice—toward the cham-bers on the left side of the court. He went directly to the chamber of purifi-cations, a room with a large mikvah in the center. Around the room on every side were three broad stone steps, on which the priests would sit to unlace their sandals, remove their clothing, or simply wait their turn to immerse themselves. About a dozen priests occupied the chamber when Honiah entered, and respect-fully exchanged wishes of peace with their revered leader. Priests from the clan of Joarib were on duty this week, most of whom resided a fair distance from

Jerusalem. As a result, Honiah did not know many of these priests by name. Across the mikvah, however, he recognized two familiar faces. Mattathias, a priest from the nearby village of Modein and a few years his senior, had already emerged from the pool. His youngest son, Jonathan, a sturdily built young man of about twenty, was descending into the mikvah. Casual conversation would have been out of place, so Honiah simply smiled and nodded a personal acknowledgment.

A temple servant unlaced Honiah's sandals while another unfastened his belt and removed his tunic. Honiah could hear the chorus of Levites intoning a psalm in the court of Israelite males, calling the people to examine themselves before daring to approach the Holy One in their midst:

O Lord, who shall dwell in your tabernacle? Who shall dwell on your holy hill?
Those who walk blamelessly and do what is right, who speak the truth from their
*   heart;*
who do not slander with their tongue, and who do no evil to a friend;
who despise the one who breaks the covenant, but honor those who fear the Lord.
Whoever does these things shall not be shaken.

Honiah immersed first his hands, then his feet, in a shallow pool beside the mikvah. Then he descended down the six steps into the mikvah itself. Even at the bottom, he still stood head and shoulders above the water. Kneeling and bowing forward, he completed the ablution. As he felt the water wash over his body, he held the words of the Levites in his mind and allowed them to pour through his heart, his soul. As he internalized them and felt afresh his deep, internal agreement with them, he arose from the mikvah feeling properly cleansed from the day's business, from the many distractions that cluttered his mind and heart from his soul's one true joy—to worship the Lord in the beauty of holiness.

A pair of Temple servants reappeared, carrying a set of vestments they had retrieved from the high priest's private office a few rooms away. Honiah dried himself with a towel and stepped into the linen breeches that were the distinctive undergarment of priests, worn in place of the loincloth so that the sight of genitalia might never disgrace the Holy Places and rites. As one tied the lacing on the breeches around the knees, another servant draped a long linen tunic over the high priest's head, binding it above his waist with an ornate sash woven from white, red, blue, and purple threads. The first servant, having finished with the breeches, now deftly tied the lacing around Honiah's forearms, so that the tunic would not interfere with his movements. The other positioned the rounded linen headdress. In this garb, Honiah was indistinguishable from the other priests. He preferred to reserve the ornate high priestly garments solely for the Day of Atonement, a dedication to simplicity that his fellow priests admired.

Honiah stepped barefoot out onto the smooth pavement of the court of the priests, the stones still warm from the midday sun, and began to walk along the southern perimeter. He passed the Office of Hewn Stone, where the other priests were discovering by the casting of lots how God would have each participate in the rites. His own part was determined by his office, though when he was prevented from attending, another priest would be selected by lot to fill his place as well. The older priests could not remember another high priest who involved himself so completely in the Temple service as did Honiah. Although he left the work of offering the sacrificial animals brought on behalf of individuals or their families to the thousand or so priests that served in a yearly rotation, Honiah himself presided over as many sacrifices performed on behalf of the whole people of Israel as his schedule permitted, and not just over the sacrifices offered at the major festivals and on the Day of Atonement, the one day that was his unique prerogative and obligation.

A few strides past the Office of Hewn Stone, Honiah arrived at the antechamber where the priests whose lot had already been determined were gathering. Once the full complement had arrived, Honiah led them in another kind of preparation. Another of his innovations, Honiah believed that the purifying of the intentions and thoughts was as necessary to acceptable service as the washing of the hands and feet. He wanted every sacrifice to be performed by priests whose hearts were fully centered on God—his own as much as everyone else's. As the priests bowed their heads in silence, Honiah closed his eyes and raised his head, allowing the cry of his heart to find its way to his lips. "O God, you are my God. Eagerly I seek you."

The gathered priests immediately recognized the text and responded instinctively with one voice. *"My soul thirsts for you; my flesh faints for you as in a waterless, barren land."*

"I have gazed upon you in your holy place, so that I might see the splendor of your glory."

"My lips will praise you, because your faithfulness is better than life."

"You have been my help, and in the shelter of your wings I rejoice."

"My soul clings to you; your right hand holds me upright."

"But those who make plans against me, to destroy me . . . " As Honiah paused for the priests to respond, he found himself listening momentarily to the voice of his own thoughts, the internal impressions that burst upon him all at once and without leave. He remembered the tone of his conversation with Yeshua and how much his brother had at stake this day and thought about the conversations Yeshua was no doubt having this afternoon. Many had plotted against Honiah in years past, and many were plotting still. *Will Yeshua be among them?*

The priests completed the verse—*"Will be brought down to the depths of the grave"*—and waited, puzzled by the silence that followed.

Honiah delivered the next cue hesitantly, fearing to pronounce sentence against those nearest him. "They shall be given over to the sword."

"Their bodies will be food for the dogs."

Honiah forced his mind back into the moment, into the experience that was his only reward and only desire as high priest. "But I will exult in God," he declared, his tone stressed by the force of will behind the statement.

"All who swear by God will rejoice, but every lying mouth will be shut," the priests concluded.

Honiah realized after the fact that he had changed the last verse slightly, inserting himself where the psalm read "the king will exult in God," but his fellow priests were accustomed by now to his instinctive personalizing of the psalm texts. Besides, what king was there to exult in God? Neither the king of the north nor the king of the south gave the God of Israel a thought.

Meir half-walked, half-ran up the crowded street toward the *agora* in the northwest corner of the city. He kept alert for any sign of undue interest in the wooden box that he was carrying, a fine chest made from smoothly planed cedar wood that his family kept on hand for such special deliveries.

The spacious market was buzzing with commotion as merchants were trying to get the most for their wares before the sun's disk touched the horizon, signaling the enforced end of the business week. Meir turned a sharp left as soon as he emerged in the *agora* and made for the row of houses ahead of him. Except for the blocks immediately surrounding the Temple where the oldest and most elite priestly families lived, some of the wealthiest Judeans maintained their residences in this quarter of the city.

Reaching the grand row of mansions, he turned right and found the home of Agathon situated on the first corner. Meir knocked on the door. After a moment, a household servant—the steward, Meir guessed from the fine tunic and chain that the man wore—opened the door. He looked Meir up and down with his painted eyes before speaking. The youth was suddenly aware of what kind of impression his appearance made with his face and arms grimy from the day's work, his clothes patched, dirty, and smelling of sweat and the charcoal fires that heated the forge in his family's shop.

"What do you want?" the steward asked with unmistakable disdain.

Meir lowered his eyes. "I have come with a delivery for Master Agathon."

"Oh, you must be the metalworker. Cutting it a bit close to evening, aren't you?" The steward sounded a little disappointed that Meir wasn't simply a beggar to be driven off. "Well, give the goods to me. I'll fetch your fee. We provided the silver, as I recall, so we owe you only for your labor."

Meir wasn't inclined to leave matters with such an unpleasant man. "With your pardon, my instructions are to present this to Master Agathon himself."

"Come in, then, and wait in the vestibule." The steward grunted and walked in the direction of the inner courtyard, stopping and adding for good measure, "And don't touch anything."

Meir took in the splendor of the house, walking to the edges of the vestibule and peering into the adjoining rooms, gawking at the frescoes, the floors tiled with polished stone, the intricately carved furnishings. The poorest item that he saw was of better quality than the finest object in his home. He very rarely set foot inside the houses of the elites, and for him it was like stepping into another world. A world of elegance, comfort, abundance. *A world without sweat, grime, and charcoal smoke.*

At the sound of footsteps, he ceased his voyeuristic tour and returned to the center of the vestibule, his eyes moving once again toward the ground.

"Ah, am I relieved to see you here." The ornately embroidered purple-and-gold Greek key design highlighting the short, finely woven tunic left no doubt that this was Agathon. "I was beginning to worry that I would not have the set in time."

Meir felt even more out of place with the appearance of the nobleman. "I apologize for any worry I caused you, Master Agathon," Meir said with some embarrassment. "My brother and I have been working all day to finish on time." He set the wooden box down on a small, decorative stone table in the vestibule and began to unwrap one of the goblets. "Is the work acceptable?"

Agathon held the silver chalice in his hand. He said nothing, but his eyes sparkled as he examined the piece. "Let me see the others."

The youth carefully unwrapped the remaining cups and the decanter, setting them all out on the small table. Agathon looked at each one in turn, comparing their decorative bases. Meir shifted his weight from foot to foot several times, uncomfortable in the silence.

Finally Agathon looked the youth in the eyes and said, "Exquisite workman-ship, young man. I do not think I could go to any city in the Seleucid kingdom and find six cups that matched more perfectly. You say you and your brother made these? Today?"

"We had forged the decanter and chalices already, but the decorations, yes, today, sir."

"Well, you have brought great credit upon yourselves with this work."

Meir lifted his face, which brightened into a smile then darkened and fell again almost as suddenly.

"What's wrong?" Agathon asked.

"I apologize, sir, for coming to your house looking like this."

"Nonsense. You're a craftsman! How else are you supposed to look?" The words were spoken kindly, but Meir felt their sting, nonetheless. "Look, you've no reason to be ashamed," Agathon continued. "Of all crafts, working with silver and gold is a noble one. Perhaps second only to the physician's craft, who plies his trade to slightly more precious materials—and rarely with such precision as you have done."

"Thank you, Master Agathon. It's just that, standing here in your house right now, metalworking doesn't seem all that noble."

Agathon smiled warmly at the young man. "What's your name?"

"Meir ben Zerah."

"Well, if you can stand it, Meir ben Zerah, come back to this house next week. I may have some more work for you." He turned to his steward. "Menes, count out twenty drachmas for this artist's labor."

"Yes, sir. Thank you, sir," Meir said, smiling back. The steward was obviously displeased at such a large fee being paid out for no more than a few days' work, but silently obliged. Meir bowed slightly, turned to leave, then turned again and added, "Good Sabbath to you, sir."

"And to you, young man," replied Agathon, already walking back to his chambers to prepare for the evening.

Complete silence filled the Temple precincts as the priests filed into the open courtyard in front of the sanctuary. Honiah raised his arms toward the Holy Place and commenced the litany that he led twice daily in the Temple, a litany in which pious Jews across the inhabited world joined, praying in their homes at the hours appointed for the morning and evening sacrifice.

"Blessed are you, O Lord, our God and God of our fathers, God of Abraham, God of Isaac, and God of Jacob, Creator of heaven and earth, our Shield and the Shield of our fathers, our confidence from generation to generation."

The whole congregation—priests, Levites, and male Israelites—responded in unison, *"Blessed are you, O Lord, the Shield of Abraham!"*

The roar of his people in harmonious agreement swept over Honiah like a wave of the sea, the oneness of God reflected in the single-hearted intentions of God's people.

"You are mighty," he continued with renewed determination to resist the other tides, "bringing low the proud; you are strong, judging the unmerciful; you are eternal, raising the dead, making the wind to blow, and sending down rain."

"Blessed are you, O Lord, who gives life to the dead!"

"Forgive us, our Father, for we have sinned against you; let our transgressions pass from your sight, for great is your mercy." Honiah prayed especially for Yeshua, whose neglect of the Sabbath was but a symptom of his growing neglect for the covenant and the things of God.

"Blessed are you, O Lord, who forgives abundantly!"

"Heal us, O Lord our God, from the pain of our heart; make weariness and sighing to pass away from us; cause healing for our wounds to rise up." Honiah's thoughts ranged from the many invalids who sat in the gates and in the streets, begging for their daily bread, to the nation itself, so vulnerable to the vicissitudes of the fortunes of the giants around them.

As if to cheer him in his distress, the congregation responded with the affirmation, *"Blessed are you, O Lord, who heals the sick among your people Israel!"*

"Be merciful, O Lord our God, toward your people Israel, and toward your city Jerusalem, toward Zion, where your glory abides, and toward the kingdom of the house of David, your righteous anointed one."

"Blessed are you, O God, God of David, the Builder of Jerusalem!"

"Blow the trumpet to announce our liberation, and lift a banner to gather our exiles."

"Blessed are you, O Lord, who gathers the dispersed of your people Israel!"

"Restore our judges as at the first, and our counselors as at the beginning, and reign over us—you alone!"

"Blessed are you, O Lord, who loves justice!"

Honiah kept his hands raised in prayer for a moment longer as the Levites began to chant another psalm, inviting the congregation to participate in the ritual with their own offerings of praise and worship through speech, thought, and gesture.

I call to you, Adonai; hasten to help me!
Hear my voice, and answer me!
Let my prayer rise up as incense before you,
and let the lifting up of my hands be regarded as an evening sacrifice.

The priests began to move to their stations for the sacrifice. Three went to a chamber on the north side of the court, emerging again with six flat loaves prepared earlier that day, a flask of wine, and a flask of pure olive oil with a measure of fine flour—all meticulously taken from the firstfruits of the produce of all the land of Israel, brought to the Temple storehouses as God's rightful portion and tribute. The bleating of a ram joined the Levites' cantillations, as the sacrifice was led out from a chamber on the south side of the court of the priests. Despite having passed through two thorough inspections for any blemish that would render it unworthy of being given to the God of Israel as part of this evening's tribute, it had to submit now to a final examination.

Jonathan ben Mattathias, who had drawn the lot to tend the seven-branched menorah that burned perpetually in the Lord's house, ascended the twelve steps and disappeared behind the first curtain. Honiah reflected, as he watched for Jonathan to return, how powerful a moment it was when he, while his father had been high priest, first drew the lot to enter the Holy Place. It was to offer the incense before the Lord during a morning sacrifice. He could remember most vividly the *stillness* of the place, the quietest place he had ever known, quiet enough to hear the voice of God. He remembered facing the inner curtain, behind which lay the Holy of Holies, the very presence of the Almighty, and falling to his knees, overcome with awe. His father had never asked what took him so long to offer the incense, perhaps because he had experienced the same thing.

By the time Jonathan reemerged, the ram had been given a drink from a golden vessel and was ready to be slaughtered. Honiah turned to face the congregation and the business of the sacrifice. Four priests lifted the ram onto a marble table near the altar, tying it down on its left side with its head hanging over the edge. The one to whom it had fallen by lot deftly cut the ram's throat with a single motion of the ceremonial knife, while another held a basin beneath the wound to catch the blood. The remaining two priests, whom Honiah recognized now as Asher ben Moshe and Salmon ben Azariah, carried the carcass across the courtyard to the shambles, a fearsome looking instrument consisting of a marble table with eight short pillars on top of it. Above each pillar was a cedar block with three iron hooks embedded in it. Even though he had seen it nearly every day of his adult life, Honiah always thought it seemed somehow out of place here.

Mattathias, the priest from Modein, now came forward and took up the basin of blood. He carried it to the northeast corner, tilted the basin slightly, and tossed some of the blood away from the altar toward the northeast. Moving to the southwest corner of the altar, he repeated the motion toward the southwest. The rest of the blood he poured out at the base of the south side of the altar. *The blood is the life*, thought Honiah. *Accept our gift of the life of this animal, poured out before you in obedience.*

Asher ben Moshe and Salmon ben Azariah suspended the carcass by driving its left legs onto two of the hooks at the knees. They began to flay the body, swiping their knives just below the skin and pulling back the hide in an almost unbroken motion, revealing the musculature and fat beneath. Cutting through the length of the animal from the chin to the genitalia, they exposed and removed the internal organs. A priest took these in a basin to the chamber on the north side of the court to be washed. Six priests formed a line near the shambles, receiving portions of the animal as the two priests butchered it, each according to the lot they had drawn. The priest who had taken away the entrails returned with them, now cleansed of all filth, and handed the basin to the sixth in line. Three more priests received the bread, wine, oil, and flour to complete the offering.

Honiah now took his station atop the altar platform at the corner closest to the curtain of the Holy Place. Once he was in place, the nine priests with the offering ascended the ramp and stood in line on the west side of the altar platform, followed by Amnon ben Imlah, who came around the east side and stood behind Honiah.

The first priest presented Honiah with the head of the ram, which Honiah received in both hands and, facing the curtain, elevated it in the direction of the Holy Place. He then handed this to Amnon, who half placed, half tossed it into the center of the fire that had been kindled in the center of the altar earlier that afternoon. Instantly the flesh of the ram's head began to crackle as the flames and hot embers boiled away the moisture in the outer layers of muscle and fat. Honiah received the hind leg from the same priest, which he elevated in the same manner and handed to Amnon, who placed it beside the head on the fire. Already the scent of the roasting lamb was wafting across the courtyard. Wisps of grayish-black smoke streaming upward like ribbons playing in the wind began to signal the transfer of the flesh from the world of the worshipers to the divine realm.

The first priest, his hands now empty, turned away from Honiah and walked back past his peers on the outside of the altar platform as the second stepped forward to give Honiah the ram's forelegs. Each priest came in his turn, Honiah raising each portion to God in the gesture of a child offering a gift to his father with the hope that the father would smile and the gift be accepted. Amnon carefully placed each portion so that all was spread out and burning evenly. The wisps of smoke quickly became a pillar, *a pleasing odor unto the Lord*. As the ram ascended, the seventh priest presented Honiah with the crater of wine. After raising it, Honiah gave it back to the priest, who then walked about the circumference of the altar, pouring out the wine as a libation as he went. The eighth priest likewise received back the flat loaves, which he placed on top of the charring remains of the ram. Last of all, the ninth priest presented Honiah with the oil and flour. Honiah poured the oil into the flour, elevated the mixture toward the curtain, and gave the bowl back to the priest to toss into the middle of the fire.

The priests and people stood silent as Honiah and the priests officiating at the altar returned to the floor of the courtyard and resumed their initial stations. The pillar of smoke rose higher and higher, bending to the east as it was caught by a higher stratum of wind blowing in light clouds from the sea. The pillar mingled with the clouds, spread, dissipated as it found its way through them and rose, in Honiah's mind's eye at least, before the very nostrils of God. The evening tribute, the perpetual sign of loyalty to their God on the part of God's people, had been duly made. The silence was shattered by the blast of seven silver trumpets sounded by the Levites to call the congregation to do obeisance before the Lord. Priests, Levites, and laity dropped to their knees and then lowered their heads to the ground in the traditional gesture of deepest reverence.

Jason stood in his reception hall. Through the outer doors, which were left standing open during the daylight hours, he watched eight men ascend the three steps to his front portico, cross the colonnade, and enter before him. They were led by Timarchos, the head of a wealthy priestly family resident in Jerusalem and a strong supporter of progress. Most wore the Greek tunic, which stopped mid-thigh, decorated with bands of embroidered geometric patterns and bound at the waist with a slender cord. One, an older gentleman with a bearded face, also sported a mantle over his shoulders. Jason had been scanning the group for this man, the gymnasiarch whom he had visited in Antioch several times before as he was gathering information about Greek educational institutions and curriculum.

"Chaire, Philostrate," Jason said with warm enthusiasm as he walked directly toward him. "You and your friends are most welcome in my home."

Jason touched his left hand to his chest and bowed slightly to Philostratos, extending his right arm slightly backward toward the inner parts of his house in a gesture of invitation.

"Chaire, Iasōn," replied Philostratos. "I am glad to visit you and your city at last. I hope our early arrival has not caused you any inconvenience."

"It has only hastened our joy," he replied with studied sincerity.

"Permit me to introduce my traveling companions," Philostratos continued. "To my right are Apollodoros and Heracleitos, citizens of Antioch." The Greeks nodded their heads slightly as the gymnasiarch announced their names.

"Though I am a resident of Cyprus," added Heracleitos.

"Just so," said Philostratos. "Heracleitos has some of the most bountiful vineyards in the world. His family has been renowned for their wines for more than a century."

"Indeed, it is because of wine that your city came to my notice," Heracleitos said, producing a chuckle among his compatriots. "I am serious. Iosephos Tobiades—I think you say 'Yoseph ben Tobiah'—was one of our best customers, a relationship that has continued with his sons. They showed me that a Jew could speak perfect Greek, deal with a Greek and his gods respectfully, and have good taste."

Some of the party's Jewish companions had stiffened at the mention of this name. Heracleitos looked from side to side in slight confusion, and Jason spoke to break the tension of the moment. "Yoseph ben Tobiah was indeed a great man who gave Judea, stuck in obscurity and poverty, its first chance at a brilliant future."

Philostratos continued with his introductions. "Over to my left is Dionysios, a Syrian born in Apamea but recently enrolled among the citizens of Antioch. Beyond him is Philon, a gentleman from your own *ethnos*, educated in the lyceum in Antioch and enrolled among the citizenry there."

"We are very interested in what you plan to do here," Philon said on behalf of the group. "My colleagues and I are eager to foster the Hellenization of Jerusalem and to lay the foundations, so to speak, for her future."

Jason did not miss the pun. "You are indeed welcome here as collaborators with us in this noble enterprise, and your investment in our future will redound to your honor here and abroad for generations to come." *Which is what public benefactors want most, after all.*

"And finally," Philostratos continued, "this is my protégé, Epaphroditos." A ruddy-faced youth, no more than eighteen, gave a slight nod of his head.

"And while we are making introductions, Lord Jason," Timarchos said, "permit me to introduce Menelaus, who has accompanied me, perhaps already known to you as Menachem ben Iddo."

"Ah, yes." Jason quickly made the connection with Simon ben Iddo, the man who had caused so much trouble for Honiah and against whom Jason aligned himself—though not entirely without sympathy for Simon's position. "Menelaus. I confess that I did not recognize you."

"I have been away from Jerusalem for some time, Lord Jason, except for my occasional rotation to serve in the Temple."

"And occasionally to serve my rotation, as well," Timarchos vaunted. "For a price." The group laughed. Suddenly realizing the impropriety of making such a joke before the brother of the high priest, Timarchos continued in a more sober tone, "Menelaus is from the priestly family of Bilgah and has spent several years in the coastal city of Azotus, facilitating trade there on behalf of several Judean families."

"But business affairs have moved me back to Jerusalem."

"He is most eager to see our plans for Jerusalem succeed," Timarchos said pointedly, to reassure his host.

"You are welcome, Menelaus," Jason said. *Though to what end I cannot imagine.*

"Your friend Timarchos has been a most able guide," Philostratos affirmed. "And your associate Agathon gave us a welcome reception at the city gate as we were entering and provided for us a magnificent tour of the city on our way to this splendid villa of yours."

"I am glad Agathon was able to greet you," Jason said. "Did he happen to show you the area we have been considering as the most suitable site for the lyceum, the gymnasium, and the xystos?"

"Yes indeed," replied Philostratos, "nestled in between the high priestly palace and the Temple. Very public, very prominent. I approve wholeheartedly."

"And what a magnificent Temple it is," Apollodoros remarked. "Of course," he added, playing to his traveling companions, "with only one Temple for only one God, I suppose you all should have been able to make it this grand. Kind of putting all your eggs in one basket, no?" His audience gratified him with their laughter.

"We heard the chants of your priests performing their evening liturgy as we passed by," said Dionysios.

"Ah yes," Jason commented. "It was the hour of our evening sacrifice, called in our language the *tamid*, one of two sacrifices made daily to God. The Levites would have been chanting hymns that have been used in worship for many centuries."

"They sound a bit dismal, like dirges, don't you think?" Epaphroditos said with a hint of derision.

Philostratos shot the youth a stern look. "We must learn to observe the native cultures of the *barbaroi* with respect and a scientific eye and ear if we are to become truly educated." Jason was not certain whether he should be pleased at Philostratos's reprimand or insulted at the obvious condescension which made an exercise in ethnography out of his people's solemn rites.

"Agathon will be joining us tonight for a banquet I have arranged to celebrate your visit. There are many more of our priests and aristocracy who wish to greet you and who are eager to see our vision take shape. I have arranged for an early afternoon reception tomorrow so that you may all become acquainted with one another."

"I hope I may look forward also to meeting the premier tomorrow," Philostratos said. "At first, I was concerned that our change in itinerary would have inconvenienced him, busy as he must be with affairs of the province. But when I learned we would be arriving before your day of rest, I was relieved since his schedule would surely be freest on that day."

Jason found himself listening to the awkward silence that followed.

"Gentlemen, tonight begins what the people of our nation call the Sabbath, a custom with which I am sure you must be aware from your broad experience. The law of Moses requires that Jews abstain from any—and I mean any—form of work on that day."

"Yes, we know of this custom," Dionysios said. "Intending no offense to my colleagues from the *ethnos* of the Jews, it has always seemed to me an excuse for idleness and for offering insult to non-Jews by putting them off every seventh day."

Jason felt both the sting of shame at the contempt with which the customs of the Jews were everywhere met and anger that a guest in his house should make him feel such shame.

"If you were to study our customs with the objectivity that, I am sure, Philostratos has employed," Jason said evenly, pushing back at Dionysios without being indiscrete, "you would find that pious remembrance of God's mighty acts lies behind the observance of the Sabbath rest. Our lore teaches that God spoke the universe into being in six days and rested on the seventh, and so the Sabbath is a witness of gratitude to the creator God in whom we live, move, and have our being. Our epics also tell of God's deliverance of the Jewish *ethnos* from slavery, and so the Sabbath is again a witness of gratitude to the deliverer God who made it possible for slaves who had no rest to be free citizens with leisure to rest."

"Though a philosopher would certainly consider the Jews still to be slaves of the worst sort," Dionysios persisted. "Not bound in physical chains, but enslaved to provincial superstitions by the adamantine chains forged by ignorance of the universal law of Nature."

"I am indeed embarrassed, Dionysios, by the way in which many of my countrymen, our premier included, cling to the ancestral traditions without regard for the circumstances, as though they were universal moral absolutes," Jason conceded. "But I am also concerned for you, lest you should be found to violate the universal laws of hospitality by your lack of sensitivity this afternoon." *And I do not need your money that badly.*

Philostratos smiled wryly at Jason's perfect riposte.

"Jason, you are indeed a Hellene in mind and spirit, and you see the challenges that beset the times in which we live. The gift of the Greeks is to bring Hellenes and *barbaroi* together for the exchange of ideas, both for the enrichment of the former and the liberation of the latter as they discover a larger world." Philostratos's tone darkened as he considered the high priest's insult. "As for the premier, whose whole duty it is to represent the civic body on occasions such as this, to choose avoidance of that duty for the sake of local tradition is, in my eyes, the *essence* of barbarism. But I understand, Jason," he continued more sympathetically, "that responsibility for his decisions is not to be laid at your doorstep."

"I am grateful for your magnanimous spirit, Philostratos," Jason said with some relief. "And I assure Dionysios, and anyone who thinks like him, that many of my nation have been liberated from the chains of tradition and are eager to discover how the universal culture of the Greeks can take shape on Judean soil." Before any new tension could creep into the room, Jason quickly added, "But these are matters that we can discuss more fully later. For now, I would invite you to refresh yourselves in your guest rooms. Sooth yourselves after your journey with a bath; take an hour's rest while my kitchen staff finishes the preparations for your evening repast."

Jason made eye contact with Castor, who mobilized a queue of servants with a gesture. "My servants will show you to your rooms and provide for your refreshment before dinner. I will send others outside to assist with your belongings."

Honiah raised his head and rose upon his knees to face the Holy Places once again. From this position, he recited what every man, woman, and child in the

Temple could have recited from memory, the creed that lay at the heart of the covenant, the foundation of Israel as a people, the core of every devout Jew's life.

"Hear, O Israel—*Adonai* is our God, *Adonai* alone. And you will show covenant faithfulness toward *Adonai* with all your heart and with all your soul and with all your might. And these words that I command you this day will remain in your heart. You will teach them carefully to your children. You shall talk about them when you sit in your house, and when you walk on the road, when you lie down, and when you rise up. Remember all the commandments of *Adonai*, to do them rather than to follow after your own heart and your own eyes in your rebelliousness. So you shall be holy to your God."

The melody of flutes and reeds filled the courtyard as the Levite singers began to chant again, intoning words that had long ago been implanted in each of the worshipers.

See, how good, how pleasant it is when brothers live together in unity.
It is like the precious oil that consecrated Aaron,
    running down his head and flowing over his robes!

Their song pricked Honiah's heart, the Levites' harmony sounding a jarring dissonance with his own experiences of brotherhood of late. He turned his attention once again to the action of the priests to distract himself from his renewed distress. The priests had cast lots anew to discover who would remove the ashes from the altar of incense behind the first curtain, and the one who had been chosen was already descending the steps from the Holy Place, carrying a short shovel and a pail full of ashes.

The Levites had segued into a second psalm, and a different priest now stepped forward with a metal bowl full of fresh incense. Taking the ceremonial shovel from the first priest, he ascended the steps. The voices of the gathered worshipers in every court grew louder, each offering prayers to God. *May my prayer rise as incense before you*, thought Honiah as the second priest disappeared behind the curtain, and he began to add his own prayers to theirs. The petitions were still ascending before God when the priest emerged and resumed his place at the perimeter of the court of the priests. Honiah allowed the moment to continue, this sacred time in which the people could pour out their needs before the Divine Benefactor and find favor for timely help.

At his signal, the trumpets blew a second time. A few worshipers brought their prolonged petitions to a speedy conclusion as the people fell once more to the ground before their God. Honiah now ascended the steps to stand between the pillars in front of the great curtain. Facing the people, he raised his arms over them and invoked God's blessing: "May *Adonai* bless and keep you. May *Adonai* make his face to shine upon you and be favorable toward you. May *Adonai* smile over you and give you *shalom*."

The people and priests responded, *"Amen, amen,"* adding their agreement and their prayers that Honiah's words should indeed be so. He lowered his hands and looked out for a moment upon the priests at their stations, the men crowding the court behind them, the women and some younger children visible through the bronze gate behind the court of Israelite males. *This is the business of a high priest,* Honiah thought. *Standing between God and God's people for the pleasure of the One and the well-being of the other.* He began to descend the steps, hesitating halfway, reluctant to return to the mire of rival factions, profane agendas, and power struggles that never seemed so petty, so wrongheaded as when he stood in this place. The faces of Simon ben Iddo, of Seraiah ben Yoseph, of young priests already neglecting their appointed times of service passed through his mind. *There is no fear of God in their eyes.* Then Yeshua's face. *Jason's face,* Honiah reminded himself. *When the day comes, at whose side will he stand?*

But for this evening, there was *shalom*. The God of Israel had been duly honored; God's people had been brought once more under the cool shade of God's favor and covenant faithfulness. It was time for rest.

Honiah recessed from the courtyard toward his private chamber. The remaining priests followed and returned to the Office of Hewn Stone to exchange their holy vestments for their own garments, save for those whose lot it was to remove the bones of the sacrifice, rake the ashes, and flush the blood down the drains. The sun was a little more than a cubit's breadth above the horizon, giving them perhaps an hour to complete their work before the Sabbath began and the commandment called all to rest with God.

Castor and his staff ushered Jason's guests from the reception hall to their apartments. Once they were out of earshot, Timarchos and Menelaus approached Jason.

"I hesitate to point out the obvious, but our cause just suffered a significant setback. A public undertaking of this magnitude requires the consent of the premier, who has just shown himself to be quite at odds with the very purpose of building the lyceum in the first place." Timarchos became more pointed. "I thought you said that you would be able to manage Honiah."

"Is it my fault Philostratos arrived early?" Jason retorted, not hiding his annoyance at Timarchos's challenge. "My brother was quite willing to accommodate us on the first day of the week."

"The greatest danger here, I think, is that these financiers may lose their enthusiasm for investing significant funds in a public project that lacks support at the highest levels," Menelaus observed from the vantage point he knew best—business. "The degree to which the lyceum and gymnasium are celebrated and embraced is the degree to which they will be honored for their gifts."

"But even if we could finance these institutions internally," Timarchos added more forcefully, "will Philostratos direct the most able teachers to us, and will he put his own influence behind the young men who study here, hoping to be introduced to the court of Antiochus, if he gets the impression that this project is just the hobby of a few Hellenophiles rather than the direction that the nation—and that means Honiah—is thoroughly committed to espouse?"

"Timarchos," Jason said reassuringly. "Timarchos ben Yoab." He overpronounced each word, highlighting the contrast between his associate's cosmopolitan Greek name and the more provincial, Judean name of his father. "Consider for a moment how far we have come in the short time of our adult lives, and therefore how much more we are destined to achieve before we grow old and feeble. You overestimate the importance of a day's delay, I think. Even if it does offer a temporary offense to these gentlemen, it certainly does not spell disaster for our plans—or for their part in it."

"Indeed, I have begun to look differently at our situation after Lord Jason's brilliant explanation to Philostratos," Menelaus interjected with reserved optimism. "Against the canvas of a—forgive me, Lord Jason—somewhat backward premier we might appear to Philostratos as all the more courageous and enlightened in our attempts to lead our countrymen to the waters of Greek culture."

Menelaus raised his right eyebrow and cocked his head slightly, signifying that he was about to reveal a shrewd analysis of the situation.

"I think Philostratos will regard our cause more sympathetically, and be more inclined to mediate assistance to ensure our progress."

"I hope you are correct, Menelaus," Timarchos replied. "A day may be a small thing, Jason, but in this case it is also a highly symbolic thing, sending a clear signal that Jerusalem is not united in its desire to escape barbarism."

"We will continue to make our way forward, Timarchos. Have no doubt of that," Jason declared. "Now, please, take some rest in one of my rooms or in the garden. We have a long and delightful evening ahead of us that, I think, will soothe any lingering sting from the afternoon."

Honiah stepped from his chamber, clothed once again in his simple tunic and cord, into the corridor that surrounded the court of the priests. He passed through the court of Israelite males and began to descend the fifteen steps into the court of all Israelites. From that vantage point, he saw Mattathias and his son lingering at the far right corner, exchanging pleasantries with two of the Levite musicians who had been on duty that evening. He crossed the court and arrived within earshot just as the four were finishing their conversation and turning away.

"Mattathias ben Johanan, you are away from home and the Sabbath is upon us. You and your son must be guests in my house tonight."

Jonathan looked at his father expectantly. Dinner at the home of the high priest would certainly be more interesting—and the fare more enjoyable—than partaking of some of the meat and bread reserved for the priests in the Temple and frittering away the evening.

"My lord Honiah is most gracious," Mattathias replied. "We would of course be honored to accept."

"Excellent. It is a joy to break bread with like-minded sons of the covenant. Come, then."

Jonathan beamed as Honiah placed his hand on Mattathias's shoulder and began to lead them out of the Temple precincts. Two pairs of Levites, carrying spears, fell in line before and behind them as they stepped into the court of all nations.

"Go home, brothers," Honiah said to his escort. "It's almost evening. Your families are waiting for you."

The guards hesitated.

"It's all right. I'm accompanied by two strong priests from the farms of Modein," Honiah urged. "You two are good in a scrap, aren't you?" he asked with the corner of his mouth turned upward in an impish smile.

Timarchos had found a cushioned bench in a shady grove in Jason's gardens.

"Lie down and rest," Menelaus urged, "and try not to worry. This will all prove to be to our advantage in the long run."

Timarchos was still far from convinced on the second point. As he began to stretch himself out on the couch, he heard approaching footsteps on the stone path.

Through a bush, he could see Heracleitos advancing. "Greetings," he said, both to welcome him and to make their presence known.

"Ah, Timarchos, Menelaus. I did not mean to intrude upon your rest," the Greek answered.

"Not at all," Timarchos reassured him. "Please join us."

Heracleitos sat in a limestone chair opposite him and next to Menelaus.

"I fear I may have caused some awkwardness in the reception hall."

"Not to worry, Heracleitos," Menelaus was quick to respond. "It might, however, be best not to speak too openly tonight of your association with the family of the Tobiades."

Heracleitos was silent for a moment, before deciding against letting the matter pass.

"I don't understand. Is that family out of favor here in Jerusalem?"

"Rivalry between powerful families happens here, Heracleitos, just as in Antioch or Alexandria," Timarchos explained. "As the two most powerful families in Judea, the Tobiades and the house of Honiah have also had the most intense rivalries."

"Yoseph ben Tobiah managed to wrest the title of premier away from Jason's grandfather, Honiah II, through his private dealings with King Ptolemy of Egypt while our land was under Ptolemy's control," Menelaus said. "A serious blow to the power of the high priest, and a major victory for a non-priestly family like Yoseph ben Tobiah's. When Judea became part of the Seleucid Empire twenty-some years later, Antiochus the Great restored the title of premier to Jason's father, Simon—in large measure because Antiochus did not trust the Tobiades due to their long and close relationship with the kings of Egypt for over a century."

"And this rivalry continues?" Heracleitos asked.

"First Yoseph and then his eldest son, Seraiah, have tried to regain what power they could through other offices and other means," Timarchos said, "primarily through their wealth."

Timarchos paused, reflecting on the feud that had been in the background of Judean politics for half a century.

"The families are ideological rivals as well. The Tobiades have been much more open to Hellenistic culture and to relations with non-Jews from the beginning. The house of Honiah has been far more—how shall I put this?—provincial in their outlook."

"But not Jason," observed Heracleitos. "He seems more aligned with the Tobiades in principle."

"But of course, family loyalties are stronger," Menelaus responded, "and so he has rallied to his brother when conflicts erupt."

The ensuing silence suggested that Heracleitos had been satisfied.

"If the two of you would excuse me," Menelaus said, "I have one matter of business in the city to which to tend before our festivities this evening. Timarchos, please assure our host that I will return as soon as possible."

"An interesting situation here indeed," Heracleitos mused out loud to Timarchos. "A new world laboring to be born, but a delivery fraught with complications. I hope it shall not be stillborn."

3

Mattathias and Jonathan accompanied Honiah at a brisk pace toward the high priestly palace, spurred on both by the increasing gusts whose chill presaged an evening rain and by the lateness of the hour. The sun had turned to deep orange as it hovered two fingers' breadth above the horizon in front of them, and the three priests were intent on making it to their resting place before the sun sank into its own. A hundred paces more brought them down the last stretch of street, across the portico, through the courtyard, and up to the main entrance to the living areas of the palace on its east side. Honiah opened the door to the welcoming scents of spiced meats roasting. Jonathan smiled broadly as he caught Mattathias's gaze. A servant immediately appeared in the vestibule to unlace their sandals and take their cloaks, while two others emerged with a pitcher, bowl, and towel and poured water over their feet.

When the servants had completed their last task before the Sabbath, Honiah led the way into the living room, where the family had already gathered in anticipation of the Sabbath. Rivkeh rose to greet them.

"Good Sabbath, my husband. I see you have brought guests."

"Indeed. This is Mattathias ben Johanan, a priest from the line of Hashmon, from the village of Modein. And this is his son Jonathan. They served with me at the evening sacrifice, with all the dignity befitting the Lord's ministers."

"You are welcome here," Rivkeh said.

"I believe you both know my son," Honiah said, "who also bears my name and will succeed me to the high priesthood when it is God's time."

A young man of twenty rose to acknowledge Mattathias and Jonathan.

"And I have no doubt that you are acquainted with Zedekiah, the grandson of the brother of Simon the Just, my father."

Zedekiah rose from his chair to greet his fellow priests. Though not much older than Honiah's son, he wore the serious demeanor of an elder. His cheeks were pale and thin from the combination of frequent fasting and infrequent exposure to the light of day.

"Acquainted indeed," Mattathias said. "I think Zedekiah spends more time in the Temple than even you, my lord Honiah."

A rustle of laughter rushed through the room. "We were just talking about that before you all came in, Mattathias," said the younger Honiah.

Zedekiah smiled weakly. "I simply ask, if a day in the courts of the God of heaven is better than a thousand elsewhere, why should I squander a single day elsewhere?"

"Perhaps you could spare a day or two to get married, and another day or two to have children," Rivkeh teased.

The banter quickly made Mattathias and Jonathan feel as if they had walked, not into the house of the high priest, but into the house of a family with whom they were quite familiar and at home.

"My aunts and female relations are most anxious to see me married," Zedekiah said to Mattathias, "but I prefer a simpler life, and one with far fewer distractions. 'One thing have I desired of the Lord. For this one thing I seek—to live in the house of the Lord all my days, to gaze upon the beauty of the Lord, and to search out his ways in his Temple.'"

"The very Scripture that went through my mind as I went to the Temple this afternoon," Honiah said. "Temple service and study are great goods, to be sure, but so is enjoying the natural and good things that God has provided."

Young Honi jumped in with authoritative support for his father's position. "Does not Scripture also bear witness that 'a good wife is a gift from the Lord'? The whole counsel of Scripture would seem to me to be moderation, Zedekiah."

"With all due respect to you, Uncle, and to you, esteemed Mattathias, priests who are married inevitably encounter"—Zedekiah's distaste was evident as he searched for the right word—"substances that disqualify them for service at least until the following evening. I wish to keep myself pure and available for God at all times, and to sanctify every hour to God."

"There is, at least, no doubt as to where your heart is, Zedekiah," Honiah said, relenting with a smile. "Indeed, I should speak more words of correction to our brothers whose ambitions are leading them, to the contrary, to sanctify fewer and fewer hours to God." Honiah's eyes clouded a moment before he shook his head and said with greater energy, "Speaking of which, this is an hour that must be sanctified. Where is Rachel?"

"I left her in the kitchen," Rivkeh answered. "She was helping the servants set out everything we would need for our meal today and for tomorrow." Rivkeh disappeared for a moment, reemerging from an inner room with their daughter and two female servants. The three male servants who had attended to Honiah and his guests on their arrival also emerged from the vestibule, as the whole household—family, servants, and guests—gathered around a ceremonial table set off to the side of the room.

Rivkeh picked up a narrow stick and walked over to an oil lamp suspended from a bronze lampstand. Holding one end of the stick in the flame, she returned with it ablaze and lit the first of two candles set out on the table.

"'Remember the Sabbath, to sanctify it,'" she said, inviting the household to recall God's act of creation and deliverance from slavery, acts that every Sabbath anchored more firmly in the historical recollection of the people of Israel. Touching the stick to the wick of the second candle, she said, "'Observe the Sabbath, to keep it holy,'" reminding the household of the command of God to set the coming night and day apart from all ordinary labor, just as God had set Israel apart from all ordinary nations.

Honiah lifted his hands in a gesture of adoration as he said, "Blessed are you, *Adonai*, our God, King of Eternity, who sanctified us by giving us your commandments, and who commanded us to observe the seventh day."

"Amen, amen," came the response from the gathered household.

Honiah, Mattathias, Jonathan, Zedekiah, and Honi all joined together to say, "May *Adonai* bless and keep us. May *Adonai* make his face to shine upon us and be favorable toward us. May *Adonai* smile over us and give us *shalom*."

Once again, priests, women, and servants affirmed together, *"Amen, amen."*

The servants began to disperse, bowing their heads and wishing "good Sabbath" to Honiah and his family and heading for the wing of the palace dedicated to their use, where they would enjoy the Sabbath meal with their own children. Honiah looked to Rivkeh, who affirmed with a nod that all was prepared. "Come, Mattathias, Jonathan. The table is ready."

Rivkeh ushered them into the dining room, Honiah and the rest of the family following. The room was dominated by a large cedar table raised half a meter off the ground, adorned with geometric patterns made from inlaid ivory, mahogany, and cherry wood. A large woven mat completely covered the floor beneath, with ample cushions placed around for seating. The table was spread with platters of roast lamb spiced with vinegar and rosemary, quails braised with cider and onion, and savory stews made from lentils and fresh vegetables. Loaves of bread, flasks of wine, and bowls of fruit and nuts completed the feast. Bowls and knives were set out for each person's use, and the family members began to move instinctively to their places.

"Mattathias, come sit next to me," said Honiah, giving his older guest the place of honor at his right side. Jonathan sat to the right of his father, leaning his left side against the cushion and propping himself up farther with his left hand against the floor. Zedekiah took a place next to him, and Honi seated himself across the table from his cousin. Rivkeh looked at Honiah, who gave an approving nod. She and Rachel then took their places at the table at Honiah's left. For any family meal, they would have naturally taken their place at the table; with guests present, Rivkeh was not certain that this would be appropriate. This was a clear signal to Mattathias and Jonathan that Honiah intended to treat them as family.

Taking one of the flasks of wine, Honiah poured some into his own cup, raised it, and said, "Blessed are you, *Adonai*, our God, whose presence fills the cosmos, who creates the fruit of the vine."

"Amen," came the response from around the table as Honiah offered the flask to Mattathias. Honi, who had not allowed himself to get too comfortable at his place in anticipation of the next rite, brought an empty basin and a pitcher of water to his father and proceeded to pour out some water over his father's hands.

"Blessed are you, *Adonai*, our God, whose presence fills the cosmos, who has sanctified us by giving your commandments and who has commanded us to perform the washing of the hands."

"Amen," the table said in unison as Honiah dried his hands on a towel and proceeded to pour water over Mattathias's hands. After Mattathias had, in turn, poured water for Jonathan, and Jonathan for Zedekiah, Honiah took one of the loaves of bread from the table and raised it up.

"Blessed are you, *Adonai*, our God, whose presence fills the cosmos, who brings forth bread from the ground."

"Amen," came the response once again, as Honiah broke a piece from the loaf and offered the remainder to Mattathias, who sent it around the table following the water.

When Rachel had finished pouring the water for Rivkeh, the mood shifted instantly from orderly ritual to family dinner. Hands on all sides of the table reached for platters and bowls, took portions for their own bowls, and began to pass the meats and stews around until everyone had taken a healthy first serving.

As the passing of plates began to slow down, Honi broached the topic that was on the minds of the whole family.

"I saw Uncle Yeshua leaving here today. He looked . . . troubled."

Honiah was visibly distressed, but spoke lightly.

"Oh, it was nothing. We have always been fighting, Yeshua and I. Sometimes I think that is the essence of brotherhood, and not 'harmony' as the sages have tried to convince us."

After a moment's silence, Zedekiah ventured to ask, "What did he want?"

Honiah looked at him and said in a nonchalant tone, "He wanted me to meet tomorrow with some out-of-town dignitaries that he had invited."

"On the Sabbath?" Zedekiah reacted, not hiding his indignation.

"Yeshua seemed keen on not doing anything to offend these visitors with our . . . local customs."

"And why are these visitors so important to him?" Honi asked. "What does he hope to gain from them?"

"His school. His gymnasium."

"To teach more of our people to observe fewer of our laws," Zedekiah said with disgust.

Mattathias stopped chewing momentarily. He was familiar with Jason's ambitions, being privy to the rumblings of the priests in the Temple and the elders in the assembly, but he had discounted them as dreams that could never be realized.

"My lord Honiah," he ventured, "every Greek city has such a school at its very heart. Wherever Alexander went, he planted gymnasia like a virus until the Greek way of life infected the whole world. Surely your brother doesn't intend to invite that into Jerusalem, into God's holy city!"

"That is clearly what he intends," Honiah said. His countenance fell as he took a sip of wine. "And it is clearly what I must prevent. I have allowed Yeshua as much room to pursue his vision as I could. When he instituted private schools for learning the Greek language, I thought it might be an asset for our youth in their witness to the Gentile world. When he encouraged the schools to teach Greek literature, I told myself that the stories they read would provide points of contact with our own stories and would demonstrate the superiority of our faith. When he imported teachers of Greek philosophy, I rationalized that it would give the faithful the tools they needed to interpret our faith in terms that the Greeks—and our Jewish brothers and sisters living for generations in Greek lands—could understand and honor. But I can no longer pretend that anyone who is trained in those schools will use his learning only to defend our ancestral ways, and a central gymnasium will only spread the disease among our elites exponentially."

The table remained silent, each person sensing the reluctance with which Honiah faced the prospect of direct conflict with Jason.

"I should never have let matters go so far, but as the premier I do have the power to see that they go no further."

"I am relieved to hear your resolve," Mattathias said.

"But is there cause to be concerned about Uncle Yeshua's resolve, if he is already that close?" Honi added.

"Indeed, my lord Honiah." Mattathias was quick to support Honi's suggestion of caution. "Yeshua is your brother and would, I'm sure, never wish you harm. But the same might not be as easily said for those families that support him."

"And with a project as large as this," Honi reasoned, "he must have considerable support from the many families that desire to become more like the nations."

"Your concern is noted, and your anxiety for my well-being appreciated," Honiah said. "But I've survived political intrigues before—and without getting distracted by politics. You all remember how, not two years ago, Simon ben Iddo, the 'president of the Temple' —"

"The 'pestilence of the Temple,' more like," sneered Zedekiah around a morsel of quail in his mouth.

"Pestilence indeed," agreed Honiah. "You remember how he tried to ruin me in the sight of King Seleucus the Fourth by suggesting that I was channeling funds from Ptolemy's allies here to Egypt, and that the money deposited in the Temple was therefore appropriate for Seleucus to seize for himself?"

Nods and murmurs from around the table signaled their recollection.

"You remember how Seleucus sent his emissary Heliodoros and a band of thugs back with that traitor to raid the Temple treasury and remove me from office? The whole city turned out in the streets and the Temple courts, crying out to God for help, calling down God's anger upon the arrogant Gentile who intended to stride right into the sanctuary and take whatever he wanted. And God intervened. God protected his Holy Places!"

Honiah closed his eyes. "I can still see the look of horror and surprise on Heliodoros's face as God's invisible hand closed in on his neck and left him writhing on the ground." He opened his eyes again, now as if seeing the scene that was imprinted forever in his memory. "Not when I was arrayed in the holy garments, not when I could hear the Levites chanting psalms at my back, not when I entered the Holy of Holies these fifteen times during my years as high priest did I ever sense the power of God like I did on that day."

He paused, pondering the strange and unpredictable ways in which their God had manifested Himself, then focused on Mattathias.

"And after such a day, should I continue to fear what human beings might plot? Who survived that gambit? Where is Simon ben Iddo now?"

"If we have enjoyed God's favor and *shalom*, Honiah, we are mindful that it is because of your steadfast devotion to ordering our common life by the Torah," Mattathias said without pretense. But he had also seen men fall down with seizures in the village in the heat of the day, men who had not crossed God as Heliodoros had done. "Nevertheless prudence is always appropriate for those whom God has set in the front lines of battle."

"We never did discover the extent of Simon's supporters, who surely are still plotting against you," said Honi, who likewise wished that his father would take a greater interest in self-preservation.

"'God will never permit the righteous to fall,'" said Zedekiah. "Uncle Honiah's foot 'shall not be moved.'"

"May God grant it to be so, as long as it serves his good purposes," Honiah said. "But enough of city politics. Tell us about the life of the country, where people plant rather than plot."

"Truly, Honiah, were it not for the joy of the Temple service, I would never leave Modein," Mattathias said. "All is so much more tranquil there than in Jerusalem. You cannot rush the winter to plant; you cannot hasten the harvest to ripen. And so there is little rush or haste. In the day we work the land and learn the patience that the earth teaches; in the evening we play with our little ones and eat the produce of the land with satisfaction—though it is not nearly so fine as the food you have set before us, my lady," he said, raising his cup to Rivkeh, who blushed, pleased by the acknowledgment.

"And at night, well . . . " Mattathias's voice trailed off. The men around the table laughed as they completed the sentence for themselves.

Rivkeh smiled and said teasingly, "Come, Rachel. The conversation has taken its inevitable turn where men are present. Now we will have to find more . . . sanctified entertainment." She turned to Mattathias and Jonathan and said, "It has been a pleasure to receive you in our house. May your next visit come quickly."

"We are truly grateful for your hospitality," Mattathias replied with a nod.

Jonathan and Honi reached for slices of fruit and nuts from the bowls on the table as the women took their leave and Mattathias resumed his account.

"Still, it is not all pleasant and peaceful in the villages. Many families have been cut off from their land—"

"Greed trumps the observance of the law of Moses everywhere," Jonathan chimed in. "There is no cancellation of debts; there is no year of release."

"It is sadly the case," Mattathias continued. "When debts are called in, families must pay or relinquish their land."

"And this happens not only in Modein, but in villages throughout Judea," added Jonathan.

"The ancient inheritance of many families—what God himself bequeathed to their lines forever—is being concentrated into the hands of fewer and fewer elites, most of them resident now in Jerusalem and Jericho."

Honiah was visibly pained, although he had heard of it many times before. "I have indeed failed in my duty to enforce the economic statutes of the Torah in this regard."

It was clear from his wearied expression, however, that it was not from want of trying.

"There are only so many places that the eyes of the faithful can watch, and there are so many ways to circumvent the law even in those places, so many loopholes for those who will not allow their hearts to be trained by the Torah to think more about their fellow Israelite than their own purses."

"I did not bring this up to be critical of you, my lord Honiah," Mattathias said. "It is just a growing concern in the villages. In Modein, we have been able to cooperate with two dispossessed families who farm our land and share in the harvest."

"You are a good-hearted man, Mattathias," Honiah said.

"I would be remiss if I were to make it sound entirely like charity, Honiah. After all, the labor of these families is giving us greater freedom to attend to our duties in the Temple as well as to be more involved in the life of Jerusalem."

"Though even so it is hard to get Judah and Avaran away from the dirt," Jonathan added.

Mattathias chortled. "Indeed, those two are more comfortable in the dust of the field than the white linen of priests." Honiah and the younger priests laughed. "Jonathan here, my youngest, has a real heart for the Temple."

Zedekiah looked at Jonathan with increased interest.

"Yes," Honiah said, "I've noticed that about him when he's on duty."

"And my oldest sons—Johanan and Simon—have a greater love for the city than the life of the farm. Their visits here are the high points in their lives, and they've taken an interest in its political life. But for me, politics is the price one has to pay for staying in Jerusalem, not one of its privileges."

Again the table broke out in laughter.

"A refreshing perspective on the maneuverings that occupy so much of our time and talent here in the city, Mattathias," Honiah said, smiling and shaking his head from side to side.

Zedekiah looked intently at Jonathan. "You went into the Holy Place this afternoon. What did you find?"

Jonathan was taken aback by the earnestness in Zedekiah's voice, and by the expectation inherent in his question that a priest would indeed find something behind the curtain.

"When I stepped behind the curtain, it was like stepping out of time into eternity," Jonathan said thoughtfully. "I felt a focus, a centeredness like I'd not experienced in any other place. I would call it . . . *shalom*."

"Indeed," Zedekiah said, visibly resonating with Jonathan's sense of the mystery and fullness of the Holy Place. "Did you hear anything? Did you see anything?"

Jonathan thought for a moment, which in itself was an answer. "No," he concluded. "Not, at least, as our prophets and seers have experienced."

"Well, we must keep listening and looking," Zedekiah said, as if recruiting Jonathan, "especially in the Temple where God's perfect realm intersects with this corrupted creation."

Honi broke in.

"You'll have to forgive my cousin," he said with a wry smirk. "He likes to collect revelations from God."

As Menelaus returned to the vestibule of Jason's house, he could already hear the sounds of conversation reverberating from the *triclinium* through the stone reception hall. He quickened his pace and entered the dining hall to find the guests already at their places on the three plush couches. The entrance from the reception hall brought him behind the right side of the first couch, the one on which the host and his family members normally sat. Today Jason shared the couch with Agathon, reclining to his right, and Timarchos, to Agathon's right. Philostratos sat in the place of honor—on the second couch, and immediately to Jason's left. Menelaus caught sight of a wooden box on the floor beneath his couch, which he presumed was the customary gift that would be offered to a guest of distinction. Next to him Jason had placed Apollodoros and Heracleitos. On the third, far couch, Philon, Dionysius, and Epaphroditos reclined. The last seemed to be pouting somewhat, and Menelaus assumed it was from being assigned the lowest place at the table on the basis of his youth.

The couches flanked three sides of an exquisitely crafted table with a large square cut out of the open side, so that attendants could step into the table, as it were, to better serve the guests. A number of appetizer trays had been laid out. Although well picked over by now, Menelaus could still see olives, bits of cheeses, grapes, sliced citrons and oranges, and bread. The room was filled with the aromas of roasting meats, herbs, and spices wafting in from the kitchen, heightening the expectation of the guests.

Jason greeted the latecomer. "Welcome, Menelaus. I trust your business was successful?"

"My apologies for my delay, Lord Jason."

"Well, you're still in good time for the festivities," Jason said cordially. "The staff is just about to begin serving the dinner." Jason gestured toward the far right of his own couch. "You would be welcome to join us here. I believe we can make room."

"Lord Jason," Epaphroditos interjected, "your guest can have my place."

Jason looked at him with surprise.

"I would not wish my host and his guests to feel cramped," the youth explained, as he rose and sat on the back corner of the second couch by Philostratos's feet. Jason nodded, though he considered it odd that a Greek male would voluntarily put himself in a place normally occupied by a wife or female companion.

The appearance of three servants bearing serving trays immediately took the attention off Epaphroditus, as the guests eagerly anticipated what would be set before them. The first servant stepped into the niche in the table and placed bowls and spoons before each diner. The second produced a large tureen of a lentil soup and began ladling some into each bowl. The aroma of cumin, garlic, and onion began to fill the immediate space of the diners, causing some to smile, some to raise their eyebrows with approval. The third servant produced a tray with several loaves of fine wheat bread. As the guests began to break the loaves and pass them around, they discovered that olives, walnuts, and cilantro had been baked into the bread.

After he had tasted the soup, Apollodoros began the conversation. "Jason, I am interested to learn what you have done to prepare your people for the introduction of the gymnasium."

"Indeed," Heracleitos interjected, "it would make little sense to build it if there is not a ready clientele."

So the probing begins, thought Jason.

"I have been in frequent contact with Philostratos over the past seven years about this very subject. Early in that period, my associates and I established several smaller schools to instruct students in Greek language, to begin to expose them to Greek literature, and even to begin training in the rudiments of rhetoric and argumentation. One of these, under my personal patronage, is free to all students who are accepted. This makes it possible for us to extend Greek primary education to those who will require both a fluency in Greek and an appreciation for Greek culture and customs to function well in their supporting roles throughout the city."

Jason could see he had already impressed Apollodoros, and so continued with greater assurance. "These have rivaled and surpassed the more traditional schools—the 'houses of instruction'—among the elite, which both demonstrates their enthusiasm for moving ahead with this project and provides a body of youths who will be ready for gymnasium-level education."

"Moreover, Philostratos"—Jason gestured toward the gymnasiarch—"has already sent several skilled teachers to Jerusalem to provide secondary training to select young men in the absence of the public institution, so that there will be a core of people already in place who can model the end result and assist others as mentors."

Philostratos nodded his concurrence. "I have also approached several of the scholars at the Musaion in Antioch about coming to teach here once the building projects are completed."

"For which we will be most grateful," Jason acknowledged with a smile.

The servants appeared again to remove the soup tureen and the guests' bowls and to supply large ceramic plates and small bowls filled with water so that they could wash their fingertips between bites.

"I understand that you have also been in touch with the gymnasiarch in Alexandria about the same," said Philostratos.

"I want our youth to be exposed to as cosmopolitan an education as possible; I mean no disrespect to your distinguished colleagues at the Musaion."

"No offense taken," Philostratos replied. "I am, on the contrary, impressed with your forethought for this project."

Castor appeared at the head of the passage that led to the kitchen, waiting to be acknowledged.

"Are we ready, then, Castor?"

"Yes, my lord."

"Very good. Proceed."

The exchange was calculated to draw the guests' attention to the procession of servants who would bring out the main courses. *A dinner that cost me this much and was prepared with such trouble is worthy of a little drama.* Jason's entire household staff had been co-opted to serve as waiters. Polydeuces appeared first, bearing a platter of sea bass and sliced citrons in a sesame-and-lemon sauce. He stepped into the niche in the table and served the guests in turn, beginning with Philostratos. When each had taken the portion he desired, Polydeuces set the remainder on the table in front of Timarchos. Niobe followed him with a smaller dish bearing grape leaves stuffed with rice, yogurt, and mint, setting this, in turn, before Agathon.

The next pair of servants advanced more slowly, giving the guests a little time to sample what they had already taken before presenting them with slices of roasted lamb stuffed with olives, almonds, and figs, accompanied by red peppers stuffed with couscous, raisins, and mint. A third pair brought medallions of beef, pan seared with dark wine and juniper sprigs, and slices of eggplant fried in olive oil with diced tomatoes. Castor himself carried the platter of quail, which had been baked in a sauce of pomegranates, wine, and walnuts, while Niobe doubled back to bear the bowl of steaming, aromatic rice. The diners' delight preempted conversation for the next ten minutes, a sign of the success of the kitchen staff.

Jason glanced around in time to see Philostratos offering a morsel of quail to Epaphroditos, who took it directly into his mouth from the gymnasiarch's hand, his lips lingering on Philostratos's fingers. The priest turned away, with only a slight narrowing of his left eye betraying his disgust.

"Lord Jason, this is a splendid banquet you have set before us," Dionysios said in a most congratulatory voice. "Lamb, quail, fish, beef, all expertly seasoned and prepared. Your bounty is such that I can't think of anything missing." He paused for a moment. "Except, possibly, pork."

"I thought it most fitting to entertain you with some of the finest dishes that customarily grace our tables," Jason answered, hoping the topic would go away.

"Is there no pork in Judea?"

"Very little, actually," Jason responded politely, quite aware that Dionysios knew the answer, and the reason, already. He added wryly, "Not many residents have acquired a taste for it."

Laughter erupted around the table at the quip. As it died down, Dionysios continued, thinly veiling his barb with a smile.

"How about you, Jason? Have you ever tried it?"

Jason resented being goaded again by this guest, but remained master of himself.

"You are no doubt aware of my fellow Judeans' position concerning the eating of pork," he replied with a serious demeanor. "Were I, brother of the high priest and a priest myself, to indulge in the eating of pork—thus violating one of the most conspicuous marks of Judean identity—what would I gain? I would gain the experience of another kind of meat, perhaps even a moment of pleasure."

He looked around the table, as if to address anyone else that harbored ideas about testing him.

"But what would I lose? I think I would sacrifice a great deal of the credibility I have been seeking to establish for Hellenization by arguing, and I hope demonstrating, that it is not entirely incompatible with our heritage. So I have exercised self-control for the sake of a much greater good."

Dionysios could find no way to challenge Jason's masterful defense, a fact that won Jason even greater respect in the eyes of Philostratos.

The gymnasiarch intervened to dispel the tension. "People are Hellenes not only by descent, but by disposition. Those who share our education are as fully Hellenes as those who share our ancestry. I have no doubt, Jason, that you are a true Hellene at heart."

The guests were slowing down in their consumption of the main course, and Castor gave a signal that the serving trays should be cleared away. Niobe and Polydeuces emerged from the kitchen, bearing bowls of sliced figs marinated in honey and wine, along with sliced apples and shelled nuts.

Reaching for a wedge of fig, Philon said, "It would seem that you are well on the way to making Jerusalem truly a Greek city."

Timarchos began to respond with enthusiasm for the prospect. "Indeed we are. Once we have the gymnasium in place, we—"

"We aren't yet speaking of a Greek city," Jason interjected, looking firmly at Timarchos. Jason softened his visage and looked across the table to Philon. "It has taken years of careful planning and maneuvering just to bring us to this point."

"But isn't that really the direction in which you're moving?" Philostratos asked, nudging Jason to admit the scope of his ambitions. "All of your careful educational reforms undertaken to date, your plans for the gymnasium, your entire vision for the shaping of Judean youth is geared toward preparing them to take part in a city that does not yet exist—a city founded upon a Greek constitution rather than, pardon my bluntness, a barbaric and xenophobic body of laws."

"And without such a shift, what citizen of any Greek city will ever feel that Jerusalem is home?" Heracleitos added.

Jason nodded to Castor, hoping that the next phase of the symposium would provide a way out from this particular conversation.

"Without changing the nation's constitution to a model of government based on the Athenian constitution," Dionysios observed, "all your reforms will amount to little more than cosmetic decoration, the outward trappings of Hellenization without its heart."

Jason redirected his gaze toward the servants who bore the first amphora of wine out to the table. They poured the wine into a large *krater* and added an equal portion of water. As the scent of the wine now mingled with the lingering aromas of the dinner, Castor remarked, "Gentlemen, this wine is made from a variety of grape introduced from Rhodes and grown in Lord Jason's estates in Har-Galil. I pray that it meets with your excellencies' approval." He gestured to a servant, who dipped a ladle in the *krater* and poured the wine into Philostratos's chalice.

The gymnasiarch sniffed the bouquet, took a sip, and swirled it around in his mouth. He swallowed with a pleased smile. "Like it was made in Rhodes itself. My congratulations, Jason, on your achievements in local viticulture."

Jason acknowledged the compliment with a nod and indicated that the servant should fill everyone's cup. As the host, Jason held his own cup and extended his arm. "May the God, the highest of all, look with favor upon our gathering, and upon this libation," he said, pouring a generous quantity of his first cup upon the ground.

"And now, gentlemen," Jason said, looking to Agathon for a look of confirmation, "I believe we have some entertainment for you."

A man in his late forties, dressed in a linen tunic with a Greek key design embroidered in purple, emerged from the reception hall, where he had been waiting for the past hour. He took his stance opposite Philostratos's couch and began his recitation:

> Capricious Fortune changes day to day,
> But those who stay the course, remaining true
> To virtue's path and to the Savior God,
> Shall rise above their station and ascend
> To glory's heights. Such was the case indeed
> With noble Iosephos, who, though born free,
> To Egypt went a slave—and died a prince!

The guests listened attentively, drinking their wine and nibbling on fruit and nuts, as the poet recounted the story of Joseph in the style of the great epics of Greece. Jason mused about the contrast between the temperate Joseph, who staunchly resisted the advances of Potiphar's wife, and his guests, who went to every symposium with the expectation that their intemperance would be indulged at some point in the evening. *Yes, you Greeks have something to learn from our heritage as well.*

The servants kept the guests' chalices filled until the poet finished his recitation. When the audience had rewarded him with their applause, Philostratos commented, "An admirable poem, though I admit that I am not familiar with the story."

"It is a story from our distant past," Philon explained. "Joseph and his brothers are the ancestors of the twelve tribes that constitute our *ethnos*."

"Fascinating," said Heracleitos. "It could have been a story from the Greek stage. The hero displays the tragic flaw of *hybris* through his dreams and incurs the envy of his brothers by accepting the special gifts from his father that disrupt the equality of brotherhood. This nemesis leads to a tragic reversal of fortune that reduces him to slavery. Unjust accusations further complicate the plot, until finally the gods deem his punishment sufficient and restore him."

"Part of that is inherent in the story itself," Philon said. "Much of it comes from the art of this poet's retelling."

"This is the heart of Hellenization as I understand it," said Agathon. "We are enriched by your artistic forms of expression and dramatic movement; in turn, we enrich the cultural heritage of the whole Mediterranean by adding to its treasury of myth and story."

"You will have no argument from me on that point." Dionysios's tone indicated that some argument was in fact forthcoming. "But I do think that, in the matter of governance, the Judean people would do far better not merely to adopt our institutional forms, but also to adopt our civic constitution wholesale."

"It does strike me as anomalous," Heracleitos said, "that one might find here, on the one hand, a gymnasium and lyceum and all the signs of a well-functioning Greek city, and then discover, on the other hand, that the city is in fact regulated by the most idiosyncratic laws of any people on the face of the earth."

"We have had this discussion many times in our own assembly—our *gerousia*," Menelaus said. "No animal designated by the law of Moses as 'unclean' and, as a consequence, no goods produced from the hides of such animals are allowed within the walls of the city, and hence are banned from its markets. No business can be transacted from sundown to sundown every seventh day. A cancellation or surrendering of debts is required every seventh year. Foreign merchants avoid places with such restrictions on business like the plague."

Jason looked with some curiosity at Menelaus. *Is he trying to advance my interests, or further alienate these foreigners?*

"And, technically, one cannot hold property belonging historically to another family line for more than forty-nine years," Timarchos said. His tone betrayed his own impatience with what he considered antique regulations. "Though, as you can plainly see, we have all found ways around that."

"Many parties in Jerusalem would be glad to see these restrictions on our economy lifted," Menelaus said with a nod toward Timarchos.

"Well of course they would," Dionysios declared. "How could anyone be expected to abide by what are, to any right-thinking aristocrat or merchant, intolerable laws?"

"I am convinced that this is the reason our whole state has experienced only a fraction of the growth that we see happening on all sides of us," Menelaus persisted, "except for a few enterprising Jewish families that became involved in international affairs and went out to connect with representatives of the Greek world."

"It seems to me," Apollodorus said, "that the real economic growth of Jerusalem and Judea can only happen by attracting new Greek and other foreign settlers to Jerusalem, and by attracting the caravans that currently bypass Judea on their east-west routes entirely, whether through the Greek cities of Idumaea to the south or through the Decapolis to the north."

"Precisely." Menelaus jabbed the air with his index finger, accenting the weight of the problem. "But why would they come through here, at least on the scale that we all would desire, when there is no Greek city anywhere in Judea?"

"The people you want to attract here," Apollodorus continued, "would only feel at home in a fully Hellenized Jerusalem where they could enjoy the privileges and predictability of a Greek *polis*, with laws that would be familiar to them from the cities that they left behind."

"And we are truly poised to put Jerusalem on everyone's map," Agathon said, trying to regain control of the conversation for Jason. "We could easily surpass the Greek cities of Galilee and the coast lands, and make our city third in the east only to Antioch and Alexandria in terms of cultural, literary, and artistic ferment. We can raise up a generation of Judeans who will be in no way inferior to Antiochenes or Alexandrians in terms of their mastery of language, philosophy, culture, physical prowess, and rhetorical skill." Adding his voice to Jason's caution, he observed, "But we can do all of that without formally shifting the constitution of the city."

"Well, for my own part, I'm not inclined to pour my resources into a gymnasium that would not be shaping its youth to be citizens in a truly Greek city," Apollodoros said. He looked at Heracleitos, as if to enlist his support. "I had, in fact, assumed that this would be the case here and am perplexed to learn that this matter is still in dispute." He leaned back, a visual signal of his waning enthusiasm. "There are other cities that are making definite progress in this direction. If we rain our benefactions upon other soil, they may produce a more fruitful harvest."

At this threat, Jason signaled to Castor to serve the second *krater* of wine. *Hopefully it will wash this conversation away from their memory*, Jason mused. Again a pair of servants emerged from the kitchen with an amphora, while two others bore a fresh *krater* and pitcher of water for mixing the wine. Castor stepped forward and announced, "Gentlemen, a burgundy made from grapes grown on my Lord Jason's estates in Hebron from vine stock imported from Alexandria." Again Philostratos was given the honor of the first sample and, with his approval, the rest were served.

The shaking of timbrels drew the attention of the guests to the doorway leading to the reception hall. Eight girls, none of them more than twenty, half-ran, half-skipped into the *triclinium*. They were dressed in loose, gauzy dresses designed in part to recall the garb of nymphs from classical art, in part to tanta-lize the viewers. Forming a circle in front of the dining table, the nymphs struck positions that demanded that their leg muscles and upper bodies tense up, show-ing them at their most shapely. Jason was amused—and pleased—to notice the degree to which his guests' level of energy and attention was heightened. *Well done, Agathon*, he thought. *If they cannot be won over with sound reason . . .*

Five musicians entered behind, bearing wooden flutes, a reed pipe, stringed instruments, timbrel, and drum. As they began to play a folk tune from Egypt, the girls performed a dance that made up in sensuality what it lacked in perfect synchronization. Their absorption of his guests' attention was a welcome relief for Jason, who was increasingly troubled by the uncompromising and, to him, impatient attitude of his table companions. *They truly have no idea how things have to be handled here.* He sipped his wine, closed his eyes, and let the plain-tive yet seductive music ease his concern. The nymphs finished their dance in a supine posture on the floor. The guests directed their applause to the dancers, and Timarchos raised his glass to his host.

"Fabulous, Jason. *'A seal of emerald in a setting of fine gold is the melody of music with good wine.'"*

"Indeed, I am very impressed with the quality of their musicianship," Heracleitos added, "especially the facility of these musicians—local, I would assume—in their treatment of foreign styles."

"I am delighted that you have been well entertained," Jason replied, turning to Agathon with an appreciative smile.

The nymphs rose from the floor and, each gauging from eye-contact or the less subtle, direct invitation which man would be most pleased by her companionship, began to take their places on the couches, sitting at the back by the feet of her chosen partner for the evening. One girl, who had taken Circe as her professional name, made her way toward Philostratos, but a sharp look from Epaphroditos stopped her awkwardly in her tracks. Heracleitos chortled, and invited her to join Baucis, who was already sitting behind him.

The musicians moved about, changing their instrumentation. One selected a seven-stringed *kithara*, another the *barymiton* with its longer strings for bass notes, another the *aulos* with its plaintive, reedy tone. The kitharist stood up, moved to the center of the *triclinium*, and began to strike his opening chords while the *aulos* established the new mode. Tilting his head back in the Greek manner, the kitharist began his recital with a hymn.

> Wisdom, your praises I will sing,
> The firstborn of God's children,
> Whose radiance first graced creation.
>
> You stood beside the Most High God
> And labored alongside him
> As a master craftsman alongside the Architect.
>
> By you, kings reign and create justice;
> You call also to the simple and humble,
> Inviting all to drink in your instruction like finest wine.
>
> More radiant than polished gold are you;
> More desirable than wealth or women,
> You, O goddess Wisdom, divine lover.

The kitharist repeated the last line, improvising a virtuoso vocal cadenza to the delight of the audience.

As the applause died down, the musicians began to play a soft instrumental tune to give the singer a respite. Timarchos turned to Jason to resume the earlier conversation. "It appears that we need to begin to lay plans for reforms of a larger scope if we hope even to enjoy those of smaller scope."

"You've planned so carefully and worked so hard," Menelaus added sympathetically. "What a pity if these dreams should be delayed or never come to pass at all."

"The constitutional basis for the city needs to be changed from the hierocracy authorized by Antiochus the Great, which shackles us to the Torah with its antiquated economic restrictions and its barbaric foreign policy, to a Greek *polis*, where everyone can feel at home—and feel secure about investing their resources," Timarchos pressed.

Philostratos concurred. "I would be very interested in seeing larger-scale developments like this as well. And I can assure you of the new King Antiochus's support for any such initiative here—for the customary pledges toward Antiochus's campaigns and other interests, which is only fitting for a city that joins itself to his elite support base."

"The fourth Antiochus," Apollodoros explained, "has grand plans for the empire of his ancestors, plans that will take him into battle with Egypt. He would warmly welcome the idea of a truly Hellenized Judea, a Judea that he could count on to watch his back as he engages the armies of Ptolemy to the south."

Jason could no longer suppress an exasperated snort.

"Do you have any idea how difficult it has been for me to get us to this point? I couldn't persuade Honiah to come to dinner with you all on the Sabbath. I would never secure his approval for a wholesale change of the constitution. We must move more slowly and patiently here, taking advantage of what openings are afforded us. It's a fine thing to dream, but let's dream of what is possible!" He added wearily, "In these matters, Honiah is a defender of the covenant first and a brother second."

"Then perhaps, for the advancement of your whole nation, you need to be more of a reformer first and a brother second," Philon said from across the table.

"I believe I've learned enough from my visit already," Philostratos announced with an air of finality. "We don't need to wait to see Honiah. We can continue our tour inspecting the educational institutions in the coastal cities and the Decapolis tomorrow." He looked squarely at Jason. "When Judea's premier can be counted upon to facilitate this process and not to impede its natural and inevitable course, then I will be pleased to do all I can. You have my word on that."

Castor came forward, leading a third procession of servants. "Gentlemen, a light red wine imported from Mount Falernus in Italy." Eyes widened around the table at the prospect of drinking a vintage from one of the most celebrated wine-producing regions in the Mediterranean. *About five minutes too late, Castor,* Jason thought.

After the guests were served, the kitharist stepped forward again and began to sing odes of a different genre.

Springtime awakens the trees into bloom
And fills the violet grapes with their bounty.
But for me, Eros knows no Winter
And needs no Spring to come alive.
Though the cold north winds blow
Over the face of the earth,
Venus keeps the flames of love alive
Deep within my flesh.

The guests were beginning to give more attention to their companions. Agathon whispered in Jason's ear that he would be taking his leave, and Jason rose to walk him to the door.

"My gratitude, Agathon, for everything you've done to arrange such fine entertainment for our visitors."

"It was my pleasure, Jason. I am sorry that things have taken the turn that they did."

"Indeed, it seems as if we are faced with an all-or-nothing situation." They reached the front portico, where Jason instructed the equerry to bring Agathon's horse. "We'll talk more of this after the Sabbath. Enjoy your family."

Jason watched as Agathon left. *Value old friends*, he remembered old ben Sira saying, *for new friends can never equal them.*

He turned back toward the vestibule and found Menelaus waiting there.

"In need of some air, Menelaus?"

"We all need some fresh air after tonight's conversations, I think." He walked up, closer than Jason expected.

"Lord Jason, I very much want to see your plans for Jerusalem succeed. So do Agathon and Timarchos, I'm sure." He looked slightly to each side before proceeding. "But I know of other parties who also wish you well in this endeavor and who have the necessary means to make your vision a reality."

"And I thought Agathon was the one providing the entertainment tonight. Have you hired some magicians then?" Jason quipped, having tasted his fill of intrigue for one night.

"My lord, I have arranged for a meeting with a friend who may hold the solution to the endless resistance to progress in Jerusalem and who has access to the extensive funds you would need to secure the right to refound Jerusalem as a Greek city."

Jason hoped his eyes did not disclose how weakened his reluctance to take this step had become during the course of the evening.

Menelaus pressed his argument. "It is surely the only way forward."

"Who is this friend?"

"I am not at liberty to say, Lord Jason. But you know him. At my signal, he will come to you here, if you will receive him in peace."

Jason turned his head away. He realized instantly who Menelaus had contacted, and argued with himself about whether or not to listen further.

"Send your signal. Seraiah can meet me in my garden in an hour."

Miryam cleared the table of serving dishes and carried them into the kitchen. She was pleased to see so little of her food remaining. The broiled fish, freshly baked bread, the stewed cucumbers—everything had been duly consumed, the sign of happy eaters. She set the dishes in a basin of water, where they would sit until the Sabbath was ended and could be properly cleaned, and stood in the doorway looking out toward the living area. Eleazar and his wife Hannah reclined on one side of the small table, Meir and Ari opposite them, with Binyamin at one of the shorter sides. All had the air of contentment that comes after eating one's fill, and perhaps a little more.

Miryam smiled, glad for the family that was here, and for friends like Eleazar and Hannah, who had stood by them throughout these difficult years. She thought about Zerah and how she missed him, with regret but not bitterness—for God had given them twenty years together and three strong sons to fill her life. She looked away from them toward the two candles that were burning across the room on a small wooden table against the wall. She thought of her other two children, a daughter and a son who both died within their first year of life. Somehow she always thought of them when she lit the two candles, perhaps because she had kindled their lives, perhaps because they were too fragile and too easily extinguished, perhaps because she hoped, as she lit the candles every Sabbath, that God would give the spark of life again to their souls for the endless Sabbath to come, when they would all sit at table together once again.

"What are you thinking about, Miryam?" Hannah asked.

"Oh, I was just thinking about Zerah and how much he enjoyed evenings like this," Miryam said, slightly embarrassed to have been caught daydreaming. Binyamin's and Meir's heads had dropped slightly at the mention of their father, partly out of respect, partly out of sorrow. "Five years later, and I can still see him sitting at the table with us and hear him laughing," she continued, walking back to her place at the table.

"Zerah was a good friend," Eleazar said. He nodded his head, as if signaling that he, too, could enter into Miryam's recollections. "I miss his companionship. His ability to bring all our conversations about the Torah down to earth. His living example of how to walk daily in the ways of God and find delight in that path."

Eleazar raised a cup of wine and looked around the table. Everyone but young Ari, who was not yet accustomed to the gesture, instinctively reached for their own cups. "To Zerah," he said, "with whom we will break bread again in the kingdom of God." Ari noticed what was going on and grabbed his cup just in time to drink with the others.

After a moment, Binyamin said, "We will be drinking to Master Yehoshua soon, won't we?"

"Indeed," Eleazar concurred sadly, "I think he will not see the morning."

Ari looked up and asked, "Is Master Yehoshua going to die?"

Miryam could see the pain in Binyamin's face at the thought of losing the man whose guidance and conversation had so eased his sense of loss after Zerah's death.

"Those who live their lives to God do not die forever," Eleazar said. "Master Yehoshua is old. His time here is done, and we will no longer be able to see him or talk to him. But God will keep him safe. 'The righteous enter into peace, and rest in their chambers.' And God will give him a new body." Eleazar's eyes widened to convey the excitement and mystery. "One that will never grow old, and that will last forever."

Ari smiled. "Like Abba will have."

"Yes, just so," Eleazar smiled. "Your father and Master Yehoshua both believed that there was nothing more important than walking in God's commandments. They knew that was only right, since God had given so many good things to them and to all Israel—and they knew that God's generosity toward his faithful ones was not limited to this life only."

Binyamin looked pensive, as if trying to recall something. "Master Yehoshua never spoke much about life after death," he said at last. "He talked about revering God as the path to Wisdom, about the commandments as the life of Wisdom, and about Wisdom rewarding her followers with long life and a blessed death. But I can't remember him saying anything about what happens after."

"What happens after is indeed a mystery, Binyamin," Eleazar conceded. He added with a wry smile, "After all, who has come back to give us a definitive report? But I've seen death come too quickly to the faithful, robbing them of Wisdom's promises. I've seen calamity and misery claim the righteous while the godless live long and grow fat. If God is anything, God is just, and this world is too evil to contain all of God's justice."

The lull in the conversation gave Meir his opportunity to solicit an expert opinion on a matter that had been on his mind since afternoon. He looked at Binyamin out of the corner of his eye, as if checking to see if it was safe.

"Master Eleazar?"

Binyamin, catching Meir's sideways glance, instantly guessed what Meir was about to ask and glared at his brother.

"Yes, Meir?"

"We have had some disagreements here about what we can and cannot do for our non-Jewish customers. Would it be permissible for us to cast or repair images of their gods"—Meir matched Binyamin glare for glare—"or must we continue to alienate them and impoverish ourselves by refusing their business?"

"Meir!" Miryam scolded. "Don't bring our guest into the middle of a quarrel!"

"It's quite all right," Eleazar said evenly. "When is a rabbi not in the middle of a quarrel?"

Even the brothers could not help but smile, dissipating the tension like a mist.

Eleazar pondered the question for a moment, then replied, "It is written, 'You shall not make for yourself any sculpted image, or any likeness of anything that is in the sky above, or that is in the earth below, or that is in the water under the earth.' I would take it from the phrase 'for yourself' that the Holy One, blessed be he, has first and foremost in mind that his people abstain from all forms of idol worship, and so not produce idols for their own use."

"There! You see, Binyamin?"

"But," Eleazar continued, "it is also written, 'You shall love your neighbor as yourself.' How, I wonder, are we showing love for our Greek or Syrian neighbor if we cooperate with their rebellion against God and help them continue to be alienated from him by means of their idols?"

Meir's face fell.

"I appreciate your desire to do all you can to help support your family," Eleazar said, leaning forward toward Meir in a manner suggesting encouragement. "It is a virtuous and honorable trait. But I do believe it is God's will for us not to contribute in any way to the folly of the Gentiles. Would it hurt us to make idols for them? Probably not. Does it hurt them if we help them call upon gods that have carved ears that cannot hear their prayers, sculpted lips that cannot give divine counsel to the suppliants, and carved hands that can do nothing to help those who plead for help? Yes, Meir, it hurts them greatly."

Eleazar leaned back again. "And perhaps it hurts God as well."

"How would it hurt God, Master Eleazar?" Meir asked.

"What—when we, who have enjoyed God's care and favor, prefer to make idols for the Gentiles for the sake of money rather than use those encounters as opportunities to testify to the grace and majesty and goodness of the Only God, what would that say to the one who looks on from above?"

Meir nodded slightly and looked down toward the table, pondering what he had heard and sorry that he had raised the topic.

The silence gave Hannah an opportunity to change the direction of the conversation.

"Enough talk about things of interest to men. So when is Binyamin getting married?" Looking at Binyamin, making him quite uncomfortable, she continued, "It's high time for finding a wife, isn't it?"

"I was talking with Eliashiv ben Joab and his wife, Helah, just a few days ago about this very thing," Miryam responded, glad for the change in subject.

"Oh," Eleazar said. "I know Eliashiv and his family. They are from Modein, a day's journey from the city."

"Yes, my father's village," Miryam resumed. "Their family and my own have known each other for generations. Zerah and I had talked about their daughter, Shoshanna, as a possible wife for Binyamin when he was only thirteen and she eight. Well, Shoshanna turns fifteen in a few weeks. Her parents and I agree that the betrothal should take place very soon."

"I hope you're looking for a daughter from a family of some means for me, mother," Meir said.

"Hush! A good woman is herself a treasure from the Lord."

Meir looked down, his brow furrowed.

"Our business is not growing," he muttered. "How can our family grow without additional money from somewhere? Shoshanna's family is in no position to help us."

Binyamin appeared to have had enough from his little brother. "Maybe you can do better for yourself, and we can all come to live in your magnificent palace!"

"Maybe I can! Maybe I won't have to bend over a forge all day only to marry a poor girl."

Ari's eyes widened, a little out of anxiety to see his brothers confronting one another, a little out of excitement to see the outcome.

Eleazar intervened, speaking first to Meir. "Do not hate toil or labor, which were created by the Most High. Honest labor with little is far better in the sight of the Lord than great wealth without integrity.'" Turning his head toward

Binyamin, he added, "But I am concerned about the needs of a growing family. If your trade is slow—and if more of that work can be entrusted to Meir—perhaps it would be advantageous to you to learn a second trade. Rabban Yehoshua was truly impressed with your aptitude for the traditions of the sages, Binyamin, as am I. Have you considered learning the art of the scribe? With some training, you would be well suited to it, and with your interests, it would suit you well."

Binyamin beamed at the idea. "Thank you, Master Eleazar. I would be honored."

Ari smirked. "It looks like Meir's now the master craftsman and Binyamin the apprentice again."

As they shared a laugh at the boy's precocious observation, Miryam looked around the table with a sense of deep satisfaction. Zerah would have been so proud of Binyamin tonight, so pleased with the opportunities that had come to him on the basis of his own virtues—opportunities that Zerah himself could not have given him. She reflected on the oversight of God, who had kept providing for them during the difficult years since Zerah's passing and whose hand seemed to shower favor upon them again today. "Master Eleazar, would you lead us in the blessing?"

Eleazar nodded with a smile and, lifting his eyes and his hands to heaven, palms upward, began: "Blessed are you, *Adonai*, King of the Universe. You gave this good and bountiful land to our ancestors for an inheritance, rescuing us from Egypt. You made a covenant with us, sealed in our flesh by circumcision. You gave us your Torah by which you made your ways known to us. We thank you, *Adonai*, our God, and speak well of your name forever and ever."

"Amen, amen," came the response from all.

"May God, the Merciful One, send an abundance of blessings upon this house and upon this table at which we have eaten. May God, the Merciful One, be praised throughout all generations, glorified always in our midst, and honored among us to all eternity."

ח

Seraiah ben Yoseph ben Tobiah had been watching from the walls of Jerusalem for the flaming torch waving from the vicinity of Jason's villa across the Kidron Valley. Together with his bodyguard—four well-armed Syrian mercenaries—he had quickly traversed the distance between the southeastern gate of the city and the hill on the brow of which sat his destination. The steady climb did not tax him in the least. Indeed, he felt himself carried along as if by his inevitable destiny—to enjoy revenge upon the house of his family's rivals by toppling one, using another, all the while increasing his own power and fortunes.

He thought about his family's ancestor, a more distant Tobiah—remembered as Tobiah *the Ammonite*, Seraiah scowled—who had become a prominent leader in Israel during the fragile years of Judah's reconstruction after Nebuchadnezzar devastated the city and who was unceremoniously expelled from his apartment in the Temple by the priest Ezra during his "reforms." Now Seraiah would expel *priests*. He left his bodyguard just below Jason's villa, where he was met by Menelaus and led into Jason's garden. They did not have long to wait.

Jason stepped out into his garden under the night sky, impenetrable with obsidian storm clouds, illuminated now and again by menacing flashes of lightning. As he moved farther from the house into the darkness, Jason remembered his father setting him on his lap with Honiah beside them on nights like this, telling stories of how God appeared to Israel at Sinai in the midst of thick blackness, flashes of fire, and blasts of thunder. Honiah drank all that in, Jason recalled, finding in the storm a symbol of the power and presence of God as God gave his commandments, a reminder of the one who watched over Israel and

85

who guarded his eternal law. But for Jason, it just meant that it would be getting wet and cold.

When he had walked about twenty meters from his house, he demanded of the air, "Well? Where is the man who has called me out on a night such as this!"

"Here, Lord Jason," said Seraiah as he stepped from the shadows.

"You've been spying on my activities tonight through Menelaus, I think, behind whose face I now find yours."

"Menelaus has helped me to understand your ambitions and your situation."

"Spying, then, indeed."

"A spy works to the advantage of the party that employs him," Seraiah protested. "Menelaus has been working for our mutual advantage—as much your own as mine."

"I will be most interested to hear how my family's enemy seeks my interest as much as his own."

"My lord Jason, our families have not always been so far apart. My grandfather Tobiah married the sister of your grandfather, the second to bear the name Honiah. My father Yoseph is first cousin to your father Simon of blessed memory. That family connection was strong enough to make your father support me and my brothers against Hyrcanus."

It grieved Seraiah even to pronounce the name, let alone admit kinship with his youngest brother. Hyrcanus had depleted the family's funds in Egypt to give Ptolemy the most extravagant wedding present of any he had received, seeking to usurp their father's place as premier and bypassing all his older brothers. Two others of Seraiah's brothers had died in the violent feud that followed. In the end, little brother gained nothing from his betrayals, for the territory passed to Antiochus III of Syria. Hyrcanus had weakened the family at a critical time, and it was not difficult for Simon the Just to persuade Antiochus to award the office of premier to him, a man from a family with no strong ties to Ptolemy and Egypt—and no history of disruptive factionalism and violence. Despite all these setbacks, Seraiah remained the wealthiest man in all Israel.

"And how did depriving my grandfather and, for a time, my father of the main political power of their office fit in to this history?" Jason interjected pointedly.

"Yoseph deemed this essential to improve international and business affairs," Seraiah offered, "and not only our own affairs, as you must be thinking. Surely you of all people would admit that Yoseph did much more for Judea in that capacity than your grandfather could ever have done with his scrupulous devotion to the law of Moses—a fact that your brother has proven by reversing many of the benefits Judea enjoyed when Yoseph was premier."

"You want to be premier, then?"

"No, Jason." Seraiah paused. "I want to make you the premier."

Seraiah savored the look of surprise on Jason's face. *He truly didn't see that coming.*

"That has never been my ambition."

"Yes, I know, Jason. And that is why your ambitions for Jerusalem continue to be frustrated." Seraiah pressed his advantage. "Honiah, like your father, looks backward. Never forward. But you have always had your eyes to the front. I have never considered you to be hostile to my goals for Jerusalem. Even when you took up Honiah's cause against us when we sought to make Simon ben Iddo the administrator of the market, I knew you did it out of kinship obligations rather than fundamental disagreement with our goals. The time has come for us to enter into an alliance, burying the rivalry between our houses in the interest of Jerusalem's future greatness."

Jason thought about the immense resources that would come with such an alliance—resources that would be used now to advance his vision rather than impede it with useless internal maneuvering—but also of the high price of such an alliance, even if it should prove to be a sincere offer.

"I won't betray my own brother. You of all people should be aware of the evils of one brother setting out to usurp another's place."

"Your loyalty toward Honiah is commendable, even more so in the light of Honiah's ungenerous refusal to use his office to cooperate with your dreams," Seraiah needled. "But you will have to choose between evils, whether to remove your brother from his position or to allow him to keep your people, your larger family, excluded from all the benefits you would bring them if you were unhindered. Hyrcanus, that perfidious son of my father, sought only his own advantage. I am asking you to do what is necessary to secure advantage for the whole nation."

Seraiah was pleased with the silence that followed. *Good. Think about it, Jason. Entertain the possibility.*

"I am prepared to stand behind you, Jason. My supporters and I have the means to secure the premiership for you. We can both have what we want for this city." Seraiah pulled his mantle over his head, turned away, and started to leave.

"Honiah is the legitimate high priest and premier. How could you hope to unseat him?"

Better still, Jason. No longer whether, *but* how. Seraiah stopped and spoke without looking back. "I will make an opportunity. Be ready."

Jason watched for a while as Seraiah, accompanied by Menelaus, walked out from the garden, skirted the eastern portico of the villa, and disappeared around the corner.

Both houses and factions working together to achieve their common vision. The redemption of countless hours that would be lost, of mental and material resources wasted maneuvering around Honiah to gain each step forward. The ability to make the most of every opportunity rather than see so many opportunities run aground on Honiah's conservatism. *So simple, so efficient. So unconstrained.*

He walked back into the house and sat in the slightly elevated chair in his reception hall.

Castor emerged from the dining hall with a cup of spiced wine and gave it to his master, who barely noticed.

As Jason sipped the drink, time seemed to be suspended, and he was fully alone with his thoughts, fully alive to the movements of his soul. Everything he hoped for was just a single act of betrayal away. *No,* he stopped himself. *Not betrayal. Courage. Patriotism.* He looked at that part of him that hesitated, that felt bound to Honiah, to the order of things as the second-born son of Simon. That part of him was a prison to which he had been sentenced before he had sinned, and within whose confines he had lived long enough. In the deepest heart that was his own, the depths upon which the light of acknowledgment rarely shone, Jason had longed for an opportunity such as this for a decade. *A way to reverse the order of our births at last.*

Jason rose from his chair and walked into the *triclinium*. Dionysios was lying on one couch, snoring audibly. A silver cup lay fallen just beyond his outstretched arm. One of the *hetairai*—the one called Thetis, Jason thought—lay draped over him, her head upon his chest. The state of her tunic left no doubt as to their activity before passing out. The second couch appeared to be vacant, until Jason spotted the balding crown of Timarchos visible behind the couch, where he had finally fallen. Jason raised himself on the balls of his feet and craned his head slightly to one side to confirm that, indeed, the legs he saw were not Timarchos's own. On the third couch Philostratos lay stretched out on his back. Epaphroditos slept on his left side beside Philostratos, his right arm and thigh draped over the gymnasiarch. *A womanish posture,* Jason thought, surprised at his own disgust. As he surveyed the scene, Jason heard the voice of his old master: *"Make righteous people your dinner companions, and make the fear of the Lord your source of pride."*

He left the *triclinium* and made his way toward his bedchamber. As he walked down the hallway, he passed the open door of one of his guest rooms. Jason did not pause long enough to decide exactly how many of his guests and their companions it would have taken to account for the number of limbs writhing upon the bed.

Now it was his brother's voice that he heard: *"Favored is the man who does not walk in the counsel of the wicked, nor stands in the path of sinners, nor sits in the seats of the scoffers."* Reaching down into the deep, he silenced the voice. It was just this sort of self-doubt that had kept him weak before his brother and before the opportunities extended within reach for so long. He answered the invisible Honiah with another scripture: *"Feasts are made for laughing; wine brings joy to the heart; and money is the answer to everything."*

Jason came at last to his bedroom, swung open the double door, and entered. He looked to the left at his own bed, the sheets and blanket still perfectly stretched out from Niobe's morning service. It beckoned to him as the Pool of Siloam beckons to the hot, dusty travelers that pass through the southern gates. He walked over to it, but only grasped a corner of the blanket that sat folded at the foot of the bed, allowing it to trail behind him as he walked to the alabaster chair on his terrace.

Meir had stood outside the house of Agathon for several minutes before daring to knock on the door. Something about the houses of the rich intimidated him, and he had never before been invited *back* to one. The door opened to reveal once again the less-than-welcoming figure of Menes.

"Ah, you've come back. After what my master paid you the last time, I can't say I'm surprised." The steward turned around and began to walk away. "At least you look cleaner this time. Wait here."

Meir's feet remained at the threshold, but after a minute he could not help but lean his body forward to take a better look at the wonders inside. In the bright daylight, he could see clearly the frescoes on the walls above the inlaid geometric design that ran throughout the atrium, one third of the way from the floor to the ceiling. To one side was a man dressed in a lion's hide, battling a many-headed snake. In the next scene a young man was trying to embrace a woman who seemed to be turning into a tree. Meir twisted his body farther to see what was on the wall beside the door. A man with a bow was shooting other men as they caroused in a large room. Each painting told a story, but these were stories Meir had never heard.

"Menes should have invited you in so that you would not hurt your neck."

Meir immediately retracted his torso and stood up straight, feeling a sudden warmth in his face.

"Not to worry, young man, though it's a habit you'll need to break. Nothing says that you don't belong among the wealthy like gawking at what the wealthy have."

"Yes, sir," was all Meir could manage. "You said that you might have more work for my family, sir."

"Indeed. I could use a steady supply of such fineries. Lord Jason was very pleased with the work, as was the intended recipient—a guest of his from Antioch."

Meir's eyes widened slightly to learn that the high priest's own brother had held his work and that it was now on its way to being displayed in the capital of the empire.

"However we may be of service to you, Master Agathon."

Agathon studied Meir for a few moments.

"Jerusalem will be growing, and I sense you have the ambition to grow with it. You could stay where you are, of course, and pass along your craft to your own children in time. But what if you could take on a dozen apprentices, train them in your craft, and become the premier supplier of metal-worked goods to Jerusalem's elite? What if, aside from the responsibility of supervision, you had the leisure to travel to learn of metalworking techniques from Greece to Egypt, or to explore other gifts and talents, or simply to expand your knowledge?"

Agathon watched Meir imagine the possibilities.

"This is a time of great opportunity, young man, and not just for those who are born to opportunity. The only question is, do you wish to be more than you were born to be?"

Meir thought about Binyamin refusing the opportunities that came their way.

"How, Master Agathon? What would I need to do?"

"You must learn Greek if you are to meet more of my associates and attract their business to your family's shop. Oh, I know you can speak some Greek, but you need to learn to speak it like you were born speaking it. You need to learn to write it and to read it. You need to be able to walk into a rich man's house and say, 'My, what a splendid depiction of Odysseus reclaiming his house from the suitors.'"

Meir began to feel the distance between Agathon's words and his own reality.

"With respect, sir, I don't see how I could do that. My brother is not likely to spend the little money we have on a tutor. I could do extra work for the money, but then I'd hardly have time left to sleep, let alone study."

"I have a Greek slave, a literate man accustomed to teaching. Come by my house in the heat of the day when you and he can do little else, and he will instruct you and give you assignments. I will see to it that you have enough work of the well-paying kind that you can relieve yourself of the work that demands

many hours of labor for little reward. Your family should not object to your working less, if the income remains the same or better, I should think."

Suspicion vied with hope in Meir's mind. "You would do this for me, a
stranger? What could I ever give you in return?"

"Make the most of the opportunity, and prove yourself worthy of my investment," Agathon replied. "And later, prove yourself a friend."

Meir beamed. "Thank you, Master Agathon. I will."

"I have no doubt. Come back tomorrow, and Menes will get you started with
Chrestos."

As Meir walked away from Agathon's house and past the other mansions, he
felt suddenly different, like he might someday actually belong in this part of town.

"Why, Master, invest in this laborer?" Menes asked, showing at once deference to Agathon and disdain for Meir as he watched the latter walking away.

"Because this is what we are about, Menes—discovering and shaping the
future citizens of a better Jerusalem," Agathon responded, staring beyond the
open door. "Education will define the new nobility and give opportunities to
those who formerly had no choices in life save to do what their fathers did. The
conservative leaders accuse us of caring only for the rich; we will show them that
we offer the only real hope for a much broader segment of the population."

"Yes, Master." Menes closed the door, bowed slightly, and turned to leave.

"And Menes," Agathon added. The servant stopped instantly and turned to
face his master. "I do not tell you this because it is your right to question me, but
so that you will understand how to treat that young man when he shows up at
our doorstep."

"*Nai, kyrie,*" replied Menes, signaling his acceptance of the rebuke.

Jason sat at his desk, examining statements from his estates outside of Lachish
and Gath. While Levites traditionally had no inheritance in the land of Israel,
many priestly families had long since acquired estates both within and outside
of Judea. Jason preferred investments in lands outside of Judah, since there was
no expectation of honoring—and thus no need of cleverly circumventing—laws
concerning the release of debts and return of the land to the family with the
ancestral claim thereto. Besides, the fertile plains closer to the coastland positioned him more readily for trade with Egypt through Gaza and with Syria
through Joppa. Tithes alone would not support Jason, or a great many other
priests, in the lifestyle to which they had accustomed themselves.

He leaned back from the table and allowed his mind to return to its primary preoccupation, from which he had been trying to distract himself. Two full weeks had passed since his nocturnal meeting with Seraiah with no word from him, nothing but exhortations to patience from Menelaus, and no change in the business of Jerusalem. *Surely Seraiah had had a plan. Did he give up?* Waiting was hard enough for Jason when he was the one arranging affairs; waiting for someone else to make a move was intolerable. Jason tried to force himself back to the reports of sales and revenue but finally pushed himself away from the table. If the proceeds were not so high, he might have indeed cared to inquire into the details. But if some manager was skimming a little here or there, well, he was managing the business of the estate so well he deserved it.

As he emerged from his study into the courtyard, he was met by an anxious Castor.

"My lord Jason, there's been"—Castor hesitated a moment—"an *incident* in the city. A messenger has arrived from your brother, my lord Honiah, requesting your presence at his residence immediately."

Jason strode out to the atrium where the messenger stood waiting.

"What has happened?"

"My lord, there's been an attack on your brother's life." Seeing the shock in Jason's eyes, the messenger continued quickly. "Your brother is not seriously harmed, but two of his bodyguard were killed. He bids you come at once."

"Castor, my horse."

"Mine stands ready, my lord," the messenger offered. "Please take it. I'll return on foot."

Jason nodded his thanks and set out. The horse handled well under its new rider and quickly carried him across the Kidron Valley and through the southern gate of the city. People darted out of his way as he rode up the main street from the Pool of Siloam to the heart of the city, turning west to reach Honiah's palace.

When he arrived, the palace was buzzing with activity. Priests and other well-wishers filled the atrium and reception hall, spilling out into the street in front of the palace. A servant who had been awaiting his arrival met Jason at the door.

"Lord Jason, my lord Honiah is within. Please follow me."

The servant cut a path through the crowd, Jason following closely in his wake until they reached Honiah's office. The servant opened the door for Jason to enter.

"Let me go in your place, Honiah." The voice was that of Eupolemus, whose father had been part of an embassy to Antiochus the Third some twenty years before. "Your arm will need tending. If you should get a fever while away—"

"My physician will travel with me," Honiah broke in. "And while I appreciate your concern, I think King Antiochus will take this more seriously if I appeal to him myself." Honiah turned back from Eupolemus to the opening door.

"Ah, Brother, thank you for coming so quickly."

"Of course, Honiah. Are you all right? What happened?"

"A gash to my arm, nothing more. But two good men are dead. I was return-ing from the morning sacrifice accompanied by my customary guards. Two men attacked from behind, slitting the throats of two of my guards!"

"Cowards!" Yoshe ben Yoezer, the priest who was also entrusted with Temple security, grunted with disgust.

"One of them managed to shout out a warning to the rest of us, or else they would have had me for sure. Hanan whipped around and pulled me toward him in time for the assassin's blade to strike my arm rather than something more vital. Hanan killed his man. The other escaped, even though—what was the young fellow's name?"

"Parosh," Yoshe replied.

"Yes, even though Parosh struggled with him courageously and gave pursuit while wounded himself."

"God be thanked, Brother, that you are alive." Jason was completely sincere, though he already knew that Seraiah had orchestrated this attack—and thus he was himself unwittingly responsible. *Never give a Tobiad carte blanche!* "Did you recognize the attackers?"

"No one has recognized the attackers," Honiah said emphatically. "No one in the street where the attack occurred, none of the Temple guards or local police who were shown the body of the dead man."

"He wasn't local," Yoshe added. "He wasn't even a Jew."

"It was an attempt at a political assassination," Eupolemus said, voicing the consensus of the group. "And that is why someone must go to Antioch to seek Antiochus's aid in investigating the matter."

"It's beyond local jurisdiction," Yoshe said, "though I have no doubt that locals are ultimately behind it."

"Whom do you suspect?" Jason asked.

"Who has been behind every attack on my leadership?" Honiah's voice betrayed a hint of incredulity at his brother's dullness. "Seraiah ben Yoseph, the same man who supported Simon ben Iddo against me in the days of Seleucus, the same man who tried to win Seleucus's favor by sending Simon to convince

Seleucus to seize the private funds deposited in the Temple. The same man who would give anything to win back the office of premier that his father lost to our father when the Seleucids won Judea from the Egyptian Ptolemy."

"You believe he'd resort to murder?"

"He'd have killed his own brother Hyrcanus if he'd had the chance."

"Honiah, it might have been members of a pro-Ptolemaic faction, attacking you as a symbol of Antiochus's rule in the south." Jason looked at Yoshe. "You said yourself that they weren't local, that they were Gentiles. Perhaps they're trying to destabilize Antiochus's government in this area in preparation for Ptolemy to regain his land."

The high priest appeared to evaluate this possibility. "No, it's Seraiah. He's got more to gain than anyone in this. He could easily have recruited foreigners for the job. His tentacles reach all the way to Antioch, which is why I need to go there to convince Antiochus to intervene."

The silence that followed suggested that everyone else in the room understood Honiah's mind to be made up.

"I agree that the matter is of the utmost importance and worthy of the king's attention, but your absence may be protracted—you know well how arbitrary kings can be about when they will receive an embassy and, even then, when they will actually decide on an action." Jason saw Eupolemus nod his assent to his observation. "I would be willing, of course, to take on your duties here during your absence. My staff can look after my affairs, and I can look after yours."

Honiah's eyes brightened at this display of brotherly concern.

"I was hoping that you would, though I hesitated to ask after I had so recently inconvenienced you."

"You set me back in regard to a pet project, Brother," Jason responded. "But someone tried to kill you. Of course I'd put myself at your disposal under such circumstances, to help you in any way that I can."

Honiah smiled and extended his right arm in Jason's direction. Jason stepped forward and clasped it.

"Thank you, Brother," Honiah said. "Tomorrow, Eupolemus will brief you on domestic and foreign matters requiring attention, and I'll ask Master Eleazar to look after organizing any chancery matters for your review or authorization in my absence." Honiah released Jason's arm and added, "Come to my home tonight for dinner, and we'll talk further."

Jason smiled, nodded, and turned to leave. As the servant opened the chamber door in front of him, he heard Honiah's voice again, half joking, half chiding.

"Now, Brother, you do remember how to officiate at a sacrifice, don't you?"

Jason found it increasingly difficult to keep his rage in check as he walked back through the city. He had half a mind to find his way to Seraiah's door and bash his teeth in for his impudence. But it would not do to be seen heading there.

As he approached the corner of the agora, he heard the voice of Agathon calling out to him. Jason stopped as Agathon made his way through the milling crowd to join him.

"Have you heard what happened to my brother?" he began before Agathon could state his business.

"Yes, Jason, and from the unlikeliest source. I've been watching here for you for the better part of an hour, hoping you'd take your normal route home." Agathon hesitated. "Menelaus is presently at my house, and he has someone with him, waiting to speak with you there."

"Seraiah," Jason hissed.

"Yes. How did you—"

"I'll explain as we walk."

In hushed tones Jason filled in the gaps in his friend's knowledge.

They arrived at Agathon's house to find Seraiah and Menelaus waiting in the inner courtyard. Jason bore down forcefully on the former.

"This was the 'opportunity' you were going to make? Murdering Honiah?"

Seraiah found himself taking a step back and raising his hands in a defensive posture. "Calm yourself, Jason. Your brother's alive, isn't he? I had two men sent against five. If killing him was my aim, don't you think I'd have chosen a different time and place?"

Jason eyed Seraiah with suspicion, checking an impulse to throttle him.

"I admit that it was not the assassin's plan to get himself killed, but that has so far proven advantageous as well. It has confirmed that the attack was not perpetrated by anyone in Jerusalem."

"Where did you find them?" Jason demanded.

"I didn't. Simon, Menelaus's brother in Antioch, had an associate of his in the seaport of Joppa hire them from among the dock rats there." Seraiah shifted forward with confidence. "Their connection to us is virtually untraceable."

"You took a significant risk with my brother's life."

"If four armed guards could not protect him from two dockworkers, Honiah himself would have been to blame for his carelessness in matters of security. But his guards did their jobs, Honiah will soon remove himself from Judea, and you will be left performing the duties of his office."

Jason could not keep the surprise from registering on his face. *How was it that Seraiah already knew this?*

Seraiah's mouth twisted up slightly on one side. "My grandfather, my father, and I have all had one gift that gave us an advantage over our rivals. We could see ten moves ahead on any game board. All that remains now is to persuade Antiochus to make the replacement permanent."

"How? Honiah is going to accuse *you* of nurturing sedition."

"Leave that to Menelaus."

Jason turned to the man, having forgotten that he was in the room, and Menelaus nodded to signal his cooperation in this plan.

"He sets out for Antioch this afternoon. He will travel light and arrive there a full day, perhaps two days, ahead of Honiah. I'd go myself, but my family's historic connections with the Ptolemies make me suspect, as would Honiah's accusations upon his arrival. Menelaus will appear to be an objective and untainted party. Besides, he can count on Simon's help in Antiochus's court."

Seraiah could see Jason's aggravation abating.

"It's a solid plan. And if we fail, well, you retain plausible deniability about being involved in any way." Seraiah bowed ever so slightly and began to walk toward the atrium and Agathon's front door, followed by Menelaus. "But we won't fail," he added as he went. "All of this is still merely four or five moves ahead."

6

King Antiochus, the fourth to have taken that name upon ascension to the throne, stepped out from the private rooms of his palace and into the courtyard that would take him to his audience hall. The business of the city of Antioch was conducted in the senate chamber in the old city, but the business of empire happened here on the island in the middle of the Orontes River, the third and most opulent quarter of the city. The air was heavy and chilled from the rains that had drenched the land the night before, though the sun would warm the island within a few hours.

Antiochus pulled his scarlet woolen cloak around his chest and over his shoulder as he began to make his way through the garden. Two soldiers, members of his personal bodyguard, fell in step behind him. A man of forty and the younger son of the great Antiochus III, he had just recently come to his father's throne after watching his older brother, Seleucus IV, manage the empire for thirteen years. *Manage. That's the word for it. Seleucus had no vision for the empire, unlike Father. Unlike me.* Despite the rumors that were still running through the streets of Antioch, Seleucus had died of natural causes. Antiochus may have seized the opportunity to place himself on the throne in lieu of Seleucus's young son, but he did not create it.

As he emerged in the audience hall through the side entrance that opened onto his courtyard, the eight cabinet members who had been milling about in conversations with one another immediately ceased speaking and turned toward their king. They lowered their heads as he passed by them to take his place on the marble throne on a raised platform on the east side of the rectangular hall, while his bodyguard stationed themselves beside the great door at the west end. The company remained standing as a priest walked over to a small shrine of Zeus carved into the northwest corner, placed a handful of incense on the heated coals on the metal tripod before the statue, and poured a small libation of wine on the ground.

"Great Zeus, king of the gods, hear, we pray, the desires and petitions of our own king Antiochus and prosper all that he intends."

"Great is Zeus, king of the gods," responded the counselors, "and great is his son Antiochus."

The priest bowed low before the shrine, then turned and bowed again to Antiochus before leaving through the western door. Antiochus took his seat, and at a gesture of his hand, his counselors took their own places in marble chairs that lined the longer sides of the room.

"I am most interested to hear from our minister of finance concerning the empire's potential for funding an offensive against Egypt."

Heliodoros, born five years before Antiochus but looking fifteen years his senior, rose in response.

"Majesty." He picked up and unrolled a small scroll that he had placed on the small table beside his chair. "The annual installments toward the war reparations imposed upon us by Rome after your father's defeat at Apamea have depleted our treasuries and drained our capacity for waging war—precisely Rome's intent in the first place. Those payments have come to an end, but recovery will be slow and we still have our annual tribute to Rome to pay. I have revisited every possible source of revenue throughout the empire. Even if we were to increase the tributes owed to us by our own provinces by ten percent, which most could not afford, it would be a decade before we had enough funds to expand and sustain our army sufficiently to think about new campaigns to seize additional lands."

"Can we petition Rome for a reduction in our annual tribute?" Antiochus asked. "We could plead financial duress in our provinces."

Herakleon, the minister of foreign affairs, rose to address the king.

"Majesty, your brother petitioned Rome many times concerning reductions to the tribute and the war indemnity. The Roman senate refuses all such petitions in order to keep us weak, to drain our resources and thereby limit our potential."

"And we dare not provoke them by reneging," added Heliodoros.

"Capturing the fertile land and the amassed wealth of Egypt will permanently relieve our empire of financial strain. I expect this council to apply its collective intelligence to discovering a way forward to that end over the coming year."

It's not entirely their fault, mused Antiochus. *They'll need some retraining after thirteen years of Seleucus.* "What business do you have for us today, Herakleon?"

"A delegation from Athens, Majesty," the old statesman responded, "with thanks for your pledge to build a temple there to Zeus Olympios."

A glance at Heliodoros reminded the king that the pledge might have been premature. The king had been too eager to establish himself as a patron of Greek culture, starting at the historic center of Greece itself.

"Inform them that I shall receive them at my table for dinner tonight to honor them and the illustrious city they represent." Antiochus turned to his personal secretary. "Alert my chief steward to make some special preparations." *And may Zeus Olympios help me find the funds to build his temple.* "Anything further?"

"A petitioner from Jerusalem, Majesty. One Menelaus, a priest and member of their governing assembly."

"Menelaus?" asked Antiochus quizzically. "Is this priest a Greek?"

A man in his late forties with heavy Semitic features rose from his chair and bowed his head slightly. "By your leave, Majesty?"

"Yes, Simon?"

"Menelaus is my brother. He was born Menachem ben Iddo, but took the name Menelaus some years ago as a token of his love for all things Greek."

"Your brother, Simon? Do you know what brings him here today?"

"Your interests in Jerusalem, Majesty."

Antiochus had not interacted much with Simon directly before his accession, but his brother Seleucus had trusted him. Indeed, he had praised him as someone whose dedication to the empire cost him his welcome in the backward city from which he had come. For this, Seleucus had rewarded him by making him a personal advisor, particularly on Judean affairs.

"I have met this Menelaus on my recent visit to Jerusalem, Majesty." Philostratos, who was Antiochus's minister of education, rose to support Simon. "He represents a sector of the Judean elite whose goals are most conducive to your own for the region."

"We will admit this Menelaus."

One of Antiochus's bodyguard pushed one side of the great door open as Herakleon went into the vestibule. He returned with a man wearing a Greek tunic.

Menelaus bowed his knee and lowered his head, offering a blessing in perfect Greek.

"May the gods look with favor upon the great king Antiochus and prosper all his endeavors."

"Welcome, Menelaus, brother of Simon," said Antiochus. "Rise and tell us what has brought you to Antioch."

"The welfare and future of my native city, Majesty," replied Menelaus. "Like many of my people, I long to see Jerusalem more fully incorporated into your empire and more closely bound to your government."

"If memory serves, Menelaus," Antiochus rejoined, "many of your people were most anxious that my father adopt a policy of noninterference toward them after he won the territory back from Egypt, contenting himself with the regular collection of tribute. That request was made by a delegation sent by the man my father had appointed as premier, the high priest Simon."

"Your recollection is, of course, perfect, Majesty," Menelaus continued. "And it is truly regrettable that the men to whom your father and brother entrusted the welfare of the province have proven to be so hostile to any change for the better. Honiah is even more fanatical about keeping Greek influences out of Jerusalem and less hospitable toward the non-Jewish peoples of your empire than his father was."

Antiochus's right eyebrow involuntarily rose, signaling his increased interest in what this visitor had to say.

"Honiah does not lead in the people's interest. He is alienated from Jerusalem's elite and refuses to cooperate with their desire to adapt themselves to the most excellent way of life of the Greeks. He inspires such dissent and factionalism that an attempt was made on his life a few days ago. That was what convinced me that I could no longer remain silent but had to come to speak with your Majesty, lest you think that an assault on Honiah, as your appointed deputy, was an act against your rule. If anything, Majesty, it was an act in favor of your rule and against a man who constantly opposes the integration of Judea into your empire."

Antiochus mulled over this information in the silence that followed.

"An assassination attempt is a serious crime, Majesty," said Heliodoros. "I suggest that the first order of business here be to support local Jerusalem authorities in a full investigation into the matter."

"Serious indeed," replied Antiochus, "but if Menelaus is correct that this was but a symptom of the larger issue, I don't see the benefit of making too much of the former without addressing the latter. Menelaus, do you have any knowledge of the origins of this attempt?"

"Majesty, any number of elite families would have cause to hasten Honiah's removal. He is a daily hindrance to Jerusalem's progress and economic development."

"It was Honiah, Majesty, who refused to remand the private funds deposited

in the Jerusalem Temple to King Seleucus," Simon interjected, "and who so daz-
zled the brave Heliodoros here with his mumbo jumbo that he willingly walked
away empty-handed rather than carry out your brother's wishes."

Heliodoros rose to his feet at this slight. "You dare impugn my courage? Go
back to Jerusalem yourself and bring the funds, if you're so brave!"

"Peace, Heliodoros," said Antiochus. "We know it's in your nature to be cau-
tious toward the gods of any land." *Though we could really have used those funds about
now.* He turned his attention back to Menelaus. "What would you suggest that
we do?"

"Majesty, if only the premier of Judea were a forward-looking friend of the
Greek way of life, like Honiah's brother Jason, we would have prosperity in
Jerusalem rather than festering factionalism."

"Jason?" Antiochus remembered Simon's explanation of Menelaus's own
change of name.

"Majesty, I have been in contact with this Jason for some time," said Philostratos. "I can bear witness to Jason's sincere desire to connect his people with the
culture and learning of the Greeks. He has been working to build a gymnasium in
Jerusalem and is a personal patron of Hellenistic learning in the city."

"Jason enjoys considerable support among other noble families in Jerusalem,"
added Menelaus, "but Honiah continues to impede their progress in Hellenizing."

"I can bear witness to that as well," Philostratos resumed. "When I visited
Jason in Jerusalem last month, Honiah refused even to see us because it was the
Jewish day of rest."

"One of many local traditions that make it difficult for the majority of people
in your empire to interact with the people in this one province," Menelaus commented. "Majesty, we are confident that, under a new deputy like Jason, Jerusalem
and Judea would flourish. Indeed, Majesty, we are so confident of the peace and
prosperity that would follow upon Hellenization, that we are ready to pledge an
additional 360 talents of tribute annually for the honor of renaming Jerusalem
'Antioch-at-Jerusalem' and refounding it as a Greek city."

Antiochus smiled. *Such an amount would put an additional six thousand soldiers
at my disposal annually.*

"Do you speak for this Jason? Will he honor your pledge?"

"Majesty, the families that crave Hellenization will honor my pledge. I would
expect Jason to show his gratitude to you even beyond this amount."

"We thank you, Menelaus, for your evident care for wedding Judea more fully
to our empire," Antiochus said. "We will consider your proposal to advance Judea's
welfare."

"Thank you, Majesty, for your beneficent oversight and gracious reception."

Menelaus bowed his knee to the ground and lowered his face once again, then left the hall.

Antiochus raised his head and massaged his throat as he continued to look ahead toward the closed door.

"An intriguing proposition. What says my counsel?"

Philostratos spoke first. "Majesty, I know this Jason. He is in his heart one of us and is even now being held back by Honiah from doing his fellow citizens great good."

"Their offer could not have come at a more opportune time," Herakleon added. "A steady source of extra income from the province of Judea if we make this man high priest in place of his brother, who by all reports is less forward-thinking than Jason anyway?"

Throughout this exchange, Heliodoros stared at Simon, who met his glare with a contemptuous half-smirk, as if to communicate victory.

"Philodemos? Apollonios? You've been very quiet this morning. What are your thoughts?"

Apollonios, commander of the Syrian armies, rose first. "Majesty, I would consider the whole of Palestine still to be a recent acquisition for your empire. Most of the people alive there can remember firsthand being ruled by the Ptolemies and would probably not care if the land reverted to them. Any course of action that would bind them closer to you and to your empire would be of strategic advantage. If the inhabitants of Jerusalem want to incorporate as a Greek city and rename their capital after yours, I could only think that this would make them better allies at your back when we are able to launch a campaign against Egypt."

"A leader in Judea anxious to promote the integration of that backward province into your empire would bring greater cohesion and strength to the whole," added Philodemos, the minister charged with internal security. "And I agree with Apollonios that this brings added value in a border territory such as Judea."

Heliodoros rose at last. "Should we not at least hear first from the *official* representative of the province?" He looked around at his fellow counselors. "We are very quickly accepting the word of a man who is, as far as we know, only promoting factionalism in Jerusalem." Heliodoros looked to Antiochus. "I know this Honiah. He is an honorable man."

"He may indeed be honorable, Heliodoros," replied Antiochus, "and still the wrong honorable man for the position. I am ready to grant that my brother may have been mistaken in confirming his appointment." He turned to Herakleon. "Recall Menelaus for us."

"Today you have become my son-in-law!" Eliashiv ben Joab clasped Binyamin to his chest and slapped him hard on the back as the villagers of Modein, gathered for this special occasion in their common life, cheered.

Mattathias stepped forward and placed Shoshanna's hand in Binyamin's as he grasped both in his own. "Blessed are you, O God of our ancestors. You made Adam, and for him you made his wife, Eve, as a helper and a support. Look with favor upon this man and this woman, who come together in betrothal in sincerity. Bring their lives to fulfillment in happiness and mercy, that they may grow old together."

"Amen, and amen!"

At once a local man began to pipe a melody on his reed flute while others began to clap or play on timbrels and hand drums. The younger men gathered up Binyamin and swept him into a circle dance around one of the fires that had been lit in the street, while the women congratulated Shoshanna, her mother Helah, and Miryam. A smiling Ari walked closer to observe the dancers, but a strong hand reached out and pulled him into the circle.

Eleazar had made the thirty-six kilometer journey from Jerusalem with the family, in part to take on the role of the father of the groom. He approached Eliashiv and Mattathias, smiling warmly.

"Zerah would have been proud to see this day, Eliashiv, as I am."

"Indeed, Eleazar," Mattathias added. "I have not known two finer men who devoted themselves more to bringing up their families in the fear of the Lord." He clapped Eliashiv's back. "Your daughter is well-matched, old friend."

Eleazar produced a small wooden box held shut with a leather strap.

"Here is the promised amount for the *mohar*, plus a little more. It may not be much, but I can assure you it was earned and saved with integrity and sacrifice."

"It is enough for Helah and me to know that Shoshanna will be well cared for by a good man all her days," Eliashiv said as he received the box. "Besides, we are in no position ourselves to help the couple in their future life together."

Mattathias looked down for a moment to master his anger and his sorrow. "Eliashiv is one of many who have lost a good part of their land to the greedy and the godless who do not honor Torah's commandments regarding the cancellation of debts or the year of Jubilee."

"My sons and I retain a third of the land that my own father bequeathed to me," Eliashiv explained. "Three bad years of crops, some illness, borrowing from the wrong people."

"Because only the wrong people, it seems, have the money to lend," Mattathias said.

"But we get by. We work our land; we work the land that used to be ours. And this"—Eliashiv raised the wooden box slightly in his upturned hands—"this may help us get part of that land back."

"May God grant it to be so, Eliashiv," said Eleazar.

"This cannot go on forever, Eleazar." Mattathias's voice grew more grave than angry. "God cannot allow the poor who fear Him to continue to be the victims of the rich who do not."

The song came to an end, and the men gave a shout as they stopped dancing. Ari looked up at the strong young man who had drawn him into the circle.

"So you're the little brother of the man who will be taking Shoshanna away from our village?" the man asked with a hint of playful menace.

"That depends," Ari replied suspiciously.

The man laughed. "Not to worry. My father has spoken well of your family, and I'm sure Shoshanna will be in good hands."

He bent over slightly and extended his right hand.

"My name is Judah, son of Mattathias."

"Ari ben Zerah."

"We grew up together with Shoshanna and her brothers. They're family to us, and you'll be family to us as well." Judah winked at the young boy and walked away toward his father and Eleazar.

The sun had begun to set and women were bringing woven mats, baskets of loaves, pots of stewed vegetables, and trays of fruits and olives from their homes and setting them out around the fires.

Miryam walked up to Ari. "Where is your brother Meir?"

"I don't know, Mother. All I've seen since the ceremony was the village spinning in circles."

Miryam smiled, shook her head, and tousled Ari's hair. "Stay close now. It's almost time to eat," she said as she walked on, scanning the villagers for Meir's face. She passed Hushai and Micaiah, Shoshanna's brothers.

"Can we help you, Mother?"

"I'm looking for Meir. Have you seen him?"

"He walked off in that direction right after the betrothal," said Micaiah, pointing to the west.

Miryam walked for a few minutes and saw Meir's silhouette against the red horizon just beyond the edge of the village. "What are you doing out here, Meir? Dinner is being set out now."

"I'm not really hungry."

Miryam recognized the pout in his voice. "Why so sullen today of all days? Aren't you happy for your brother?"

"Not if this is also all that I have to look forward to, Mother."

"What do you mean *all*, as if this is not enough? A good woman with whom to share your life and raise children, God willing? The ability to work with your hands to provide for yourself and them? Walking in the covenant and enjoying the favor of the Almighty God? What more is there that you should want?"

"Why should we continue to be content with this, when there are avenues to getting more?"

Meir surprised even himself with the vehemence of his response. "Should we be grateful for lentils and bread when the rich eat meat? Should we be glad to have to work today just to have some food tomorrow? I want more for my life, Mother—a better way of life than bending over an anvil and sitting by a forge all day."

"What way of life is better than the one God provides?"

Meir could see the pain in his mother's face at his rejection—he realized too late—of the life that his parents had labored to give him.

"Aren't you afraid of insulting God with your low estimation of his provision? Now stop casting a shadow on your brother's day of happiness and join your new family in celebration."

Miryam left no room for retort, and Meir followed her back into the village, his only protest being to lag a few steps behind. He thought of Agathon and learning Greek, of *goyim* bringing him gold to work into who-cared-what, of becoming a master metalworker over a dozen apprentices who could work to make him rich.

It was already dark as Miryam and Meir walked past two groups seated around their fires. Around the third they recognized Shoshanna's family with Binyamin, Ari, Eleazar, Mattathias, and several of Mattathias's sons, two of them accompanied by their own wives.

"Ah, good. You're here," said Mattathias. "We were beginning to be afraid that you were looking around for more of our village's daughters for your other sons."

The others around the fire laughed. Meir scowled but said nothing as he dropped down to sit beside Ari on a mat.

Mattathias rose and lifted a round, flat loaf in his hands. The people grouped around the fires fell silent.

"Blessed are you, O Lord our God, King of the Universe, for you bring forth bread from the earth."

"Amen!" shouted the village in response.

He bent down to receive a cup filled with wine from one of the young men beside him. Raising it above his head, he said, "Blessed are you, O Lord our God, King of the universe, who creates fruit from the vine."

"Amen!"

Mattathias looked down at Binyamin and Shoshanna, seated across from him, and said, "Blessed are you, O Lord our God, King of the universe, who created joy and gladness, groom and bride, delight, love, peace, and companionship."

"Amen!"

Around each fire, the people raised their cups to bless the couple and drink to their future. Then each circle gave its attention to passing the food around and beginning the evening's festivities. The food was plain but plentiful. The local musicians continued to play familiar tunes, while occasionally some of the women stopped their eating and conversing long enough to sing along to a favorite.

"I don't know, Miryam, if you and your family have met all of my sons." Mattathias gestured at a young man of almost thirty seated next to a woman ten years his junior. "This is Johanan, my firstborn, and his wife, Michal. Next to him are Simon, my second son, and his wife Salome." Mattathias turned to look at the man immediately to his right. "This is Judah, my third son. And the mountain over there," he continued, indicating a man who sat almost a head taller and a span broader than any other in the circle, "is Avaran, my fourth son, and strong as the rest of them put together, I think."

John, Simon, and Judah made gestures of "no contest" as the others around the circle laughed.

"You won't find Avaran in Jerusalem unless I, together with two oxen, have dragged him away from this village."

"Where is Jonathan?" Eleazar asked.

"I left him in Jerusalem, where he's stayed for the past month now thanks to the hospitality of some friends," Mattathias replied. "Someone in the family needs to have an eye on what's happening there these days."

Food was passed around a second time, and cups filled afresh with locally made wine. Miryam and Helah shared the stories of their betrothals so long ago and spoke warmly of the many years that followed. Together with the older men, they remembered some of the struggles of marriage along the way, all the time assuring Binyamin and Shoshanna that God had been faithful to see them through all of them, as God would do for them as well.

Ari looked up at Judah, Mattathias's third son.

"Shouldn't you be married by now? You're a lot older than Binyamin."

Judah laughed. "The soul of my dear mother returned in the body of an urchin!"

"Judah prefers to let all the women of our village dream about marrying him," Avaran teased, "rather than be so cruel to so many as to marry any *one* of them."

The commotion of hoofbeats, a hasty dismount, and a rider tripping through seated guests and food distracted Judah from landing any rejoinder. He rose to his feet as his hand instinctively moved to the hilt of the dagger in his belt. Mattathias rose a moment later.

"Who are you, friend?" the elder asked.

"Joram ben Levi," said the rider through heavy breaths. "I've come from Yoshe ben Yoezer of Jerusalem."

Mattathias placed his hand on Judah's shoulder to signal that he could stand at ease.

"Forgive my intrusion on your festivities here."

"Sit, Joram, and tell us what brings you here in such haste," Mattathias said.

"Perhaps it would be better if we went inside?"

"Perhaps if you sit, Joram," Mattathias urged, "everyone that you just stumbled over will assume that everything is all right and return to enjoying a carefree evening." Mattathias motioned to his fellow villagers that nothing of import was happening. The din of conversations and music once again began to fill the night air.

"Master Eleazar," Joram said as he scanned the faces around the circle. "This news is for you as well. A messenger came from Antioch to Jason this morning. Honiah has been removed as premier of Judea, and Jason has been appointed in his place." Joram's voice became more impassioned. "Honiah is forbidden to return to Jerusalem."

The group sat in stunned silence. Finally Eleazar asked, "What explanation has been given?"

"None," Joram replied. "Jason has convened an emergency meeting of the *gerousia* for tomorrow afternoon to discuss—his words—'policy changes,' which is why Yoshe sent me here. He wanted to be sure that you, Master Mattathias, and you, Master Eleazar, would be present and your voices heard."

"But Honiah is the high priest," Simon objected. "How can he be banned from Jerusalem?"

"Jason will continue to serve as high priest in his absence," Joram replied.

"How could this have happened?" asked Eleazar. "Honiah was a blameless high priest and a faultless premier. The Seleucids' tribute was never lacking."

"I don't know for certain about this, mind you," Joram said, "but I heard that Menelaus was also in Antioch this past week. It could be unrelated."

Mattathias lowered his head and clenched his fists. "Slander—the death of many a righteous man!" he exclaimed. "We know that Menelaus is a friend of Hellenization and, like his brother Simon, no friend of Honiah. What lies did he take to Antioch to get Honiah deposed?"

"In league with Jason?" Judah ventured.

"I would hate to believe it—his own brother!" answered Simon.

"Give me the dung of the field rather than the dung of Jerusalem politics any day," Avaran said, spitting into the fire.

"And may God deliver us from living under the heels of the *goyim*, who have such power to meddle in our affairs!" Judah exclaimed.

"The nations have power over us, Judah," said Eleazar, "only because we have been so careless in keeping covenant with God."

Mattathias slapped his hands on his thighs.

"We will ride back to Jerusalem with you at first light, Joram. Eat and rest here with us tonight. Tomorrow we'll see what Jason intends and offer Honiah's family what help we can."

"I'll come with you, Father," offered Judah.

Mattathias nodded in consent. "We'll have a horse for you as well, Eleazar."

Eleazar signaled his appreciation with a nod.

"I am sorry, Binyamin, Shoshanna, that these matters have intruded into your celebration."

"When would such news *have* been timely, Master Mattathias?" Shoshanna responded.

"You should come with me, Binyamin," said Eleazar. "As my apprentice, it is not too early to learn how the scribe's work is not all study, but often the messiest and most dangerous kind of work—dealing with those in power."

"For the remainder of this night, however," said Mattathias, "let's talk of family, of love, and of all the good things that God will bring into the lives of this favored couple."

The men around the fire voiced their agreement. The wineskin made its way around the circle once again. All raised their cups again to Binyamin and Shoshanna as, for the time being, they allowed the music and singing around them to rise above the clamor in their hearts. Miryam wished she could prolong this night for her oldest son and newest daughter. The shadow cast over the evening was likely to lengthen rather than abate come morning.

7

The ride back to Jerusalem took Eleazar and Binyamin five hours. Mattathias and Judah had ridden harder and faster, in order to confer with Honiah's family in Jerusalem before the meeting of the *gerousia*, while Joram kept pace with the older priest as a safeguard. Eleazar and Binyamin refreshed themselves at Eleazar's home, eating the midday meal in near silence before heading to the Temple. As they immersed their hands in one of the *mikvoth* outside the Temple courts, Eleazar said, "I fear we may need such purification again upon *leaving* the Temple this day." He stood for a moment looking up at the Temple, imagining it without Honiah presiding over its sacrifices and protecting its purity and the sanctity of the whole city. *Just as Master Yehoshua had feared barely one month ago.*

They made their way to the inner court and entered the Office of Hewn Stone which, in addition to serving as a gathering place for priests before sacrifices, was also the traditional meeting place of the *gerousia*. The semicircular rows of stone benches were beginning to be filled with the heads of priestly and elite lay families, some of whom had brought their sons to witness what they sensed would prove to be one of the more momentous meetings of their lifetimes. Others were still standing in conversation with one another, speculating about what was to be announced and what had led to this sudden change. As Eleazar and Binyamin surveyed the assembly, they noticed Yoshe expressing clear opposition as he spoke with vehemence to the men gathered around him. The faces of considerably more men reflected confusion, but a surprising number of the attendees wore a look of excitement, even triumph.

"Remember, Binyamin," said Eleazar, "say nothing. You have no voice in this assembly, and I would not want the first impression you make to be your eviction."

Jason entered, followed closely by Menelaus, Agathon, and Timarchos. Conversations around the room ceased with unusual suddenness in anticipation. Those standing on the open floor quickly parted before Jason as he took his place upon the president's chair facing the semicircle. Menelaus, Agathon, and Timarchos remained standing behind him to signal both their support and their prominence in the new regime. Jason surveyed the semicircles of senators with an air of deliberateness, allowing the gravity of the moment to become his own *gravitas* before drawing a deep breath to speak.

"Truly great and surprising things have come upon us as a result of our noble King Antiochus's interests in and forethought for our city. He has extended to us the privilege of becoming incorporated as a city with rights and political standing equal to those of the other great cities of his empire from Antioch to Seleucia. In his benevolence, he no longer wishes to treat us as conquered provincials but as peers."

Jason's tone became more subdued as he continued.

"Sadly, the king could not see a way to move forward with Honiah representing Judea to his government. Despite my efforts to protect him from his own entrenchment in the ways of the past, he continued to neglect my advice to his own detriment. It was impossible to hide his opposition to progress from King Antiochus any longer. The recent attempt on his life was heard in the court of Antioch as the cry of our city for a new leader who would facilitate, rather than fight against, the good things that our partnership with the larger world around us will bring."

Jason paused.

"It has pleased the king to name me as Honiah's successor to this office, and thus as president of our senate."

At this, a full third of the assembled company rose to their feet and applauded Jason. Another third rose to join them as the applause and shouts of acclamation continued.

Once a sufficient number had expressed affirmation, Jason motioned for the assembly to take their seats again. "Thank you, brothers. It lifts my spirits to know that I will have your support in the challenging work ahead of us as we re-create our city."

Eleazar rose to his feet to speak, as was the custom in the assembly. "What has become of Honiah?"

"It fills me with regret to bear this news"—there was a sincerity in Jason's voice that even his opponents could recognize—"but the king has decided that, both for Honiah's own safety and in the interests of preserving unity, Honiah should take up residence elsewhere for the time being."

Sounds of surprise through the room told Eleazar that not all the messengers involved in convening this meeting had been as forthcoming as Joram had been.

Elam ben Jacob rose next. "Honiah is the nation's high priest!"

"Naturally, as next in line to Honiah," Jason responded, "I will continue to serve as high priest as well."

"Forgive my confusion, Lord Jason." The voice came from Eupolemus, a younger Judean dressed in a Greek tunic. "Wouldn't Honiah's son succeed him to this office before his brother?"

"These arrangements were confirmed by the king himself," Jason replied. "And as it happens, also by Honiah before his departure for Antioch."

"When Honiah was expecting to return to the place you were supposedly *holding* for him," Yoshe ben Yoezer said, pointing at Jason in agitation. "What right does a Gentile king have to interfere with the high priesthood?"

Menelaus stepped forward. "A Gentile king has the right to determine what is in the best interests of his empire, which in this case is Honiah's absence from Jerusalem. The selection of a new high priest is merely a consequence of this necessary action. If anything, it was serendipitous that the man whom Antiochus deemed reliable to protect the king's and the city's interests was also of the same high priestly family."

"You speak of re-creating our city, Lord Jason," Amnon ben Imlah said with a tone of suspicion. "It is written, 'The Lord has laid Zion's foundations.' What new foundations do you—or perhaps I should say, does King Antiochus—propose? In whose image would you re-create Jerusalem?"

"King Antiochus has granted us the privilege of founding a new city—Antioch-at-Jerusalem—within the old. This will become the administrative center of Jerusalem and, with it, Judea. It will have a Greek constitution, modeled after the constitution of Athens itself, and all the necessary institutions that go along with it."

"Lord Jason," Amnon ventured, "we have a constitution. It is the Torah given to us by *God*. The Torah provides us with our principles of jurisprudence, economics, and ritual observance. It cannot be replaced as the foundation of our polity."

Eupolemus spoke again, less timidly than before. "My father, John, was part of the embassy that went to the father of this Antiochus, asking him to confirm our right to govern ourselves by our own law. That, too, was a royal privilege."

Eleazar raised his voice in support. "God has chosen us to be different from the nations around us, not to seek to be like them," he said as gently as he could. "He has called us to be holy to himself and has given us the Torah as our securest path to well-being. 'The fear of God is the starting point for all wisdom; in every wise action there is the doing of God's law.' What you are proposing is not in keeping with wisdom."

A younger priest named Eliakim, who had in recent years taken the name Alcimus, stood up to answer.

"Master Eleazar, we have nothing but respect for you and your lifetime of devotion to the old ways, but I cannot accept your claim that Torah is the only source of wisdom. Even our recently departed teacher of blessed memory, Yehoshua ben Sira, devoted himself to learn the wisdom of the Greeks and of the Egyptians. Surely the God who created all who live and move and have being did not shine the light of wisdom only upon Mount Sinai."

Yoshe answered his nephew impatiently. "God did indeed shine his light upon the *goyim*, and does so each new day—but they grope about in darkness today as they always have. Whom do they thank for the light that rose upon them today? Whose laws do they honor?"

He turned his gaze squarely on Jason. "We're not just speaking of setting aside one set of human-made political arrangements for another.

> "The Creator of all things gave Wisdom an order,
> and assigned her a place for her tent:
> 'Make your dwelling in Jacob,' he said,
> 'and in Israel shall be your inheritance.'
> So Wisdom took root in an honorable people,
> in the Lord's portion among all the peoples of the earth.
> This is the book of the covenant of the Most High,
> the law that Moses commanded us,
> the inheritance of the assemblies of Jacob."

Yoshe turned to the assembly, accusing them with his eyes as he asked: "This is what you would now set aside?"

Timarchos now stepped forward from behind Jason to meet Yoshe's challenge. "This is indeed not about exchanging one set of political arrangements for another. It's about exchanging an outdated, backward way of doing business for one that will allow Judea to prosper."

Timarchos addressed himself to the assembly. "We're not living under David or Solomon anymore, brothers. One could fantasize about the wealth of the nations pouring into Jerusalem under them. Five hundred years later, it's a very different picture."

Menelaus added his voice against Yoshe's attack. "Ben Sira may have thought that the Torah was God's gift to Israel, but what has it brought us in the face of the Assyrians? The Babylonians? The Greeks? How many more centuries would have to pass before you'd admit that Torah just hasn't worked for our nation?"

A murmur of disapproval met Menelaus's final words. Zedekiah, who had been sitting silently on the ground by the doorway, rose to his feet, shaking visibly.

"Sons of Korah, and not Aaron!" he shouted, pointing at Menelaus and Jason. "Supplanters of the righteous! Would you so boldly lead the nation into apostasy? If we haven't enjoyed Torah's promised blessings, it is because we have not submitted to its yoke." He paused to fix his gaze on Jason. "It is because you have not submitted to its yoke. When this assembly leads the nation in righteousness, then will our light shine. Then will God exalt us above the nations once more. You are bringing God's curse upon our nation!"

Eupolemus rose again, speaking in a diplomatic tone, obviously intended to defuse the growing tension. "The third Antiochus, like the Ptolemies who ruled us before him, respected the right of all Judeans to observe the traditions of our ancestors. They wisely decided never to make our people choose between loyalty to God and loyalty to them."

"The fourth Antiochus intends nothing different," Jason assured him. "Separate markets will be maintained to protect the purity of food for those concerned about such things. Sabbath observance, the covenant of circumcision, the rituals of our holy Temple—none of these things will change for those who care to observe them. But," Jason added triumphantly, "following all such regulations will be a matter of conscience, not superstition, not slavery to tradition enforced by the state."

"Conscience, Lord Jason?" Judah exclaimed. "The conscience of the rich will never be sufficient to safeguard the lives of the poor." He looked around the room, seeming to focus on some of the more affluent members as he continued. "Come to Modein and see how your conscience has affected your brothers and sisters in Israel. Come see how your conscience has deprived families of their land and livelihood already, in complete disregard for God's law."

Menelaus did not attempt to hide his contempt for Judah's point of view. "An economy that has to start over every seventh year is impractical, just one more local, idiosyncratic practice that has made it next to impossible for people of other nations to create long-term economic ties with us."

This has gone on long enough, Jason thought. "I had no illusions that this assembly would be unanimous in its support for these changes. But as they do not affect your individual piety, except insofar as that piety will no longer be imposed upon the progress of the nation, I do not see that any injustice has been done."

Jason watched the faces in the hall carefully, noting that the majority were signaling at least resignation, if not pleasure, with the new direction.

"I also do not see a place for an official vote," Jason continued.

Yoshe scoffed. "Coward! Are you so unsure of the value of these 'privileges' you are promoting, Jason? Are you so afraid that this assembly is not buying what you're selling?"

"This is, ultimately, the will of King Antiochus," Jason said forcefully. "A vote against him would amount to a declaration of revolution. Are you prepared for that?" Jason looked around at the assembly, challenging them with his eyes. "Is anyone here prepared for that? I shouldn't think so: the advantages he offers us are more than equally matched by the disadvantages that would follow upon opposition."

Eupolemus offered in an even tone, "On the other hand, Lord Jason, would it not be advantageous for our relationship with King Antiochus to be able to report that his offer was received positively by the vote of the *gerousia*?"

Clever Eupolemus, Jason thought.

"An unofficial poll, then." Jason looked up to the assembly. "All who are in favor of accepting the king's offer to allow us to found Antioch-at-Jerusalem and to receive citizenship in a peer city of his empire, stand and be counted."

"Lord Jason," Eupolemus protested, "ought not a ballot on such a sensitive issue be taken confidentially?"

"Eupolemus," Jason replied. "You heard Yoshe. This assembly is no place for cowardice. All who favor receiving the king's offer, stand and be counted."

At once several dozen men stood to their feet. Jason waited. Another dozen arose to join the party of those standing. Jason continued to wait, surveying those who remained seated. More stood, one-by-one, as he met their eyes.

"A clear majority," he announced, then added with feigned benevolence: "I will not make those who oppose the king stand and declare themselves. Perhaps some of you will yet have a change of heart." Jason motioned for those standing to seat themselves. "In the meanwhile, we will proceed with the proposed changes. I expect all members of this assembly to act in line with the will of the majority. We have heard quite a bit from the late ben Sira today, from whom I also will draw: 'Fear God; honor the high priest.'"

Judah would not allow the old master's voice to be co-opted in this way. "'Who deserves honor? The person who fears the Lord! Who deserves contempt? The person who departs from the commandments.' You may convince the people in this assembly to accept these departures from the covenant, but you will never convince God. You are no successor to Honiah, but a usurper!"

"Is this hothead your son, Mattathias? Does he speak for your whole family?"

"As for me and my house, we will serve the Lord."

Jason decided not to indulge the distraction further.

"The new constitution calls for the enrollment of those who will constitute the citizenry of Antioch-at-Jerusalem. Citizenship brings significant privilege; it carries international recognition and ensures the special protection of King Antiochus. Naturally, such privileges carry additional expectations of support for the king's government, as is fitting for a city that now has a greater stake and degree of enfranchisement in that government."

"Aha!" Yoshe exclaimed. "Now we come to the point. How much did your new office—and Honiah's exile—cost, Jason?"

Jason had just expended his last reserves of patience. "You are well beyond insubordination, Yoshe," he said through his teeth.

Menelaus did not flinch at the question. "Three hundred and sixty talents," he said matter-of-factly, as if Yoshe's objections ultimately did not matter. "And that was quite a bargain, as any man of sense here knows."

"What were we talking about?" Jason asked. "Ah, yes. Citizenship. Those who are not enrolled as citizens will be politically classified as *metokoi*, people with right to property and residence but no political voice or vote except through a citizen acting as his representative. We will adjust the membership of the *gerousia* accordingly to function as the senate of Antioch-at-Jerusalem."

Jason paused long enough to give moment to what followed.

"Each of you may apply to become citizens of the new Antioch-at-Jerusalem and to have a place in the senate of our new city. We will seek to be as inclusive as possible, but we will also want to avoid getting bogged down in the same old debates every time we want to make an improvement." Jason looked at Yoshe and Mattathias with a glimmer of anger in his eyes to intimate that his next words applied particularly to them and those of their mind-set. "Your applications will be carefully considered."

Jason rose to signal that the meeting was about to end.

"I will contact Philostratos with the news that the premier and senate of Judea are fully supportive of the transformation of the city and all it entails. Building the gymnasium and *ephebeion* can begin at once, to fit our young elites and the next generation for even more distinguished and prosperous futures in the larger world. I believe that concludes this day's business. We stand adjourned."

As Jason walked through the Hall of Hewn Stone toward his private office, he was warmly congratulated by the stronger supporters of the new measures. He signaled for a scribe to follow him into his office and disappeared. At first Yoshe thought it odd that Jason's closest partisans—Menelaus, Timarchos, and Agathon—did not follow him, but he reasoned that they were left to mingle with the crowd to encourage those who had stood in support of Jason's policy changes and to "overhear" the conversations of the less convinced.

Yoshe, Mattathias, and a few others communicated through eye contact that they should leave the chamber separately and process elsewhere what had just transpired.

Mattathias and Judah made their way across the court and passed through the great Nicanor Gate into the women's court, pausing at the gate long enough for Yoshe and Amnon to see them. They waited at the bottom of the steps for their peers to catch up.

"I am sorry, Father, for my outspokenness in the assembly," Judah said.

"I was certainly thinking what you were speaking," Mattathias offered reassuringly. "Though some of it," he continued with a half-smile, "was perhaps better thought than spoken."

"I would have liked to have said a thing or two more," said Yoshe as he approached.

"If it will ease your mind," Mattathias ventured, "I can't think of anything you left unsaid."

Mattathias caught sight first of Binyamin and then of the wispy form of Zedekiah passing through the Nicanor Gate and motioned for them to join their conversation.

"It is difficult to look at today's meeting as anything other than a decision to relegate our sacred law to second place and become like the nations," Mattathias observed. "I fear that we cannot yet begin to imagine the implications of this for the everyday life of Jerusalem."

The group suddenly became aware of the presence of Eupolemus, standing just outside their circle.

"Shouldn't you be congratulating Jason right about now?" Yoshe asked, clearly communicating the lack of welcome.

"I see little reason to congratulate anyone today," he replied.

Mattathias stepped toward him. "Yet when it came time to stand and be counted, you stood alongside him. That hardly makes you a friend of the covenant."

"You think the best path is to alienate yourself from Jason completely and find yourself with no voice in the government?" Eupolemus countered. "Who will speak, then, to protect the Torah and the people tomorrow? In the face of the unavoidable, minimizing the damage may have more value in God's sight than bold—and perhaps ultimately selfish—statements of protest."

Yoshe grunted his disagreement.

"I am no more in favor of these changes than any of you, and not just because it throws away my father's careful work and diplomatic achievements for the nation," Eupolemus said. "And I can support others in the assembly who feel this way as well. Don't presume that there's only one way to fight against these innovations."

"Diplomacy and compromise too often go together to sit well with my soul," Mattathias replied, "but God is your judge, not I."

"How can God accept the offerings of a high priest who has purchased the office from the *goyim*?" Zedekiah complained.

"Don't worry, Zedekiah," Yoshe said. "I doubt Jason will actually officiate in the Temple any more than he has to." Yoshe's humor was not lost on anyone but Zedekiah. "But this turn of events is just one more example of the impossibility of keeping faith with God while under the yoke of Gentile domination and the arrogant interference of the *goyim* in our covenant relationship with God."

"More immediately," Eupolemus interjected, "does anyone know what will become of Honiah and his family?"

"We met with the younger Honiah earlier today," Mattathias said. "He plans to take his mother and sister to Egypt for the time being, far out of harm's way and beyond easy reach, even for Antiochus. They hope that the elder Honiah will join them there, but they suspect he may try to remain closer in an effort to intervene on behalf of his people at some point."

"Will you join them, Zedekiah?" Yoshe asked.

"I will not leave the holy land of our God. I will seek his guidance, but not here. His spirit is gone from this place." Zedekiah looked sadly about the courtyard and toward the Holy Places. "It stands now under his judgment."

"Where will you go, then?"

"Where God has always bent down to speak to his prophets—the desert." His eyes seemed to focus on some point inside his own mind rather than on the faces around him. "There I will inquire for all of us. There I will listen."

Jason emerged from the high priest's office and proceeded to the colonnades of the Temple that led back to the city.

"Lord Jason," a voice called out. "A moment, please?"

Jason and his entourage stopped and turned.

"What is it, Master Eleazar?"

"Jason," he began gently, "I did not want to challenge you openly in the assembly, so as not to engage you in a contest of honor. But permit me to speak with you privately, here, about the direction in which you are leading us."

"I hardly have time for a further lecture, Eleazar," Jason said in a vain attempt to silence his former teacher.

"Nor should you need a further lecture. How can you not remember the lessons that first Rabban Yehoshua and then I tried to instill in you when you were a young pupil? Surely your own memory tells you daily about the holy God who chose this holy city for his own dwelling, and who gave us the Torah to teach us how to keep the place and ourselves holy to the Lord who ransomed us from Egypt, who made us a distinctive people, and who holds our future."

"We are agreed, then," Jason said, attempting again to free himself not only from Eleazar's persistence, but from the nagging voices buried within, "that I need no further lecture." He turned to walk away, but Eleazar's voice kept its grip on him.

"Jason, what are you chasing after as you run away from your training? Will you not find that you, like Solomon in his straying, have been chasing the wind? Something that will ever elude you and, even if you could catch it, will never fill you?"

Jason could feel the earnestness in Eleazar's pleading.

"Only living in the awareness of God can give meaning to this brief vapor of life, not those things for which you are turning away from God. As Solomon himself learned, 'God gives wisdom, knowledge, and joy to those who please him. To those who offend God, he assigns the task of hoarding and accumulating only to give it all to others. This too is pointless and a chasing after wind.'"

Jason paused for a moment, not so much thinking about Eleazar's words as about whether or not to open up such questions again in his own mind.

"Thank you, Master Eleazar, for your evident commitment to the well-being of the nation. Once the newly constituted senate is convened, you can expect that one of its first acts will be to honor your retirement after a lifetime of distinguished service."

Binyamin sat in the workshop until late afternoon turned to evening. An obvious cloud hung over his head as he absentmindedly worked to smooth the surface of the bronze disk that he had cast and that was destined to become a mirror. Miryam emerged from the inner house to bring him a cup of water and a snack of dried figs and nuts while she and Ari finished preparing the evening meal.

"Still upset, Binyamin?" she said, nudging him. "You should be thinking about Shoshanna today and your future together, not about intrigues in the assembly."

"You weren't there, Mother. Our elders all but repudiated the covenant today."

"You are making too much of what goes on in high places," Miryam said as she sat down beside her son and put her hand reassuringly on his forearm. "Whether under a Ptolemy or an Antiochus, whether under Honiah or his brother, we will still follow the law of Moses and traditions of our ancestors. 'Do not worry yourself because of evildoers,' Binyamin." Miryam gripped Binyamin's forearm more firmly before releasing it. "God will never abandon his faithful ones."

Miryam returned to the kitchen, while Binyamin went back to polishing the bronze disk. After a short while, Meir burst into the workshop from the interior of the house.

"Where are you going in such a hurry, Meir?"

"Hello to you, too, Binyamin. I'm going to Master Agathon's house."

Meir continued passing through the workshop and was about to step out into the street.

"Why? Does he have more work for us?"

"No, not today."

Miryam emerged to announce that dinner was ready.

"Then why?" Binyamin persisted.

"I'm going," Meir declared defiantly, "because he's taken an interest in helping me succeed in the new Jerusalem taking shape around us." He modulated his tone as he explained further. "He's having one of his slaves teach me Greek. Look." Meir lifted the wax tablet he was carrying and pointed to the foreign letters on it. "Soon I'll be able to write and speak Greek better than anyone in our quarter."

"While you leave us to do the work around this place?" Binyamin objected.

"Master Agathon has promised that he will send enough work in silver and gold my way to more than make up for my time away from the shop here. It will be good for all of us."

"Who is this Agathon?" Miryam asked. "Is he a Greek?"

"No, Mother," Meir said. "He's also a Jew, like us."

"Not a Jew like us," Binyamin interjected. "I saw your Agathon today, Meir. He stood with Jason the usurper against Honiah, the legitimate high priest."

"Master Agathon is one of Lord Jason's oldest and closest friends," Meir said in defense. "That makes him one of the most powerful men in Jerusalem today."

"Why would this man do this for you?" Miryam asked. "What does he want in return?"

"I don't know," Meir said with some perturbation. "Perhaps he sees something more in me than a poor metalworker. Why can't you?"

"Your father was a 'poor metalworker,' Meir," she replied, "but I saw something more in him—deeply rooted reverence for our God and his law, and the assurance that gave me that I'd never have cause to be ashamed of him or sorry that I had married him. That's the only 'something more' I need to see in his son as well." Miryam paused and took a breath. "Now come eat dinner, while it's still hot," she said, disappearing into the interior of the house.

Binyamin got up from his workbench and walked toward Meir, shaking his head slightly from side to side.

"You can't touch pitch, little brother," he warned, "without it sticking to your fingers. And if you hang around this Agathon, you'll soon find yourself polluted by the apostasy infecting our whole city. Today they've chosen friendship with the *goyim* over friendship with God."

"Agathon's a Jew, too, Binyamin," Meir protested. "Maybe his way is just as good as yours."

"Or just as good as our father's? Are you the only one who can't see how your actions of late dishonor his memory? Because our mother certainly sees it."

"I'm tired of you judging me, Binyamin. You do what you think is in our family's best interests, and I'll do what I think best advances us. Your inability to accept that is hardly reason for me to do otherwise."

"No, but honoring our mother should be reason enough. 'With all your heart honor your father, and do not forget the labor pains of your mother. Through your parents you were born; what can you give back that equals their gift to you?' Don't go another step down the path that brings Mother grief and shames the memory of Father, Meir." Binyamin pointed in the direction of the agora and Agathon's house beyond. "That path."

Jason was reclining on a couch beside a table under a canopied pavilion. Its long, white, gauzy curtains moved gently with the breeze. The sun shone through cloudless skies. Jason was laughing and reaching for a cup of wine. Agathon, Honiah, Seraiah, and Eleazar were also seated around the table, sharing stories and passing trays of nuts and olives. Honiah said, "How good, how pleasant it is, when brothers live in unity together."

Adoni? A woman's soft voice was calling to him. He turned around but could see no woman in the room. Agathon looked at him as if to ask what was wrong. *Adoni?* the voice said again. He felt a hand on his shoulder and turned around. His wife was standing beside his couch. She placed her right knee on the couch as if to sit with him.

"Adoni?" Niobe said yet again, this time shaking Jason's shoulder slightly.

Jason's eyes shot open as he raised his head and shoulders a half-meter from the pillow on which he had been sleeping. The sun was full in the morning sky, streaming into his bedroom. The sight caught him by surprise, and he raised himself up on his arms.

"What's the hour?"

Now it was Castor's voice that he heard. "It's the third hour of the day, my lord," he said as Niobe propped several pillows for Jason to lean back upon. "I was about to send for the doctor to feel for your pulse."

Jason smiled. He looked out onto his veranda, where a loaf of bread, bowl of fruit, and cup were sitting, no doubt for several hours now.

"You have appointments in the city starting at the fifth hour, so I didn't dare wait longer to rouse you," Castor explained.

"Thank you, Castor."

Jason rose from the bed, walked out onto the veranda, and leaned against the railing. He drew in a series of deep breaths as he gazed at Jerusalem in the bright morning sun. *A new day for Jerusalem*, he thought. *A new day for me.*

BOOK · 11

The Temple

In the 140th year of the kingdom of the Greeks (172 BCE) . . .

1

Meir hurried along the portico of the gymnasium to the main atrium, where an older man in a Greek tunic was speaking to a couple with two young sons in tow.

"You'll find the facility and its grounds to be in no way inferior to the gymnasia of any city of this size throughout the empire."

The old man noticed Meir approaching.

"Ah, here comes Hilaron now."

The director of the gymnasium, a Greek from Antioch, stepped back and motioned for Meir to enter the circle.

"You sent for me, Master Zenon?" Meir asked in well-pronounced Greek.

"Yes, Hilaron. This gentleman is Sarpedon, recently arrived to serve as captain of the Syrian cohort resident in Antioch-at-Jerusalem."

Sarpedon was no taller than Meir, but of exceptionally sturdy build, dressed in a heavy Greek tunic bound with a leather belt at the waist and wearing military sandals that reached almost to his knees. He nodded curtly to the young man.

"Your director has spoken very highly of you, Hilaron," Sarpedon said, "calling you one of the finest pupils from the local population."

"I am honored to have Master Zenon's confidence," Meir replied.

"This is my wife, Hespera," he continued, indicating the lady dressed in a long tunic with a golden cord bound under her breasts, "and our two sons."

"These young men," Zenon said, "will begin their formation here at our gymnasium in just a few days. Show the family what we have to offer them."

The director turned to Sarpedon and Hespera and said, "I leave you in Hilaron's capable hands for the next hour. Please find me again before you leave."

Meir led the family back along the portico from which he came.

"The gymnasium complex wraps around the southwest corner of our Temple Mount," Meir explained as they walked. "This courtyard and its porticoes are frequently used for instruction," he said, pointing to a few groups of students of different ages, gathered around their teachers or working on their lessons. "So is the building directly ahead." Meir paused at the base of the stairs leading into the lyceum. "Younger students first learn how to read and write the Greek language and then begin to read Greek literature from Aesop to Homer to our native Scriptures."

"I thought the Jews' sacred texts were written in Hebrew," Hespera said.

"They are, ma'am," Meir replied, "but the most important parts have been available in Greek for a hundred years already, thanks to the Greek-speaking Jewish community in Alexandria." He resumed his tour speech, already given to many a new arrival. "Older students learn logic and rhetoric, since being able to formulate arguments and speak persuasively are among the most nec- essary skills for participation in government, whether here or anywhere in the empire."

They proceeded to walk up the stairs into the classroom building.

"We also learn arithmetic, geometry, music, and astronomy."

They passed a number of rooms, some with small groups studying, most empty.

"It's fairly quiet now," Meir observed. "Most instruction happens midday when the sun is too strong for athletics."

"I've had the impression that Judea is not very open to foreigners," Sarpedon said. "My wife is concerned that she and our boys may not feel at home here."

"Many, many families such as yours have come to Antioch-at-Jerusalem," Meir responded. "Lord Jason's building projects have brought many master builders and craftsmen from Syria and Egypt, along with their families. This, in turn, brought more merchants, suppliers, teachers, physical trainers, and performers, all now residents of Jerusalem." Meir looked at the young boys as he continued. "Many of these people came with children of their own, and many are now enrolled in the gymnasium alongside Judean youth."

"The founding of Antioch-at-Jerusalem has given many of us the opportu- nity to give our children a faster track to citizenship in a Greek city," Sarpedon confessed. "A military man like myself can generally look forward to citizen- ship upon retirement, but that would be too late to give our boys the education and start they need. My commission here means that we can gain this citizenship and its benefits much earlier."

"It has helped many of us here in Jerusalem as well," Meir replied. "I myself am the son of a metalworker, but I have enjoyed the sponsorship of a local nobleman named Agathon, who has been exceedingly generous toward me and my family. I could never have hoped for the privilege of education at a gymnasium otherwise."

Meir paused for a moment before continuing. "I would be lying, ma'am," he said, remembering Hespera's concerns, "if I told you that all of our local population supports the direction that the city has taken. But most of the people you will meet in the public buildings and markets of Antioch-at-Jerusalem will be very welcoming."

They emerged from the lyceum and came upon the *palaestra*, a large courtyard covered in sand, surrounded by porticoes, with an entrance to another building at the far side. The *palaestra* was buzzing with activity. In the nearer part, a group of about thirty young men were moving through a series of well-choreographed exercises. A young man played a rhythmic tune on a reed instrument, setting the pace for the exercise, as the trainer walked between the others, pausing to correct this one's posture or another one's movements. Farther away, some students as well as adult males were engaged in wrestling matches, boxing, and the long jump.

"Of course we practice running, the discus toss, and the javelin throw, as well. Lord Jason is constructing a stadium just outside the city wall, about a fifteen-minute walk from here."

"I see you let some of the adult population train here," Sarpedon remarked.

"Of course," Meir replied. "The new sports are very popular among both our local nobles and newer residents like yourselves. Four years ago we had very little like this in Jerusalem—at best, the men would wrestle or spar with staffs for physical activity."

Meir watched the young men moving through their exercise regimen as he led the captain and his family along the east portico.

"And we certainly never thought about our bodies in the way that our Greek trainers have taught us—taking care to stretch and firm up every sinew, every part, giving careful attention to diet and hygiene."

They entered the building at the far end of the *palaestra*.

"Speaking of which, this is the bath complex. We have one side dedicated for men's use, another for women's," Meir explained. "There are several small pools of cold water, and a number of basins and the means for heating water for the warm bath after exercise."

"Altogether fine facilities," Sarpedon said approvingly. He looked at Hespera, finding confirmation in her smile. "I'm glad our sons will have the opportunity to study here as well, and I hope they shall turn out to be such fine gentlemen as you appear to be. What are you called again?"

"Hilaron," Meir said.

"Well, Hilaron, I am sure our paths will continue to cross here. Thank you for your time."

"The pleasure was all mine, Captain," Meir said with a bow of his head. "Shall I take you back to the atrium?"

"We'll find our way just fine," Hespera said. "Please go back to whatever it is you need to do."

"Ma'am," Meir said, acknowledging her also with a nod of his head. He turned to leave the baths and return to the *palaestra*. He walked along the western portico until he came to a hallway that took him to an external portico running the length of the lyceum, *palaestra*, and bathhouse. He followed this to the south until he found his cohort of students seated in a circle with Apelles, a Syrian-born Greek who had been his tutorial instructor for the two years since Meir's admission to the gymnasium, following his preliminary work in Greek language and writing in Agathon's house.

"Ah, good, Hilaron," Apelles said as Meir approached. "You're back. We've been discussing the story of the rebellion of the Titans against the gods and how we should understand its meaning."

"I said that the 'gods' in this story were really the angels who abandoned heaven to take up with human women," said Ariston, "and that the 'Titans' were the giants who were born to them, who ended up destroying the earth."

"So, Ariston," Apelles prodded, "you think that your native tradition provides the key to interpreting the traditions of the whole world?"

"What about the explanations of Euhemerus," Meir ventured. "He was a Greek, and he said that the Greek's gods were originally just great kings or founders of cities who were treated more and more like guardian spirits and gods in the generations after their deaths. In this case, perhaps the story of the Titans has its roots in succession crises, where the kings' children were in too much of a hurry to gain power for themselves."

"But why," Apelles persisted in the manner of Socrates, "could our gods not indeed be gods?"

"Because there is only one God," another young man ventured. "The gods of the Greeks, Egyptians, and others are perhaps just aspects of the one God, imperfectly captured."

"Besides," Ariston added, "these gods do many things unworthy of the divine. They commit adultery against one another, they are spiteful and vengeful, and they use human beings like game pieces in their contests."

"Yes," Apelles said coyly, "or wipe out all of humanity because they could not persuade them to virtue, or harden the hearts of rulers just so they can show off their powers more impressively, or incite a group of refugees to commit genocide against the residents of an entire region?"

"Or kills a baby because the parents committed adultery," added Telamon, a son of a Syrian architect who had come to Jerusalem at Jason's invitation, "or holds such a grudge against one king that he refuses to turn away disaster from the land no matter how much that king's successors try to appease him? I haven't heard much about your God that persuades me he's so much better than our own."

"Indeed, Ariston," Apelles said to bring home the point of his lesson, "you should be as rigorous in examining and critiquing your own tradition and religion as you are in critiquing that of other peoples. This is the mark of an educated person."

"Some of the most revered philosophers," Meir suggested, "seemed to point to the belief in one and only one God as ultimately correct. Xenophanes did not approve of thinking of the divine in terms of the gods of Homer, or as beings that could be represented as humans like us."

"Quite correct, Hilaron," affirmed Apelles. "And this is a point, gentlemen, in favor of the Judean religion. They push us," he said, looking at the Syrian and other foreign students in the circle, "to discern the one God behind the many forms and to remember that God is beyond any image we could make for Him."

He turned his attention to Meir, Ariston, and the other Jewish students in the group.

"But what can you learn from us?" he asked, his tone indicating that he would soon provide an answer. "Perhaps, first, that the one God is not exactly as your tribe has imagined him to be. If there is only one God, then that God cannot possibly be concerned only with one particular tribe of people to the exclusion of investing himself in all others, can he?"

Apelles paused long enough to indicate that this was a genuine question, but Meir and his peers had nothing to say in response at the moment.

"If there is but one God, he must be the God of all—Greeks and barbarians, or Gentiles and Jews as you like to divide the world. This brings us back to a lesson we had last week on the difference between the universal law that the divine has established and the particularistic rules and customs of each nation or people."

Apelles leaned forward slightly, as if imparting a great mystery.

"Justice, courage, self-control—these are universal mandates from God. But every nation adds a thousand more restrictions and practices, enslaving men and women with human-made rules. So perhaps Greeks must look beyond their gods to perceive the true nature of the One, while Jews must look beyond their ethnic customs to perceive the true nature of God and what God requires."

Apelles sat back again, indicating that the morning's climax had been reached.

"Our commitment to dialogue means that we can each help the other on this path to genuine discovery of the Divine that is beyond our limited notions."

Meir and his peers remained silent for a moment, processing what their teacher had said.

"Perhaps that's enough for this morning," Apelles suggested. "Your eyes indicate that your brains are full. Go, digest. Tomorrow I will read from Plato's *Euthyphro*, which should extend our conversation about piety quite nicely."

Zedekiah knelt beside the Qilt, the small stream that had kept him alive for most of the three years since he had left Jerusalem. He filled his water skins and rose to walk back up the southern hill of the valley to the cave in the rocky crest above that he had made his home. He had left Jerusalem with a number of possessions, the most treasured of which had been his scrolls of the Torah, the prophets Isaiah and Jeremiah, and the Psalms. And he had left with sufficient silver for his modest needs, which journeys to nearby Anathoth had provided—stores of dried fish, two new tunics in as many years, papyrus for writing. There were sufficient date palms, olive trees, and citrons in the valley for most of his meals.

His contacts in Anathoth also allowed him to keep up with the news in Jerusalem and even to exchange word with Mattathias and Yoshe on occasion. Nothing he read in their letters and no insight he had received in his meditations had convinced him there would be any merit in returning. Pollution heaped upon pollution, sin upon sin. In his desert cave by his seasonal stream, there was holiness. There was purity.

He set the skins down inside the cave, opened one, and poured its contents into a stone that had been hollowed out, through centuries of sitting in the flow of the stream below, into a basin. He rinsed his hands in the water, dried them on a linen cloth, gently picked up his scroll of Isaiah, and sat down at the mouth of the cave to pray. He unrolled the scroll to expose a few columns and began to read. By this point he needed little more than the first words of each oracle to recall the rest.

The sound of small rocks rolling down the hill and the crunching of loose stones under sandals intruded upon his meditation. He looked up to see three men in long, white tunics, their heads covered with a fold of their robes, approaching his cave. He started, unsure of their intentions.

One of the men looked up at him.

"We know who you are, Zedekiah, 'God is my righteousness.'"

"We know that you live up to your name," a second said, "and that you are the faithful remnant of the family of Simon the Just."

"We have observed you for many seasons," said the third, "and we know that your heart is pure and that you seek God in all sincerity."

The first man uncovered his head, revealing his gray hair and sun-dried face. "Come with us, and we will show you the answers you seek."

Meir emerged from the gymnasium into the market. Most of Jerusalem's residents had already sought out the day's provisions, so the square was relatively quiet in the heat of the day. Nearing the southern end, he saw Eleazar sitting in the shade of one of the porticoes, surrounded by young children—Meir guessed that the oldest might have been twelve. When he passed the row of columns, Ariyeh, who was sitting with his back resting against a column, came into view.

Eleazar happened to glance toward Meir, and Ariyeh followed the teacher's eyes.

"Meir!" Ari shouted.

"Ah, shalom, Meir," Eleazar said. "Come sit with us for a few minutes."

"Begging your pardon, Master Eleazar, but I am in a bit of a hurry."

"Come," Eleazar said again, "sit with us. Children, this is Meir ben Zerah, the son of one of the most upright men I have ever known."

A few children scooted out of the way to make room for Meir on the step next to Eleazar, and Meir resigned himself to stay for as short a time as he could.

"You're looking exceptionally well, Meir," Eleazar observed. "Your studies and training at the gymnasium seem to agree with you."

Meir suddenly became aware of how out of place he was in this circle, dressed in a Greek tunic, freshly bathed, oiled, and fragrant with balsam.

"I have been enjoying it very much, Master Eleazar," Meir replied. "I hope some of you," he said to the gathered children, "may have such an opportunity someday."

"Ah, well, for many of them the informal tutelage of an old priest will have to suffice. I wonder, Meir, if you could help us with our lesson."

"I am sure I could add nothing to what you would be able to—"

"We were just talking about Daniel, taken to the court of Nebuchadnezzar along with his three friends. Who can tell Meir what happened to them when they first arrived?"

A young boy of about nine, whom Meir recognized but could not place, spoke up.

"Daniel and his friends refused to eat the food that the Gentile king provided, asking to be allowed to eat only vegetables and other clean foods."

"And what happened as a result?"

"At the end of ten days, their guardian saw that they were more fit than the other young men in the school and put all the others on the same diet."

"So from early on, Daniel was a witness that God's ways were the best ways for everyone," Eleazar commented. "Now we'll learn from Meir what happened next. Do you remember, Meir?" There was just a hint of challenge in Eleazar's voice.

Meir could see where this was going, but he could not walk away now and be thought ignorant.

"Of course, Master Eleazar," he replied. He turned to the children and related the story in a somewhat lifeless manner. "After Daniel and his friends grew up, the king had a disturbing dream and called all of his counselors together to give him the interpretation. He wanted to be sure that they wouldn't be lying, so he commanded that they should first tell him his dream and then he would trust their interpretation. Of course, they couldn't. Who knows a dream except the dreamer? So Nebuchadnezzar sentenced all the wise men of his court to death. When Daniel and his friends heard of this, they prayed to God, and God showed Daniel what the king had dreamed and what it meant. So Daniel was brought to the king, who spared all the wise men and promoted Daniel and his friends to the inner circle of his friends."

"Very good, Meir," Eleazar said, showing pleasure that Meir had not forgotten the stories that his father, Zerah, had taught him. "Isn't that a marvelous story, children? Now what would have happened to Daniel and his friends if they had sought to make their way at court by becoming like their Gentile masters in every way?"

"They would have died along with the others," Ari said, not wanting to be shown up by his older brother.

"Indeed they would have!" exclaimed Eleazar. "So because Daniel and his friends kept faith with God all those years growing up in the king's court, God kept faith with them when they needed him the most—and the wisdom God gave them made them more valuable advisors to Nebuchadnezzar than all his Gentile sages."

Eleazar turned to Meir.

"Thank you for sitting with us, Meir, and reminding us to be sure what kind of wisdom we will need in the future before we alienate the one and only God who can help us."

"Master Eleazar," he said with a nod of his head and a smile at the none-too-subtle lesson, before rising and resuming his journey home.

Binyamin knelt on a small mat in his father's workshop, pumping air into the space beneath the small charcoal furnace till the coals glowed bright yellow. The bronze in the iron cauldron set inside the furnace began to liquefy. Shoshanna came out with a cup of water, freshly drawn from a cool stone jar in the kitchen.

"You're dripping, Binyamin!"

She set the cup down on a worktable, went back into the kitchen, and returned with a cloth soaked in water.

"Why don't you rest for an hour until the heat of the day has passed?"

He paused from pumping while his wife wiped the sweat off his forehead and smiled. He took the cloth from her hand and wiped his neck and chest.

"I'm fine, really. I want to finish casting this piece before evening." He handed the cloth back to her. "Thank you," he said, holding her fingers in his before releasing the cloth.

Shoshanna returned to the kitchen where, two years ago, she had set up a small warp-weighted loom purchased with a portion of the *mohar* that had been given to her family at her betrothal. It was sufficient for making clothing for the family, though several pieces of the cloth she wove would need to be stitched together to make any one garment. She sat down on a mat in front of the loom and resumed her work.

"I look forward to the day when you can make a single garment from one of your pieces of cloth," Miryam said.

"I'd need a much bigger loom, Mother," she replied. "We wouldn't have the room even if we could afford it."

"I wasn't thinking about a bigger loom." Miryam raised an eyebrow. "I had in mind a smaller body."

At the sound of laughter from the kitchen, Binyamin rose from his work and entered the kitchen, carrying the empty cup. "What are you ladies conspiring about now?"

"The usual subject, Binyamin," Shoshanna said as she gave Miryam a playful stern look.

Binyamin exhaled loudly in mock exasperation. "When it happens, Mother," he said as he filled his cup from the stone jar, "I promise you'll be the third to know."

"I'm not pushing." Miryam looked at Shoshanna. "Am I pushing?" she asked, as if the answer would have to be no. "Of course, when Zerah was your age he was already holding you over his shoulder."

"Father did not inherit two younger brothers and a mother at the age of fourteen," Binyamin replied matter-of-factly.

Miryam reached up and cupped Binyamin's face in her small hands.

"Oh, my responsible son!" she said, half-teasing. Her face suddenly became more serious. "God give you ten years of happiness for every year you gave me since Zerah's death."

Binyamin smiled and went back to the shop. As he left Miryam called out after him, "And give me a grandchild!"

He had just sat back down when Meir entered from the street.

"Will you deign to get your hands a little dirty today with work, Brother?"

"No, Binyamin," he replied defiantly. "I'm only here to change clothes. I need to get to Master Agathon's house within the hour."

"You still have duties here, Meir. You've barely put in a day's work all week."

"I work smarter now. One day working on a silver piece for one of Master Agathon's friends brings in more money than a week working bronze. And he gives me extra money for you, specifically to keep you off my back."

"We give away the extra money to the poor."

Meir's face flushed with anger.

"Oh yes," Binyamin continued. "Mostly to the poor back in Modein—those whom people like Agathon and his friends have deprived of their land. I don't mind money earned, but I won't have my family beholden to Agathon for his 'gifts.'"

"You take great pride in your principles and poverty, don't you, Binyamin?" Meir held up his hand as he looked away. "I'm not going to argue with you today. This is an important night for me. I'm going to dine with Lord Jason himself."

"And you take pride in hobnobbing with the great and having no time for your family?" Binyamin retorted. "Do you even know what begins at dinnertime today, Meir?

Meir resented the questioning but searched his mind for some occasion he might have overlooked.

"It's the Sabbath, Meir. The time to be with family, giving thanks to God and hallowing the day?"

Meir was embarrassed, but hid it by scoffing, "There'll be another in seven days. How often does one get to have dinner with the high priest and his closest advisors?"

"You can be impressed with yourself for that, if you like," Binyamin retorted as Meir disappeared into the house, "but I still remember the high priest whom Jason trampled upon to climb where he is."

Binyamin stoked the coals of the furnace, upset with himself that every conversation with Meir became an argument within a few sentences, upset that his brother was taking such a different path. He heard the sound of muffled conversation as Meir no doubt explained to his mother where he would be late into the coming night. Then the house grew silent.

A few minutes later, Meir reemerged wearing a finely woven tunic with gold embroidered work surrounding the opening at the neck, clearly a gift from Agathon for the occasion.

"Just take care, little brother," Binyamin said, his voice meant to convey only concern. "Remember that someone far greater is watching you from on high tonight. He's the one you need to impress."

ז

M̲eir paced in the atrium of Agathon's house.

"Keep that up and I'll have to have those stones filled in." Menes had certainly warmed up to Meir over the years and come to accept him as part of the household.

"I can't help it, Menes. I'm nervous about tonight."

"I don't blame you one bit, Hilaron." Menes affected a deathly seriousness. "Sitting among the great and powerful is like walking upon a razor's edge—one misstep and you'll slice yourself in half."

"Honestly, Menes," Agathon said as he emerged in the atrium, "the way you amuse yourself sometimes is perverse."

"Sorry, Master," he said, giving Meir a wry smile as he walked away.

"You must be excited about this evening, Hilaron. I know I am. I've looked forward to presenting you to Lord Jason for some time."

"I'm grateful for your confidence," Meir said, "but I am nervous."

"To be expected, and no doubt appropriate," Agathon acknowledged. "You only have one chance to make a first impression. A few words about etiquette, then, before we go?"

Agathon seated himself upon a cushioned wooden chair and gestured for Meir to do the same.

"You'll have to strike a balance between being self-promoting and being reserved. The former will turn people off, the latter will result in their not taking note of you. Regard the words and smiles of the powerful as tests of your character and intentions. Don't rush forward into the house when the door is

136

opened to you, or peer about into its rooms like a nosy boor who doesn't really belong."

At this last sentence, Agathon raised an eyebrow and looked at Meir with mock accusation, remembering an early visit the young man had made to his house. Meir blushed slightly, and Agathon smiled as he continued.

"You'll be surrounded by all kinds of wonderful foods, but don't lose sight of what is most important for your future: the company you will be keeping and the impression that you will be making. Everything else will pass through your system by tomorrow night."

Meir chuckled and broke out into a smile.

"Don't be greedy for the dish that's slow in being passed around. Be the last to reach out your hand for food and the first to stop eating. When you're asked a question, speak concisely: say a lot with a little. And don't worry." He smiled at Meir. "You'll do fine."

The ornately carved wooden door swung open to reveal the marble atrium of Timarchos's house. An older slave wearing a tunic and the gold chain emblematic of his position as steward greeted Agathon and Meir, leading them through the inner courtyard to the *triclinium*. Jason was the first to notice their arrival.

"Welcome, Agathon," he said warmly, "and welcome to your young guest."

"Jason, Timarchos, Menelaus," Agathon said as he acknowledged each of the parties seated on their couches, "may I present Hilaron, son of Zerah of Jerusalem."

Meir bowed his head. "I am honored to be in your company this evening."

"You are welcome in my house, young man," said Timarchos. "Agathon, you and Hilaron may take the couch opposite me."

Agathon sat on the part of the couch that butted up against the middle couch, where Jason sat in the place of honor, while Meir sat to Agathon's left.

"Agathon tells me that you've excelled in your studies at our gymnasium," Timarchos continued. "What have you been learning?"

"Today we were talking about the God of Israel and the gods of the nations," Meir answered. "We talked about how our own forebears had been right to insist on God's oneness, in keeping with the thinking of the wisest Greek philosophers, but wrong about God's exclusive interest in a single people group."

"And what do you make of this, young man?" Jason asked with sincere interest.

"Perhaps this is a way forward for Israel to become indeed 'a light to the nations,' as Isaiah had prophesied?" Meir responded.

Jason's face lit up.

"Indeed it may be," he said. "Other nations have much to learn from us about the oneness of God and the poverty of their representations of God in their idols and myths, but why would they listen to us as long as our message is that this one God likes us better than anyone else?"

Meir swelled with pride to have provoked such enthusiasm from the high priest.

"I prefer the opinion of Epicurus," interjected Menelaus, with an obvious lack of enthusiasm for the conversation. "The gods, if they exist at all, do not trouble themselves with human affairs. There is no fate but what we make for ourselves."

"What was that famous quatrain of his?" asked Timarchos. "'Nothing to fear from God; Nothing to feel in death—'"

"'The good can be enjoyed, the evil can be endured.'" Menelaus finished the maxim.

A man wearing an ornately embroidered tunic—in his late fifties, Meir guessed—entered the *triclinium* accompanied by several young women, two of them carrying a flute and a cithara. At their arrival, Menelaus and Timarchos became visibly more energized.

"Are we late? You know how long it takes women to get ready for any social event."

"Your timing is perfect, Seraiah," Jason said wryly. "Menelaus and our host were just praising the 'virtues' of the Epicurean philosophy."

"Seraiah," added Timarchos, "this is Hilaron, the young man Agathon has been telling us about."

"A pleasure, Hilaron. And these ladies," Seraiah continued, indicating each in turn, "are Callista, Briseis, Shammiram, and Persephone. They'll help us pass the evening more enjoyably."

Seraiah led Callista, his usual companion at social functions, to the middle couch and seated himself next to Jason.

Agathon leaned over to Meir.

"I didn't expect this tonight. I hope it will not make you feel uncomfortable."

"Not yet, Master Agathon," he replied.

"Yes, well, the evening is young." He looked intently at Meir, to steel him. "Don't feel pressured to do anything tonight against your conscience."

Briseis and Shammiram set their instruments out of the way on a table by the wall. Persephone remained standing in front of the table, hesitant to make eye contact with the men on the couches. She was visibly younger than the others, perhaps no more than sixteen. Meir could sense her discomfort and instinctively felt protective of her. He was almost startled when Menelaus spoke.

"Why don't you come sit with me—Persephone, was it?"

A surge of adrenaline sped Meir's thinking.

"Master Menelaus, it's generous of you to invite the least experienced girl to your place, but a man of your sophistication would no doubt better enjoy another's company."

Seraiah laughed out loud. "He's saying she's too young for you, my friend."

Menelaus shot Hilaron a glare.

"No, Master Menelaus, that was not—"

"Oh don't worry, young man," Seraiah said. "Whether you meant it or not, it's true. Come, Persephone, sit with the young buck."

Menelaus looked slightly wounded but was soon consoled by the arrival of Briseis, while Shammiram settled in next to Timarchos.

Once everyone had found a place on a couch, servants began to appear, placing trays of food on the table at the center and keeping everyone's wine cups full. Meir had eaten at Agathon's house before, often taking his midday meal there during the year he was being tutored in Greek, but he had not encountered such delicacies as were now set before him. A servant presented a tray of whitish flesh still attached to hard, red shells. His heart began to race when he realized that he was looking at cooked shellfish—and then saw some of the Jews at the table reaching for them. He observed with relief that Jason did not and decided that he would partake only of the dishes from which Jason ate.

"I have exciting news," Jason announced. "Antiochus himself is coming to Jerusalem in three months as part of his tour of the southern regions of his empire."

"That's wonderful, Jason," replied Agathon. "He'll finally get to see all that you've accomplished here."

"All that *we've* accomplished," Jason corrected, looking around the *triclinium*. "This visit will also mark his formal acknowledgement of Antioch-at-Jerusalem as a colony of Antioch. I have asked Zenon to arrange for games to celebrate the event."

"We'll need to move quickly to complete the stadium," said Timarchos.

"Every available craftsman and worker will be taken off other public works projects and reassigned to the stadium," Jason assured him. "It will not be finished, but it will be serviceable."

Menelaus looked across the table at Meir.

"Perhaps you'll even compete in the games."

"Hilaron is actually quite accomplished at running and throwing the discus and javelin," Agathon said. "I would expect that we'll see him in quite a few events."

"And of course, we'll send out invitations to the gymnasia of the other Greek cities to the north and in the coastlands to enlist their athletes for the competitions," said Jason. "We'll give Antiochus a good show."

"Let's make sure it's one that rivals anything he might have seen in the other Greek cities of the region," Seraiah urged. "Tell Zenon to spare no reasonable expense; my friends and I will help sponsor the games."

Menelaus's lip curled into a smirk. "Antiochus will see one thing here at our games that should make the event memorable."

His dinner companions waited for him to finish his thought, but he only raised an eyebrow and returned their gaze. Finally Callista giggled, the first to make the connection. She twisted to her right side to face Seraiah and tapped his chest with her left forefinger.

"He's talking about that special thing you do to your wands," she said.

"Ah," Seraiah said as he looked away toward the other men. "Yes, that will no doubt attract attention, if not comment."

"Well," Jason added, "it should make it easy for the crowd to recognize the home team and know when to cheer."

Laughs around the table greeted the high priest's quip.

"Why do your people do that to their sons?" asked Briseis.

The other women giggled at the directness of the question.

"Well, I've wanted to ask that before," Briseis said defensively, "but normally the circumstances where it crosses my mind haven't been right."

"Yes, it would be a real mood-spoiler, I suspect," agreed Callista.

"It is an ancient tradition," Jason explained, "marking us as part of the tribe of Abraham, our great ancestor with whom the God of the universe made a special pact."

"A kinder god would have just introduced a secret handshake," said Callista, provoking strong laughter around the table.

"I think that God was quite kind in requiring this mark," ventured Meir.

"If you mean, kind to require that it be done on the eighth day of life before we could remember it," Seraiah said, "I heartily agree."

After that wave of laughter had died down, Jason gestured to Meir, indicating that he should say more.

"Well, the desire for sex is one of the strongest passions, isn't it? By choosing to mark us there, God has given us a visible reminder, whenever the deed is before us and our minds are least apt to be thinking straight, to heed his commandments concerning how, when, and with whom to enjoy God's gift of love."

Meir's answer left the other guests silent for a few beats after he finished—some because of a twinge of embarrassment to be confronted with the distance they had traveled from their own ancestral teaching, others because the youth clearly possessed genuine virtue.

"An excellent answer, young man," said Jason at last. "You are living proof that a generous education may enhance, rather than undermine, our native strengths."

Timarchos motioned to a servant to bring more food for the trays that were beginning to look bare. As the conversation continued, Meir thought about the gulf that separated the men at the table. Jason was clearly a man of vision and high standards, even if many people—including Eleazar and his own brother—criticized him as misguided, even apostate. As for Menelaus, in place of vision, in place of some ideal, Menelaus had only . . . Menelaus. He struck Meir as almost soulless.

As if sensing Meir's scrutiny, Menelaus lifted one of the recently restocked plates. "You haven't tried this one yet," he said as he extended the plate of roasted, light-colored meat to Meir.

Meir did not recognize the meat, which had a pungent aroma. He did not, however, see either Agathon or Jason eat from that plate.

"Thank you, Master Menelaus," Meir replied, "but I think I've eaten too much heavy food tonight already. I'll have to start training all the more tomorrow now that I know King Antiochus is coming."

Menelaus lowered the plate back to the table, looking somewhat disappointed. "Someday, perhaps, you'll take a taste."

"That's perfectly fine, Hilaron," said Jason, glaring sternly at Menelaus. "It's not for everyone."

"But it is for everyone else throughout the known world," said Seraiah, taking a mouthful of the meat. "Just one more of those many differences that will always remind Greeks, Syrians, Egyptians, and others that we'll never really be one of them, nor they one of us."

Seraiah took a swig from his wine cup to wash down the mouthful and smiled at Meir. "Briseis, Shammiram, play something for us."

"Of course," Shammiram said as she and Briseis rose from the couch and retrieved their flute and cithara.

"Perhaps over there," Seraiah said, indicating some cushions beside a pillar set between the *triclinium* and the interior courtyard, "to provide some nice background music for our conversation."

The duet began to play a tune in the Phrygian mode, each displaying considerable talent at her instrument. The others at the table listened for a while until Seraiah spoke.

"Hilaron, the conversation is about to get a bit more mundane. Perhaps you and Persephone would like to take some time to get better acquainted in Timarchos's lovely courtyard?"

Meir looked at Agathon, who nodded his concurrence.

He rose from the couch and gallantly extended his hand to the girl.

"Will you walk with me?" he asked, as if the choice were entirely her own. She smiled, put her hand in his, and rose from the cushion.

"You're not like the others that I usually find at dinners like this," she said as they stepped into the courtyard.

"I'm not usually *at* dinners like this," Meir confessed.

They walked to the middle of the courtyard and sat down beside the central pool.

"I was looking forward to tonight," Meir continued. "Agathon thought I was ready to meet Lord Jason—finally, after almost three years of studying Greek at the gymnasium."

"You speak almost like a native," Persephone said. "It's very good."

"You're not from Jerusalem?"

"I was born near Seleucia. My mother died ten years ago, giving birth to my younger brother. I also have a younger sister—she's thirteen now. My father moved us here almost three years ago, since he would have steady work as a stone mason with all the new construction."

Persephone grew quiet.

"Is something wrong?"

"About a year ago, there was an accident at a work site," she continued. "My father died from his injuries. His leg had been crushed and became gangrenous. It was cut off, but the gangrene returned."

"I'm sorry," said Meir, as he dropped his eyes.

"I was left here to look after my sister and brother. That's when I came to Callista's attention, and through her to Lord Seraiah's. He's provided well for our needs."

They sat in silence for a few minutes, listening to the new tune that Briseis and Shammiram had begun. A woman started singing.

"It seems that Callista has grown tired of the conversation at the table," Persephone surmised.

"Did your parents name you Persephone?"

"What? Don't you like my name?" she asked in mock indignation.

"Well, she's kind of a sad character, isn't she? Six months in the sunlight, six months in the underworld with a husband she doesn't much like?"

"It's a good name for me, I think."

Meir thought about his companion's story for a moment.

"Because you don't much like the men you're around?"

"See? You're pretty smart when you put your mind to it," she teased. "Much of my life I spend with my sister and brother, and that's pretty good. For the rest, I'm expected to entertain Seraiah's guests and friends. So I took the name Persephone . . ."

"As a kind of quiet protest," Meir finished.

"Yes," she said simply. "I think you're the first man who got it."

"So what's your real name?"

"My mother named me Tavitha." Meir could see her smile and bite her lower lip in the moonlight, remembering her earlier days.

"Mine's Meir, actually."

She looked at him with surprise.

"Many of my people have adopted Greek names in the hope of fitting into Greek society more naturally. Even Lord Jason—he was born Yeshua, I'm told."

"So escorts aren't the only ones who change their names to get in bed with the Greeks." Tavitha smiled and looked into his eyes. "Well, *Meir*, I have been provided for your entertainment tonight. And I think that, for once, I won't really mind. What would you like me to do for you?"

Meir gazed at her young, beautiful face glowing in the moonlight and thought about what he really did want from her.

"Be Tavitha when you're with me, and not Persephone," he answered.

Her head tilted slightly as her smile brightened. "You really are different, aren't you?"

"I appreciate your position, Lord Jason," Menelaus continued, "but Seraiah's point stands. Only when we make non-Jews feel fully at home and unconstrained by our native prejudices will we attract not just those who are willing to put up with the limitations but also those whose social level makes them intolerant of such limitations."

"And basic to feeling at home for these people," Seraiah pressed, "is the ability to build shrines and temples to their gods."

"This is inevitably where Hellenizing has to take us," Menelaus added, "and has been taking us from the start—religious pluralism, toleration, respecting the gods of all our citizens."

"You say you appreciate my position," Jason replied firmly, "but clearly that's not the case. We've made great and quick strides toward allowing our non-Jewish residents to live according to their own religious rules and not be burdened by ours. I have lifted restrictions on the marketplace on the Sabbath, leaving it open for Gentile merchants and Gentile buyers."

"And Jason has endured criticism for that both from Jews who feel that the Sabbath is being violated," Agathon said in support, "and from Jews who are just angry that their Gentile competitors have an extra day on which to conduct business."

"Many violations of the Torah no longer carry criminal or civil penalties," Jason continued, "with the result that observing our traditions is a matter of conscience—or often lack of conscience, as you gentlemen demonstrate time and again. Residents can expect to be judged according to a body of laws that is in almost all respects identical to what they would find in any Greek city."

"But aren't you still imposing our religion on non-Jewish residents," Seraiah pressed, "when you forbid the construction of religious sites dedicated to any god besides Israel's own?"

"There is also a limit to what I can impose upon our *Jewish* residents!" Jason's insistence intensified as he rose to a sitting position, still leaning upon his left arm. "Support for what we have done here is tenuous at best and is rejected outright by many in the city and most in the villages as apostasy. Once they are able—justifiably—to link Hellenizing with idolatry, there will be no containing the outcry and the resistance that would follow."

"You admit that we don't enjoy the support of the masses," Menelaus said. "So why do you hold back to please them, especially when we do enjoy the support of the king—and his soldiers?"

"You're eager for a civil war, then, Menelaus?" asked Jason incredulously. "You want to bathe the land in our people's blood? For what? What more do we need to do to enjoy a civilized and civilizing Jerusalem, recognized by King Antiochus himself as a peer city within his empire? No, gentlemen, I will not be pushed further than I have gone, and you would do well to stop pushing."

"We've come such a long way in three short years," Agathon said, trying to be conciliatory. "Jerusalem is a more multicultural metropolis than it has ever been before. The opportunities our youth have for education and we have for business and connections beyond our province are greater than ever before. Let's enjoy what we have gained and allow the city to develop its course naturally from here."

"I agree that we have made remarkable strides," Timarchos added. "I'm sure Menelaus and Seraiah do not mean to detract from these accomplishments."

Taking the hint, the two nodded their assent.

"Good, then," said Timarchos. "Perhaps we should turn our attention to lighter diversions for the remainder of the evening."

Seraiah called for the ladies to rejoin them on the couches. One of Timarchos's slaves appeared with his own cithara and began to pluck its strings casually.

"I should take my leave," said Jason as he rose from his couch. "Thank you, Timarchos, for your hospitality this evening. Friends, your company is always enjoyable," he added with a smile, "even when we disagree."

"I'll see you home, Jason," offered Agathon. "Let me check on Hilaron first."

"I'll wait for you in the vestibule. Gentlemen," Jason added, "I bid you good Sabbath."

Four members of the Temple guard had been instructed to wait outside Timarchos's house from the second watch of the night to escort the high priest, but Jason would not spoil what was perhaps his friend's excuse to leave before the entertainment became unsavory.

Agathon took a few steps into the courtyard, and then called out to his protégé.

"We're here, Master Agathon."

Meir appeared, holding Tavitha's hand.

"Lord Jason is leaving; I was thinking of accompanying him. I didn't want to desert you."

"Thank you, Master Agathon," Meir replied. He looked at Tavitha and added, "Perhaps it's time for us to leave as well. Do you think Master Seraiah would allow me to escort the lady to her home?"

Agathon smiled.

"I think that would be a fine idea. I'll let him know."

"Our apartment is this way," Tavitha said as she led Meir down a side street off the main *agora.*

They walked up the street in silence, saying all they needed through their clasped hands, until they arrived at the set of stairs that led to her second-floor apartment.

"May I see you again?" Meir asked.

"I'd like that," Tavitha replied, looking appreciatively into his eyes. "Any time Seraiah doesn't have need of me," she added, admitting the limitations with a cock of her head.

They stood facing each other in silence for a moment, as Meir thought about kissing her. She placed her left hand around his upper arm, signaling her consent.

3

Zedekiah sat in the shade of an olive tree, where he had spent the past two days reading and meditating upon three scrolls that had been given to him by the "sons of Enoch," as the men who had come to visit him called themselves. They had led him several kilometers farther along the Wadi Qilt toward the Dead Sea to a small oasis and set of caves in the wall of the gorge that had been their retreat in the desert for almost two decades. There a handful of men, never numbering more than ten, had created a life where purity and covenant observance stood at the center of their existence.

Zedekiah might have had many questions for them, but he instinctively felt them to be such kindred spirits that he had not asked anything more of them than what they had revealed before handing him the three scrolls. He had read them slowly, devouring their contents like the hidden revelations that the sons of Enoch claimed them to be, pausing frequently to close his eyes and reflect or pray over the words. His hosts brought him water throughout the day, and he never felt the need to ask for food, as the words were food enough. He continued to read as his hosts gathered to pray the previous afternoon and that morning, their chanting of the psalms lifting Zedekiah to a place of near ecstasy as he thought he could see before him the very visions written down in the scrolls.

Ephraim, the senior member of the sect, saw from his cave that Zedekiah had set down the last scroll beside him and was still sitting quietly under the tree. He made his way down to him.

"What have you discovered? Have you found answers to your questions?"

Zedekiah looked down at the scrolls beside him, searching again through their contents in his mind.

"I have heard the story of the Watchers before," he replied, "the angels who left their posts in heaven to have intercourse with human females, begetting a race of giants. I had not before contemplated the evils that this act unleashed upon the earth as I have read in this scroll."

"When the angels defiled themselves with women," Ephraim said, "they crossed boundaries that God had said not to cross. Only pollution, violence, and chaos could result."

"They taught the arts of working metal into weapons," Zedekiah remembered.

"To make violence and bloodshed abound on the earth," Ephraim responded.

"They taught people how to mine for silver and gold—"

"To make greed fill the hearts of human beings."

"They taught women to paint their faces and cast spells—"

"To inflame lustful desire among the sons of men, spreading defilement throughout the earth."

"And their offspring, the giants, waged war against one another and devoured all for which human beings toiled—"

"Devouring the people themselves in their thirst for blood!"

Zedekiah considered the scroll that he now held in his hands.

"You received this from Enoch?"

"No, but from the God from whom Enoch also received his wisdom and secret knowledge," Ephraim replied.

"How can this be?"

"The same God who revealed the secrets of ancient times and the causes of the flood still reveals his secrets according to his pleasure and purpose," Ephraim explained. "We have followed in the way of Enoch, who was a righteous man in the midst of a corrupt generation. Therefore God removed him from the pollution all around him. We call ourselves his children because we, too, have sought God's righteousness with all our minds, all our hearts, and all our strength, and God has taken us up out of the midst of the defilement in Jerusalem and throughout the land."

Ephraim stood up from the ground and paced to the north and to the south as he continued.

"Are we not now living in the midst of giants battling one another over possession of the land and devouring all its produce? Are not boundaries being crossed even now, as we prostitute ourselves to the empires looking down upon us from on high, making the land unclean?"

"And God has shown you what he once showed to Enoch?"

"Yes!" Ephraim said with fire in his eyes. "God has restored his revelations for his people in these last days, before his judgment comes upon the face of the earth once again!"

"God will once more judge the powers and the giants that ravage us," Zedekiah said, as if seeing now what Ephraim could see. "God will cleanse the land of all their defilements—"

"And raise up the righteous once again to lead the people into all obedience," Ephraim said with assured finality.

Zedekiah rejoiced in his heart to find people who knew, as he did, that God could never have remained silent when his people were in such need of his guidance, but all this time he was listening for that word in the wrong places—the places of corruption.

"In this second scroll I find the same stories that Moses wrote for us in his first and second books, but told quite differently."

"I believe that, in *this* scroll, we find Moses' true intentions," Ephraim said. "For one thing, time is not counted in some haphazard manner, but divided in an orderly fashion in accordance with the divine principle of the Jubilee."

"And this narrative confirms what I have always believed," Zedekiah added. "The law of God is eternal and has always sanctified God's people, even before it was revealed afresh and in its totality to Moses upon the mountain."

"Precisely! Abraham would not have been accounted righteous before God had God not revealed his law for Abraham to follow."

"It illumines much in the Scriptures that I have known from my youth," Zedekiah said appreciatively. He laid his hand on the third and longest scroll. "This one fills me with greatest dread. If it is correct, we have been wandering in transgression since before I was born."

"Indeed, Zedekiah, 'God is my righteousness,'" Ephraim replied, "it is correct. God set the greater light to rule the day and the lesser light to rule the night. Surely God intended for his chosen people to follow the greater light in all their undertakings, leaving the lesser light to the Gentiles who grope about in the darkness."

"When rule over Israel passed from Egypt to Syria, my great-uncle, the high priest Simon the Just, adapted our calendar to that of our new overlords, following the movements of the moon and the addition of the thirteenth month every third year."

"And therefore," Ephraim observed grimly, "you did not keep the festivals on their appointed days, but veered off the course set for you by God like the wandering stars. But we have charted the movements of the sun and moon day by day with great care and written them down, so that when the time is right, the observances in the Temple can be restored to their rightful days."

"Though my great-uncle's heart and Honiah's heart were pure," Zedekiah concluded, "still they did not observe the covenant with the accuracy demanded by the holy God."

"And thus has corruption been multiplied in Jerusalem. Jason was merely the instrument of God's judgment upon Honiah, and Jason will be judged in his turn, until a righteous high priest arises who will restore the Sabbaths and festivals to their proper days, bringing Israel into alignment once again with God's own rhythms of work and rest."

Zedekiah stared off into the valley, mulling over the import of what he had learned.

"Teach me to hear what God is speaking and to see what God would reveal."

"We will, Zedekiah, 'God is my righteousness.'" Ephraim raised Zedekiah to his feet and placed his hands on the young man's shoulders. "Surely God has appointed you for this very thing, and to lead us as that high priest who will restore God's Temple to its former holiness."

Binyamin sat on the stone slab that served as a step between the pavement and the entrance to his metal shop. Six young teenage boys clustered around him at the side of the street. Ariyeh had spent the morning playing with some of them, and they gravitated, as they tended to do on such Sabbaths, to Miryam's kitchen to enjoy some of the foods that she had left out from the night before. After they had filled up their loaves of flat bread with tasty, spiced lentils, marinated olives, and bits of cheese, they came out to sit with Binyamin and spend the early afternoon doing what God had ordained for the Sabbath—talking about the commandments, binding them, as it were, to their minds. Sometimes Master Eleazar would join them, but increasingly Binyamin had taken over their Sabbath day lessons.

Binyamin unrolled a small scroll—a recent purchase of which he was particularly proud. He, Shoshanna, and Miryam had agreed that, if he were to continue to teach the covenant to the young, he should begin to collect some of the scrolls most vital for that purpose, so that he could read to them and quote accurately. They had used some of the money that Meir had brought from his patron, and Eleazar, who made up the difference, had arranged for the scroll to be copied from the Temple chancery. Binyamin's choice for his first scroll was the fifth book of Moses, as the fullest expression of the commandments and the covenant.

"Make no covenant with them and show them no mercy," he read aloud to the boys as they ate. "Do not marry with them, giving your daughters to their sons or taking their daughters for your sons, because that would turn your children away from obeying me, to worship other gods. Then the Lord's anger would flare up against you, and he would destroy you at once."

Binyamin looked at the boys in the circle around him, remembering the first flushes of attraction to the opposite sex.

"Maybe it's not too early to talk about this commandment. I mean, I'm assuming that you gentlemen have noticed that there are a lot of girls around in this city."

Embarrassed chortles through mouthfuls of bread assured Binyamin that his instincts were correct.

"Yair has a girlfriend," one ventured.

"Shut up, Boaz!"

"All right, all right," Binyamin intervened. "So Yair has a girlfriend. What's important in light of today's reading is that Yair's girlfriend is also a daughter of the covenant."

Yair's mouth dropped in disbelief that even Binyamin would know his secret.

"You are a little obvious about whom you like, Yair," Binyamin teased. "But it's all right—her parents are on to you and will keep their daughter safe."

The other boys laughed while Yair put on a show of being offended.

Binyamin drew them back to the lesson. "Why would Moses our lawgiver command us so strongly not to become involved with Gentile women?"

Boaz attempted an answer.

"Because we are drawn to our God, but they are drawn to their gods. We would be pulling in different directions."

"And the women usually win," Ari added with a smirk.

Again the group broke out in laughter.

"We laugh," said Binyamin, "but history proves Ari's point, doesn't it?"

The boys thought about it for a moment.

"It happened when our ancestors were wandering in the desert," Yair said at last. "Our ancestors became involved with the Moabite women, and they ended up worshiping their gods."

"That's right. In fact, we are told that this was Balaam's strategy for saving Balak and the Moabites and for defeating God's plan to give this land to our ancestors. Do you remember what happened?"

"Yes," said Ari with a gleam in his eyes. "Phinehas." He pronounced the name as if it told the whole story.

"Phinehas was awesome," Boaz agreed.

"Yes, he was," Binyamin said. "An Israelite man and his Moabite wife flaunted God's command right there in front of the congregation. Phinehas fetched a spear, entered their tent, and thrust the spear through both the man and the woman as they were consummating their unlawful marriage."

He paused as the boys relished one of their favorite action scenes from the books of Moses.

"And because of Phinehas's zeal for the covenant," Binyamin concluded, "the plague that was sweeping through the congregation was stopped."

"And God made a promise to Phinehas, that he and his descendants would be priests forever."

"Exactly, Yair."

"Where are heroes like that now?" Ari asked, his voice betraying his disappointment. "All our lives, all our parents' lives, all our grandparents' lives—and for how long before that?—the Gentiles have had power over the land again."

"And our leaders are trying to make them more at home," Yair added, not hiding his bitterness, "instead of protecting the land's holiness."

The boys fell silent.

Binyamin hoped they had the mettle to be new Joshuas and Calebs. He held out the scroll of Deuteronomy in front of them. "When we keep faith with God again as He commanded us, God will renew the blessings He promised under the covenant. Have confidence in that."

Shoshanna had been standing for some time in the inner doorway separating the shop from the living areas, watching Binyamin and thinking what a good father he would make someday, doing for their own sons and daughters what his father had done for him, what he now did for the children in the neighborhood. Hearing him come to what seemed like a good stopping point, she walked across the shop to the outer door and made her presence known.

"If you sages are done debating the finer points of the law for one Sabbath, perhaps I could have my husband back?"

"Yes, I think we've solved the problems of the world," Binyamin replied. "Come back next Sabbath," he said, smiling to his circle, "and we'll solve them all over again."

"*Shabbat-tov*, Binyamin," the boys said as they got up to leave.

"Good Sabbath, gentlemen."

"Thanks for the food!" Boaz said to Shoshanna.

"You're quite welcome," she replied.

She placed her hand on Binyamin's shoulder. He reached across his chest to place his hand on hers as he rose to his feet.

"I thought we might walk together for a while, and make our way to the Temple for the evening sacrifice," she suggested.

Binyamin smiled and nodded, and called to Miryam to let her know they were leaving.

The couple started unhurriedly up the street toward the city's center, exchanging Sabbath greetings with neighbors sitting at their doors, talking with each other about the week that was passed and the one that lay ahead. They entered the market, where several stands and tables remained open for business.

"I mustn't allow myself to grow accustomed to seeing this on a Sabbath," Binyamin said. "It's been, what, three years since the decree to allow non-Jews to do business on the Sabbath? It would be too easy to start seeing it as normal."

He continued to look around the market as they walked through. He came to a sudden stop.

"What's wrong?" Shoshanna asked after noticing she had taken two steps without him.

Binyamin stepped slightly behind her and gently guided her a few steps off to the side of the *agora*.

"That's Meir," he said, gesturing to a stand stocked with breads and cheeses diagonally across the square.

"He's with a young woman," Shoshanna observed.

"The same one I saw with him about a week ago," Binyamin responded.

"Yes, I remember you telling me. You were walking past the gymnasium around midday and saw them sitting and eating together in the shade of one of its porticoes."

"I've been waiting for an opportune time to talk to him, but was hoping he'd first choose to mention it to me."

They watched as the young woman paid the vendor for a loaf of bread and some cheese and then walked away hand-in-hand with Meir.

Binyamin took a step forward as if starting on an intercept course. Shoshanna reached up to grasp his shoulder.

"I'm not sure this is the best time, Binyamin," she suggested, sensing his fury.

He remained tensed for a moment, but then succumbed to Shoshanna's wisdom.

"That woman is a Gentile, Shoshanna," he said, "or at the very least an apostate. She's leading him even further astray."

"I know, Binyamin," she replied calmly. "Come. We have one more reason now to go to the Temple."

She stroked his upper arm soothingly and gently nudged him in the direction of the Temple Mount.

They walked up the inclined paths leading to the Temple entrances and paused by the pools outside of the Temple precincts where they knelt and immersed their hands. Such rituals were not required by the Torah, but they provided a welcome and often necessary moment for internal preparation to enter into God's presence. Binyamin immersed his hands several times, allowing his preoccupation with Meir to drain away along with the water.

Already the Levite choir was chanting psalms for the evening sacrifice. Binyamin and Shoshanna allowed the sound to fill their minds and souls as they crossed from ordinary into sacred space. This threshold had become more pronounced, more palpable, for Binyamin during the past three years, as if it now required more effort to step over. The Temple had become, for him as for many faithful Jews who shared his mind-set, an oasis of holiness, as the law of Moses came to govern less and less of life in what had once been a holy city.

They came to the Court of Women. Binyamin offered to stay there with Shoshanna, but she encouraged him to go on up the steps into the Court of the Israelites to participate more fully and to be more attentive in his prayers. As the priests went about their work, lifting up the parts of the sacrificed lamb to God before casting them upon the fire to transfer them to God's realm in the form of smoke, Binyamin lifted up his prayers for Meir, for wisdom in reaching his brother, for the directions that the city and nation were taking. He tarried there for a few moments even after the benediction, until he felt clean from all the anxieties that had been possessing and polluting him. At last he went down the stairs and returned to Shoshanna.

"Your step seems a little lighter," she said, greeting him.

"I left a heavy burden behind with God," he replied with a smile.

The couple left the Temple precincts, lingering on the ramparts for half an hour to watch the sun set before returning to their house. They entered the living area to find Miryam and Ari sitting down to eat. Meir emerged from the kitchen with a flatbread heaped up with cold lentil stew.

"Ah, Meir, what a surprise," Binyamin said. "I thought you'd already eaten."

His tone put Meir on alert. "Who can resist mother's cooking?" Meir replied as he sat down on a mat by the low table, fighting the warm flush of his sudden anxiety.

"Why don't the two of you get some food and join us?" Miryam said.

"That sounds good," Shoshanna replied. "Will you come?" she added, tugging Binyamin's arm.

Binyamin remained fixed where he stood, his focus on Meir unbroken.

"I haven't seen much of you these past few weeks," Binyamin observed. "Perhaps we could go for a walk together in the cool of the evening."

Meir was relieved that, whatever was on Binyamin's mind, he wouldn't force the conversation in front of the whole family.

"I'd like that, Brother."

"Can I come?" asked Ari.

"No!" Binyamin and Meir replied in unison.

"We need some time to talk," Binyamin said to assuage Ari's feelings.

"That sounds like a good idea," Miryam chimed in. "I've been worried about the way the two of you have been going at each other for years now. Walk together and remember that you are brothers, two fingers of the same hand."

Shoshanna looked at Binyamin imploringly, underscoring Miryam's desire for harmony between them.

"I'm not hungry just yet, Mother, but thank you," Binyamin said. "I'll be in the shop when you're done with supper, Meir."

A few minutes later, Meir emerged from the house and stood across from Binyamin in an awkward silence until Binyamin walked toward the outer door and signaled with his head for Meir to follow. They walked a few dozen paces before Binyamin began to speak.

"So do you want to tell me about her?"

"No, Binyamin, because you wouldn't give her a chance."

"You're right, Meir, not when I see her leading you into the market to do business on a Sabbath Day."

"So you've been spying on me?"

"And you've been hiding things from your family. That says something about the uprightness of your actions."

They took a few more steps in silence.

"She's not even a Jew, is she?"

"She's a person, Binyamin, a beautiful person."

"'Don't be misled by a woman's beauty, or allow a pretty face to lead you astray.'"

"I'm familiar with the proverb, thank you very much, and I'm not just talking about her appearance," Meir retorted. "She was recently orphaned. She takes care of a younger sister and brother. She knows duty and, in her own way, piety."

"She worships other gods, Meir, and your calling that 'piety' is proof of the wisdom of the commandment forbidding us to get involved with Gentile women."

"Oh, please. That commandment might have been important when Israel was first becoming a people in this land, but we've grown past such xenophobia."

"So you think because you didn't drop dead the first time you touched a Gentile woman, God doesn't avenge sin? You think because you neglect God's Sabbath for the sake of your precious gymnasium—yes, I know you've been there on the Sabbath—that God doesn't take notice? 'Both mercy and anger are with God, and both go forth at the moment God chooses.' Turn back quickly, little brother, before your time of punishment comes."

"Don't lecture me like one of the street boys you gather around yourself."

"I don't *have* to lecture them like this—they already know better than you. You've forgotten everything Father taught you."

Binyamin paused for a moment to let some of the heat between them dissipate.

"I don't know who you are anymore," he began again, his tone conveying more regret than anger. "I mean, I literally don't know who you are anymore. Someone came to our house with a package for 'Hilaron' two weeks ago. I told him he had the wrong house, but he finally convinced me that he meant you. So who are you?" Binyamin paused, but Meir said nothing. "You're not the person our father was raising, so I guess it's fitting that you shouldn't be called 'Meir' anymore."

"Father's long dead, Binyamin," Meir retorted, "and the one God didn't do anything to stop that from happening. Did keeping all those minute commandments bring him the 'length of days' that God promised? No, it left him poor and allowed him to die young."

"Father lives with God," Binyamin shot back. "He will live eternally in the resurrection."

"We needed him *here*, Binyamin."

They took a few more steps in silence before Meir continued. "I've found a way that provides for us better than Father's way. You may not see it now, but you will." Meir met his brother's glare with a new confidence. "The support we've enjoyed from Master Agathon is just the beginning. Lord Jason himself has joined him in sponsoring me as I train for the games. I make far more for the family by my activity at the gymnasium than I ever could working in the shop. I'm starting to make important connections with important people—the high priest, Binyamin!"

"No one is more important than a person who reveres the Lord, Meir, and that is not Jason. As for that accursed school and everything it's done to you, 'Better is a person who lacks an education but fears God than the highly educated person who transgresses the Torah.'"

"A popular proverb among those who lack an education, I imagine," Meir retorted.

Binyamin felt the barb but did not bite.

"Our father named you Meir because he hoped that you would grow up to shine with the brightness, the splendor of God—the one God—and that this radiance was all the glory you would need. Do you really wish to trade your birthright for a bowl of Greek stew?"

Meir took a few steps back from his brother as he responded. "I still worship God in his Temple, Binyamin. I don't bow down to other gods, I don't eat forbidden meats, and I don't have sex even when it's offered to me. I haven't traded away my birthright. But I am willing also to inherit what Father could not leave us—and make this part of my own children's inheritance when I have them."

He turned toward home and took a few more steps. Then he stopped and turned to face his brother for one more comment.

"And Binyamin: Hilaron still means 'brightness.'"

Ephraim and Zedekiah sat together in one of the smaller caves toward the upper crest of the south hill overlooking the valley oasis of the sons of Enoch. Since his arrival two months ago, Zedekiah had spent most of his days in prayer, reading, and meditation, taking part in the group's morning and evening worship and conversing with them late into the night after the evening meal. He had now been fasting for three days, however, taking only water and devoting himself fully to prayer in preparation.

Ephraim had built a small fire toward the mouth of the cave, and Zedekiah sat behind it, looking out into the night sky. Ephraim threw another handful of dried resins and gums upon the fire, which produced a fragrant smoke that filled the cave, then he sat down again, outside of Zedekiah's line of sight.

"Keep your mind clear and open your heart to what God is showing you," he said slowly, hypnotically. "See with your spirit, not with your eyes."

They sat in silence, sensing the presence of God's timeless eternity rather than the passing of the hours of the night. Zedekiah suddenly drew in a sharp breath as his mind's void took form.

"What do you see?"

"I see the statue of gold, silver, bronze, and iron," Zedekiah said distantly.

"Ah! God is showing you Nebuchadnezzar's dream, even as he once showed Daniel. Keep looking, Zedekiah. Let God shape what you see."

Zedekiah sat in silence again, staring through the fire into the night sky.

"The metals are moving apart. They are taking new shapes . . . beastly shapes."

Ephraim remained silent.

"There the gold head is becoming a winged lion . . . The silver chest and arms are becoming a great bear, snapping up people and chewing on their bones!"

Zedekiah's eyes widened in fear and horror as if the vision continued to unfold in the sky before him.

"The bronze part has become a fierce leopard, flying over the whole earth with its wings. It has not one head, but four! Nothing can withstand it."

He paused, his eyes straining as if to see through a fog.

"Uglier than anything that came before. The iron legs . . . they have become some monstrosity, some Behemoth. Horns are rising up out of its skull—ten of them! It gnashes its iron teeth and tramples the Holy Land, breaking everything in its path under its bronze claws!"

Zedekiah continued to watch the drama unfold.

"Three of these horns have been plucked out, and a new horn is arising from the monster's skull, growing more exalted than all the other horns. It has a face, and it speaks defiantly toward heaven!"

Zedekiah's eyes grew wide again as a new image formed. "I see . . . the throne of God! Fire shoots forth from it to consume the monster! Now a man steps forward and receives authority from the Ancient One. He is exalted over all the nations that formerly trampled the Holy Land!"

Zedekiah continued to stare, breathing heavily until the vision faded. He began to collapse backward but stopped himself by bracing himself on his hands. He turned his head to seek his teacher.

Ephraim pressed his palms together and placed his fingers in front of his mouth. "The spirit of Daniel rests on you, Zedekiah." Then he reached for some blank sheets of papyrus and a reed pen and placed them in Zedekiah's lap. "Write these things down. These are true words of God!"

4

Antiochus Theos Epiphanes, "the god openly revealed," entered Jerusalem through its western gate. He rode clad in a gold breastplate seated upon a magnificent white horse. Several of his advisors rode closely behind him on horses of their own, escorted by a detachment of one hundred cavalry bearing spears. Jason stood in the middle of the road, holding the reins of his own horse in his right hand, ready to greet the king. The nobility of Antioch-at-Jerusalem were similarly gathered in the street, some with horses, awaiting the king's arrival. Young women and men were scattering handfuls of flower petals into the air above the king's entourage as they passed through the gate while musicians played festive Greek dances to celebrate their arrival.

Jason extended his left arm slightly, still gripping his horse's reins with his right hand, and bowed till one knee rested upon the ground. The rest of his nobles followed suit.

"A heartfelt welcome, Highness, to the *polis* of Antioch-at-Jerusalem. Your presence graces us and our city."

"It is a joy to finally see the results of your bold experiment in this land that neither I nor my predecessors ever thought to integrate so fully into our empire," Antiochus replied. "You are to be congratulated, Jason, along with your colleagues here."

He signaled for them to rise.

"We have much planned for your visit, Highness," Jason said, "but perhaps now you are tired from your journey and wish to rest?"

"Rest would be welcome," the king replied, "but first I want to see your civic improvements—your gymnasium and senate house especially—and perhaps also your famous Temple."

"With pleasure, Highness," Jason said as he mounted his horse to lead the king to the city center of Antioch-at-Jerusalem.

Several of the local nobility, including Seraiah, Agathon, Timarchos, and Menelaus, took to their horses as well, joining the king's entourage and basking in his reflected glory.

"We've planned a banquet in your honor for later this evening, Highness," said Jason, "after you and your company are refreshed. Tomorrow we propose to hold Olympic-style games in your honor in our new stadium, to celebrate your official recognition of the city."

"Athletes will be coming from cities throughout the region," Menelaus added, "as well as some notable local competitors. It should be a show worthy of a city bearing your name."

"Wonderful," the king said with a smile that revealed sincere admiration at what Antioch-at-Jerusalem was becoming. "I'll look forward to the event."

Jason was beaming as they neared the city center, proud of his accomplishments and of the recognition the king was certain to give them. The entourage passed the senate chamber, the gymnasium, bustling with activity as athletes spent their last day in training before the games, and the main *agora* with its columned porticoes.

"This is remarkable, Jason," Philostratos remarked. "In three short years you have transformed this backward place into a Greek city."

"Indeed," Antiochus concurred, "this rivals much of what I might see in the coastal cities that have been part of the civic network for more than a century."

Seraiah responded to the king's compliment. "Yes, Highness, you'll find everything here that you would find in any Greek city of your domain—except temples to your gods, of course. You can do just about anything here that you would in Antioch, except worship."

Antiochus raised his eyebrow, but then gave a shrug of understanding.

"The people of Judea have always been intolerant of any god but their own."

"They have indeed, Highness," Jason interjected, hastening to regain control of this conversation. "But they have had to learn a great deal of toleration in other respects during the past three years for us to have made the progress that we have been able to see. I fear we've been moving too fast as it is, with the major shifts in constitutional law, economic practice, and the like. Master Seraiah's family has always pushed against the limits more than most."

Antiochus rode a few paces in silence, as if to weigh the importance of this trait. Such pushing might be required eventually to make room in Jerusalem for all the peoples of his empire.

"I'm sure you have made some provision for your Greek citizens and other immigrants to worship according to their customs," Philostratos prodded.

"We have indeed, Philostratos," Jason replied quickly. "Our non-Jewish citizens and residents are free to worship as they will in their own homes. They are even permitted to bring in idols and create shrines in their homes, as long as they respect the need to keep them covered when transporting them through the city."

"Thus hiding their devotion," interjected Seraiah. "We would chastise the person who is afraid to show his or her gratitude to human patrons openly, but here non-Jews must hide their gratitude toward their divine benefactors."

Jason could hear murmurs of disapproval among Antiochus's other counselors.

"And we Jews would be outraged," Seraiah continued, "if the authorities in Antioch or even Alexandria were to forbid us to build synagogues in their cities. Yet we continue to deprive immigrants here of such courtesy. But I do not wish to make your visit unpleasant, Your Excellency, by airing these issues further."

"I appreciate your passion for the religious freedom of all your citizens, Seraiah," Antiochus said, "though I am sure that Jason is attentive to such matters as well and moving in a manner that the delicacy of this issue—here more than anywhere else—requires."

"Thank you, Highness," said Jason, suppressing his anger at Seraiah's challenge. "May I lead you and your associates back toward my palace, where guest chambers have been prepared for you, and where my servants can attend to your refreshment before tonight's banquet?"

"Yes, I think we've seen enough for now," Antiochus concurred. "Tomorrow we'll see what kind of person your gymnasium produces."

Eleazar sat in a portico of the *agora* as people milled past him toward the city gate that led to the stadium. The sound of a lone cantor reverberated down from the Temple Mount, chanting psalms as part of the preparation for the morning rite of the whole burnt offering. He looked out at all the faces of priests in the crowds that passed by, priests who a few short years before would have been in attendance in the Temple. One group of priests caught his attention in particular.

"Bad luck for Berechiah and the others," said one of them, "to have drawn the lot for Temple duty this morning. They're going to miss half of the events!"

"Someone had to stay and do it," another replied, chuckling. "The people expect it."

"God expects it!" exclaimed Eleazar, rising awkwardly to his feet. "Listen to yourselves! So taken up with these new entertainments that you forget what a privilege has been granted to you, to serve the one God in his holy Temple!"

The young priests stopped dead in their tracks at this rebuke, taken aback at the energy of the old man's vehemence. One met Eleazar's glare defiantly, but the others shifted uncomfortably. At last one of the latter said, "Come on, let's go," and the group moved on. Eleazar shook his head sadly and turned to make his way toward the Temple Mount against the stream, focusing on the lone Levite's psalm and blocking out the clamor of the excited crowd as he left the scene.

The crowd that had gathered between the market and gymnasium began to cheer as Antiochus himself approached from the direction of the high priest's palace on horseback, attended by Jason and Antiochus's bodyguard. The athletes and other young men from the gymnasium, now joined by the competitors who had come from cities throughout the coastal plains, rushed out of the complex to greet him and pledge to win victories that day in his honor.

Antiochus and Jason, followed by their counselors and the highest nobles of Jerusalem, set out for the stadium. The athletes followed not far behind the king's entourage. Some of these were clad in simple tunics. Others wore a short cloak draped over one shoulder, just long enough to cover their hips. Some also wore the traditional broad-rimmed hat associated with the student body of gymnasia throughout the eastern Mediterranean. They were smiling broadly and raising their fists high as pledges of triumph, basking in the cheers of people lining the streets and falling into procession behind them as they passed.

The king, his counselors, Jason, and the other elites passed through the first gate in the northern wall, now with the stadium complex rising before them just a hundred meters outside the city.

"This will be most impressive when it is finished, Jason," the king admitted.

"Thank you, Highness. We chose this site since the Tyropoean Valley area is so sparsely populated. We hope eventually to extend the city walls to this area and make it a focus of new construction."

Jason was distracted by a commotion breaking out behind them. The king's bodyguard jumped to action, surrounding the king and his nobles. Jason stood slightly in his saddle to try to locate the source of the disruption. The athletes were just now passing through the gate, and people were hurling citrons and other fruits, seasoned with insults, at the young men wearing the broad-rimmed hats. The guards relaxed slightly to discover that no actions were directed toward them or the king.

"What is going on there, Jason?" Antiochus demanded.

"I don't know, Highness."

The pelting stopped as suddenly as it had begun and the perpetrators had vanished back into the crowd or otherwise disappeared. The athletes seemed unharmed and had already continued their procession toward the stadium.

"Whatever it was about, it seems to be over," observed the king. "Come, let's proceed."

They dismounted outside the stadium, and Jason led the king, his party, and the Jerusalem nobles up a staircase to a spacious, canopied box located at the midpoint of the south stands of the stadium. As they took their seats, servants brought goblets of new wine and trays of fruits and breads for them to enjoy during the games.

After a few minutes, Menelaus blurted out, as if just receiving a revelation, "It's the hat."

The others looked at him quizzically.

"The source of the commotion?" He smiled with disbelief and shook his head slightly as he continued. "The hat that many of the foreign athletes were wearing is a symbol associated with the Greek god Hermes, right? We have some residents who are well-enough educated to know that, but not well-enough educated to admit the athletes without taking offense at their attire."

Jason nodded, affirming the explanation.

"There is, Highness, admittedly a sizeable portion of the population that looks for any excuse to criticize our reforms and our efforts to make room for elements of Greek culture as an affront to our traditional religion."

"It is not enough for some that there are no images of Hermes here or in the gymnasium," Menelaus added.

"As far as I am concerned," said Jason, "our traditional faith and the new order can exist in complete harmony, like Solomon and Sheba."

"But you will remember," Eupolemus said with a smile to blunt the directness of his warning, "what happened to Solomon when he surrounded himself with too many Shebas and forgot that he was a Jew."

The conversation was brought to an abrupt halt by a fanfare sounded on trumpets and reeds by musicians located directly beneath the box. Several dozen athletes, well-oiled, some naked, some minimally covered, glistening in the sun like mythic heroes, ran out onto the field. The audience met them with thunderous applause. The sight of the naked bodies was so contrary to expectation that it took a full five seconds to register with the majority of the crowd. The applause was partially replaced by inarticulate sounds expressing surprise, shock, in some cases revulsion. A handful rose indignantly and quit the stadium. Others who were initially offended felt compelled by the setting, by the presence of the king, and by the sheer momentum of the course that their city had taken to resume their applause until the last of the athletes had emerged.

Antiochus rose and walked forward to the stone railing of the second-story box. He extended his arms, palms upward, in a gesture of invocation to the crowd and announced in a loud voice, "Let these games, which celebrate the inauguration and official reconstitution of this city as 'Antioch-at-Jerusalem,' begin!"

The musicians sounded their fanfare again as the audience cheered with a renewed—though for a sizeable minority somewhat forced—enthusiasm and the first athletes took their places for the opening events. Twelve of the athletes had registered to compete in the five events that made up the pentathlon. Meir took his place among them beside the long, thin sand pit for the standing jump. The others came for but one or two of the other events, which included long-distance races, boxing, and the no-holds-barred *pancratium*. These remained off the field, engaging in stretches, exercises, or shadow boxing.

The first contestant took his place at the starting marker at one end of the pit. In each hand he held a sling with a five-kilogram weight in its pouch. He began to swing his arms and flex his knees and hips in rhythm, building up momentum for his first jump. Finally he launched out and landed just shy of three meters away. He repeated the process till he had jumped five times to a total of fourteen meters, to the cheering of the crowd. The other foreign contestants followed suit, some disqualifying themselves by stumbling and falling to a knee on a landing.

Meir went first among the Jerusalem contestants. As he approached the starting line, he caught sight of Tavitha in the stands, smiling at him and raising her fists before her chest as a wish for victory. The flush of adrenaline gave him just over three meters on his first jump, an advantage he carried to a fifteen-meter total, the best score to that point. The audience cheered excitedly for him. Above the din, he thought he heard Jason's and Agathon's voices congratulating him from the box. The remaining four contestants, who had never beaten Meir in practice, performed to their own expectations. An official walked to the center of the stadium.

"The winner of the standing jump—Hilaron of Jerusalem!"

Meir beamed to hear the crowd roar once again, raising his arms proudly to acknowledge and accept their acclaim.

"That's the kind of person our gymnasium is crafting," Jason said proudly.

Antiochus smiled at Jason and nodded to acknowledge his achievement.

The javelin throw followed. This time, however, victory went to Callisthenes of Ptolemais, with Meir placing third. Meir emerged the victor a second time with the discus throw, with Callisthenes placing second. The official of the games brought the two contestants to the middle of the field. He raised Meir's arm and announced, "The winner of the *triagmon*—Hilaron of Jerusalem!"

The crowd roared in response. Even Agathon and Jason found themselves on their feet to applaud the local boy's triumph thus far in the Greek games.

The contestants for the pentathlon left the field as others took their places for the five-stade race. Telamon, one of Meir's classmates and a fellow competitor, slapped him on the back.

"Well done, Jew!" he said. "It seems your lack of a foreskin hasn't robbed you of balls."

"Crude, Syrian, crude," Meir replied with mock disapproval and a shove to his shoulder.

"There's your competition," Telamon observed, pointing to Callisthenes. "He's good, and he's got ten kilograms on you."

Meir watched Callisthenes rubbing his upper right arm and complaining to an older man, possibly his trainer.

"So he'll win at wrestling," Meir guessed, "but running is my event."

"Good luck, Hilaron. Since I'm not going to win, I hope it'll be you."

Meir smiled at the Syrian's sincere good wishes, and clasped his outstretched forearm. He returned to the warm-up area outside the stadium to find Tavitha running up to him. She grabbed him by the shoulders and pulled his head down to meet hers in a full and passionate kiss.

"I'm so proud of you," she exclaimed when she finally pulled away. She put on a playful pout and added, "But now that you're a celebrity in Jerusalem, how am I going to keep all those other women away from you?"

Meir pulled her close for a second, calmer, lingering kiss.

"You'll just have to do a better job not letting me out of your sight."

Tavitha gave him a smack on his chest as she stepped back and lifted the small woven sack she was carrying.

"I brought you some lunch to keep up your strength," she said, handing him the sack. "Do me proud this afternoon." She smiled at him over her shoulder as she walked back toward the entrance to the stands.

Meir opened the sack, nibbled on some fish and fruit, and took a drink from the vat of water made available for the athletes. Then he gave his attention to stretching out before the *stadion* sprint, working tendon by tendon, muscle by muscle.

The winners of the long-distance races were announced, and places for the one-stade sprint called. Vendors were moving through the crowd in greater earnest as midday approached, and servants brought fresh trays of meats, breads, cheeses, and fruits for Jason and his guests in the box.

Meir and the other pentathlon contestants ran a leisurely lap around the interior of the stadium to complete their warm-up before the race, coming to a stop at the south, interior end of the "U" that was the field. The twelve men took their places side by side at the starting line. The official of the games ascended the steps to Jason's box and presented Antiochus with a square cloth that had been dyed a bright red, giving him the honor of starting the race.

Antiochus smiled at the gesture, walked to the edge of the balcony, and raised his arm dramatically. After an appropriate pause, he released the cloth. It had not fallen two meters before the runners had catapulted themselves forward toward the marble finish line inlaid across the far side of the stadium.

Meir quickly found his stride, gained the lead, and maintained it through the first three-quarters of the race. In the last stretch, Meir saw a darker-skinned young man approaching and passing him in his peripheral vision. He reached deep inside and began to push himself with his last bit of determination when, to his complete surprise, a wispy frame passed them both on Meir's other side and crossed the finish line, with Meir finishing third.

"The winner of the *stadion*—Epimenes of Marisa!"

The crowd cheered politely, if not enthusiastically, for the lanky Idumean.

Meir leaned forward with his hands upon his thighs and drew in labored breaths, disbelief at the outcome furrowing his brow. After several minutes his breathing returned to normal and he began to walk around, to keep his legs from cramping.

The official called for the boxing match and the *pancratium* and the competitors took to the field and gathered around the central, round sand pit. Meir continued walking to the open end of the stadium and around to the outside of the complex. He fought against the urge to give up in light of the fact that he knew himself to be less accomplished in wrestling than he was in running. He had, as he suspected, placed well ahead of Callisthenes in the race, but that hardly mattered now that he had not only lost, but placed third.

He scanned his memory for something that might help him get his mind back into the game. He tried to find something from a Greek text about competition, wrestling, or even courage. Finally he went to a story his father had told him about a young man who took down a giant against impossible odds, and to another about two young soldiers wreaking havoc in an enemy camp. As he rubbed his body afresh with olive oil, he smeared onto himself the assurance that the weaker force could overcome the stronger and shook off the demoralizing thoughts hounding his mind and weakening his will.

The judges had determined that only three of the twelve contestants could potentially win the pentathlon by winning the last event, the wrestling match, so they decided to restrict the last event to these three. Epimenes looked at Meir and Callisthenes, lowered his head, and moved his two hands from side to side in opposite directions in front of him, signaling that he would not be competing in this event. Clearly, he had counted on winning by doing better in the initial events, though he had at least placed second in the standing jump.

"If I understand the rules for scoring correctly," Menelaus said, "Callisthenes can win the pentathlon if he wins at wrestling."

"That is correct," said Antiochus. "Winning two events and coming in second place in a third would just edge out your favorite."

"But even if Hilaron loses to Callisthenes in the wrestling match," Agathon objected, "he's still won two events and finishes second in wrestling."

"Ah, but no one comes in second in the wrestling event," Antiochus answered. "There's only a single winner—and multiple losers."

"But in the classic pentathlon as practiced in Athens before Alexander's time," Philostratos interjected dryly, "there simply wouldn't be a winner unless a single contestant won three events outright."

"True, true," Antiochus acknowledged with a smile, "but who wants to watch a day-long competition with no winner?"

The king leaned back in his chair and looked at the contestants.

"I'll put ten talents on the uncircumcised Callisthenes," he said, "if anyone would like to take the wager."

Jason looked at Agathon, who shook his head imperceptibly from side to side.

"Come now," Antiochus goaded, "I'll give two-to-one odds."

"I'll take a piece of that action, Highness," Seraiah ventured. "Two talents."

"Only one of you believes in your athlete, then?"

"I'll put three talents on Hilaron," Jason said at last. "I was just trying to remember how much cash I had laying around the house."

The group laughed at the quip, and all eyes returned to the field with renewed interest.

Meir and Callisthenes faced each other and orbited the center of the sand pit like twin planets, each looking into the other's eyes to judge when best to strike. They both launched at the same time, each grasping the other's shoulders, each keeping his legs well braced and his body balanced even as he pushed against the other. Meir could feel Callisthenes's greater strength bearing down on him, but Callisthenes was too good, too attentive to balance to allow Meir to use Callisthenes's greater weight against him.

Meir felt his own shoulders caving beneath his opponent. Soon he would be vulnerably off balance and the match would be lost. He shifted his grasp suddenly, bringing his hands under Callisthenes's armpits and landing them on the inside of his shoulder. He felt his opponent's right shoulder give momentarily after contact and saw a wince of pain cross Callisthenes's face. *He injured himself winning the javelin throw*, Meir realized. He immediately gambled on this insight. Pulling his arms free, he put both hands on Callisthenes's right shoulder and pushed in with his full strength. Callisthenes's shoulder gave way as he tried to muffle a roar of pain, his face red and his tendons straining. Still pushing on the shoulder, Meir brought his left leg around Callisthenes's right and brought him to the ground. He jumped on him, straddling his chest and forcing both shoulders into the sand.

The crowd stood up all at once and cheered as the official escorted Meir from the sand pit to the center of the stadium.

"The winner of the wrestling match and the pentathlon—Hilaron of Jerusalem!"

He placed a wreath of laurel upon Meir's head as the crowd continued to cheer. Meir acknowledged the crowd once again by raising his arms. Then he looked up to the box, fixed his eyes on Antiochus and Jason, and bowed deeply to them.

"Well done, boy," Antiochus spoke in a voice just loud enough for those around him to hear. "Well done. Jason, it appears I made a hasty wager. I'll have the six talents delivered to your palace by morning."

"Let my nation, and not one man, profit from this wager," Jason said. "Shall we just deduct it from the annual tribute due your majesty?"

"That would be fine, Jason, and much more convenient. And you, Seraiah," Antiochus said, "how shall we settle up?"

"Highness, we are all so indebted to you for your sponsorship of the improvement of Jerusalem, I could never presume to collect."

"Come now, a bet is a bet!"

"Highness," Seraiah suggested after a moment's pause, "perhaps you would consent to keep the four talents and accept my invitation to dine with me this evening?"

Antiochus folded his hands in front of his mouth and puffed out a single exhalation. Then he turned to Jason and said, "Your hospitality has been magnificent, Jason, and you have probably gone to some lengths to prepare for a dinner tonight. But I don't spend four talents on my most expensive state dinners. Perhaps you would accept a reduction of your tribute by another two talents as recompense to your honor, so I can still save myself fifty-some kilograms of silver by accepting this invitation."

"As your highness wishes," Jason said, casting Seraiah a suspicious glance.

"And I want to congratulate this young man in person," Antiochus added. "Have him come to meet me this evening."

Meir's friends and fellow-competitors from the gymnasium had run out onto the field and lifted him up on their shoulders. For people like Telamon, the disappointment of not winning themselves could be sublimated by celebrating the fact that at least one of their own had beat out all those contestants from other— and better established—Greek cities. A number of the spectators also made their way to the field to acknowledge the contestants personally and congratulate the winners of the various events. Meir spotted Tavitha making her way through the crowd and jumped down from his comrades' shoulders, welcoming her into the circle with another kiss. His friends hooted their approval of the display, and they all walked off the field together, feeling like the lords of the city.

They entered Jerusalem and made their way back to the gymnasium. As they passed the corner of the marketplace, Meir caught sight of Eleazar, sitting in a portico, surrounded by the younger boys he was teaching. He thought for a moment of how neither of his brothers had come to the games; how Eleazar had not; how his own father, if he were alive, would probably have avoided the stadium like a place polluted. Eleazar raised his gaze from his scroll and met Meir's eyes. Involuntarily, Meir's head tilted back, as if pushed by a wave of shame. Eleazar looked down sadly, and Meir heard his father's voice speaking to him in memory: *Those who fear the Lord will seek his approval—not the admiration of the godless who have no knowledge of God.*

Tavitha reached her hand to his cheek, and he allowed her to redirect his gaze to her face, smiling and looking inquisitively up at him. His ears filled up again with the sounds of his friends reliving the day's events and celebrating their performances. Meir breathed in deeply, allowed his chest and spirits to rise again, and relished his victories anew as they turned away from the market place and toward the gymnasium.

ℸ

Antiochus lay on his back across the middle couch of Seraiah's *triclinium*, his head and shoulders propped up by two luxurious cushions. Seraiah sat upon the first couch; Timarchos shared the third with Menelaus. Four of the king's bodyguard, bearing spears two meters long, stood at their stations at the four corners of the room; two dozen more were stationed around the exterior of the mansion and in the inner courtyard.

"A fabulous meal, Seraiah, and all for such a small party," Antiochus acknowledged. "Your kitchen staff did marvelous work, especially on such short notice. But perhaps you did not release four silver talents simply to impress me with your staff's culinary magic?"

"It is worth that and more to have your majesty grace my home," Seraiah replied, "and to be granted these hours in which to become acquainted. But I do confess that I am also solicitous for my nation, and want to make sure that your direction of our affairs is not only informed by the picture that our high priest paints for you."

"I suspected as much," replied Antiochus as he rolled back to face Seraiah, propped up by his left arm. "And I remain as interested in multiple perspectives as when Menelaus was first introduced to me in Antioch three years ago."

"Sire, Jason has accomplished much during his three years as premier, of that there is no doubt," Seraiah began. "But he has also made it clear that there are limits to how far he is willing to go to accommodate a multiethnic population here in Antioch-at-Jerusalem."

"These limits fall far short of what a non-Jew could reasonably expect of a colony of Antioch," Menelaus added.

"The issue of prohibiting the construction of places of worship for their gods or conducting such worship in the open is a major one," Seraiah continued, "and one that continues to deter non-Jews from settling here."

"That one is troubling," Antiochus concurred. "My father gave substantial concessions to your people in the area of religion, and your historic disregard for the gods of your neighbors is legendary."

"We need someone at the helm who can take us beyond this impasse and repair our reputation," Seraiah pressed, "if we are truly to become a Greek city worthy of your empire."

Seraiah gave Antiochus a few moments to reflect on what had been said.

"Then, too, there are economic concerns directly related to these questions," he continued. "Jason is supposed to present you with the annual tribute before your departure?"

"That is part of our business for tomorrow, yes."

"You'll find it to be in arrears again," Menelaus said.

"And Jason himself is ultimately the reason," Seraiah added, as though receiving the baton, "because he's only gone partway toward making the other peoples of your empire feel welcome in Judea."

Timarchos finally spoke up. "In a sense, sire, we're almost in a worse way than we were under Honiah. We've moved toward becoming a Greek city just enough to alienate a large part of our . . . less educated population, but not far enough to truly make people of all nations feel at home."

"Economic growth in this province will continue to be slow," Menelaus added in support, "unless we make a clear decision about our civic identity, a decision Jason is unwilling or unable to make."

"Now, sire, I personally made up the deficit in our annual tribute during the first year of Jason's tenure," Seraiah said, bringing the conversation to its most practical level. "I could not in good conscience do so during the second year nor can I now during the third, since, in my opinion, Jason is not doing all that is necessary to secure our nation's well-being. I would be willing to do so this year, however, if we had a leader in Jerusalem in whom I could have greater confidence. Moreover, we're so certain that new leadership would bring an economic boom to Judea that we would be willing to see our annual tribute increased by, say, three hundred silver talents."

Antiochus raised an eyebrow at the offer. "You have a candidate in mind, I imagine?"

Seraiah nodded his head forward in the direction of the man seated across from him. "Menelaus."

"Menelaus is a priest, like Jason," Timarchos said to add his support, "and could lead both as high priest and premier."

"And he's much more progressive and open-minded than Jason," Seraiah continued. "He'll do what would be necessary to make you yourself feel at home here, which, as our king, you should."

Antiochus pondered this in silence for a few moments.

"I have been significantly impressed with Jason's accomplishments on this visit," he said at last, "but I am struck by the concerns you raise. I will speak with him about these matters tomorrow and will give you my answer concerning your proposal."

Antiochus shifted his weight to his other arm, as if to signal a change in topic. "Now where is this young man who won today's competitions? Did any of you arrange for him to come to me?"

"Of course, Highness," said Seraiah, gesturing to his steward. "I believe he's been here for some time."

At the steward's summons, Meir entered the room clad in his finest tunic, having been called away from a celebration of his victory at Agathon's house by Seraiah's messengers.

"Come in, young man," said Antiochus, gesturing with his fingers. "Why don't you sit there beside Master Seraiah here so we can raise a cup to toast your accomplishments."

Meir was embarrassed by the honor and could only manage a "sire."

"Winning athletes often feast with kings—what was your name?"

"Hilaron, Majesty," Meir replied meekly.

"Winning athletes often feast with kings, Hilaron," the king said with a smile, "so you may wish to start getting used to it."

A servant had begun filling everyone's cups afresh with wine, providing one for Meir as well. Antiochus raised his.

"To Hilaron of Jerusalem!"

The company echoed the king's toast and added their own congratulations for his performance.

"You did not participate in the games naked, after the Greek fashion," Antiochus observed.

"Respectfully, sir," Meir replied, "that would be considered a public shame here."

"But not elsewhere," Antiochus countered, raising his index finger. "With the proper training, you could have a future in Antioch itself."

"Thank you, sire, but I think even there it would be problematic for me to compete naked."

Antiochus nodded, as if in understanding. "Yes, that barbaric mutilation of your member that Jewish parents inflict upon their young," he said sympathetically. "You know, there's an operation that can restore the prepuce. I'm told it's terribly painful for a number of weeks, but in the end it's almost perfectly normal again."

"I'll keep that in mind, sire," Meir said, fully intending to put the thought out of his mind as soon as possible.

"Well—Hilaron," Antiochus said emphatically, "you performed splendidly today and brought honor to your city."

Antiochus extended a closed fist over the table toward Meir. Meir tentatively placed his hand beneath it. The king opened his fist to release a number of gold coins into his open palm.

Meir's eyes widened to what seemed twice their size. "Thank you, sire!"

"I hope we'll be hearing more about you in the future. Be well," Antiochus added with a flick of his wrist signaling the end of the audience.

Meir rose from the couch, bowed deeply, and turned to leave. As he exited the room, he heard the king comment, "This city is indeed full of potential." His face flushed at the compliment and his pace quickened to seek out Tavitha.

The king continued to stare off in the direction of the boy's departure, tapping his fingers on the couch. *Maybe it does need a stronger push.*

6

Antiochus left Jerusalem on the third morning of his visit, with an additional cart bearing the tribute of Jerusalem and Judea in his train. Noticeably fewer citizens gathered in the streets to see him off than had gathered to welcome him as he entered. Late on the previous day, a proclamation had been made in both the senate house and the Temple concerning a change in his appointed leadership of the region. Menelaus had arranged for a troupe of trumpet and reed players to accompany the king's retinue as they processed from the high priestly palace through the streets and out of the western gate, where the majority of their guard had been encamped and now stood prepared to fall in line on either side of the king's entourage. The musicians continued to play from the gate until the king was three hundred meters distant. In the ensuing silence, Antiochus thought that he heard a sound of lament faintly emanating from the city.

Meir, alongside the winners of lesser events in the games, had been among those who accompanied the king to the gate, feeling somewhat unclean for having to do so in light of the intervening day's developments. He also could not miss the reception in the gymnasium's inner courtyard that immediately followed, a reception that Menelaus had organized ostensibly to congratulate the winners in the games before sending the foreign competitors home, but more to congratulate himself and his coterie on their coup. Meir had no appetite for the foods offered, nibbling only on some bread and fruit. The only bright spot in his morning was that Tavitha had been able to join him at this reception, though she was visibly uncomfortable at Seraiah's presence there.

After staying for what Meir felt was an acceptable minimum, he began to lead Tavitha toward the side exit that led to the market and the road to Agathon's house.

"Is the most celebrated winner leaving so soon?" Seraiah's voice boomed out.

Meir and Tavitha suddenly found themselves the center of attention, and returned somewhat meekly into the courtyard.

"Forgive me, Master Seraiah, Master Menelaus," Meir said. "It's just that I think I'm taking ill from all the strain of these past few days."

"I'm sure Lord Menelaus would join me, then, in wishing you a quick recovery." Seraiah took a few steps toward Tavitha. "I must confess, Persephone, that I was most displeased at not having been able to reach you two nights ago when I was entertaining the king."

Tavitha looked down and away, saying nothing.

"Master Seraiah," Meir ventured, "so many nobles have been willing to honor me for my victories. Perhaps I could ask a boon of you as well?"

Seraiah now found himself the focus of attention. "What can I offer our local champion?"

"A small piece of local real estate in Your Excellency's possession," he said. "A small apartment."

Meir pulled out ten gold coins from his pocket.

"Sir, you may remember that King Antiochus graced me with these from his own hand. This would be a more-than-fair price for the property, even without the added value of having been touched by his highness."

Tavitha's eyes brightened as she looked up at Meir.

"I would, of course, allow the current tenants to remain," he added, looking at Tavitha, "so you needn't be concerned about them further."

Seraiah knew he could neither refuse the request nor accept the king's gift as payment.

"I understand completely," he replied with open magnanimity. "What future can a young and promising citizen have without a place in the world to call his own? Receive the apartment as my gift to you, with every good wish."

Those onlookers who had remained interested in the exchange broke out in applause for Seraiah's generosity and for such an award to so worthy a recipient.

Meir stepped forward and bowed graciously to Seraiah.

"Well played," the latter said through a smile and under his breath.

"Many thanks," Meir replied.

Meir bowed again to acknowledge Menelaus, raised his hand to bid the other guests and his friends farewell, and escorted Tavitha out of the gymnasium. As soon as they emerged in the street, she jumped in front of Meir and held him in a tight embrace, laying her head on his shoulder for what seemed like an age.

"Thank you," she said, as she stepped back.

"Being able to do this makes everything else I did up to this point worthwhile," he answered, looking into her eyes. "Though we may ultimately have Seraiah's vanity to thank," he added to lighten the moment.

They walked hand-in-hand up the familiar path to Agathon's house, into which Menes now welcomed them as part of the household. They found Agathon in the atrium speaking with Eupolemus and Alcimus, and waited respectfully at a distance until the conversation had ended. As Agathon's guests took their leave, they exchanged greetings with his young protégé, though the mood was remarkably different from the atmosphere Meir and Tavitha had just left. Here it was as though someone had died.

"Master Agathon?" Meir did not really know what to say or how to form a question that would not sound stupid under the circumstances.

Agathon nodded to acknowledge the awkwardness.

"Jason was not inclined to accept Antiochus's invitation to be his guest in Antioch for an unspecified time during this period of transition. Even I don't know where he went, though I do have a few ideas."

Agathon dropped heavily into a cushioned chair and let his head rest against the back.

"'From morning to evening conditions change,'" he muttered, remembering the maxim. "Hasn't that proven to be the truth!"

Meir and Tavitha sat down together on a small couch across from Agathon.

"I'm concerned about you, Master Agathon," Meir said after a brief silence.

"What have you heard that concerns you, Hilaron?"

"This morning, Timarchos approached me at the gymnasium. He said he was impressed with me, and that I should break my ties with you and come under his wing instead. He said that you have no future here, and neither would I as long as I remained under your protection."

"And what did you tell him?"

"I thanked him for taking forethought for me, but said I could not repay your many kindnesses toward me and my family by abandoning you at the first sign of trouble."

Agathon smiled at the young man. "Your loyalty is a sign of your nobility of spirit. You are a credit to your parents." Agathon rotated his head and neck in an effort to relieve the tension that had lived there of late, then made two gestures to Menes, one getting his attention and the other pointing to his neck and shoulder.

"I'm not surprised by his offer. You're a rising star who even caught the attention of King Antiochus. You would adorn Timarchos's entourage, to be sure. Remain cordial toward him. It's an opening into Menelaus's circles that we may be able to exploit—or that you might indeed need later, should we fail."

Meir looked at Agathon quizzically.

"Oh, Jason didn't go through all that trouble just to allow some lackey of the house of Tobiah to supplant him."

Agathon allowed Menes to continue for a number of minutes before rising from his seat.

"But for now," he said with obvious resignation, "Menelaus has convened the entire senate, and I must go pay court to him and learn what he intends for Jason's city."

Menelaus strode from the high priestly palace, of which he was the recent beneficiary, toward the senate chamber. A dozen Temple guards escorted him, clearing a wide path and keeping a keen eye on the people for any signs of trouble. The first few weeks of a new regime, before it could establish itself and begin to appear routine, were always the most dangerous.

Menelaus himself was not worried for his well-being, however. The power of King Antiochus stood behind him, and he could almost feel its power coursing through him as its channel. He had lived with resentment his whole adult life. Born into an undistinguished priestly family, Menelaus perceived himself to have been condemned, not privileged, to serve the Temple—to serve a system that would never serve him as it had the family of Honiah and others who had come before, all because of an accident of birth and the rigidity of Israel's internal bloodlines. All that had now changed. He had stifled his resentment, hidden it beneath flattery and obsequiousness, covered it over with the smooth plaster of seeming to devote himself to advancing the interests of those around him. But now he would release it at last—in decisive action against the old ways that had kept his fathers, had hitherto kept himself, and would have otherwise kept his male offspring fettered in perpetuity to a system in which there was no possibility of advancement.

A crowd of men had gathered in the portico of the market opposite the path to the senate house. Most were common folk, though Menelaus recognized a few familiar faces in the crowd—like that of Yoshe ben Yoezer. If Menelaus had had any doubt about him being one of the ringleaders behind the gathering, Yoshe swept it away as he stepped forward, pointing to Menelaus as he approached.

"Look, Korah returned from the underworld to rebel again against the family that the Lord chose!"

The crowd began to jeer, several men raising and shaking both fists to signal their rejection of the new regime. Over the din, Menelaus could hear a number of specific complaints shouted out.

"The holiest office is for sale now, going to the highest bidder!"

"You are unfit to enter the Holy of Holies and to make atonement for the people!"

"You may put on the turban and breastplate, but we have no high priest!"

"You are not worthy of the Temple!"

This last gibe pushed Menelaus beyond his limit. He turned on the demonstrators with such force as might make the shock wave of his anger felt across the square.

"The Temple is not worthy of me!" he shouted. "But have no fear: I will make it worthy."

Menelaus all but shoved the two guards nearest him toward the demonstrators and ordered the rest to join them in breaking up the crowd.

"If they resist, start sticking your spears through the ones in front."

He signaled to a pair of guards to remain with him while the others carried out the orders, sending protestors scurrying back through the market and down into the old city. Yoshe stood his ground during their retreat until he stood alone before the advancing guards, who stopped three meters away from their former commander.

"Your God-appointed task is to defend the Temple, not this usurper," he instructed them as if still their chief. "Remember that in time to come."

Yoshe took a step back, nodding solemnly as he surveyed the group, and then turned around and walked away.

Menelaus fought to gain control of his anger as he neared the senate chamber. The members of the senate had gathered punctually, as each was most anxious—some with anticipation, others with dread—to learn what this change of leadership would mean for the city. They were already in their seats, most speaking to one another only in hushed tones, when Menelaus entered, attended by Seraiah and Timarchos. A handful of senators rose from their seats at his arrival; the majority were not yet prepared to make even that token gesture to acknowledge Menelaus's appointment.

Menelaus nodded slightly as he surveyed the room, registering their reluctance, and motioned those standing to take their seats.

"This is the will of King Antiochus," he said simply. "If you disagree with his policies, I suggest that you take it up with him. Until you succeed in changing his mind, I expect your full cooperation and support as his appointed representative for the province."

Menelaus sat down in the president's chair without taking his gaze from the senators.

"My predecessor's experiment, for all its successes, faltered in a number of essential respects. This is not my opinion; nor is it open for debate. It is the opinion of King Antiochus, as my sitting in this place bears witness. And I have been appointed, in large measure, to remedy these deficiencies."

Alcimus rose to speak. "It is surely the king's privilege and right to appoint whomever he wishes to represent Judea as his premier in this province," he began, mustering as much respect as he could, "and I have every confidence that he appointed you with good reason."

Menelaus acknowledged the comment with a suspicious nod.

"I do wonder how he came also to appoint you to serve as high priest. The king's father, the third Antiochus, was careful not to make such appointments contrary to the laws governing the Temple. This fourth Antiochus's last appointment also did not contravene these laws."

"Laws, Alcimus?" Menelaus asked, feigning ignorance. "To what laws do you refer?"

"A member of the family of Zadok has served as high priest since the time of the first Temple," Alcimus answered.

"Ah!" exclaimed Menelaus. "You refer to custom, to tradition—and not, in point of fact, to law." He leaned forward slightly in his chair to press his point. "Would it surprise you to know that I have read the Torah quite carefully and quite often over the years? Nowhere does it prescribe that a high priest must come from this particular family—in fact, Zadok's name does not appear at all in Moses's legislation." He moved forward in his seat even farther to deliver his coup de grâce. "But even if it did appear legislated therein, what difference would that make to us now? For this city and this body are not governed by those provincial laws any longer, nor have we been for the past three years of Jason's tenure."

Menelaus sat back in his chair and continued to speak over the surge of murmuring that arose in the hall. "And your question is hardly disinterested, Alcimus, since you are also part of the line of Zadok, as are Honiah and Jason."

Menelaus raised his hand to summon the assembly to silence and order once again.

"Jason's greatest failure was not to implement fully that which was also his greatest success, namely, our transformation into a colony of Antioch, a true city of Antiochus's multinational empire. Since this failure is most evident in the symbolically important world of religious practice, it pleased our king to name me high priest as well as his deputy. We are no Greek city as long as the peoples of Antiochus's empire are allowed no place to worship nor to express their piety—a matter of equal importance to them as to us—within our walls. We lie to the rest of the empire when we advertise ourselves as a place where any citizen can be at home, and then, once they arrive, impose old tribal customs on them—customs such as prohibiting them from bringing into the city the meats or hides or any product made from animals our ancestors once labeled unclean. And we cannot allow the Temple that dominates this city to remain a symbol and reminder of our ancestral contempt for our fellow-citizens and their gods."

About twenty senators, many of them foreigners who had come as citizens of the new Antioch, stood and began to applaud Menelaus at his declaration of intent. The clear majority, however, erupted into sounds of disapproval, some in the form of comments made to one other, some with comments directed at Menelaus himself.

Eupolemus rose to his feet and tried to quiet both groups. "Lord Menelaus," he began, his voice a model of diplomacy, "you name so many important issues and raise the possibility of so many changes all at once. I'm sure we will have the opportunity to consider each of these and any other proposals separately with the detailed examination each deserves and to vote on each as a body."

"Vote, Eupolemus?" Menelaus asked, feigning surprise. "Why would we need to vote again on these issues? These are all decisions that we already made. I sit in this chair simply to implement your will, to put into place at last the measures you approved three years ago."

"Jason never threatened the holiness of the Temple of the one God," Eupolemus said evenly but firmly.

"Is it not written, 'My house shall be a house of prayer for all nations'?" Menelaus recited, savoring the irony of his application. "And where is Jason now?" he asked pointedly. He redirected his gaze to the assembly as a whole, as he announced the answer. "He's a fugitive on the run, a man in disgrace!"

He arose from his chair. "The king gave us, at our own request, a very great privilege. He is most concerned, however, that we abuse the privilege no longer in our treatment of his non-Jewish subjects in our midst. May I inform the king that I have the support of this body, or are there further objections to carrying out his will?"

Menelaus scrutinized the assembly under his gaze during the tense moments of silence that followed his challenge.

"Good," he concluded. "He will be pleased to learn of your unanimity."

Seraiah followed Menelaus into the high priest's office and closed the door behind him on the assembly that still sat in stunned silence.

"You enjoy a very strong hand, Menelaus," Seraiah said, half amused and half aghast by the man's lack of diplomacy, "but you didn't have to play it all at once."

"The senate needs to understand that I will not indulge in perpetual negotiations with them, nor yield to their sentimentality about the old ways as Jason did."

"Then mission accomplished, I dare say," Seraiah replied as he took a seat beside the writing table in the center of the office. "I appreciate your energy for rigorous action, Menelaus, but we need to proceed gradually—any one of these changes will be difficult for our local population to swallow, and we must not cram them all down their throats at once or we risk an uprising. We'll begin with allowing our non-Jewish citizens to sponsor the construction of what public shrines to their gods they deem most needful on land they purchase privately, and delay any other major shifts for at least the first two or three years."

Menelaus had listened impassively, and not with his full attention.

"I'll take it under consideration."

"I beg your pardon?"

"Thank you for your advice," Menelaus said more deliberately. "I'll consider its merits."

"You'll consider?" Seraiah asked with indignation.

"The high priest does not take orders from private citizens," Menelaus said, as if Seraiah had forgotten to whom he was speaking. "You will need to come to terms with the changed dynamics of our relationship, and I would suggest you do so quickly."

"You are high priest because I made you—"

"I am high priest because Antiochus made me such," Menelaus said decisively. He softened his tone and eased his bearing slightly before continuing. "I have valued your support, and value it still. I would like for you to remain foremost in my inner circle of advisors. But," he added with a formerly hidden strength, "I am no one's puppet."

Seraiah quietly rose from his chair and nodded to Menelaus. "I'll take it under consideration," he said evenly. He paused before opening the door and looked back at Menelaus. "I wonder how long you would be high priest without my financial backing—that is, should you fail to deliver Antiochus his money."

Menelaus smiled at Seraiah. "I have the key to the largest treasury of silver and gold between Alexandria and Antioch, and you think I'm worried about being hard-pressed for cash?"

Four well-armed mercenary soldiers watched as a solitary traveler approached on horseback. The horse moved slowly, its wearied rider swaying slightly from the heat and exhaustion.

"That's far enough," their squad leader declared. "Who are you, and what's your business?"

The rider pulled his cloak down from around his head.

"I am Jason," he said hoarsely, "he who was high priest in Jerusalem. I am here to see your master."

The squad leader looked him over for a moment before speaking again. "Leave your horse and any weapons here."

Jason dismounted, drew out the long dagger he was wearing at his waist, and handed it to the nearest soldier. He opened his cloak to show that he was concealing no other weapons.

The squad leader ordered two of his command to remain at their posts and signaled to Jason and the fourth soldier to follow him. They escorted Jason along the dusty path that led to the gate of the fortress city that was home to Jason's only hope. As they entered the city and walked along its main street, Jason observed with satisfaction that a disproportionate number of the inhabitants were clearly military men, many sporting Egyptian weapons and armor. They approached the entrance of a palace, parts of which were still under construction.

"Wait here," the squad leader instructed Jason, signaling to his lieutenant to remain with the stranger. Jason turned his gaze back to the street and the surrounding buildings, continuing to gauge the military strength of the master of this city. A voice interrupted his mental tally sooner than he anticipated.

"Jason of Jerusalem?"

Jason turned back toward the palace to see a well-dressed, perfectly groomed man approaching him, flanked by two seasoned bodyguards.

"This is probably the last thing I expected when I woke up this morning," he continued. "Welcome to Araq el-Emir." At his signal, two servants appeared bearing cool water and fresh fruit. "What brings you to this side of the Jordan?"

"Hyrcanus ben Yoseph ben Tobiah," Jason said with a slight nod. "Your brother Seraiah has betrayed me. I have come to ask for your help."

"My help to do what?"

Jason gulped down a cup of water, then brought his gaze back upon Hyrcanus.

"To kill him and take back my city."

7

Yoshe ben Yoezer strode up the road from the old city, past the market. In the three years that had passed since Menelaus had become high priest, several houses along the street had been converted into temples dedicated to Astarte or Baal-Shamen or Isis. Sacred symbols were clearly carved into their facades, and images of the gods' attendants before the buildings welcomed worshipers into the inner shrines where, no doubt, far more ornate images of the gods themselves awaited their devotion. Altars stood in the porticoes of the market and gymnasium, erected against the walls. Yoshe spotted a Jerusalem resident walking up to one to throw some incense upon the fire that burned in its center, bowing her head in prayer to whatever god. These altars no longer had images of their gods on them—it had proven impossible to protect them from vandalism and too costly to continue to replace them.

Though it had been nearly three years since the first shrines began to appear, the sight continued to sear Yoshe's soul every day, as if he were witnessing the pollution of the Holy City afresh for the first time. It was a wound scraped open anew every time he moved from one place to another in his city, with no respite given even for a scab to form, let alone for it to heal. He arrived at last at Eleazar's door. A teenage boy sat against the wall under the shuttered window and looked up at him. Yoshe rapped on the door.

"May my eyes fall out if they ever become accustomed to abomination!" he declared as he was admitted into the house.

The voice of Mattathias answered him. "Our visits to Jerusalem are painful indeed. In all honesty, we make them as infrequently as possible. How much worse for you who must live day after day in the midst of the desecration."

"Welcome, Yoshe," said Eleazar. "As you can see, Mattathias, Judah, Eupolemus, and Amnon are here already. And I've brought Binyamin in as well, as someone whom I trust completely."

Yoshe clasped the hands of Mattathias and Judah, acknowledged the others with respectful nods, and sat on the mat next to Judah.

"Who's the sentinel?" he asked, nodding toward the window.

"That would be my youngest brother, Ariyeh," Binyamin ventured.

"He'll give us warning if he sees anything suspicious," Eleazar explained, "and keep spying ears from listening at our window. At this point, our gatherings could easily be interpreted as sedition. Eupolemus?"

"Thank you, Master Eleazar." The young senator appeared to be fighting to retain his composure as he began. "Brothers, I know some of you questioned my loyalty to God when I chose to remain a part of the senate under Jason and, again, under Menelaus. But you also know how hard some of us on the senate fought to turn Menelaus away from some of his plans for the city. Admittedly, we had to remain silent in the face of some evils in order to speak out against greater evils. But we did so out of the same love for God and Jerusalem that burns in each one of you."

Yoshe folded his arms in front of him and cocked his head, signaling his continued skepticism.

"We have focused our efforts on keeping Menelaus from touching the Temple," Eupolemus resumed, "so that it, at least, would remain a sanctuary for our people. It seems that we have finally failed."

Everyone in the room leaned forward in anxious anticipation of what details would follow.

"Menelaus has given the order to begin some . . . 'improvements' in the outer court open to people from all nations. Work crews have already begun breaking up an area of the pavement for the planting of a grove, a space for the worship of certain nature gods and spirits. He is also preparing an area for a large 'sacred' stone that will serve as an altar in the outer precincts."

Yoshe rose to his feet, tugging at the neckline of his tunic until it ripped.

"How long will you watch, Lord God, and do nothing?" he roared, raising and shaking his hands to plead with the unseen deliverer. "How long will you let those who trample your laws and defile your courts see the light of day?"

Judah stood and placed his hand on Yoshe's shoulder to reassure him that he was not alone in his distress and gently led him back down to a sitting position.

"I think news of Antiochus's forthcoming visit is what finally motivated Menelaus to overrule our concerns," Eupolemus continued. "From this point, I have little hope of restraining Menelaus. He seems to be using his knowledge of the covenant to direct his policies at every turn, instituting whatever Torah prohibits."

The men sat in silence for what seemed an eternity. Finally Judah spoke. "We, too, are lawbreakers, as long as we sit off to one side and watch this desecration continue."

He looked at Yoshe. "Should we suppose that God has not raised his arms and shaken his fists at us, shouting to us: 'How long will you watch and do nothing? How long will you let these lawbreakers trample my laws and defile my courts?' For three years we have sat by and watched and complained as Menelaus has defiled God's Holy City."

Yoshe nodded as he remembered words from the fifth book of Moses: *This is how you shall deal with them: break down their altars, smash their pillars, cut down their sacred groves, and burn up their idols. For you are a people holy to the Lord your God!*

"We have kept ourselves from the pollution," Judah continued, "but we have not kept God's Holy Land and Holy City from pollution as he has commanded us."

"Remember how Moses and the Levites purged Israel of the golden calf and struck down many who had bowed down to worship it," Yoshe added, nodding his agreement with Judah. "And how Elijah led the people to rout and kill the priests of Baal who had been deceiving God's people and defiling the land?"

"What can you hope to do?" Eupolemus asked incredulously. "Menelaus has the power of Antiochus and his empire behind him."

"And don't we have the promise of someone stronger fighting for us," Judah countered, "if we have the courage to walk in God's ways? Remember even what ben Sira used to say: 'The person who fears the Lord will not be timid, nor play the coward, for God is his hope.'"

"We could appeal to Antiochus," Eupolemus interjected. "Send an unofficial delegation, stand upon his father's policies of protecting our native religion and laws."

"It's too late for that," Mattathias replied. "Every appeal to Antiochus has brought us to a worse state than the previous one. It's time to appeal to God, and to allow him to decide whose cause is right."

Mattathias turned to address Yoshe. "We need to begin to organize resistance here in Jerusalem and throughout the countryside as well. We'll need to do this quietly, organizing in bands of small numbers like Moses's groups of tens, until we have a sufficient movement to begin to strike in force."

"We can use our estate outside of Modein as a training ground," Judah added, "and we'll need to begin acquiring weapons from whatever sources we can."

"I know where to begin among the Temple guard and some other pockets within the city," Yoshe volunteered. "Master Eleazar, will you help us?"

Eleazar smiled weakly and looked down.

"You know that I will support you in my spirit and pray on your behalf every day," he said, "but I am an old man. I have no influence, no power anymore to affect the course of this nation."

"Master Eleazar," Amnon objected, "you still command great respect among the faithful throughout the city."

"They still look to your example," Binyamin concurred. "You're a powerful symbol of covenant loyalty, a reminder of a more faithful time."

"I appreciate your attempts to reassure me, friends," Eleazar said, "but I see how my influence has faded. You can count on me to continue to sit in the market and teach the young about our God and his law, in fulfillment of the commandment. You can count on me to speak well of all that you do for the sake of God. You can count on me to open my doors to you at any time. And you can count on me to pray to God to deliver his people, his city, and his Temple." He looked around at the men in the circle with unmistakable weariness. "But what can an old man do beyond this?"

Eupolemus, realizing that he could not dissuade them from what they were planning—and knowing that he had no solid ground on which to urge them to entrust their city to any alternative course of action—spoke up. "What can I do to assist?"

"From now on, you're our eyes and ears in the senate and everywhere else Menelaus moves," Mattathias responded.

"And find out who else among the senate would be sympathetic to God's cause," Judah added. "They might not be willing to fight, but they might be willing to pay for weapons and supplies."

"From today on," Mattathias said solemnly, "we dare to love the Lord our God with our whole heart, our entire life, and our full strength."

8

In the 143rd year of the kingdom of the Greeks, Antiochus Theos Epiphanes, "the god openly revealed," marched his great army from Antioch toward the gates of Egypt. They moved south through the coastal plains like a plague of locusts, trampling and devouring all the crops in their path, raiding villages and cities, "requisitioning" supplies. Antiochus left the army to encamp near Ashkelon, where Apollonios and his other generals could finalize their plans for their initial assaults on Pelusium, while he took his most trusted advisors, along with five hundred soldiers and cavalry, east to Jerusalem.

"Set up your camps a hundred meters out from the walls," Antiochus told the division commanders. "Spread out a bit. Make an impressive display for the residents here to remember."

Antiochus turned to his advisors Herakleon, Heliodoros, and Simon.

"Shall we go see what sentiments will be at our backs as we engage Ptolemy?"

He pressed his heels into his horse's sides and moved forward toward the city gates, followed by fifty mounted soldiers.

Menelaus stood at the gate to welcome Antiochus. He allowed himself to feel a wave of satisfaction with himself for his readiness for this moment. He had declared the day of the king's arrival a public festival and provided, at state expense, a feast for the local population. Seemingly out of deference to Jewish sentiments, he offered kosher meats from the Temple sacrifices in locations throughout the old city to the south of the Temple. Here, near the west gate, he catered to the tastes of the immigrant population with roasted pork and music in Syrian and Greek styles, guaranteeing that the area through which Antiochus passed would be teeming with the people most enthusiastic about the new order. He had instructed the senate to appear in full force, and to make sure that their whole households and all their dependents were present as well, to greet the king and reinforce the impressions of support.

Antiochus entered the city to shouts of acclamation in his native Greek. Young women rushed forward to offer garlands of flowers to him and his entourage. The young men enrolled in the gymnasium came forward, carrying palm branches and laying them down in his path chanting *"Antiochos Nikēphoros,"* "Antiochus, bearer of Victory," in anticipation of his Egyptian campaign.

Menelaus, at the head of a group of senators, bowed deeply before Antiochus. The king recognized several faces, among them Timarchos, standing to the side of and just a step behind Menelaus, and Seraiah, farther back in the group than Antiochus would have expected.

"Welcome once again, Highness, to Antioch-at-Jerusalem."

"My thanks to you, Menelaus, and to the citizens of this city for this warm reception. I have heard encouraging reports of how you have devoted yourself to improving the conditions of the people of other nations living among you."

A spontaneous cheer erupted from the people surrounding them. Menelaus clasped his hands in front of him and lowered his head slightly to acknowledge the acclamation.

"I am grateful, Highness, for the opportunity you have given me to serve them. They are just as much my people as my native race."

The residents once again cheered Menelaus for this statement. Antiochus saw no insincerity as he looked into their faces.

"Please accept my invitation to you and your counselors to refresh yourselves in my palace after your long journey from Ashkelon. We have prepared a reception for you on the grounds of the gymnasium later this afternoon, to be followed by a banquet at my home." Anticipating the king's question, he added, "Tomorrow, Highness, it will be our pleasure to render you your due tribute in full."

"Your forethought in all these matters is most appreciated, Menelaus," Antiochus replied.

As Antiochus proceeded down the road leading to the center of Antioch-at-Jerusalem, the people lining the streets waved their arms and shouted words of welcome and greeting. Several people did the same from the second-floor windows of their dwellings, drawing Antiochus's attention upward in time for him also to glimpse several people scowling as he passed, some even closing their shutters. He returned his focus to the people lining the streets, returning their greetings with the waving of his own arm. At the same time, he leaned over slightly to instruct Herakleon and Heliodoros.

"Keep your eyes to the upper windows and the doorways. Take note of how many residents do *not* seem glad to see us here."

Eupolemus left the gymnasium before the festivities were over. He had dutifully paid his respects to King Antiochus and Lord Menelaus, expressing his wishes for the king's campaign in Egypt in terms that could be understood as praying for his success. In his heart, however, he hoped that Ptolemy would prove more than the king's match and decimate his armies. Eupolemus made his way to the edge of the party so that he could disappear as Menelaus invited the king to offer a libation and incense at the shrine of Zeus that had been erected in the gymnasium complex out of deference to Antiochus's patron god. Not having been invited to the dinner that would follow, Eupolemus knew that he would not be missed for the rest of the night.

He walked to the market and wandered through the stalls with their thoroughly picked-over offerings, but his gaze was not on the produce and wares he pretended to browse. His eyes scanned the other people, especially those that entered the market shortly after he did. Satisfied that he was not being followed, he doubled back into the residential area west of the Temple and made his way to Eleazar's home. He had sent Amnon earlier by another way to collect Yoshe and anyone else deemed useful. As he approached the home, Eupolemus recognized the boy sitting in front of the window, even in the dusky gray that had settled on the city with the evening.

He knocked on the door and was admitted by Binyamin. Yoshe, Eleazar, Amnon, and Judah had already assembled in the living area. Small talk would have been out of place, so Eupolemus came immediately to the point.

"We knew that the main purpose of Antiochus's visit was to collect whatever he could of the tribute due him from our province, together with the additional sum promised for the rights he conferred on the city."

"Menelaus's bribes, you mean," Yoshe said, as if spitting.

"Yes, Yoshe, one could put it like that," Eupolemus conceded. "Despite the fact that support for Menelaus has eroded among the elite, we've not fallen behind in either payment, and I think I know why. Menelaus has been stealing from the funds deposited in the Temple to make up the difference. I've checked the financial records carefully. There could be no other explanation."

Eupolemus tried to quiet the circle's expressions of disgust and horror at Menelaus's further violation of the holiness of the Temple.

"Unfortunately, it gets worse. He has invited Antiochus, his advisors, and a detachment of his soldiers to accompany him through the Temple courts and into the treasury itself to receive this year's tribute."

"He's going to take a Gentile into the court set apart for the priests of Israel?" Yoshe's voice was resonant with incredulity. "I'll kill them both myself if they cross the threshold!"

"No, you won't, Yoshe!" Eupolemus said with a firmness that surprised even himself. "If Antiochus's five hundred soldiers camped outside our city aren't reason enough for you, consider the fifty thousand he's left in Ashkelon awaiting his return."

"Eupolemus is right, Yoshe," said Eleazar. "We do not want to provoke Antiochus or his soldiers."

"We must do something!" interjected Judah. "If we just sit by while God's Temple is further profaned, he will not hold us guiltless."

"I would advise doing precisely nothing, brothers," said Eupolemus. "Tomorrow afternoon Antiochus—and his soldiers—will be on their way. We should do nothing that would make him stay longer or feel as if his interests here are in jeopardy."

"Exactly the sort of attitude that has brought us to this place to begin with!" Yoshe objected.

"So you'd rather stage an attack tomorrow when Menelaus has five hundred of Antiochus's soldiers at his back than wait till the third day when he has only his local police force?"

Yoshe did not have an answer, so Judah stepped in.

"God will be watching us tomorrow, Eupolemus. What witness will we be giving if we bury our heads beneath our pillows because we're afraid of Antiochus's soldiers?"

"Will God be pleased with us for acting after his Temple has been thus violated, if we could have acted to prevent it?" Yoshe added, having recovered his balance.

Binyamin preempted what would have been a less-than-diplomatic reply from Eupolemus.

"Masters, you have all spoken wisdom here. If I might venture to make a suggestion?"

"Please, Binyamin," Eleazar said encouragingly. *If it just gives the others time to cool their heads, it will have been worth sharing.*

"Would God not be pleased if we simply did this time what our high priest Honiah led us to do the last time a Gentile threatened to cross the threshold into the Court of Israelites?"

Eleazar, who had been present that day, sat up a little higher and began pointing repeatedly to the air in front of him.

"Yes, Binyamin, yes. Eupolemus is correct that we must not provoke Antiochus, lest we bring death upon our city, but Yoshe and Judah are correct that we cannot ignore this threat to the Temple's holiness."

"God protected God's Temple last time," Yoshe interjected, "because Honiah did everything well in God's sight."

"Surely it will be enough," Eupolemus replied, sensing this to be the best compromise, "to leave it to God to decide the case this time as well."

Yoshe and Judah reluctantly nodded their assent.

"At first light, we will begin to rally the people to the Temple for the morning sacrifice," Judah began to plan out loud, "warning them of what might come."

"We will instruct them to take no weapons and take no action," Amnon insisted, "except to call upon God to protect his Holy Places and to protest with tears and lamentation."

"Both God and the king will know where the people of this city stand on the matter," Eupolemus concluded. "If Antiochus proceeds, the guilt will be on his head and not ours."

Ariyeh jumped up from the ground as Yoshe and Judah opened the door, bid their brothers shalom, and walked out into the street.

Following after them, he called in a semi-whisper, "Master Judah!"

Judah stopped and turned around as Ari closed the distance.

"*I* would fight for the covenant."

"Yes, little lion, I believe you would. Now run along home to your mother," Judah said, teasingly.

"You've got a bit of milk there," Yoshe added, touching the corner of his own lips and grinning.

Ari was undeterred.

"I'm not the boy you met at Binyamin's wedding, Master Judah. I'm sixteen. I can hold a sword or a spear."

"But can you push it through a man's heart?" Judah countered.

"I have as much experience as you," said Ari.

Judah paused for a moment.

"You're right, little lion. This is new ground for us all. Even Yoshe here has only killed in his dreams. You're welcome in Modein—but only with your mother's blessing."

Menelaus escorted Antiochus, his advisors, and ten of his bodyguard from the high priest's palace to the courtyard of the gymnasium, where a light breakfast had been prepared. Members of the senate had been milling about the courtyard for some time, anticipating the king's arrival. The young men enrolled in the *ephebate*, the body of the future citizens of Antioch-at-Jerusalem, puttered around the tables making sure everything was perfect for the king's arrival. Zenon, the gymnasiarch, had asked Meir to be present, both to help oversee the catering staff and to fulfill Menelaus's request that he be visible during Antiochus's stay as a point of positive connection with his previous visit to the city.

Upon Antiochus's entrance, people throughout the courtyard fell silent, turned, and greeted the king with a deep, reverential bow. He acknowledged the gesture by reaching forward and out with upturned palms, signaling for them to rise and resume their conversations. Several senators bid him good morning as he moved toward the tables in the center of the courtyard, laid out with freshly baked breads, slices of fruit, clusters of grapes, cheeses, olives, and nuts. Meir dispatched two young ephebes, one to bring the king new wine mixed with water, another to bear an empty platter and to place on it whatever the king wished. He and Zenon followed them to the table.

"Good morning, Highness," Zenon began, "and welcome once again to our gymnasium. I hope you will find our hospitality sufficient for your needs this morning, but if you find something lacking, we stand ready to make up any deficiency."

Antiochus looked at the variety of foods on the table with an air of satisfaction. "What you have provided will be quite adequate, and I remain most appreciative of the city's hospitality." The king noticed the young man standing beside the gymnasiarch and cocked his head slightly. "You look familiar to me. Did we meet on my last visit?"

"Yes, Highness, I had that honor after I won the pentathlon in the inaugural games over which you presided."

"Of course," Antiochus responded with greater animation. "You performed splendidly, I remember, though I confess that I don't recall your name." Antiochus pointed to some bread, certain kinds of fruit, and other items on the table, and the ephebe arranged appropriate portions of each on the plate.

"Hilaron, Highness. I remember your immense generosity toward me on that occasion, and I remain truly grateful to you."

"I hope it proved helpful to a young man getting his start in the world."

"It did indeed, Highness," Meir replied. "Thanks to you, I was able to buy a shop and furnish it for silversmithing. Four apprentices work under my supervision, leaving me free to spend more time here at the gymnasium as a tutor and trainer."

"Very glad to hear it, young man."

"And I've married—a beautiful woman from Seleucia named Tavitha."

"Heartfelt congratulations, young man. And may all Jews and Syrians live together as happily as Hilaron and Tavitha."

Menelaus, who had signaled for another ephebe to hold a plate for him as he selected his breakfast, pointed the king in the direction of a group of couches that had been set out under a canopy. After Antiochus's advisors had filled their plates, the senators, who had only viewed the buffet with anticipation since their own arrival, descended upon the table.

Heliodoros took his place on a couch next to Antiochus, and Meir hovered nearby, directing an ephebe to keep the company's cups full of water and new wine.

"Sire, may I speak freely?"

"Of course, Heliodoros," Antiochus replied. "When have you done otherwise?"

Heliodorus smiled, acknowledging the truth behind the question.

"Sire, why antagonize the Jewish population of this city—and perhaps their God—by transgressing their customs? What do we truly stand to gain by this? Why not just let the Jews bring the tribute out from the Temple to you?"

Simon ben Iddo signaled his scorn with a sharp exhalation. "Here he goes again. I'm surprised you've been silent this long, Heliodoros."

"You weren't there, Simon," Heliodoros retorted. "No, you stayed in Antioch because you were too ashamed to face your own people after what you had done." He turned his attention back to his king. "But I have firsthand experience, sire. I stood at that barrier between the outer and inner courts of the Temple, and I know what happened when I tried to cross it. I beg you not to endanger yourself."

"That barrier separating Jews from the people of other nations," Menelaus interjected, "represents everything that is wrong here in Jerusalem. And the absurd idea that God enforces those boundaries is what accounts for the longevity of my people's xenophobia. I intend to show the people of this city once and for all that they are wrong, and to change everything about this Temple that has, for so long, symbolized and reinforced that wall of hostility between our people and all the other peoples of this empire." Menelaus signaled for his cup to be refilled.

Meir began to tremble as he realized what was being planned for the king's visit to the Temple. Straightaway, he fell to his knees and placed his forehead to the ground in front of the king's couch.

"What's this, then, Hilaron?" asked Antiochus. "Do you seek another favor from me?"

"Only that I may speak freely in your presence, sire."

Menelaus began to flush with anger.

"Speak, Hilaron," Antiochus said. "The voice of Jerusalem's future deserves to be heard."

"I beg you, sire, to heed the wise counsel of Lord Heliodoros and not to cross a threshold that has been honored for centuries." Meir thought about his brothers, the kinds of men with whom they were rubbing shoulders, and how inflammatory the situation could quickly become. "I fear for the stability of your city, should its traditions be despised so openly."

"You see, Highness," Menelaus declared, "this is exactly what I'm talking about. A Jew might be able to win a pentathlon, but years later he still can't conquer his own superstition."

Menelaus turned to Heliodoros. "And if you hadn't lost your nerve and fainted seven years ago, this city would have moved toward this level of enlightenment that much sooner." Menelaus turned back to Antiochus. "Forgive me, Highness, for my bluntness."

"Your frustration is understandable, Menelaus," said the king. "Still, I do not hear superstition in this young man's words, only a recommendation of prudence."

The king turned his attention back to the suppliant. "Hilaron, you have great promise indeed. Someday there may be a place for you in the government here. Nevertheless, I cannot accept your advice."

Meir's hope plummeted.

"A king does not accept the restrictions of local customs," Antiochus continued, "and local populations need to learn that their local customs are not binding on kings. And I happen to agree with Lord Menelaus: the idea that your God favors one people to the exclusion of all others is inherently reprehensible and will be a persistent hindrance to Jerusalem's assimilation into the empire."

Meir rose to his feet and bowed his head to Antiochus before returning to his duties.

The king noticed Menelaus glaring at the youth as he retreated. "Oh, don't be angry with him, Menelaus," Antiochus chided. "There is not a single nation in the world that is not protective of its sanctuaries." Then he added for the whole company, "Although every other nation would welcome its king into those sanctuaries."

Sarpedon, who had maintained his command of the Syrian cohort serving as the local police force, approached Menelaus and the king.

"Excellencies, the morning Temple service has been concluded and my forces have taken up positions to secure the area for your visit." He turned his attention fully to the king. "Highness, a cohort of your soldiers has entered the city to transfer your due tribute."

"Very good, Sarpedon," Menelaus responded. "Sire, if you have satisfied your needs?"

"By all means," Antiochus said, "let's see this fine Temple of yours."

Antiochus rose from his couch. His bodyguard fell into formation around him and his advisors as Menelaus led them toward the Temple Mount. Sarpedon and a detachment of local police acted as vanguard, while one hundred of Antiochus's soldiers, about twenty of them detailed to move the two carts that would carry the bulk of the tribute, brought up the rear.

The streets were eerily quiet as the company made their way. A murmuring could be heard, however, wafting down from over the Temple courtyard's walls.

Antiochus began to be a bit uneasy. "Surely I couldn't be the first non-Jew ever to enter the Temple!"

"Not at all, sire," Simon assured him. "King Nebuchadnezzar of Babylon went in, did as he pleased, and took whatever he wanted. Then for good measure, he came back ten years later and destroyed the place after taking everything that was left. And how did God punish him? By giving him another twenty-five years of prosperous rule after the event!"

They ascended the great ramp that led into the Court of All Nations. As they emerged, they saw several thousand of the city's residents crowded into the edges of the courtyard and its porticoes, the local police having cordoned off a wide path from the ramp to the inner courts. Antiochus was impressed with the vastness of the space and with the sight of the sanctuary itself, visible over the walls separating the courtyards, gleaming as the morning sun reflected off its polished marble surfaces. Several of the women in the crowd were lamenting as if for the dead, while a group of men were chanting *"Qadosh l'Adonai! Qadosh l'Adonai."*

"What are they saying?" asked Antiochus.

Eupolemus had worked his way up to the front of the group of senators that had followed the king from the gymnasium. "'Holy to the Lord,' sire. They are trying to remind their high priest of the laws that protect the sanctity of this place."

"I have entered many such temples before throughout my realm—and have proven to be the benefactor of many." Antiochus looked ahead toward the towering facade of the sanctuary. "This place is no different from the others. They will come to understand that." *But to be safe,* he thought, *perhaps we had better let two of our bodyguard precede us.*

Lost in his own thoughts, Heliodoros walked out into the courtyard. He looked around, half-expecting to see angels on horseback bearing down on him as before, but there was something different about the place this time. He felt nothing of the presence of that power that had moved upon him years ago and stopped him dead in his tracks.

Menelaus led them past the recently planted sacred grove. As he looked to the stone altar opposite the grove, he noticed that someone had freshly scratched on it the word *Bdelygma*—"Abomination." He signaled for Sarpedon to come to him.

"I want this investigated," he said sharply under his breath, "and I want somebody punished for it."

As Antiochus drew closer to the threshold of the inner courts, the crowd grew more vocal and agitated. Many were now erupting into spontaneous prayers, calling upon God to defend his sanctuary from "the encroacher," apparently referring to some ancient law. A number of conservative priests broke through the police line and rushed to the space ahead of Antiochus's path. His bodyguard snapped to attention, but the priests made no further threatening action. Rather, they prostrated themselves on the pavement, lying down in the king's path. Antiochus felt oddly amused by the sight and put his left hand on his chief guard's right forearm to forestall any action on his part.

Sarpedon signaled several of the police to drag the priests out of the way as the crowd jeered at them for touching the priests with their profane hands.

As Menelaus approached the steps leading to the threshold of the inner courts with Antiochus and two of the latter's bodyguard, the Temple guard stationed there stepped forward and placed his hand on the hilt of his sword. The two bodyguards immediately drew their swords from their sheaths and stepped in front of the king. The standoff sent ripples of tension throughout the entire outer court. Menelaus stepped in front of Antiochus's bodyguard and stared directly into the temple guard's eyes.

"Stand down!" he ordered, then with greater intensity as he leaned in to the unmoving guard. "Stand . . . down . . ."

Reluctantly, the guard allowed his arms to fall to his sides and stepped back and off to one side.

"You are relieved of duty," Menelaus said, and then under his breath, "I'll deal with you later."

Antiochus waited for the guard to walk away from the area before gesturing to the two bodyguards in front of him to proceed.

Yoshe ben Yoezer recognized the dismissed Temple guard as Hanan, who had once protected Honiah in the assault on his life. Yoshe moved through the crowd into Hanan's line of sight and signaled him to come over.

"You've just made a powerful enemy but secured for yourself a more powerful Ally for all eternity." He put his hand on Hanan's shoulder. "I believe that when Moses asked, 'Who is on the Lord's side?' you would have rushed to stand shoulder-to-shoulder with him."

"I hope so, sir," Hanan replied to his former commander.

"It won't be safe for you here. Gather up your family and what goods you must and go to Modein. Men like you have a place there."

The guard nodded his appreciation and assent, and moved quickly and discreetly from the Temple precincts.

Antiochus watched as first Menelaus and then his two bodyguards crossed the barricade. A loud wail went up from the crowd of Jews in the outer courtyard. Antiochus paused at the threshold, then took a step forward into the Women's Court. He paused again, almost looking for signs of divine displeasure, then took another few steps into the center of the courtyard. *Rather anticlimactic*, he thought.

Antiochus's advisors—except for Heliodoros, who remained discretely outside the barricade—and the remainder of his bodyguard followed him through the Women's Court and up the stairs into the Court of Israelite Men, after which they disappeared completely from the sight of the crowd below.

Binyamin stood among the crowd next to Eleazar.

"Why does God allow this? Why doesn't he intervene?"

"I was present, Binyamin, when God struck down Heliodoros when he tried to enter the Temple to claim funds for King Seleucus," Eleazar said as if from a fog. "But that was under Honiah's leadership. God has since suffered terrible affronts from Jerusalem's leaders—and many of its people. He has cast us off once again; he has withdrawn his protection."

They continued to watch as the captain of Antiochus's bodyguard emerged from the Women's Court and signaled to the chief of the cohort waiting outside. The majority of the soldiers marched without hesitation across the Court of All Nations into the Women's Court and beyond, with no unseen hand barring their way, no portent signaling God's displeasure. At the sight, the crowd gave in to renewed laments, concluding that God had abandoned both his Temple and his people.

Yoshe called out from the edge of the crowd to the senators who remained gathered in the courtyard.

"You see now the result of abandoning the covenant? God's presence here was your glory, and for what have you exchanged it? What are we, if the Holy One does not live in our midst?"

From his place in the crowd, Eleazar began to weep and to pound his fist against his chest. Binyamin took hold of his forearm to stop him from hurting himself, and Eleazar bent over in grief.

"Master Eleazar, you have done nothing against God. None of this is your fault."

"What does that matter? God has still turned away. And how can we seek atonement with him? What sacrifice would God ever find acceptable in such a Temple from such a priest as this Menelaus?"

Soldiers began to appear again, descending the great staircase separating the Court of Israelite Men from the Women's Court, each carrying a considerable quantity of silver, some in the form of bars, others in the form of loose items in wooden chests. They spilled out into the Court of All Nations and continued to flow toward the gate.

Yoshe heard someone shouting out behind him. "They're taking the money made sacred by the Temple!"

Others around him began to denounce the soldiers. "Temple robbers!" they cried out, surging forward against the police cordon.

Yoshe remembered his agreement to help forestall violent resistance while Antiochus had so many soldiers in and around the city, and turned to address the more hotheaded. "Hold your places, brothers! Why would you prevent Antiochus from taking this silver? Why would you save him from God's vengeance?"

The men around him paused.

Satisfied that he had gotten their attention, Yoshe continued. "God is angry with us for our leaders' abandonment of the covenant, and so he allows his

Temple to be polluted. But do you think God will let these Temple robbers go unpunished? This silver will cling to them like burning pitch. It marks them as targets for God's judgments. Think about the profane uses to which they will put this silver—they will cast idols, they will use the chalices to carouse with their whores, they will give the coin to their men of violence and their prostitutes. And then what will God do? Remember Belshazzar, and think what God will soon do to this new Belshazzar and his false priest!"

Antiochus emerged with Menelaus from the Court of the Israelites, the king's bodyguard taking flanking positions as they descended the staircase. Yoshe could not have been more pleased with their timing. He looked into the faces of the men around him and began to chant *"Mene, Mene, Tekel, Upharsin! Mene, Mene, Tekel, Upharsin!"* The others smiled as they caught his meaning and took up the chant themselves, which spread through the crowd.

Antiochus emerged from the Court of Women and paused to listen.

"What are they saying?" Antiochus asked suspiciously. "I don't recognize the words."

"These are just the remnants of the old, xenophobic Jerusalem, Highness," Menelaus said dismissively. "Their ravings are not important."

Eupolemus, still at the front of the cluster of senators, stepped forward. "Perhaps we ought to let his majesty decide whether or not it is important."

Eupolemus turned his attention to Antiochus. "Our people tell a story about King Belshazzar of Babylon. One night he was giving a party for his friends and courtesans and thought it would be fun to serve them using the sacred vessels that his father Nebuchadnezzar had taken from the first Temple that stood on this ground. After the holy vessels were put to such polluting use, an invisible hand wrote four words on the wall of the king's hall: *Mene, Mene, Tekel, Upharsin.* A wise courtier named Daniel was summoned to interpret their meaning. Daniel said that the king had insulted God in his arrogance, that God had weighed him in the balance and found him lacking, and that other nations would take possession of his kingdom. Belshazzar died that very night. At least," Eupolemus concluded with a smile, "that is the story to which the people are referring, Highness."

"And what do you think, Senator?" Antiochus asked.

"Sire, only that it would be a frightful thing to fall into the hands of the living God." Eupolemus gave a respectful bow and stepped back into the company of senators.

Antiochus raised an eyebrow momentarily, then shrugged off the moment and proceeded to follow his soldiers from the Temple complex. The bulk of the silver was loaded onto the carts waiting at the bottom of the ramp, and the cohort proceeded to transfer the funds to the camp outside the city walls.

"I came to find out what I'd have at my back as I fought Egypt," Antiochus said. He turned back toward the Temple as if to allow the continued chanting to signal the answer. "You have your supporters here, but I wonder about your ability to maintain the loyalty of the people—and to maintain peace in a situation that is more volatile than I suspected."

"We are indeed at a critical juncture, sire," Menelaus explained. "Our progress meets with resistance from those whose loyalty is first to their ancestral customs and not to your empire, nor to their fellow citizens of other races. But as long as the old ways persist, Judea will not be a secure possession within your domain."

"I am aware that I set you in place of Jason to advance the program of integration more fully," Antiochus conceded, "but I was not aware of how great local resistance would be. I cannot afford a revolt at my back."

Antiochus paused as his mind raced to improvise a strategy to forestall such a possibility. After a moment, he nodded decisively. "I will leave one hundred—no, two hundred additional soldiers here as a peacekeeping force."

He turned to a soldier from Phrygia named Philip, the lieutenant of his personal bodyguard. "You will remain behind in command of the garrison. Your primary responsibility will be to safeguard the non-Jewish citizens and residents of Antioch-at-Jerusalem. This is a situation of significant ethnic and religious tension, so work to defuse it rather than provoke it, if possible." Antiochus surveyed the lay of the land in that part of the city. "You'll need to construct some sort of fortification for yourselves, something that gives you a commanding position both over the Temple and over the city."

"If I might be so bold, sire," Menelaus ventured, "most of our foreign nationals are located to the immediate south and west of the Temple."

"So then, a fortification on this side of the Temple makes good sense. Make it as large as you need to do it right, Philip." Antiochus looked in Menelaus's direction. "There's plenty of silver and gold here to cover the costs."

Zedekiah, Ephraim, and several others of the sons of Enoch sat on the ridge of one of the mountains east of Beth-Shemesh. The walk from their camp had taken several days, but Zedekiah had felt compelled to come to this spot to fast and to pray. Before the others had heard a sound, Zedekiah rose and looked down and to the east. Antiochus and his three remaining cohorts began to appear around a bend in the mountain pass. To Zedekiah they seemed a single, monstrous serpent winding its way down from Jerusalem. He kept watching as the company slithered south at the western opening of the pass, disappeared behind another mountain ridge for some time, then reemerged farther in the distance as they continued to follow the road west toward Ashkelon.

Ephraim had risen to stand beside Zedekiah and join his prayerful vigil.

"How long will God allow these giants to rampage, these unholy monsters who know nothing but war, who lust for power, who suck the lands dry to satisfy their cravings?"

Zedekiah answered as if from a trance as he continued to stare off in the direction of the army. "He returns and moves to the south, but ships from Kittim will come against him, and he shall lose heart and turn back." Zedekiah winced. "In his anger, he will assault the holy covenant. He will listen to those who forsake the covenant. They shall occupy and defile the temple and the fortress. They shall remove the burnt offering and set up an abomination that leaves the sanctuary desolate, until the end that God has decreed comes upon the desolator."

Ephraim and the others received Zedekiah's words, as they had so many others, as a gift from God, well worth the trouble of the journey to this place of revelation. "Blessed be our God forever and ever," exclaimed Ephraim. "He reveals mysteries and hidden wisdom."

"He sees what is in the darkness," added a companion, "what our eyes cannot penetrate, and reveals this to his holy ones!"

"Zedekiah, 'God is my righteousness,'" Ephraim said, placing his hand on the prophet's shoulder, "it is time to collect what God has given you and to send it to the faithful in Jerusalem, to prepare them and to encourage them."

Zedekiah nodded his assent, still staring off as the serpent's tail slithered beyond view.

Menelaus sat at his desk in the office within the high priestly palace, a map of the city spread out before him and stacks of property records to either side. Seraiah entered and stood before the desk.

"With your typical heavy-handedness," Seraiah began, "you alienate the Jewish population even more."

"What I have given them today is another dose of the antidote to their native superstition."

"The people did not take their medicine well, I think. I have to admit that I felt embarrassed for you, to have the king see so many residents voicing their dissent, let alone one of your own guards opposing you."

"It was a significant embarrassment, but not without its compensations. Today there are two hundred more soldiers at my disposal than there were yesterday—which is why I have asked you here, by the way, and not so I could explain myself to you."

He pushed the map forward on his desk toward Seraiah.

"We have two hundred soldiers to billet, and I want them concentrated in these two areas," Menelaus said, pointing to the north section of the old City of David and the area southwest of the gymnasium and senate house. "I want you to head an inquiry into which families in these areas are not loyal to our regime and to find some grounds to relocate enough of them to house our garrison. I've heard reports that some properties have already been left vacant, which should make your job easier."

"Menelaus," Seraiah said in a conciliatory tone, "we have always wanted the same things for Jerusalem, but we could have accomplished everything without the militarization of the city. Just as Jason would not move far enough because of his regard for the conservative Jewish population, you move too far, too fast, in utter disregard for the same people."

"I will continue to advance the interests of the non-Jewish citizens of Antioch-at-Jerusalem," Menelaus countered. "The Jewish citizens and residents will need to adapt." He eased more securely into his chair. "And Antiochus will see to it that they do."

9

Menelaus stood on the southern end of the Temple platform, looking out at the rising citadel before him. Throughout the summer and fall, every available artisan, stonemason, and worker had been diverted from other projects throughout the city to focus on the construction of the fortress—the "Akra," as the Syrian cohorts called it. The soldiers themselves worked on it in shifts as well. Children gathered to watch the bustle from a short distance, swearing that they could see the fortress grow in the space of each hour. Under the general umbrella of this project, Menelaus had also ordered what he referred to publicly only as "renovations" to the Temple. Stonemasons had worked throughout the summer extending the platform of the great altar of burnt offering on the side facing the Holy Places and erecting three stone tables on the extension facing the north, west, and south. Two small limestone buildings were under construction in the southern part of the Court of All Nations, one to the east, one to the west, and both facing north. He was careful to hide his purposes from all but his most trusted friends, since he had never discovered who in the senate had leaked word of his intention to take King Antiochus into the inner courts and, thus, had enabled the rallying of such a demonstration. He spoke merely of improving the facilities for worship and left the rest to speculation.

Beginning in the fall, however, Menelaus ordered the inner courts temporarily closed due to the ongoing renovations. A few carefully selected priests were allowed to enter the premises to fulfill their duties. Black smoke billowed up over the inner court twice each day, assuring the people that God still regularly received the sacrifices that betokened the people's loyalty to him and to the covenant. These priests still received animals brought by a dwindling number of the devout as offerings of thanksgiving or of purification, and transferred them from the Court of All Nations to the inner courts themselves.

For the most part, however, keeping the pious out of the Temple had not been a problem since Antiochus's visit. Many now regarded it as unclean, a place from which the Spirit of God had finally been driven. As a necessary part of the "renovations," a steady stream of Jewish and Gentile artisans and workers freely entered and exited the inner courts without discrimination. Members of the senate had worked up the nerve to challenge Menelaus about this practice on one occasion, but he had answered them easily: "Antiochus's safe passage through that space proves that God doesn't object to Gentiles entering that space; why, then, do you?"

Timarchos emerged from the Temple and stood beside Menelaus on the outer platform. "The master craftsman reports that the work is finished. He asks that you inspect the pieces before they are set in place on the altar."

Menelaus's attention was drawn, however, to a group of Jews in a portico of the market, on their knees and facing the Temple Mount.

"Look at them, Timarchos. Praying no doubt for God to 'purify' his temple and city." Menelaus's eyes narrowed in contempt. "Absurd, to regard one form of religion as pure and every other as pollution. That very idea—that's the pollution here, and I will cleanse Jerusalem of it at last."

He went into the Temple and crossed into the inner courts to inspect the work. Pulling back large canvas sheets that covered the carved limestone, he viewed the craftsmanship with satisfaction.

"Put these in place as we discussed," Menelaus ordered the foreman of the work crews. He looked at Timarchos with an air of triumph. "I believe we are just about ready for our grand reopening."

Menelaus closed the Temple to the public for ten days, beginning on the fifteenth day of Chislev, the month that begins the winter season, to complete his renovations. The smoke still ascended twice each day, but no other sacrifices were performed. A decree was read publically by heralds throughout the city: "A great service of thanksgiving and rededication will be held on the morning of the twenty-fifth day of Chislev celebrating the unity of the citizens and residents of Antioch-at-Jerusalem. All who love their king, who honor their fellow citizens, and who respect their civic duty are commanded to attend."

When the day arrived, the city gathered in the public spaces to the south of the Temple. The entire garrison was present, stationed all along the stairs and the ramp leading to the south entrance of the Temple complex. An overwhelming number of the foreign citizens and residents had turned out. The senators in their white Greek tunics could be seen gathered in a group at the foot of the ramp, to have the honor of being among the first to enter. Immediately behind them were a group of the young men of the *ephebate*, also clad in white tunics bound with a white cord at the waist.

Menelaus appeared on the Temple platform above the crowd, wearing priestly vestments, but not the traditional garb of the high priest with its twelve stones representing the tribes of God's particular people. Rather, he wore the long white linen tunic and scarlet-embroidered sash of a priest of Zeus.

"Citizens," he began, "residents, guests. We do not gather today as Jews here, Syrians there, and Greeks over there. We gather today as one body, one city, under the supreme God who watches over all. From today on, this is your Temple, a Temple for all the citizens and residents of Antioch-at-Jerusalem."

The soldiers banged their swords against their shields as many in the crowd below cheered and waved to Menelaus.

Eupolemus stood among the senators, listening to the roar about him as if in a dream. Alcimus and Amnon ben Imlah were standing near him, the former making a pantomime of clapping.

"What's he done in there?" Eupolemus could not help vocalizing the question, even though he knew neither of his companions could answer it.

"A better question: what are we doing here?" Amnon replied.

Menelaus extended his arms in a gesture of invitation. "Come and worship!"

The people began to move forward up the central stairs and ramps, first the soldiers and then the senators leading the way into the Temple precincts. Groups of foreign residents were singing songs, presumably hymns to their gods, in Syrian and in Greek as they processed.

As the senators entered the Court of All Nations, they were greeted by the sight of white-robed priests to the east and the west gathered by the limestone buildings, now fitted with altars of incense and altars for animal sacrifice. As Eupolemus passed these shrines, he was able to catch a glimpse through their open doorways of what was inside. Each structure now housed an idol—the one to the east a male figure holding a cup and a large bunch of grapes, the one to the west a female figure with one breast exposed. A number of barely-clad young women stood outside the entrance to the second shrine. Eupolemus closed his eyes in horror and folded his hands in front of his mouth, open as if to pray a prayer he did not know how to begin.

Menelaus continued to lead the procession of soldiers, senators, foreigners, and Jews into the inner courts. As those in front ascended the stairs to the innermost court, they looked upon the greatly enlarged altar of burnt offering. Amnon ben Imlah recoiled against the wall of the stairway and remained frozen there while others crowded by. He stared up at the two large limestone statues that now flanked the north and south sides of the raised platform, each with a marble altar in front of it. The west side, the one facing the sanctuary proper, had an identical altar, but no image. Alcimus forced himself to continue forward and to enter the altar area.

Eupolemus lagged behind. He noticed that the barricade that had marked the point beyond which non-Jews could not cross had been removed. Now he felt a surge of fear and adrenaline as he contemplated crossing the line that no longer existed. As he stepped into the first inner court, he saw Elam ben Jacob, a conservative senator who had been uncomfortable under Jason and nauseous under Menelaus, pushing against the stream to find his way out of the Temple. Tears were streaming down his face, his expression equal parts disgust, horror, and rage. Eupolemus crested the stairs leading to the innermost court in time to see Menelaus ascend the altar platform, attended by two associate priests.

"Zeus Olympios," Menelaus intoned, facing the image to the north with upraised arms; "Baal Shamen, lord of heaven," he continued, facing the image to the south; "God Most High," he said, facing the imageless altar to the west: "God of many peoples, known by many names, we gather before you as one people to honor you and invoke your blessing together upon our city."

Menelaus's associate priests threw handfuls of incense into the flaming tripods standing beside the altars of Zeus and Baal and then poured a small amount of wine into the fire as a libation. Several ephebes emerged from a side chamber, leading several animals toward and then up the ramp. The first pair of young men led a goat to the priest of Baal who muttered a prayer over its head before slitting its throat. The two ephebes heaved the twitching animal onto Baal's altar and held it as the priest disemboweled it and inspected its organs. Satisfied that the entrails were free of bad portents, he raised each organ in turn toward the image before taking a few steps to the great fire pit and tossing it onto the coals.

Eupolemus reversed his direction in horror, backing down the stairs through the crowd, each person behind him only too happy to move forward into the space he vacated. He caught up with Amnon, who had also begun to withdraw once he had recovered from his initial shock at seeing the idols of the Greek and Syrian deities in the one God's holiest courts. Together they moved into the western portico of the Court of All Nations and exited through a side gate.

Though they looked at each other several times as they made their way back down into the city street, neither could speak.

Above the festive sounds being made in the streets by the non-Jewish residents who had been unable to fit into the Temple complex, Eupolemus and Amnon heard the sound of Hebrew chanting and moved toward it. As they drew closer, they could begin to understand the words:

> *The Lord has rejected his altar and disowned his sanctuary;*
> *he has delivered it into the enemy's hands;*
> *his house was filled with a great clamor,*
> *as though on a festival day.*

They entered the market area, where they saw Eleazar, Yoshe, and many others of the faithful gathered together in the portico, kneeling, many with their hands raised toward the sanctuary and toward the God whom they believed to have abandoned it, chanting Jeremiah's laments. Eupolemus approached Eleazar and stood beside him. The older man looked up with a start and ceased chanting. Eupolemus helped him to his feet.

"Our inheritance has indeed been handed over to strangers, Master Eleazar," he said, quoting from Jeremiah himself.

Yoshe, Mattathias, Judah, and Binyamin also rose and moved deeper into the shelter of the portico with the two senators.

"It's unthinkable," Amnon said, almost afraid to give voice to what he saw. "Shrines to Dionysus and Cybele stand in the outer court with their own idols, priests, altars—and prostitutes!"

Eleazar shut his eyes in sorrow.

"He has built a second set of altars over the great altar of burnt offerings," Eupolemus added. "Images of Zeus and Baal were there, and sacrifices were made according to the Greek and Syrian custom."

Judah grasped his scalp with both hands. Mattathias pulled at the neckline of his garment until it ripped.

"That's all we saw before we just had to leave." Amnon looked hesitantly back up toward the Temple. "I feel unclean for having witnessed what I did."

"We will kill him for this," Yoshe declared, his eyes reflecting pure rage and hatred for Menelaus. "This blasphemer, this desecrator will not live!"

"It is the 'abomination of desolation' about which we were reading."

The voice was that of Joram ben Levi, a faithful Levite and Temple guard who had long since removed himself from the Temple. The others looked at him.

"In a book of visions from the prophet Daniel," he explained, "recently delivered to us by the faithful in Anathoth and given to them by Zedekiah."

"Why have we not heard of this book?" asked Eleazar.

"In God's providence, the words were made secret and sealed up until the time of the end—the time in which we are now living. The fall of Antiochus's empire and all its evils is growing close, as is the day that God will restore the kingdom to God's holy ones. This desecration is a sign."

"May it be so, Joram," said Yoshe. "Brothers, it is time to rise up against these evils, if only to acquit ourselves of guilt before God in the face of this unthinkable affront."

"I agree, Yoshe," Mattathias replied. "We need to start bringing our fighters-in-training back into the city and lodge them where we can."

"And we need to put the leaders of the cell groups throughout the city on alert," added Judah, "releasing them to take action."

"In the meantime," Eleazar suggested, "let all who are loyal to God and to the law boycott the Temple and separate themselves from the pollution. Let no faithful Jew lend legitimacy to what Menelaus has done by appearing in its precincts!"

"And when our brothers and sisters ask us how they can remain right with God without taking sacrifices to the Temple?" asked Amnon.

Eleazar recited something he had learned from Yehoshua ben Sira, words more apt now than ever before: "'The person who keeps the Torah makes his offering; the person who heeds the commandments sacrifices an offering of well-being. Return a kindness, and you make a grain offering; give alms, and you make a thanksgiving offering. Forsake wickedness, and you make an atonement offering.'"

The priest officiating at the altar of Zeus had completed his transfer of the organs of a heifer to the realm of the god, and Menelaus now offered the traditional morning sacrifice of a ram. Two Jewish priests assisted him in carving the animal on the middle table and tossing each part into the fire pit in the center of the platform.

"It may be that we have performed some aspect of these rites amiss," Menelaus declared, "in which case we offer to Zeus Olympios the traditional sacrifice for such unwitting transgressions."

Two ephebes now emerged from the side chamber. A murmur rippled through the crowd among the few Jewish citizens and residents who had remained as these acolytes came around from behind the altar, revealing that the animal they were escorting was a sow. Even Alcimus drew in his breath sharply as the animal was led up the ramp to the platform. The priest of Zeus slaughtered the animal, and the three officiants in cooperation tossed it whole onto the fire. The carcass crackled on the flames and its smoke billowed up. Alcimus caught a whiff of the scent, an odor that he knew from certain quarters in the streets of Jerusalem but that had never before penetrated these sacred spaces. He held his breath almost instinctively to prevent inhaling more of that polluting air. He closed his eyes and, after a moment, allowed himself to complete his cycle of inhalation and exhalation.

Menelaus extended his hands over the worshipers from the top of the platform.

"May Zeus Olympios bless and keep you. May Baal Shamen make his face to shine upon you and be favorable toward you. May God Most High smile over you and give you peace."

BOOK · III

The Sacrifice

In the 145th year of the kingdom of the Greeks (167 BCE) . . .

1

Meir and Tavitha walked together toward the market. The sun shone brightly upon the city, though it was still early enough that the air was cool. Meir had spent an hour inspecting the previous day's work of each of his apprentices and giving them instructions for the day ahead. He now had an hour of leisure to spend with his wife before he was due at the gymnasium to attend to his duties as trainer and tutor.

As they emerged from their street into the public spaces opposite the market, they saw a large group of Jews gathered in the open courtyard beneath the Temple, between the market and the imposing Akra. Meir estimated a group of more than a hundred people, some standing, most on their knees, almost all with arms outstretched toward heaven. It was now a familiar sight. Every morning, at the hour of the daily burnt offering, people who formerly gathered inside the Temple now gathered outside to offer prayer.

"Why do they all face away from their Temple?" Tavitha asked innocently. "I thought they believed that your God lived there?"

Meir had not yet grown used to the sight himself, so counterintuitive it was to the practice with which he had grown up, the practice assumed in the psalms he had prayed from childhood.

"They believe that God has withdrawn from his Holy Place because of its defilement and that they must look for him elsewhere for now."

Tavitha had never pressed questions of religion with Meir. Today, however, as she watched yet another demonstration of the people's fervency and unflagging commitment, she did. "But the God of Israel still has an altar in the Temple—the one with no image before it."

"The first of all the commands God gave to my people was that there should be no god worshiped alongside the One," Meir explained. "The second was that we should never make images for the purpose of worshiping the One or any other god. Now we violate both in God's own house." He looked up to the Temple, his face reflecting the sorrow deep in his heart. "God has surely turned his back on the Temple; why shouldn't they?"

They began to walk again toward the market.

"No other god ever took an interest in helping our people," Meir said after a moment's silence. "The One revealed himself to our great ancestor Abraham, delivered us when we were slaves in Egypt, and made of us a kingdom that once rivaled the great powers of its age. So I can understand how angry the One must be to look down upon such disloyalty and ingratitude in his own house."

As they neared the market, Meir caught sight of Binyamin and Eleazar praying in the southeast portico. He stopped for a moment and watched, long enough for Binyamin to become aware of his presence and look up. Immediately Meir was rewarded by Binyamin's usual flush of anger, but this time, instead of returning it with his own look of defiance, he offered a face of sympathetic regret. Binyamin's countenance visibly eased, and he nodded to his brother, who returned the gesture.

A clamor in front of the Temple immediately drew the attention of both brothers. Menelaus was approaching at the head of a procession, flanked by armed guards. Several priests in white robes and skullcaps were carrying a platform on which stood an image of Antiochus IV. Others were chanting hymns in Greek and swinging censers.

"It's the twenty-first," Tavitha said, referring to the monthly celebration of the king's birthday.

As Menelaus approached, the Jews who now found themselves in his path quickly withdrew into the crowd and found new stations for worship. The pious were careful to shift their bodies away from him, so that their worship could not be interpreted as a participation in any rite that Menelaus was about to perform. One shouted out, not toward Menelaus but clearly to him: "Misery to you, godless ones, who have trampled God's law! You will have children only for calamity and groaning! You will fall, and there will be joy; you will die, and inherit your curse!"

Another began chanting the 115th psalm, which those around him and soon the whole gathering took up.

Not to us, O Lord, not to us, but to your name give glory,
For the sake of your covenant faithfulness and love!
Why should the Gentiles scoff, "Where's their God now?"

If there had been any doubt that the choice of this psalm was motivated by protest, that doubt was removed as the statue of Antiochus, followed by the increasingly uneasy Greek and Syrian residents on their way to make sacrifices in the Temple for the king's health and success, passed through the area occupied by the pious.

Our God is in the heavens and takes whatever action he wishes.
But their idols are silver and gold, the product of human hands.
They have mouths, but can't speak; eyes, but can't see.
They have ears, but can't hear; noses, but can't smell.
They have hands, but can't touch; feet, but can't walk.
May all who make them and worship them become as they are!

Menelaus stopped for a moment to speak into the ear of Sarpedon, who was in charge of the armed escort detail, then began his forward motion again.

As the procession began up the ramp that would lead to the Temple platform, the guards held their places at the ramp's base. Once the procession had disappeared into the Temple courts, the guards turned to face the pious, most of whom were still on their knees in worship.

"Your hate-speech will no longer be tolerated," Sarpedon announced. "Slander against the gods of your fellow citizens will be punished for what it is—sacrilege and subversion of the peace and unity of Antioch-at-Jerusalem!"

Sarpedon caught the eye of one of the watch posted along the parapet of the Akra, held up two fingers, then curled them and brought his arm down. The watchman barked an order in Greek and, within seconds, archers lined the parapet with bows drawn against the crowd.

"Disperse!" Sarpedon commanded. At once his soldiers began to attack the closest worshipers, banging them across their faces with their shields, striking them with the hilts of their swords, and kicking them with their boots. The pious scrambled to retreat from the soldiers, daring to offer no resistance under the bows of the Akra. Those who rose tripped over others who were still kneeling in prayer, but continued to crawl away until they could recover their footing and run.

Sarpedon caught the eye of the man he knew as Hilaron at the edge of the crowd, protectively leading his wife out of the melee and he nodded a greeting. Once he saw they had turned the corner to safety, Sarpedon again signaled the watch commander with a gesture over his head. Again the latter barked an order in Greek and the archers began to let fly their arrows, carefully aimed toward the open spaces of ground or toward the columns of the portico, so as to increase the protesters' eagerness to clear the square. It was inevitable that a handful of the pious would step into the line of fire or that a soldier's blow would prove lethal. Within minutes the crowd had been dispersed and the soldiers began the task of removing the six or seven bodies of the fallen to the Akra, where they would be kept for a day or two to be claimed by their relations. Hymns to Zeus sung triumphantly in Greek descended from the Temple courts into the dead silence below.

A cloud of sorrow still hung over the pious three days after the attack. Binyamin had seen Eleazar safely home, then had spent the days working quietly in his shop, seeking solace for a while in the routine and in not thinking past the piece of metal before him. Ari worked alongside him. Binyamin had thought him a little distracted, catching him more than once looking over his shoulder at the sun as it rose higher into the sky or scanning the faces of passersby, but he had said nothing. After the violent attack on their fellows, anyone who was not displaying either anxiety or melancholy—to which Binyamin was himself more prone—was the one to worry about as far as Binyamin was concerned.

Ari stood up and walked toward the outer door of their shop, pausing there for a moment before stepping out into the street. Binyamin had looked up to see him standing in the doorway, but turned back to his work before Ari disappeared, missing his opportunity to ask him where he was going.

Ari walked up the street toward the city center, passing his friend Boaz, who sat in front of his home, along the way. After Ari passed, Boaz got up, walked a few paces up the street, then turned up a side alley. Fifty meters later, Ari passed the home of another friend, Yair, who emerged from his house and headed up the next side alley leading toward the western part of the city. Ari emerged at last at the north part of the old city and began to head west himself, past the gymnasium and the high priest's palace. He turned south down another main road just in time to see Joram ben Levi emerging from a side street into the same road. The target was just twenty paces farther down the street.

Joram pulled out a linen scarf, tied it around his face to cover his nose and mouth, and pulled the fold of his cloak over the top of his head. He allowed the hammer concealed in his sleeve to drop down into his hand. Ari quickly followed suit. As they descended upon their target, Ari saw four other figures emerge with their faces and heads covered, all wielding hammers. Together they burst into the shrine of Astarte that had been established within a converted shop and began to smash the cult statue, the small altar that stood before it, and any other paraphernalia they came across. A few devotees fled the building, fearing that the intruders would run out of objects upon which to vent their fury and turn on them instead.

The men completed their work in short order and emerged again into the street. One of them, whose voice Ari immediately recognized as that of Judah ben Mattathias, boldly shouted the words of the law above the panic in the street: "'This is how you shall deal with them: break down their altars, smash their pillars, cut down their sacred poles, and burn up their idols. For you are a people holy to the Lord your God!'"

While he was speaking, another member of his group drew out a flask filled with paint and a horsehair brush. He poured some paint on the brush and wrote three Hebrew letters on the outside wall of the shrine. As soon as he was finished, the six men ran off in different directions. Two braver Syrians tried to pursue two of the attackers, but all they found were linen scarves on the ground.

The young Syrian named Telamon ran past the market, across the open court, and up to the entrance of the Akra. Two soldiers stopped him from barging into the fortress itself.

"Please," he gasped, suddenly aware of how out of breath he was from his sprint, "I have to speak with the commander. There's been an attack."

The senior of the two guards nodded at the young man, put two fingers into his mouth, and whistled loudly toward the interior of the fortress. Another pair of guards appeared at once.

"Accompany this fellow to the commander," he ordered. "There's been another one!"

The soldiers led Telamon across the interior courtyard of the Akra into the administrative offices. They could hear a commotion as soon as they stepped into the hallway.

"Quiet!" the garrison commander, Philip, shouted from behind his desk. "I can't hear the man speak!"

Telamon listened as another citizen, who had apparently arrived just minutes earlier, described an attack on a shrine in the southeast district of the city very similar to the one that he himself had just witnessed in his own quarter. When he had finished, Philip looked up at Telamon, still standing in the doorway.

"And you—a similar story, I'm guessing?"

"Yes, sir," Telamon sputtered. "Five or six men, their faces covered, came out of nowhere and smashed up the shrine of Astarte in the western city—"

Philip help up his hand, indicating that Telamon did not need to continue.

"You're the fifth person to come into my office in the space of a half hour. These attacks have been taking place all over the city."

He rose from his chair and turned to Sarpedon.

"Divide your cohort into companies of twenty. Go with these citizens back to the sites of the attacks. Begin to make inquiries, see what you can find out."

Philip pointed to the soldiers who had escorted Telamon.

"You in the back—find the other cohort commanders and tell them to meet me in the courtyard." Philip looked at a group of senators who had witnessed several attacks in the more public spaces of the city and had come seeking his help. "We'll turn out the whole garrison and restore order before noon, gentlemen. Have no fear of that."

Philip strode from the room with Sarpedon at his heel.

"This was a highly coordinated attack, sir," Sarpedon observed. "From what the witnesses described, these were all different groups acting together in some kind of united effort."

"So it would seem, Captain. Today was just an initial announcement of their presence, I fear. Get me names."

Sarpedon quickly mustered his cohort and divided them into five details, sending one to each reported attack site. With his twenty, he himself accompanied Telamon. As they passed by the marketplace, Sarpedon paused to look at the altars in the porticoes there. Each had been smashed irreparably. A single word consisting of three Hebrew letters had been written in red paint over each one. He looked around for a moment and grabbed a local standing nearby and hauled him in front of the wall.

"I know you—you're a Jew," he roared. "What does this word mean?"

As the man looked at the graffito, he straightened up under Sarpedon's grip and, jerking his shoulder free of Sarpedon's hand, he replied, "The word is *ḥesed*, and it means 'loyalty to the covenant.'"

2

Jason crouched slightly, clutching a shield that was strapped to his left arm and brandishing an iron sword in his right, waiting for an opening. His opponent, a well-built Egyptian soldier who was similarly armed, moved from side to side, feigning to strike, testing Jason. Finally the Egyptian launched an attack to Jason's right shoulder. Jason blocked it with his shield while bearing his own sword down on the Egyptian's leg. The Egyptian lowered his shield enough to defeat Jason's thrust and brought his own sword around and under Jason's shield. In a single movement, Jason drew his sword back, up, and to the left, deflecting the blow, and brought his sword up against the Egyptian's throat. The latter froze as Jason held his blade there for a moment. The circle of soldiers around the pair began to applaud as their commander, a Greek from Egypt named Antigonos, stepped forward and playfully slapped the Egyptian on the back of the head.

"You're dead, soldier," he said gruffly. "Slain by a priest."

The soldiers laughed as Jason and his sparring partner nodded to each other in respect.

"Five years ago it would not have been so," Jason said to defuse any shame the soldier might have been feeling. "You have all been excellent teachers."

Since his arrival in the Transjordan, Jason had devoted himself to learning the art of war with the same studiousness he had shown toward Greek culture earlier in life. He was now just as comfortable in his leather armor as his linen tunic, as confident with a sword as with a stylus. Not only had he trained almost daily since his arrival, but he had accompanied Hyrcanus's soldiers on several skirmishes undertaken at Ptolemy's behest, pacifying Arabian nomad-warriors and even journeying once as far as Nubia to help protect Egypt's southern border. But he did it all with one goal in mind—to lead Hyrcanus's soldiers into Jerusalem and sink his sword into the breasts of Menelaus and Seraiah and anyone else who stood alongside them.

It was almost noon, and the air was hot and dry. Jason began to strip off the leather cuirass and head for the baths when one of Hyrcanus's servants came to summon both Jason and Antigonos to Hyrcanus's audience chamber.

"We've had an envoy from King Ptolemy this morning," Hyrcanus announced as the two entered the chamber. He smiled at Jason. "It would seem your opportunity has come at last."

"It's about time!" Jason exclaimed.

"I know that waiting has been difficult for you, but we are not our own masters," Hyrcanus said sympathetically. "And as these are technically not my soldiers . . ."

"I understand," Jason replied, shaking off his outburst.

Hyrcanus gestured for two slaves to bring wooden chairs for Jason and the commander before continuing.

"Antiochus is moving south through the coastal plains once again with a great army. It is clear that he is initiating a second attempt to take Egypt. As his actions represent a clear violation of their truce, King Ptolemy has authorized me to send our forces to seize Jerusalem. He hopes that the action will draw Antiochus away from Egypt to defend the territories at his rear."

"Are we on our own?" Antigonos inquired.

"King Ptolemy will not be sending reinforcements," Hyrcanus answered, "though our spies report that the city is still protected by only three hundred or so of Antiochus's soldiers."

"I have maintained contact with my own supporters in the city," Jason said. "We can count on help from inside."

"Speaking of those contacts," Hyrcanus added, "your usual messenger also arrived this morning. I've sent him to your wing of my palace to wait."

Jason nodded his acknowledgment.

Antigonos had been staring at the ground in front of him as if plotting the attack on the city. "The most important thing, it seems to me, will be not losing time and men trying to get into the city. We don't have enough of either for a siege."

"And there's no way we can move this many soldiers toward Jerusalem and not be noticed," Hyrcanus observed. "They will have the city locked down before our force can get close."

"I've been thinking about that," said Jason. "For years, in fact."

He knelt down on one knee and made the outline of a large circle over the ground with his finger. Indicating the major gates of the city along the circle, he continued: "Over the next few days, we send in soldiers in civilian dress through each of these gates, perhaps three or four per gate per day. They'll carry no weapons or armor, only construction tools and equipment in the event they're searched. My people will send servants to meet them at each gate, and greet them as masons and workers being hired for projects at their masters' homes. I've also had allies among the Temple guard and merchants stashing armor and weapons with my friends—a leather breastplate here, a sword there, over five years it adds up. Agathon will arrange everything from the inside."

He tapped the floor where the bottom of the circle would be.

"We can approach the city from the south and camp between these southern gates. Let all their scouts see us coming from that direction. They'll concentrate their forces in the southern part of the city to repel our assault. At a preset time, the soldiers we've sent in, accompanied by my allies on the inside, will seize and open the western gate while we charge around the southwest corner. Our cavalry will get there long before Menelaus's soldiers. It will take them almost as long to move through the city to reach the western gate as for our own infantry to arrive from outside. Our people inside will have to hold them off for a matter of minutes at most while our forces enter."

Antigonos leaned back in his chair and looked at Hyrcanus. "It's a good plan." He turned, nodding his approval to Jason. "A good plan."

Hyrcanus remained quiet for a moment, impressed with his guest's transformation from priest to military strategist. "You do realize, however, that Antiochus will come against you in force."

"Antiochus is a practical man," Jason said. "I will make peace with him before he ever arrives at Jerusalem. Once Menelaus is dead, he'll come to terms with me, and Jerusalem will be his secure possession once again. And you will have access to your funds in the Temple and succeed to your brothers' estates."

Hyrcanus raised an eyebrow and smiled slightly at the thought. If Jason had waited five years for his revenge, Hyrcanus had waited thirty. How different life would have been for him had the fifth Ptolemy not lost to the third Antiochus at Paneas, and Jerusalem had remained under his own master's control!

"Antigonos, the details are yours to work out," Hyrcanus said as he rose from his chair. "Perhaps Jason's visitor can escort the first 'workmen' back toward Jerusalem."

Jason and the commander rose and nodded their assent to put the plans in play. Jason, still grimy from the morning's workout with the soldiers, went to the baths before returning to his chambers. One of Hyrcanus's slaves had brought a tray with meats, bread, and fruit for his lunch. As he sat down to eat, the messenger from Jerusalem appeared at his open door.

"Menes," Jason smiled, "welcome. Have you eaten?"

"Lord Jason," he replied, "I have been looked after, thank you."

"Sit," Jason said, gesturing to a chair across from him.

The slave was clearly uncomfortable, not so much because of Jason's hospitality but because of his uncommonly good spirits.

"What's wrong, Menes? What could possibly be wrong, today of all days?"

"Lord Jason," he began, finding it difficult to look into his eyes. "I bear difficult news."

Jason adjusted his demeanor accordingly in anticipation.

"There's no easy way to say it, master. Your brother is dead."

Menes watched the color and energy drain from Jason's face.

"Apparently he could no longer sit by in Egypt with all that Menelaus was doing to the Temple and to your more devout countrymen. He went to Antioch to denounce Menelaus and to present his case before the king on behalf of his people before the situation erupted into open bloodshed.

"Well, Antiochus was entirely concerned with his military plans at this point and was in no rush to see Honiah. There was enough time for Menelaus to get wind of this, to send bribes to this and that person in Antioch to make sure that Honiah would never get in to see the king, and to accuse Honiah himself of acting on Ptolemy's behalf to divert Antiochus's eyes from Egypt and disrupt a stable city in Antiochus's southern frontiers."

Menes looked down at the ground again before continuing with the worst. "So Antiochus moved south without listening to Honiah, and Menelaus used one more bribe to get a man named Andronicus, one of Antiochus's captains of the guard, to assassinate your brother."

Jason closed his eyes tightly and turned his head away. He saw Honiah as he had sat behind his desk so many years ago, refusing to give a centimeter. *Would either one of us have been so inflexible had we foreseen what was to come?* He forced his grief to retreat to the back corners of his mind and opened his eyes once again.

"The time has come for us, Menes, to strike back into the hearts of our enemies. The commander of the garrison here has a mission for you to carry out and instructions for you to take back to your master and my friend, Agathon. Tell him I will see him in Jerusalem soon."

Jason rose, nodded to Menes, and walked to the window as the latter bowed and left to find Antigonos and to carry out whatever was laid upon him. Jason looked off to the northwest, toward Jerusalem. He saw in his mind's eye what had been described to him: the desecrated Temple, the Akra, and the pious— who could once count on him for at least a modicum of protection for their sentiments—exposed to everything hateful. He felt Honiah's spirit looking down upon him, reproaching him for taking matters into his own hands only to lose control over them. It was all on him now to bring the situation back to center, and not for his sake only.

He could not resist the impulse to pray.

Antiochus sat on a portable throne in his war tent near the shore east of Alexandria. Within a month of his first encounter with Ptolemy's border troops, he had pushed through to the capital itself. A breeze had been blowing in from the northwest late into the afternoon, adding to Antiochus's pleasure as he listened to the reports of his generals over the not-so-distant din of saws and hammers constructing the siege towers that would soon hand Alexandria over to his control. Apollonios, the senior general, was in possession of the latest news from the island of Cyprus, a part of Ptolemy's empire that was insultingly closer to Syria than to Egypt.

"Our fleet admiral reports that he is getting the better of Ptolemy's ships south of the island and has been able to land significant ground troops, who are securing the east and heading toward Paphos. If the Egyptian fleet remains there to fight, we will destroy them. If Ptolemy should recall them to aid him here, we can finish landing our troops at the capital, secure Cyprus, and still pursue and overtake them."

"Meanwhile," added Bacchides, a battle-scarred veteran who thought it best to command from the front lines, "the few ships we have supporting us here have proven able to drive off a good many of the boats attempting to supply Alexandria. A decisive victory in Cyprus will free our fleet to set up a more effective blockade. Our cohorts to the west and south of the city remain in complete control of the land supply routes."

"I shall be disappointed if we need to rely on starvation to give us this city," said Antiochus, goading his officers.

Nicanor, a talented strategist who had risen to the rank of general well below the typical age, was in charge of the siege proper. "By all accounts, starvation is at least six months away, Highness," he said. "You shall have victory in one."

Antiochus smiled at Nicanor's willingness to take the bait and impress his king.

"The siege towers will be completed in a matter of weeks. It would be done already if there were decent trees in this country, but my messengers report that the last transport of lumber from Syria is arriving within days."

Nicanor stepped forward to the rough model of the city on the table in the war council tent. "Two rows of catapults stand ready to bombard a space of a hundred meters surrounding the gate, leaving spaces at these four points for the advance of the towers. The prisoners of war from Pelusium have been set to work quarrying and transporting the stones that will unleash Hades upon Alexandria's eastern defenses while we make our move."

Nicanor walked to the side of the table representing the east and extended his hands to their full breadth behind the model towers as if preparing to push them into place. "Gathering the projectiles is what's going to take the most time. We will need to keep our forty catapults firing almost constantly, alternating between the two rows as fast as we can reload them so as not to give Ptolemy's men the chance to breathe, let alone get off any shots at us. The longer we can pound the parapet and the city beneath before we begin, the better for our men—I'd allow a full hour, about 480 stones. The better part of an hour to get the towers against the wall, fifteen minutes for our archers atop them to thin remaining resistance, fifteen minutes for the four cohorts to move up the tower and rappel down the inside, fifteen to thirty minutes for them to secure and open the gate. I figure that's another 960 stones, all cut to particular weights to cover different distances, and all roughly rounded to do the most damage upon landing."

He took a step back, still looking at the model as if assessing the plan for flaws and finding none. "After that, it's up to Bacchides's ground troops."

"Just get those towers finished before my men forget that they're soldiers, not carpenters," Bacchides huffed.

"I'll show you how to hammer out the iron plating, if you'd like to speed things up, old man," Nicanor retorted with a wry smirk.

Antiochus sat back in his chair, satisfied that his generals were not going to disappoint. Apollonios began to report about supplies in hand and plans to requisition more, matters about which Antiochus was content to half-hear as he allowed his gaze to wander about the camp and off toward the sea. A small ship with a sail bearing thick red-and-white stripes caught his eye. Apollonios noticed the king's new focus, stopped speaking, and turned around himself.

"It's a Roman galley, a light ship, one bank of oars on either side," he said.

The king squinted in the direction of the ship with his head cocked slightly, as if trying to discern its purpose by looking harder, and then rose and began to walk with his bodyguard toward the makeshift landings that his soldiers had constructed. He stepped off the road of crushed stone into the sand by the sea. A figure clad in the distinctive white toga with the broad purple band that denoted senatorial rank disembarked and began to walk up the dock toward the shore, flanked by two fully armed soldiers on escort detail. Antiochus continued to walk toward the dock, westward now into the descending sun, which made it difficult for him to make out their features until they were within fifty paces. When at last the figure emerged from the sun's cloak, Antiochus recognized the face of Pompilius Laenas. The features had aged twenty years, but it was unmistakably Laenas.

As Antiochus closed the distance he was transported to the Eternal City, his mind suddenly far from the concerns of the siege of Alexandria and giddy with the flood of forgotten memories of his escapades with Laenas's sons as a young man in Rome—and his flirtations with one of his daughters. He remembered how Laenas had all but adopted him into his family during his years living in Rome as part of his father's guarantee of obedience to Rome's wishes. Antiochus's eyes brightened and his mouth widened into a smile. He reached out his hand to greet Laenas, surprised when it closed upon something cold and cylindrical rather than warm flesh. It was a scroll enclosed in a diplomatic case carved from ivory, marked with the seal of the Roman consul. Antiochus looked up from the scroll to Laenas's face, searching his expression for an explanation. The latter never broke into a smile, but not from ill feelings toward his old acquaintance. Antiochus saw rather the determination of a man resigned to his commission, with a hint of distress that it had to be his task.

"You and your forces are required to quit Egypt."

Antiochus could not master the absurdity. Encountering Laenas here out of nowhere—without the old senator's betraying any sign that Antiochus had eaten a hundred meals at Laenas's table. Being ordered by a Western power with no business interfering in his conquest of Egypt to pack it in and go home like a child being sent to his room. He surprised even himself when he burst out into a brief but boisterous chortle.

Half-hoping Laenas would return the laugh and give up the charade, half-afraid that Laenas was in fact dead serious, he said simply, "You're joking, right?"

"This is the will of the Senate and People of Rome."

The solemn, formulaic reply, uttered on so many similar shores by similar envoys to—Antiochus hated to admit it and hated Rome for reminding him at this moment—similar minor kings living in the lengthening shadows of Rome, sent a deadening wave of dismay through his heart. As the implications of the moment bore down upon him, Antiochus heard his own blood pounding in his ears and thought for a moment about killing this Roman—for it was no longer Laenas who stood before him, but Rome. He would take Alexandria and mobilize for all-out war against Rome itself, wiping out the memory of his father's defeat at Apamea decades ago.

But then he saw Rome's certainty of its own power, represented in sending a mere three men to stop an army. He saw, in his mind's eye, his father cowering at the "peace" of Apamea. He saw the grandeur and might of Rome as he first experienced it as a boy taken as a hostage to ensure his father's support of that peace. All life drained from his face as the inevitable defeat of his dream of reuniting Alexander's territories under one rule, the stillbirth of the renewed Greek empire, sank into his consciousness. *This is how the dream dies? With a withered Roman issuing a command?*

Antiochus tried to reaffirm his own stature and gravity. "I'll consider it in consultation with my advisors," he pronounced weightily.

Laenas touched the sand in front of Antiochus with the thin rod that was the emblem of his office as *lictor* in Rome. He walked around the king, drawing the circumference of a circle.

"Consider it here."

Antiochus drew in his breath as he felt the heat beneath his cheeks. *Unyielding, the power of Rome. Insensitive to any attempt to save face.* He exhaled with resignation.

"It will be our pleasure to honor the request of the Senate."

Relief swept across Laenas's face as his countenance and posture relaxed slightly, a wave of relief that reached Antiochus as well, despite the death of his dream on that shore when it had been within his very grasp. Laenus extended his hand at last, and Antiochus received the gesture in a warm clasp. Business was done; he was no longer facing the grim-faced envoy of the implacable power to the west, but his old friend.

Laenas gestured toward Antiochus's encampment and the two began to walk back together in that direction, followed by their respective bodyguards.

"You have to understand," Laenas explained. "If Rome allowed you to take Egypt, you would suddenly look like a major competitor in the Mediterranean—and therefore a threat. Rome doesn't want to have to treat you like a threat."

Antiochus understood exactly what that would mean.

Laenas stopped walking and turned to Antiochus, speaking in hushed tones to give his words added gravity.

"There are people in the Senate—I'm not going to hide it from you—who wanted to allow events to unfold in precisely that way. With you taking Egypt and spread so thin, they saw an opportunity to secure the entire Mediterranean for Rome in an all-out war with you."

They began walking again, and Laenas continued in his normal speaking voice. "As for Palestine, well, Ptolemy claims it should be returned to him, but I've convinced the Senate that your claim is stronger, and that the first Ptolemy ought to have ceded the region to your glorious ancestor, the first Seleucus, over a hundred years ago. The price he pays for keeping you out of Egypt is that Ptolemy will not move on Palestine again."

They arrived at the pavilion, and an attendant brought each of them a cup of wine mixed with water. Laenas sat down opposite the king. He leaned forward slightly in his chair, as if to press his words into Antiochus's consciousness.

"There is no room for your ambitions in the west, Antiochus," Laenas said earnestly. "A lesson, I might add, that you should have learned from your father. But the East? Rome doesn't much care what happens there. It's not nearly as well developed as Asia Minor or Egypt, but you may recall that it was sufficient to hold Alexander's attention."

Antiochus began to look a little less sullen.

"And for your cooperation today," Laenas continued, "Rome will grant you amnesty from one-half your annual tribute for the next five years."

Antiochus raised his head higher upon hearing this.

"As long as you refrain from moving against Ptolemy again, that is," Laenas added.

"Keep my hands off Egypt and I get to keep my money."

Laenas smiled and leaned back in his chair. "Rome may take away with one hand, but it knows how to give with the other. Build your empire, my old friend. Build it up from the ground where someone else hasn't already planted. That's what made Alexander great; that's what will make your memory great as well."

The king was still angry, but he realized that Laenas had taken some pains to work out a deal in the Senate on his behalf. And he had already been thinking about expanding his eastern frontier. He managed a half-hearted smile.

"I certainly did not see the day ending this way when I woke up this morning," he said, "but since you've come all this way I trust you will join me and my generals at our table this evening."

"We can talk of old times in Rome," said the envoy.

"And you can tell me what your sons have been up to for the last two decades."

Early the following morning, Antiochus's generals began to supervise the breaking up of the camp. Nicanor had been so looking forward to seeing his strategy put into play that he seemed more sullen and irritable than even Antiochus as he barked his orders to his lieutenants concerning the dismantling of the catapults for transport and recovery of what resources could be taken from the nearly completed siege towers. Bacchides was preparing to embark in a heavy war galley for Cyprus, where he would declare a cessation of hostilities and arrange for the orderly withdrawal of Antiochus's troops. Laenas had launched off in his galley at first light, heading back to the warship anchored outside the harbor that would take him back to Italy. Antiochus himself had slept in and was only now being roused by attendants who had taken a basin of fresh water and a breakfast tray in to the monarch's tent.

With the entire camp turning itself inside out to return north, the arrival of three messengers galloping in at full speed on horseback occasioned little notice. The lead rider jumped off his horse and half-ran, half-stumbled to the war counsel pavilion. He was surprised to find it unattended. He leaned against the table for a moment, closing his eyes and taking deep breaths to recover his senses after riding through the night. Noticing a pitcher of water on the table, he reached for it, gulped down several mouthfuls as he walked back outside the pavilion, and poured the remainder over his head.

He began to take stock of what was happening in the camp around him. Scanning the faces, he found Nicanor and set off in his direction.

"General, sir," he said as he caught up with him.

"What is it, soldier?" Nicanor did not immediately recognize that this man was not from among the troops pressing the assault on Alexandria.

"I bring urgent news from Jerusalem," he replied. "I must convey my message to his majesty."

Nicanor began to pick up on the gravity of the man's demeanor and his evident anxiety about the information he carried.

"Come with me," the general said. "We'll see the king together."

As they approached the king's tent, Nicanor barked at one of the guards at the entrance.

"Has the king awakened?"

"Yes, sir," the guard replied, "though only recently."

Nicanor showed no signs of slowing his approach, so the guard merely stepped out of the way—a courtesy extended only to the three generals. The messenger was swept along in Nicanor's wake.

"Majesty," Nicanor said simply.

The king lay stretched out on his back, one arm folded over his eyes. He had—quite intentionally—drunk to excess the night before.

"Nicanor," Antiochus grunted.

"Sire, a messenger has arrived with news from Jerusalem."

"My head is the size of Jerusalem," Antiochus replied wearily. "Can't it wait?"

Nicanor studied the messenger's face for a moment.

"I don't think so, sire."

"Very well, then," Antiochus said as he pushed himself up into a sitting position against the headboard of his couch. He opened his eyes briefly to reach for the cup of new wine on his breakfast tray, gesturing with his other arm to the messenger before leaning his head back and shutting out the daylight once again.

"Your Majesty," the messenger began, "there's been a revolt in Jerusalem."

Antiochus's eyes snapped open.

"Several days ago, Jason appeared at the head of an army of about four hundred men. The city was locked down, but he had help from the inside. He entered through the western gate and has been wreaking havoc on the cohorts there. There have been heavy losses on both sides—I'd say about half our garrison, including Philip himself, who fell on the second day of fighting. The rest of our force and the senate were taking refuge in the Akra. Menelaus dispatched five of us to seek help while we could still get word out of the city. Three of us made it, sire."

Antiochus pressed his palms into his temples, trying to stop the pounding that this news had only exacerbated.

"Where did Jason get an army?"

Antiochus looked down and snorted an answer to his own question. "Damn you, Ptolemy, trying to undermine my empire even while I'm camped out at your very door."

He swung around on his bed and planted his feet on the floor. He started to stand, but his head convinced him to take things more slowly.

"Nicanor, find Apollonios. Tell him I want two hundred cavalry and two thousand infantry ready to march for Jerusalem in the morning. Send out an advance party yet today to begin to set up supply lines to our projected campsites along the coastal route."

He drained the cup of new wine and sent the metal vessel clattering across the plank-wood floor.

"Send ten of your catapults and two of your siege towers as soon as you can, in case the city is not impressed with the size of our force."

"I'll bring them up personally, sire," volunteered Nicanor.

"No, general, I want you here to supervise the withdrawal of our main force. I'm not going to leave our most valuable asset to underlings."

"Yes, Majesty," Nicanor replied, not hiding his disappointment to be deprived yet again.

"Don't be so sour, Nicanor," Antiochus chided. "There are plenty of strongholds to be besieged among the Parthians to the east and beyond, once we take care of this business in Judea."

3

Jason sat on the edge of his bed in the high priestly palace. The fact that it was once again his bed eased his mind of the pain being inflicted by the servant changing the dressing on his left arm, which had sustained a blow during the second day of fighting. It did not deter him, however, from returning to the fray by the fourth day of fighting. A glancing blow to his right thigh on the fifth day, which his attendant had already cleaned and re-dressed, convinced him to leave the fighting thenceforth to the professionals. He would have suspected Antigonos's soldiers of taking it easy on him during all those years of training, had he not sent nine of Menelaus's soldiers to Hades himself.

He heard someone approaching in the hallway outside his chamber.

"Now you're a soldier! Before you were just playing. How are your wounds?"

Jason smirked at Antigonos's greeting, until the servant's ministrations turned it into a wince. "The wounds aren't as bad as their treatment," he said, scowling at the servant.

Antigonos grunted his sympathies.

"I've just returned from visiting the battle lines around the Akra. Menelaus and his soldiers have locked it down pretty well, but we've taken up positions on every side. No one will get out without a fight. I've stationed archers on the Temple fortifications to pick off anyone inside the fortress careless enough to show a few centimeters of flesh."

Jason nodded his appreciation for his commander's preparations. "We can't afford to wait long enough to starve them out. Antiochus will no doubt have already heard about what's happened here and will at the very least send a portion of his forces to retake the city."

"I know," Antigonos said. "We'll have to take the citadel with a frontal assault. I've set the carpenters and mason in the gymnasium to work on my battering ram, as well as some oversized shields to protect the men operating the ram from Menelaus's archers. Tomorrow, I trust, we'll finish this."

Around noon, far from Jason's palace, a number of men started to gather in the shade of the portico beside the Pool of Siloam in the southernmost part of the city. Ari and his friends, Boaz and Yair, had spent the entire morning skirting about the city, getting word to one or another person about the time and place. It had been the first day since Jason's advance that it was remotely easy to move about the streets again, but with all the action now focused in the city's center—and Menelaus and his party locked down in the Akra—there was a strange feeling of freedom in the southern quarter.

Yoshe and Mattathias looked around at the fifteen or so men that had gathered so far and then at each other, agreeing that it was time to begin.

"It's clear that God's hand is at work in these events, brothers," Mattathias began, "but difficult to discern where he is leading us and how to cooperate. But none of us can deny that there is an opportunity."

"I know some of us have already taken advantage of the situation," observed Eupolemus. "A number of bodies have turned up in places where there wasn't actually any fighting."

Yoshe snorted and crossed his arms.

"Menelaus's own brother, Lysimachus, was found in an alley with his throat slit," Eupolemus continued.

"Let's make that the start of a family reunion," Joram suggested, eliciting grim chortles around the circle.

"Antiochus is still king," said Eupolemus. "Let those of us who have been members of the senate take this opportunity to go to him. We can petition him to restore us to our former status and to return to the protections and privileges his father legally gave us. If anything, Jason's attack and Menelaus's incompetence will both argue in our favor."

"Antiochus is dead!" Joram exclaimed. "Why else would Jason dare to attack Menelaus now?"

"We've had no such news from the Egyptian front," Eupolemus cautioned. "We should be mindful of how he would view whatever actions we take."

"We should be mindful of how God will view our actions," Mattathias interjected. "What would *he* have us do?"

"Brothers," Eupolemus urged, "if you will not appeal to Antiochus, then our best course of action is to cooperate with Jason now to destroy Menelaus. Let's help him take the Akra, and then strike terms with Jason for the reinstatement of the Torah as the constitution of the land."

"Fight to help that traitor to his brother and to the covenant?" Yoshe asked incredulously. "No, I'll never fight alongside that son of Satan." A murmur of agreement rippled through the group.

"Jason never touched the Temple," Eupolemus said. "To my knowledge, he never personally violated the prohibitions against idolatry, forbidden foods, or many other practices of our people. I'm sure that he hates what has happened here as much as any of us."

"Have you forgotten, Eupolemus, that Jason is the one who started us down this path?" Yoshe roared. "He's the one who made a covenant with the Gentiles to change our very constitution."

"Honiah's dead now because of him," Joram added.

"Let's put the blame where it belongs," Amnon said. "Menelaus is the one who got Honiah killed."

"But Jason is the one who put him in harm's way to begin with," Judah countered.

"This is our chance to be rid of both apostate high priests once and for all," Joram declared.

"The time to take back our city has come," Yoshe said in agreement, "now that these two giants have worn each other down to size."

"If that's to be the way of it," Amnon ben Imlah said, "we should at least wait until Jason and his forces have done all the damage they can to Menelaus and his troops."

"They've done enough," said Hanan, the former Temple guard whom Mattathias had brought back into the city. "We can take it from here. Jason's been a great help. Now let's show the sinner out—that, or send him to hell!"

"I'm inclined to agree with these brothers," said Judah. "Jason is clearly the lesser of two evils and might even look attractive in hindsight, but he's still an evil. We should not forget that."

"Exactly right, Judah," said Yoshe. "Let's not settle for one high priest just because he won't abuse God's covenant as much as the other."

A consensus was emerging around the circle. Eupolemus and Amnon looked at each other, but neither spoke further in favor of compromise.

"It's settled, then!" Yoshe declared. "We have hundreds in our networks throughout the city. We'll gather them together, fall upon Jason's soldiers, and take over the siege of the Akra."

"I appreciate your zeal, Yoshe," Mattathias interjected, "but we need an actual plan."

"Brothers," Judah offered, "we are growing in number, but our strength thus far has been in stealth, unpredictability, and suddenness. We should build now on those strengths."

Judah exuded such clarity of vision that even Yoshe was content to listen.

"Simply, we need to find out where their strongest forces are concentrated, and then attack them everywhere else, preferably at multiple points at the same time. When they reposition themselves, we attack at the unexpected, under-manned points again, and so on until we've worn them down."

"If we go up against their main force," Mattathias said in support, "we'll be lucky to trade man for man. This way, we might get five, or even ten of theirs for every one of ours."

The others nodded their assent to the strategy. Judah leaned in and spoke more quietly. "I've got some ideas about where to start."

The heavy footfall of military sandals upon the polished limestone floor of the high priestly palace echoed through its dark corridors as a soldier, led by a servant with a lamp, made his way to the audience hall that had been converted into officers' barracks for Antigonos and his lieutenants. The soldier stood over his commander's cot.

"Sir, wake up, sir."

Antigonos stirred, then snapped into a sitting position. "What is it, man?"

"Sir, there's been an attack on some of our men in the gymnasium," the soldier exclaimed between labored breaths. "The soldiers on watch were overpowered first. Then the others' throats were slit or their heads bashed with hammers as they slept."

"How many?"

"A dozen, sir."

Antigonos rose up wearily to his feet as Jason came limping down the corridor from his bedroom.

"What's happened?" he asked

"An attack on our men in the gymnasium," Antigonos said.

Before Jason could make further inquiry, both men were distracted by a commotion at the front door and the sound of other soldiers running into the hall.

"Commander," one said as he leaned over with his hands on his thighs attempting to catch his breath. "The men on watch across from the southeast and southwest corners of the Akra. When they didn't send in to report at the beginning of the third watch, we went to check in with them. They're dead, sir, all of them!"

Antigonos looked up at him in disbelief.

"Menelaus's soldiers?" asked Jason.

"No," responded the soldier. "No, none of them could have made it out of the Akra without being noticed by someone, even if they scaled down the walls. These attacks came from somewhere else."

"Locals," Jason surmised, remembering the hostility that some had harbored against him.

"Well-organized locals, at that," added Antigonos

"Any leads as to who?"

"No one saw anything," said the solider, "at least no one that was left alive. There were no bodies left for us to identify except those of our own men. They just came out of the night and evaporated back into it."

Antigonos thought about the attacks, three different ones coordinated to happen at the same time.

"I think they mean to keep doing it," he concluded. "Rouse the men. We need to be on our guard tonight."

The remainder of the night passed without incident, though neither Jason nor Antigonos slept again. The soldiers were on edge, every second man being ordered to keep alert while his comrade tried to catch at least a little sleep. Antigonos strapped on his armor before first light and went with an escort of a dozen soldiers to the forward command post he had set up behind the front portico of the market. He sent another ten men to the gymnasium to fetch the battering ram and bring it on a large cart to the market place. Ten men would operate the ram, fourteen more would bear two shields each, to protect themselves and to cover the rammers. Archers would keep up a steady fire at the Akra's parapet to discourage any attacks from above their heads.

He watched from his station for an hour as the sun began to rise, focusing not on the Akra, but searching the periphery of the large courtyard, peering down into the side streets, looking for any sign of the local resistance. At last the soldiers had been mustered for duty and those on the ram detail stood waiting.

"Where is my battering ram?" Antigonos barked.

An adjutant signaled to four soldiers to come with him as he ran off in the direction of the gymnasium.

Antigonos remained seated, tapping the table with his left index finger. Jason arrived at the command post, limping up the three steps with some difficulty. Antigonos looked up to acknowledge him, returned his gaze to the space before him, and suddenly made a connection. He leaped up, sending his chair tipping over behind him, and walked out to the twenty-four soldiers allocated to the ram.

"With me," he ordered simply, and they fell in line before him as he half-ran after his adjutant. He caught up with him and his escort in the eastern portico of the gymnasium, bending over the bodies of ten soldiers, trying to staunch the flow of blood in the two or three who were still showing signs of life.

"Damn these rebels to Hades!" Antigonos shouted. "You twelve, get to the palace and get these men some help. And be careful! Get out your swords, be ready for anything." He surveyed the carnage again and suddenly realized what was missing.

"Where's the ram?"

Once the surviving wounded had been taken back to the palace, Antigonos returned with his soldiers to the market. He was not prepared to be besieged himself—and that when he was stuck out in the open while pressing a siege against the Akra. Clearly the local rebels intended to take his forces down by tens rather than fight out in the open like men. It was cowardly, in his opinion, but it would be effective, since he had no reserves upon which to call.

He began to confer with his lieutenants about how to redeploy their dwindling forces to maximize their defensive capacity while building a new ram when a soldier rode up to the command post from the west, leaped off his mount, and ran to the commander.

"Sir, our scouts have reported that Antiochus's forces are advancing on Jerusalem, about two thousand men plus cavalry. They should be here before nightfall."

Antigonos looked through the portico at the still-solid gate of the Akra and slammed his fist on the table.

"Well we're not getting in there before then," he announced with a curse.

"We can close and barricade the city gates," Jason said. "That will buy us weeks. My father fortified the walls substantially."

"We didn't come with supplies to withstand a siege, Jason," said Antigonos. "Menelaus didn't have time or warning to lay in stores before our advance that we could take advantage of. We don't have weeks. And your own countrymen here seem bent on killing us before we have the chance to get into the Akra."

"Surely," Jason said tentatively, "you're not thinking of giving up."

"It would be different, Jason, if we had killed Menelaus early on, or if we had the time to starve him out. But while we're out here and he's still breathing and safe in that fortress, Antiochus will simply slaughter us and liberate his duly appointed deputy."

Jason shook his head incredulously from side to side, unable to process the turn of events.

"Our primary mission has been accomplished—Antiochus has withdrawn from Egypt to deal with us. No need to stick around now to be slaughtered. I'm sorry, Jason, truly, but we have to go."

Antigonos quickly devised an exit strategy, withdrawing through the west gate and turning immediately south. His archers protected their rear flank as they left the market and processed down the main westward thoroughfare, in case either the local resistance fighters or Menelaus were disposed to attack from the rear.

As their retreat became known, pockets of cheers rose up throughout the city. The resistance groups, along with citizens who were now emboldened by the sight of one enemy leaving, began to stream into the market and around the Akra, brandishing knives, hammers, and swords. Some began to chant:

Sing to Adonai *a new song because he has done wonderful things!*
His own strong hand and his own holy arm have won the victory!

Mattathias and Judah made their way warily through the crowd as if the celebratory mood were a dangerous intoxicant and found Yoshe seated at the table that Antigonos had left abandoned in the market.

"One night of terror, Judah," Yoshe declared, "one night and they scamper off like frightened children!"

"We didn't drive them off," Mattathias said. "We scored a few good hits, but not nearly enough to have weakened their resolve like this."

"Do you not remember what Elisha showed his servant when the godless camped against him?" Yoshe asked, heady with victory. "It is as though God's armies fight with us and have frightened them off from the skies."

"Antiochus must be close," Judah surmised. "It's the only explanation for the haste of their withdrawal."

"You do not give yourselves—or God—enough credit!" said Joram.

"Their retreat is a sign that God is with us," declared Yoshe. "If Antiochus comes, we will lock down the city, purge it of its defilements, and wait for God's deliverance. In the meanwhile," he said, pointing to the battering ram sitting on the ground beside his table, "we can take action against the arch-defiler in the Akra."

He rose from the table, walked through the portico, and shouted up toward the Akra: "'Rebels and sinners shall be destroyed together; those who forsake Adonai shall be consumed.'"

First only those nearest him in the crowd, then an increasing number, took up the promise of Isaiah as an invocation against the apostates and the foreign soldiers sequestered in their fortress, as if they could make its walls collapse merely with the pounding rhythms of their incantations.

Rebels and sinners shall be destroyed together;
those who forsake Adonai *shall be consumed.*

Eupolemus approached Mattathias and Judah. "I was able to learn from one of Jason's friends in the city that Antiochus is indeed bearing down on us with a large force, perhaps even before the day is over. You have to convince Yoshe and the others not to resist him."

Mattathias and Judah looked at each other, trying to determine where their course should lie.

"If we shut the gates against Antiochus," Eupolemus insisted, "we become the rebels fighting against him and his deputy. If we let him in, we're the loyal subjects who drove off the rebel Jason—and who might be in a position to get some concessions from him against Menelaus."

Yoshe was walking back toward the table now. He did not need to hear Eupolemus's words to know what he was urging.

"No! We will not allow Antiochus to come in here and reinstate Menelaus. We have been faithful to God, and we are fighting in God's cause. 'Though an army encamp against me, still I will not cower!'"

"Are you so sure of yourself that you're willing to bring death down on the heads of all the people around you?" Eupolemus challenged. "Would you risk the lives of hundreds, even thousands of the innocent residents here who will surely get caught up in the slaughter?"

Yoshe looked at the fighters gathered around the portico and began to speak more to them than to Eupolemus. "Shall we abandon the Temple to Menelaus a second time?"

With one voice, the men around him shouted "No," drawing the attention of yet others in the crowd, who began to listen.

"Shall we give the city back to Antiochus, or back to God?"

"To God!" came the reply.

"'The Lord is with me like a fearsome warrior!'" shouted Yoshe, reciting words from Jeremiah.

"Therefore my enemies will stumble and not prevail!" The crowd was in a frenzy, ready to climb the very walls of the Akra were the order given.

"We will take the gates and lock down the city," he declared. "Then we will take that ram"—he paused to point dramatically toward the Akra—"through that door."

Mattathias simply nodded. There was no point arguing any further.

"I share your zeal and your hopes, old friend," he said as he took a few steps back. "May God indeed fight alongside you and give you victory."

Judah and Eupolemus followed Mattathias to the portico on the far side of the market. Tears had begun to form in the corners of Mattathias's eyes.

"Everyone who stays in this city to fight Antiochus will die," he said. "We should gather at least our own cell groups and anyone else who will listen to reason and leave for our farms outside Modein."

"We can't abandon our brothers, Father," objected Judah. "If we can't persuade them, we owe it to them to stay to fight with them."

"If we die with them today, Judah," Mattathias replied, "who will fight for God's people tomorrow?"

ч

Jason walked through the open door of his villa overlooking Jerusalem. Wind caught the dried leaves covering the floor of the vestibule and set them rustling through the deserted audience hall. Something scurried away, alarmed by his footfall on the limestone floor. Agathon had seen to it that Castor, Niobe, and the others who had been in Jason's service were well cared for from the sale of Jason's estates north of Judea shortly after his departure. Most of the furnishings and decorations were gone, but Jason was pleased to find his alabaster chair still in place on the balcony off his bedchamber. He threw his cloak down over it to cover the bird droppings, sat down, and watched the city.

He heard the sound of footsteps crossing the bedroom behind him.

"I thought I might find you here."

Jason smiled, rose from his chair, and extended his right hand to Agathon, who clasped it sympathetically.

"I could hardly leave without saying good-bye."

The two searched for words that would not seem trivial after all they had been through together. A quotation from a Greek tragedy? A proverb? Nothing seemed equal to the moment. Finally Jason smiled as a sign of giving up the search.

"I must ask of you one last favor, and that without any hope of repaying your kindnesses henceforth."

"Please," Agathon demurred, "what can I do?"

"Go to Egypt and retrieve the proceeds of the sale of my properties that you have deposited there on my behalf. Give the funds to Honiah's son in Leontopolis. He may hate me, but he's still family. You should stay there with him yourself for some years to come and take whatever wealth of yours with you that you can. If you haven't liquidated enough, by all means take what you need from my accounts. You'll be hunted out as an enemy of the state here for helping me."

Agathon nodded his assent.

"What will you do, Jason?"

"Oh, I'll join up with Antigonos tonight at his camp south of the city and return to Hyrcanus. I may make my way to Egypt eventually, or perhaps even Greece."

"Won't you need this money yourself?"

"Don't worry about me, Agathon. I've stored enough away for the short time I have left on this earth."

Agathon was not comfortable with Jason's answer but did not press him.

"You've been a good friend to me, Agathon," Jason said, putting his right hand on Agathon's left shoulder. "I pray that God will yet reward you in this life for your loyalty, for," he added with a smirk, "I fear I will never be able to do so."

Agathon searched for fitting words, but his eyes said what his mouth could not.

"You should make your preparations and go quickly. Besides, I want to spend a few quiet moments here before I leave."

"God be with you, Jason," Agathon said.

"May the Lord bless and keep you, Agathon."

Jason watched Agathon leave and sat down once again in his chair. The sun had begun to set, sending its red glow over the city. Despite its beauty, it seemed to Jason a portent of blood. As he looked beyond the city into the setting sun, he could see Antiochus's forces approaching, like an oozing black river pouring over its banks toward the city. When the flow was still about three hundred meters from the city, it began to split to the north and to the south as if it had hit an invisible wall. Finally it separated into four separate, stationary blocks.

Darkness was creeping over him, swallowing him up as the sun receded below the horizon and the blackness descended from the east. He thought about the pleasant fiction he had spun for Agathon, but he would not return to Hyrcanus. He doubted he could even get up from his chair, so crushing was the weight of failure, the weight of regret. No, he could live no life other than the one he was born to in Jerusalem.

As he watched the last touch of rose disappear beneath the horizon, he pulled the dagger that he had stored in his belt and opened the veins in his wrists.

The siege engines arrived on the third day after Apollonios and his lieutenants had set up the camps. A more than ample number of projectiles had
been gathered in those intervening days, so that the assault could begin early
in the morning on the fourth day. The catapults released a steady bombardment of boulders at and over the parapet of the wall while the two siege towers
were moved forward into place against the wall. Archers on the top quickly dispatched anyone who left some body part exposed to view, and the soldiers began
to pour up the stairs of the towers and to occupy the wall and drop down into the
city below. The meager numbers of fighters that had remained in place, huddled
against the gate to avoid being struck by the projectiles, were quickly overcome,
and the western gate was opened to Apollonios's main force well before noon.

"We must congratulate Nicanor on his siege tactics when we see him again
in Antioch," the king said to Apollonios as the latter gave the order to enter the
city.

The resistance fighters attempted to make their stand west of the market, but
the street was too broad to provide their smaller force any advantage. Apollonios's
soldiers hacked their way mercilessly through their ranks, killing both those who
stood their ground and those who turned to flee. Yoshe and Joram had left the
command post to fight alongside their men and shout encouragement to them.
After less than half an hour's fighting, they had been pushed back east of the
market into the most open spaces of the city center.

It was at that moment that Sarpedon led a charge out of the Akra, more out
of a desire to be found on the battlefield by Apollonios than out of any actual
military need. The remaining Syrian soldiers streamed out from the fortress and
caught the resistance fighters from behind, pressing them between themselves
and Apollonios's main force like grapes in a winepress.

Yoshe called for a retreat, though most of his fighters had already intuited that
it was time to abandon their position. Many broke away south, running down
one of the streets that would eventually lead them to one of the gates on that
side of the city. Some headed north, hoping to escape through the gate beside
the Baris, the old fortress to the north of the Temple, built during the time of
the Ptolemies' occupation. Those in between charged through Sarpedon's lines,
preferring their chances against a beleaguered few than Apollonios's fresh and
seemingly numberless force. These fared the worst. The time they lost tangling
with Sarpedon was all the time the soldiers from the west needed to subdue
them, and by that point, they were more intent on taking prisoners to execute as
examples than on outright slaughter. Few made it to escape through the pedes-
trian passages in the eastern gates.

Joram and Yoshe, together with some of the more experienced fighters, stayed to the rear of the group that was fleeing south through the city. Keeping their faces to the advancing Syrian forces, they engaged them just enough to slow down their progress, giving the rest a few more precious minutes to secure, open, and escape through the gate beside the Pool of Siloam. They took no chances with attacking thrusts that would leave them exposed, devoting their attention fully to defensive parries and holding ground.

"Break!" Yoshe ordered.

At once the five fighters turned and ran down the road about fifty meters, the Syrians following three meters behind.

"Has anyone given any thought to how we're going to get away?" Parosh asked as they ran.

Yoshe spotted an abandoned cart in the road ahead.

"Turn!" he ordered.

At once the five were again engaging the pursuers, buying time for themselves as well as their comrades. Yoshe fixed on a plan.

"Break!" he ordered again. As they ran, he said, "Go around the cart on the left side. We'll spin it toward the right to block the road."

Parosh and two others ran ahead and behind the cart. As soon as Joram and Yoshe cleared the right side, they started rotating it. The five of them pushed against the cart to hold it in place as the Syrian forces struck it from the far side. Yoshe found a foothold against a raised paving stone on the right side of the road. He dug in his heel and pushed his back against the cart.

"Get out of here!" he roared, his voice strained.

Three of the fighters started running as fast as they could. Joram held his position on the left side, looking for a way not to sacrifice Yoshe.

"Yoshe, let them push it forward," he said, gesturing with his head to the raised stone.

Yoshe understood, and let his muscles slacken just enough for the cart to slide slowly toward its target. The Syrians pushed the cart forward until one of its thick wheels caught against the stone. It took them a crucial minute to figure out that they needed to push only from the left side to spin the cart out of their path. By the time they did, Yoshe and Joram had dashed well out of their range. The soldiers continued their pursuit to the city gate and just beyond, though now with less than complete commitment. They could see dozens of men scattering over the landscape, heading for any one of a thousand hiding places. Their detachment leader called off the chase and gave them a few minutes to rest. An officer on horseback emerged through the gate and demanded a report.

"The rebels escaped, sir," the detachment leader said. "I did not believe that further pursuit on foot would attain our objectives."

"No shame, soldier," the officer replied. "Your men fought bravely. The city is retaken."

"Thank you, sir."

"Take your men back up this street and conduct a house-to-house search. Some rebels might have taken refuge inside rather than taking a chance on making it to the gate."

"Yes, sir!"

As the officer rode back toward the Akra, the detachment leader organized his men into search teams and set them to their task. The streets were completely quiet. Most of the residents had bolted their doors, shuttered their windows, and sequestered themselves in their innermost rooms or upper floors to stay as far out of the way of the slaughter as possible. Soldiers began banging on the doors. Bolts could be heard sliding back, followed by the slam of doors against walls as the soldiers rushed in, prepared to encounter any kind of resistance.

One team of four burst into a house on the west side of the street. Two women sat huddled against the inner wall along with a child and an older man. The soldiers began to toss the contents, looking for any kind of weapon that might signal the presence of a hiding rebel. One of the soldiers kept his eyes firmly on the thirty-year-old man who had unbolted the door for them.

"You seem to be fairly sweaty," he said. "Been running out in the streets today?"

"No, sir," the man said, looking down. "It's hot in here, is all. And we've all been pretty nervous with all that's going on out there."

The soldier took a step closer to the man.

"I saw you out in front of the Akra earlier today," he goaded, hoping to provoke some sign of guilt. He called to one of his comrades. "Isn't this one of the guys we saw fighting earlier today and chased down here?"

Before the other soldier could answer, the man said "No, sir, I swear. We've all been locked up in here all day. We don't want any trouble."

The second soldier stared at the man for a moment. A look of genuine recognition appeared on his face and he opened his mouth to warn his comrade. In an instant, the old man had pulled out the sword upon which he had been sitting and ran it through the thigh of the soldier. The younger man pulled a sword out from behind the front door and swung it upward through the first soldier's throat and into his skull. The second soldier fell to the ground, holding the gaping wound in his thigh while the older man finished him with a blow to the neck.

The other two soldiers who had been ransacking the inner rooms rushed out. One struck the old man in the back while the other impaled his stomach after he had fallen. The two bore down together on the younger man, who fled through the door. He had not gone ten paces before running into another team of four soldiers, emerging from the house they were searching. They quickly disarmed him, forced him down to the ground, and started to tie his arms behind his back with leather thongs.

"I knew there were some rats hiding here," the detachment leader said as he congratulated the team that had made the collar.

He crouched down on one knee to speak into the captive's ear. "There'll be a sharpened pole waiting for you at the end of the day, Jew."

The two surviving soldiers emerged from the captive's house with the women and child in their grasp.

"What about these, sir?"

"Take them to be held in the Akra. They'll be sold off as slaves to help pay for the damages here. Keep searching, men—and don't be off your guard." He knelt down again and lifted the captive's head off the ground by his hair. "There could be another of these in any one of these houses waiting to kill you."

By nightfall, Apollonios had declared the city pacified. His lieutenants had stationed troops at every gate and drawn up details for police duty in the streets throughout the night, but the general had no expectation of further fighting. Several dozen rebels had been impaled outside the city by the western gate, where they would remain—alive and writhing for a day or two, dead and rotting for weeks to come—as a vivid and effective antidote against thoughts of renewed sedition.

Antiochus had entered the city himself around sunset, after Apollonios had signaled an initial "all clear," and proceeded to confer with Menelaus and the surviving officers of his garrison concerning the events of the past weeks.

"It was definitely Hyrcanus's forces that supported Jason," Sarpedon explained. "I recognized their captain from a skirmish I fought when I was stationed on the Idumean frontier. And Ptolemy pulls Hyrcanus's strings."

"I'll deal with Hyrcanus soon enough," Antiochus responded, "if he has the courage not to take his life first. I'm more disturbed by the popular revolt in your streets. Matters are more volatile here than I had been led to believe."

"This volatility only began to make itself known recently, Highness," Menelaus interjected quickly. "Certainly many of the more backward residents were unhappy about opening up the city's Temple to the worship of the gods of all its citizens, but there were no acts of violence until recent weeks."

"It's true, sire," Sarpedon confirmed. "And those initial attacks were the first sign we had of their strength. They were well-coordinated."

"Well, we dealt any rebels quite a blow today, but I'm not going to take any chances here. I'm leaving an occupation force of five hundred men, which will bring your total to well over six hundred. Six hundred soldiers to keep peace in a terror-stricken city." Antiochus eyed Menelaus with some displeasure. "You should be able to handle the situation from here. Apollonios, I'll leave you here long enough to oversee the new organization of the garrison. Then I want you to take charge of the force in Samaria until Judea is truly stable, in case backup is needed."

Apollonios, who had been helping himself to some meats that had been set out on a serving table in the conference room, turned to the king with evident surprise in his expression.

"I know, we have an eastward campaign to plan," Antiochus explained, "but what's the point until we are certain that this province will remain pacified?"

Apollonios reluctantly signaled his assent and turned his attention back to the late supper.

"Majesty," Menelaus ventured, "I would like to be allowed to take more drastic action."

"Revenge, Menelaus?"

"Rooting out the source of rebellion, Highness." He sat down at the table across from the king.

"These rebels call themselves the *Hasidim*," Menelaus sneered, "the 'men of covenant loyalty.' You can see their acts of vandalism throughout the city, along with their watchword, *ḥesed*, painted everywhere. They've made the law of Moses their rallying cry. They've used its specific commands to promote acts of sacrilege against the sacred shrines of our non-Jewish citizens and to justify these attacks as the will of God. It's this idea of a covenant with God that gives them the boldness to try to stand up against even your armies."

"What do you suggest?"

"The law of Moses, together with the people's attachment to it, has to be eliminated, Highness."

Apollonios had taken an interest in their conversation and drew up a chair. "Menelaus is correct, sire," he said in support. "We all know that the Jews' peculiar law is the source of their hatred of foreigners. You'll never achieve a unified kingdom as long as its barbarism is tolerated."

"The law of Moses hasn't had legal force for almost ten years, since Jason petitioned you to allow us to adopt governance under a Greek constitution," Menelaus continued. "But its practice in the private sphere continues, in no small measure thanks to the edicts of toleration granted to Judea by your esteemed father. The situation here has gotten to the point where I think it's time to reverse that policy."

Antiochus seemed to be thinking over the implications of such a shift.

"Sire," Apollonios said, "as long as these people continue to hold on to a law that makes no room for other gods, for other people, or for other ways of life in this city, it will remain forever divided into an 'us' and a 'them,' and further violence—even further rebellion—is inevitable. It won't matter what kind of impression we made today."

Antiochus thought for a moment longer, then nodded his assent. "Very well, Menelaus, do what you think necessary to assure peace in this city." He rose from his chair, at which the others rose as well. "And now I'm tired. I want a good night's rest and to leave for Antioch tomorrow at first light. This has been a very disappointing week."

As Antiochus emerged from the Akra, the twenty soldiers detailed to his bodyguard snapped to attention to escort him out of the city to his pavilion in the army's camp.

Menelaus summoned Sarpedon and Memnon, the commander of one of the cohorts newly detailed to Jerusalem. "I want the two of you to attend to two tasks in the weeks ahead. First, hunt down the rebels who fled from here today."

"With all due respect, sir," Sarpedon objected, "they could be hiding anywhere in that vast desert of a countryside. We don't have the forces to conduct a search."

"They'll be making contact with people in the nearby villages within the next day or two, since they'll need food," Menelaus answered. "You'll find them through those contacts. Second, a lot of backward and divisive Jewish practices are about to become illegal. The main body of the garrison will assist in enforcing the new decrees here, but the two of you will take the decrees to the villages and put them in force there."

The two commanders nodded curtly.

"That will be all for tonight," Menelaus said. "Report here at first light."

Menelaus signaled for a scribe to come and sit near him.

"Now, then," he began, talking chiefly to himself, "what makes a Jew . . . a Jew?"

5

Ari and Boaz had left their post at the two-kilometer mark outside of Modein and were walking back toward the village at the head of several dozen men, women, and children. Simon and Jonathan, who were keeping the early morning watch at the one-kilometer mark from their base of operations, could see that most of these people were carrying bundles of possessions and were staggering somewhat as they kept their forward pace. They had clearly been walking all night before encountering Ari and Boaz.

Boaz shouted out ahead of the group.

"These people are coming from Jerusalem. You'll want to hear what they have to say."

Simon and Jonathan quickly closed the distance between themselves and the refugees.

"I am Simon ben Mattathias and this is my brother Jonathan. What has been happening in the city?"

"May God bless your father, that man of covenant loyalty, and all his sons," said an older man in the group. "I am Salmon ben Azariah, and I used to serve with your father as priest in the Temple—when it was a Temple."

"I know your name, Master Salmon, and your reputation for piety," Simon acknowledged. "I'm surprised you could tolerate Jerusalem for so long."

"I prayed daily for the city," Salmon said. "I hoped that God would intervene. But now?" He shook his head hopelessly from side to side. "New decrees have been issued. This rebellion has given Menelaus the excuse he needed to make war on the covenant itself. Circumcision, lighting the Sabbath candles,

248

even possessing a copy of the Torah—these have all been made capital crimes. Soldiers led by apostate priests raided the Temple library and every synagogue in the city, gathering the sacred scrolls and burning them in front of the Akra. The people were given three days to bring every scrap of parchment or papyrus on which some portion of the Torah was written and throw them on the same fire."

He lovingly unwrapped the bundle in his arms to reveal a collection of scrolls.

"But they won't burn this copy," he said, "or these," he added, gesturing to similar bundles in the arms of his fellow refugees.

Simon felt tears welling up behind his eyes as he considered the plight of Jerusalem and the devotion of the older priest before him.

The voice of a younger man beside Salmon drew his attention back to the moment.

"Menelaus is seizing property throughout the city to accommodate the new cohorts left by Antiochus and to reward his mercenary auxiliaries and their families. The houses of revolutionaries who were killed or fled were the first, with any surviving family members thrown out into the street—some of these women and children here, widowed and orphaned not three days ago. Then they took the houses of people who were too outspoken in past months about Menelaus's 'reforms.'"

Simon and Jonathan nodded sympathetically and spoke to each of the refugees in Hebrew, asking about their names, their families, their circumstances. While they were interested in them as people, at the moment they were more interested in listening to their accents and their facility in the religious language of the covenant. It was one of the few tests they had for ferreting out spies gathering intelligence on the surviving resistance.

"There's not much farther to go, friends," Simon reassured the travelers. "Jonathan will show you the way to safety."

Jonathan began to usher them off the road.

"We're not going to Modein?" a woman asked.

"Modein is not completely committed to the cause," Jonathan explained. "We have doubts about a few families. They don't cause trouble for us, since they're afraid of us. Still, the less they know . . ."

"Jonathan will lead you to our family's farmlands," Simon reassured the group. "There will be food, water, and shelter for you there."

The group reluctantly trundled off into the surrounding scrub, following Jonathan.

"You're not taking them to the camps in the hills?" Ari asked.

"Not yet," replied Simon. "Best to keep those secret for now, to protect our freedom fighters there and any other survivors that come our way from Yoshe and Joram's forces."

Simon looked thoughtfully in the direction of Jerusalem.

"Let's cast our nets a bit wider," he said at last. "Round up some of your friends from our camp and have them watch the roads closer to Jerusalem. Many more people will be leaving the city, and I suspect that many of them would be willing to fight to take it back if they thought they had a good chance. Send them in this direction."

Ari and Boaz nodded approvingly as they imagined bands of refugees swelling into an unstoppable army of God.

Meir escorted Tavitha to the market. The city was smoldering in quiet tension. Soldiers patrolled every street, effectively intimidating the Jewish residents who were inclined toward peace and causing those inclined otherwise to seethe and simmer in silent resentment. Meir could sense that it was only a matter of time before the lid blew off the pot once again, and the explosive force would only become worse the more Menelaus pressed down upon that lid. In the past week, after the expiration of Menelaus's "grace period," soldiers had broken into several homes upon being informed that law scrolls were being kept inside. In the case of three of these houses, the information proved true. The male head of each household was executed, the remaining residents were sent to Joppa to be sold into slavery, and the homes were requisitioned to billet more soldiers.

Meir left Tavitha in the market and made his way into the district just west of the Temple Mount, where some of the richest priestly families had established their homes. Turning north onto the second street brought him to his destination. He approached the open double door and found his way blocked by a servant.

"How may the household of Timarchos be of service?" the servant asked in a tone that indicated anything but a desire to be of service.

"Please tell your master that Hilaron ben Zerah is here and humbly asks to see him."

The servant recognized the name, gave a curt nod, and walked off into the house. He returned momentarily to usher Meir into the inner courtyard, where he found Timarchos sitting comfortably on a couch and Alcimus in a chair opposite him. Between them lay a short, portable table with breads, fruits, nuts, and cheeses.

"Hilaron ben Zerah." Timarchos pushed himself up slightly upon his arm to acknowledge the young man's arrival. "What brings you—at last—to my door?"

"Master Timarchos, Master Alcimus," Meir began, acknowledging both priests, "I am deeply troubled by what I see going on around me in Jerusalem. Our sacred place and practices have been changed with no regard for our long-standing tradition. Our people are now forbidden to practice the religion of their ancestors. The rule of law is daily trampled by the boots of the soldiers. What I see today is as contrary to the ideals of Greek culture and politics as anything that might have been practiced here before Lord Jason began his reforms."

"I would not invoke that name too freely in this city, young man," Timarchos warned.

"I am sorry, Master Timarchos. I know you are Lord Menelaus's friend, and I have no wish to antagonize you. But I am deeply concerned about what his decrees will mean for . . . many in the city."

Meir was thinking chiefly about his own family—about a brother who kept scrolls of Deuteronomy and a few other books in his house, about a mother who would never cease to light the Sabbath candles.

"Forcing people to abandon their long-cherished customs and adopt new and foreign rites—that's what I read about tyrants doing to Greek populations, not proper rulers," Meir continued.

"What do you want me to do, Hilaron?"

"Can you talk to Lord Menelaus?" he replied earnestly. "Could you help him see that stamping out devotion to our ancestral practices will only result in the deaths of many peaceful residents and fan the flames of uprising?"

"That's quite a favor you're asking from me now, isn't it?" Timarchos said, harboring a pocket of resentment for Meir's earlier refusal of his patronage.

"Master Timarchos," Meir said, bowing his head slightly to signal his repentance, "I beg you not to remain angry with me. Your offer was most generous, and it was never my intention to slight you. But what kind of client would you have taken on in me were I to prove disloyal to the man who was then my patron at the first signs that he was in distress?"

Timarchos softened a bit at this evident attempt to apologize and to satisfy his honor.

"You're right, Hilaron; you acted nobly. Besides," he added with a smile, "if Jason had had his way, I would no doubt be approaching you for your help right about now."

Alcimus, who had watched the exchange in interested silence, added, "And in times like this, all of us need to look for allies wherever we can."

Meir understood from the look in Alcimus's eyes that this was meant not only to justify the young man's presence here, but Alcimus's as well.

"Do you think I like where the city has gone?" Timarchos asked. "But all this will pass. You have to understand, Hilaron. Menelaus is under a lot of pressure. The city is divided by all kinds of factions. Antiochus expects order—and the steady flow of tribute that only an orderly society can produce. He's spent more on Judea than he's gotten from her this year. Menelaus has to think about all that."

Timarchos paused for a moment, thinking about Menelaus's responses thus far.

"Power and pressure never bring out a person's best qualities."

Alcimus nodded his agreement with this judgment. "Timarchos and I both have problems with how far Menelaus has gone—even before these most recent steps."

"You want me to say it?" Timarchos interjected, as if this had been the very topic of conversation before Meir's entrance. "Things were better here under Jason. There, I said it. The Greeks and Syrians here might have been treated a little like second-class citizens, but many concessions had been made and many were coming to make their home here. Now even Gentile citizens are looking to move abroad. Who wants to live in a police state? Or in a city torn by ethnic and religious conflict?"

"Seraiah, the man who put first Jason and then Menelaus in the seats of power, hasn't set foot in this city in over a year," Alcimus added. "He just stays on his estates in Jericho and beyond to the north. Even he's not pleased with what's happening here."

"He's not pleased with Menelaus forgetting who put him in power," Timarchos interjected.

"I'm sure even Seraiah never intended for matters to go this far. The point is," Alcimus asserted, "Menelaus and his policies won't last forever." He raised his hand placatingly toward Timarchos. "I know he's your friend."

"You're right. I'm not arguing with you. Jerusalem has certainly not prospered under his leadership. And with decreasing support from rich Judeans like Seraiah, we've been paying our annual tribute increasingly from the Temple treasury. That's not going to last forever."

"We just need to do what is necessary to survive longer than Menelaus," Alcimus counseled the young man.

"He wouldn't have lasted this long, I think, were it not for the uprisings," Timarchos said. "Well, if Antiochus were to replace Menelaus under these circumstances, he'd be admitting that he made a mistake putting him in power to begin with. He's not ready to make that admission, and certainly not in a situation where revolutionaries might take advantage of it by stirring up revolt against Antiochus's management of the province altogether."

Meir could see in the eyes of both priests that wheels were already turning. *Seraiah must not be just pruning his vines and counting his money in Jericho.*

"I appreciate your counsel," he said, "but what about those who will not be content to do whatever it takes to survive because they regard their duty to God to be far more compelling?"

Their change of expression showed that his question came out more sharply than he had intended.

"What I mean, masters, is that silence on our part now leaves the person who will not join in Menelaus's sacrifices to foreign gods, or who will not hand over the sacred scrolls, or who will not violate the covenant in some other particular in grave danger."

"Hilaron," Timarchos said reassuringly, "it is not our intent to remain silent. I will speak with Menelaus about reexamining his policies, though I can't promise to be successful. In the interim, you would do well to show yourself supportive of his agenda. Show up at the Temple and be seen worshiping alongside your Greek and Syrian fellow citizens. Come to dine with us some evening at Menelaus's palace, and let him see you eat some pork or crab, so that he'll know you're a friend. All at once, any suspicion attaching to you because of your dedication to Agathon—and thus to Jason—will evaporate, and you'll find significant opportunities opening up for you."

Meir felt his cheeks flush at the suggestions. He loved much about the Greek world; he loved a Syrian woman and had now been together with her for years. But he continued to live as a Jew—at least in his own understanding, if not Binyamin's.

"Who knows?" Timarchos continued. "A few small compromises like these, and you might find yourself in a position to turn Menelaus toward a new way of thinking."

"Or at least to use your influence to protect those about whom you are most concerned," added Alcimus.

"I am grateful to you both for your advice and for anything you can do to help those who are presently in danger," Meir said, bowing slightly to the two priests.

"You are welcome, Hilaron," Timarchos said. "And you are welcome henceforth in my house. Take heart, young man. Better days are coming."

Meir bid them good-bye and returned to the market. He found Tavitha sitting on a limestone bench under a portico on the sunnier side of the square.

"Will they be able to help, do you think?" she asked.

He dropped down heavily beside her on the bench. "I don't think so. They're working on some other angle and aren't going to go out on a limb for the ordinary folk who still love their God."

She touched his upper arm reassuringly.

"I thought we were part of something that was going to be good for Jerusalem." He thought about the exchange of ideas in the gymnasium, the thrill of competition in the stadium, the excitement of watching Jason's plans for the city unfold and being in the forefront of it all. "But now look at the harvest of those seeds that were planted with Jason's rise to power."

"Meir, we don't have to stay here. Neither does your family. We can all go to Alexandria, where Agathon has gone, or some such place. You've done well here. You'll do well there. We can all start anew where they'll be safe . . . Where you'll be safe being the brilliant, Greek-educated Jew that you are."

She said these last words with a smile, craning around in front of him to catch his eye and drive away the melancholy that had settled upon him.

He looked at her but could not return her smile.

"I don't have the right to start over somewhere else," he said soberly. "I can't just walk away from a mess that I helped make." He drew in a sharp breath and sat up a little straighter on the bench. "We ruined Jerusalem. We ruined her when we embraced a different constitution for the city other than the one our God gave us along with this city, when we rose up against God's anointed high priest . . ."

"You didn't do any of that, Meir," Tavitha asserted, trying to ease his conscience.

"I didn't do anything to stop it or to protest it, either. Everything I have, everything I am, comes from having thrown in my lot with Jason's party."

"You have me because of that as well. If you hadn't done all of that, you would never have been invited to a dinner where Seraiah would have brought me—and I'd probably still be entertaining his friends somewhere."

"You're the one good thing that came from all those years," Meir said to reassure her. "But even there I failed. God's covenant demanded that I take thought first for leading you to the worship of the one God, and only after that take thought for the pleasures that we found together."

"I love you all the more for not having done that. You and I prove that Jew and Syrian can live together in peace, mutual respect, and love, without either one having to become something else. Besides, don't you think I've learned a lot about your God during these years with you? When I first came to Jerusalem,

I thought of your religion as full of strange and silly superstitions. Now I see a lot more of the superstitions in my religion, and see a lot more of the truth of a creator God who is beyond any image and without peer."

She turned her gaze toward to the Temple Mount. "I believe I liked your Temple better the way it was before Menelaus made it a house for any and every god, even if I could only go so far and no farther. It was special then. It was unlike anything else in the world."

Meir remembered dozens of arguments with his brother about the seriousness of the covenant and the dangers of not living by God's instructions in God's holiest city. "Binyamin was right," he said aloud. "There has to be a way back . . ."

His voice trailed off as he heard his father's voice from somewhere deep in his mind reciting a portion of the Torah over Sabbath dinner, as was his custom. *"If you return to the Lord your God, and you and your children obey him with all your heart and with all your soul, just as I am commanding you today, then the Lord your God will restore your fortunes and have compassion on you."*

It was the first time Nadav ben Jonah saw Syrian soldiers in Modein. They had arrived mid-morning from the north, rather than from the east as he would have expected for the Jerusalem-based cohort. Apparently they were making the rounds of the villages surrounding Jerusalem and had ridden out from Ramathaim that morning. There would not be a better opportunity for him to rid himself of Mattathias and his family of bullies, and to make sure that the troubles in Jerusalem did not disturb his family home.

Most of the villagers had been gathered into the open space just inside the primitive gate of Modein, spilling up into the main street that led past the synagogue. Nadav had offered his services to the soldiers, helping to spread word of the required assembly. At last, Mattathias arrived, his rough clothing, hands, and face begrimed with dirt. Bits of chaff and other grasses clung to his hair and beard, and he carried a long shovel over his shoulder. His sons came through the gate with him, similarly showing the signs of having been in the field all morning.

"You're here at last, Mattathias," said Sarpedon, who had led this particular detachment of twenty soldiers to Modein. "I almost didn't recognize you underneath all that mud."

Nadav did not suppress a smirk of contempt for the elder of the village who didn't know better than to work like a peasant. Mattathias pushed past him to stand five meters opposite Sarpedon, while his sons fanned out behind him.

"You could have left your dung-encrusted shovel in the field, Mattathias," Nadav goaded, waving his hand in front of his nose.

"What brings you to Modein, Captain?" asked the priest.

"Recent events in Jerusalem have demonstrated how dangerous our divisions are to the peace of the city and the well-being of its citizens," Sarpedon answered, his tone containing a hint of accusation. "The king, in his deep interest for stability and harmony, has decreed that all his subjects in Judea put the sources of our disunity behind us."

Sarpedon angled his body to reveal behind him the makeshift altar that his soldiers had erected.

"He has ordered that we all acknowledge one another's gods and live together in peace henceforth. To that end, we have come to give you all the opportunity to demonstrate your loyalty to the king by offering a small sacrifice in honor of Zeus, Baal Shamen, and, of course, your own deity."

The tension in the square increased palpably.

"As an acknowledged leader both here and in Jerusalem, I thought it most appropriate to invite you to be the first to take this step toward peace." Sarpedon kept his gaze fixed on Mattathias, while his soldiers braced for any sign of trouble.

Mattathias relaxed his stance and took a single step back.

"Come now, Mattathias," Sarpedon persisted. "Surely you don't want more lives to be lost here."

Nadav seized the opportunity. "Excellency," he said as he pushed through Mattathias's sons to the front, "please do not regard this man as a spokesperson for Modein. Many of us are happy to live in peace under the king's rule." He approached closer and bowed extravagantly in front of Sarpedon. "Allow me to offer the first sacrifice on behalf of my village."

Nadav felt brave for perhaps the first time, knowing that the king's soldiers would protect him once he proved his loyalty. He turned around to face his fellow villagers, as if offering himself as an example to follow and promoting himself as the new leading elder. As he scanned their faces, he noticed several strangers in the crowd, which should be impossible in a small village that he had inhabited so long. These strangers were edging closer to the front, and Nadav could see that each was carrying a pitchfork, scythe, or other sharp farming implement.

Nadav's eyes widened as he understood the situation at last. He drew in a breath and spun around to warn Sarpedon of the attack, but all that came out of his mouth was a spatter of blood. Mattathias had whipped his shovel around from off his shoulder, sending the decoy shovel head flying and revealing a javelin with a thirty-centimeter spearhead. He lunged forward to thrust the javelin through Nadav's back, catching his sternum and pushing him forward toward Sarpedon. The captain instinctively took a step back against the altar and extended his arms against Nadav's shoulders to keep Nadav's body away, not realizing what was propelling the man toward him. Mattathias continued to press the javelin forward. It broke free of the sternum, burst through Nadav's chest, entered Sarpedon's stomach, and exited through his back.

In an instant, Judah and his brothers threw off their muddy cloaks, swords and small round shields already in their hands. The sight of Sarpedon's convulsing body gripped the soldiers' attention just long enough to give Judah and the others time to dispatch the nearest targets. By the time the remaining soldiers had drawn their swords and identified the combatants in the crowd, they were similarly beset by the strangers who had infiltrated the gathering—all of them freedom fighters from Mattathias's camps. In minutes, all twenty soldiers lay dead or dying, and the revolutionaries began the task of collecting their weapons and stripping them of their armor. Mattathias placed his foot firmly on Nadav's back and pulled the javelin back out of the two bodies. Then he placed his foot on the top rim of the altar and toppled it to the ground with a look of disgust.

The crowd that had drawn back in fear of the fighting began to move forward once again, instinctively waiting for Mattathias to speak.

"Brothers, sisters," he began, "you know how things stand in Jerusalem, and you see that the defilement will not stay there, but will spill out over this whole land. Now not only is everything that is unlawful permitted in Judea, but everything that is lawful before God is forbidden on pain of death. The middle ground has been completely swallowed up. You must each determine on which side of the chasm you stand."

Mattathias looked at the faces in the crowd, most of them familiar to him since his own birth or theirs. "Reprisals will follow for what we have done today. Modein is no longer safe for the people who are loyal to God's covenant. But I promise you that it will also no longer be safe for the people who would make themselves enemies of God's covenant." He paused to nudge the lifeless body of Nadav with his foot. "If you are on the Lord's side, if you are willing to fight for the covenant, come with me."

Silence hung in the air for a few seconds.

"We're with you, Mattathias!" the voice of Eliashiv rang out.

"We're with you as well!" a younger voice declared.

More and more of the villagers declared their intentions. Mattathias stepped forward, raised his right arm, still holding the javelin, and began to shout. "For God and the covenant!"

Soon the crowd took up the chant, raising their fists above their heads. *"For God and the convenant!"*

Judah looked at his brothers and then to the faces of those who had come with him from Jerusalem and smiled appreciatively at the spirit of his village. He walked up next to his father and raised his hand, calling for silence. "We would do well to leave before sunset. Gather blankets, food, tools, weapons. Meet us at the far side of our family's fields. From there we'll head into our camps in the hill country. You are part of God's army now."

The villagers shouted again, then dispersed to prepare for their evacuation.

Judah spotted Ari and Boaz at the edge of the crowd and crossed over to them.

"We can't allow ourselves to be surprised by the enemy, not today," he said. "I want you, Ari, to take a horse and go five or six kilometers up the road to Jerusalem to watch for troop movements. Boaz, you do the same on the road north to Ramathaim, in case Sarpedon had reinforcements coming. First sign of trouble, you get back here with a warning."

"Will do, Judah," said Boaz as he darted off to the stables.

"Judah, I'll stay long enough to cover your escape," said Ari, "but then I need to get back to Jerusalem. I'm worried about my family. They might need me."

Judah was reluctant to lose any fighter, especially one as reliable as Ari. "I understand. But come back quickly. God's cause needs you as well."

"Whether I'm here or in Jerusalem, I serve God's cause, Judah. You know that."

Judah smiled, slapped Ari on the back of the head affectionately, and watched him jog away toward the stable. He was surprised by a sudden anxiety that he would not see him again.

Shoshanna rose to the sound of a soft rapping at the door of their house. Even though their windows were closed, the families gathered together inside the living area knew that the sun was already beginning to sink below the horizon. Shoshanna returned, ushering an older couple into the room and offering them a place on a thick mat.

Binyamin looked around at the faces in the room, illuminated only by a few small, smoky oil lamps. Here was Israel. Here were God's people. He knew that other groups like this were gathering throughout the city. He even knew where some of them would be, since Eleazar had been one of the elders principally responsible for recruiting leaders for these meetings from among his former students and those like Binyamin whose walk he had personally nurtured. Since Menelaus's desecration of the Temple, Eleazar had forgotten that he was an old man. *And I've forgotten that I'm a young man*, Binyamin thought. He smiled to think about the energy and purpose that had been coursing through Eleazar. The old priest would never think of himself as a revolutionary like Mattathias or Yoshe, but he was no less zealous for the Torah and no less active in his commitment to resistance.

"Brothers, sisters," Binyamin began, "as I think about us gathered in this room, I can't help but think about Daniel, that man of covenant loyalty who was taken away from Jerusalem as a boy and spent his whole life in Babylon. Throughout the course of that long life away from the Temple, surrounded by the gods of the people who had power over him and over Israel, he never wavered in his loyalty to the one God.

"I can't help but think of the time some malicious men, bent on securing their own power, convinced the king to authorize some foolish decrees trying to force people not to offer prayers and fulfill their duty to the Divine in the ways that they had been taught from birth. How many Jews in Babylon obeyed the king, fearing his power over them more than God's power? How many continued to worship God, but took care that no one should know? These deprived their neighbors of the encouragement of their example, and they deprived the Gentiles of the all-important witness that the one God is worthy to be served and obeyed above all.

"But what did Daniel do? He went to his upstairs room, opened his window, and prayed toward Jerusalem just as he had done the day before the king issued his senseless decrees. He raised up holy hands and bore witness to all that no threat of pain nor promise of reward altered one's duty to God, and that he would honor God according to God's merit, not according to any human's pleasure or disapproval."

Binyamin paused to study the faces around him once again. He thought he saw a little less fear in some of them than a few moments ago.

"Like us tonight, Daniel did not know what would happen. But he didn't decide what to do based on what he thought might happen. He decided what to do based on who God was and on who he himself was as a part of the people whom God had taken into a special relationship. This is what he would encourage us to do as well. Antiochus and Menelaus can't make God to be less than he is. Don't let them make you less than you are."

The people in the circle nodded in agreement and looked into one another's faces for encouragement. Miryam beamed with pride at her oldest son.

"Binyamin," she said, "I'm finding it a little stuffy in here. Perhaps you could open up the windows?"

He released an amused grunt at his mother's suggestion and looked down thoughtfully.

"Yes, Binyamin," another man said. "It's a beautiful evening. Why are we all shut up in here?"

Binyamin stood up and looked around the circle once more. He saw only encouragement in their eyes, and so he crossed the room, unlatched the shutters, and opened the windows. He looked for a moment into the thin alleyway that ran beside the house. There was little danger in having the windows open anyway, but Daniel's example necessitated at least this gesture. He remembered a saying of Master Yehoshua's. *Don't be ashamed of the Most High or of his covenant.* This wasn't a time for closed windows.

Shoshanna went into the kitchen and emerged with a thin piece of kindling, one end blazing with fire from the hearth. She approached the table that stood against the east wall and carefully lit the two candles set upon it. Everyone in the room began to chant together.

> *Blessed are you, O Lord our God, King of the universe,*
> *who set us apart and made us holy by giving us your commandments,*
> *and who commanded us to light the Sabbath candles.*

They performed the ritual washing of their hands, the blessing of the cup of wine, and the blessing of the bread, which they passed around the circle. Binyamin produced the scroll of Deuteronomy that he now kept carefully hidden behind a loose stone in the hearth, unrolled it to the place appointed for that day, and handed it to the eldest man in the circle, who fought back tears as he read.

After the Sabbath had been duly hallowed by the prayers and the word, Binyamin and his family bid their guests good night and sat down together in the kitchen for their evening meal. They ate in silence together, feeling the weight of the threat that loomed over them for doing this night as they had done since their births. Finally Binyamin broke the silence.

"I want you to go stay with your parents in Modein," he said to Shoshanna.

Shoshanna looked startled by the suggestion.

"Just for a little while," Binyamin said reassuringly, "until things calm down here in the city."

"Will you come with me?" she asked.

"I would like nothing better," he answered, "but I don't feel that I can."

Shoshanna was silent.

"They're not your responsibility, you know," she finally said.

"Whose are they, then?"

Another silence followed.

"I'm not leaving without you," she declared.

He placed his hand lovingly upon her rounded abdomen.

"If our child is a boy, and is to be circumcised on the eighth day, you will need to take him far away from here."

"There are still flint knives here in Jerusalem."

"And then I will have to watch you and him hanging by the neck on the city wall?"

"You talk about Daniel obeying where it is forbidden, not hiding."

"And what do we read of Daniel's wife and unborn child?"

Shoshanna was silent.

"Exactly," Binyamin said. He took her forearms in his strong hands and drew her closer. "You are where I am most vulnerable. If you are here, I may not be able to be as brave as God would have me be. A perfect man could do what you say; I'm just trying to be a good man. If you stay, I might not, in the end, even be that."

She looked into his eyes and nodded slightly, forcing back her tears after two escaped down her cheeks.

He looked across the low table at Miryam. "I'd like for you to go with her, Mother."

Miryam understood that he needed Shoshanna to be safe so that he could be strong, but she believed she needed to stay for the same purpose.

"You want me to let those godless men run me off, Binyamin?"

"You have to go, Mother. How will Shoshanna ever manage without your advice?" Binyamin said, trying to tease her into assenting.

"Your father brought me from my father's house to this place," Miryam said with unmistakable earnestness. "Here I bore him five children, and here we raised the three of you who survived. Here I closed his eyes. Here I will close my eyes, too, so that it will be easier for us to find each other in the hereafter."

Binyamin nodded his surrender.

6

"Our troops have now been fully withdrawn from Egypt," Nicanor reported. "They are being restationed, for the most part, to the east, near Europus and Arbela, in anticipation of your eastward campaign."

"My eastward campaign," echoed Antiochus. "And what are the chances of my undertaking such a campaign in the near future?" he asked his cabinet with a hint of accusation.

"Highness, Menelaus is making progress repressing rebellion in Jerusalem," Simon answered. "He reports that more Jewish citizens have been participating in the Temple rites alongside their Greek and Syrian neighbors and that open agitation against your order has abated. The most recent decrees appear to be achieving their effect, although," he added, "there have been a few incidents."

"Incidents, indeed," Heliodoros interjected. "I don't believe that Menelaus's brother intends to paint the full picture for you, sire. I have heard reports of old men sheltering copies of their law in their homes, knowing that it would mean death for them. Menelaus had them slaughtered in the streets when the scrolls were discovered. I have also heard reports that new mothers chose to have their infant sons circumcised. Menelaus had these women dragged through the streets of the city with their babies hanging from their necks, and threw them off the city wall to their deaths."

"There are also reports," Philodemos added, "of attacks on soldiers sent out by Menelaus to the villages to enforce the decrees. Revolutionary activity is still very much alive there, and harsh measures are called for."

"Sire, these people are not going to give up their ancestral way of life," Heliodoros added, "and Menelaus's measures will only incite more resentment and, eventually, greater violence against your rule."

"Are the Jewish residents of Jerusalem the ones to dictate to the king on what terms they will be ruled?" Simon interjected indignantly, deflecting any blame against himself by appearing to defend the king's prerogatives. "Do the subjects determine the king's policies?"

"And would you prefer, sire, to return Jerusalem to its former state, with a segregated Temple and the inequality of its citizens?" Philodemos asked. "Would you sacrifice the rights that have been gained for the people of your own blood because the Jews cherish their prejudices?"

Antiochus thought in silence. Everything had been the opposite of what it was supposed to be, and he was getting tired of the constant provocation. Rome interfering in Egypt. Jason and then the local rabble rebelling in Jerusalem. Now even old men and young mothers flouting his authority. The prospect of displaying his power over their bodies and their wills—of exercising power that was rightly and still his—was darkly appealing.

"Perhaps it's time for me to intervene again personally. Menelaus is unable to enforce his decrees; perhaps the people of Jerusalem need a more compelling demonstration."

"Majesty," Heliodoros pleaded, "is it really wise to make war on a god?"

"I'm not doing anything of the kind, Heliodoros. When I withdrew General Apollonios from Jerusalem and sent him to inspect our forces in Samaria, did I give him orders to interfere with their worship of the God of Israel? No. But then the people there are not in revolt against my government."

Antiochus paused, concerned to find more evidence against the possibility that he was, in fact, inciting a god against himself. He raised his hand with index finger extended as he remembered another instance.

"And when some citizens here in Antioch petitioned me just last week to issue the same decrees here against the practice of our Jewish residents as were issued in Jerusalem, did I indulge them? No. And I have no intention of doing anything of the kind. Let them worship their God, as long as they respect my government."

"Though you have to admit," Philodemos interjected, "that there must be something perverse about their way of life to make their fellow citizens wish to see it stamped out. I do think, however, that your time is far too precious to waste on such matters, Highness. I would give your deputies in Jerusalem more time to sort this out."

"As long as I'm here in Antioch, I'm wasting my time waiting for them to fix the problem."

"These matters are indeed too slight to merit your personal attention, sire," Simon said, adding his weight to Philodemos's suggestion more to keep Antiochus at a safe remove from inspecting his brother's work firsthand than out of concern for Antiochus's time.

"My presence will then be felt more weightily, its effects all the more decisive. By making our strongest play now, we will nip in the bud any further thoughts of rebellion. Besides, we cannot begin an eastern campaign against Parthia until matters in the south are settled. If we leave matters to Menelaus, who knows?" Antiochus looked squarely at Simon. "My empire might shrink even further."

Heliodoros decided to make one more attempt. "Highness, I would urge you to consider the merits of returning to your father's more tolerant policies toward Judea. He enjoyed a peaceful relationship with the people of Jerusalem throughout his reign, as did your brother Seleucus before you, even after that one incident—instigated, may I remind you, Highness, by this same Simon here. I am grieved that this Menelaus has led you away from your father's example."

"Heliodoros," Antiochus said, "I appreciate your position, and I will not say that you are wrong. But the time for tolerance is past. The armed rebellion in Jerusalem has made it impossible. We cannot retrace our steps, or we will appear hesitant and weak—and be overrun."

"Religious persecution is not our way."

"No, but it is the necessary form that reinforcing our appointed government in Judea must take."

Antiochus rose from his throne, signaling an end to the cabinet session. "Philodemos, make all the necessary preparations for us to travel safely to Jerusalem and to conduct our unfortunate business there. I want to be ready to leave the day after next. Send a courier to Menelaus. All violators of our decrees are henceforth to be held for my arrival."

Elam ben Jacob kept the company of men, women, and children in his care staggering forward through the rocky tracks of the desert east of Anathoth. They had fled Jerusalem and sought refuge in Anathoth after Menelaus had issued his terrible decrees and begun to show himself earnest about their enforcement. There they met up with other refugees—some of the *Hasidim* who had fled earlier after their defeat by Antiochus's army. Now, with soldiers from the Jerusalem garrison traveling out to the villages throughout Judea, it was not safe even there.

The group had traveled all of yesterday and part of the day before, hoping to make it to their destination before sundown as they lacked the necessary supplies to remain in the wilderness through a Sabbath. Elam noticed that the scant scrub was beginning to give way to greener, fuller vegetation. Over the next hour of their eastward journey, the desert seemed to be coming to life all around them. At last they spotted two figures in the distance, bent over a widening in the stream, rinsing garments. A few dozen meters farther, and they began to see other signs of activity at the mouths of caves and on the slopes of the ravines to the north and south. A few men here and there were dressed in long, white robes. Perhaps a hundred other men and women were dressed in more ordinary clothes, some sitting by makeshift grinding stones making bread, some gathering the fruits growing in the wadi, some mending garments, some meditating over opened scrolls.

"Israel could not worship her God in Egypt, so God called Israel out of Egypt into the wilderness and there provided for her for forty years."

The words came suddenly from a younger man, wrapped in a white cloak, who was walking down the side of the ravine toward Elam and his party, his face significantly wrinkled and darkened from his years in this place. "Here in this wilderness we have found the simplicity of covenant obedience once again and known God's intimacy as then, during the honeymoon of God's marriage to his people. You are most welcome here."

"Are you . . . Zedekiah?" asked Elam.

"I am, Elam ben Jacob."

The older priest looked surprised.

"You see, I've not forgotten you. I've not forgotten any of God's faithful in Jerusalem. I pray for you daily."

Zedekiah gestured to Elam and his company to follow him as he led them farther eastward along the wadi.

"Our camp has grown considerably since the wicked Menelaus raised up his desolating sacrilege in the Temple of our God, but never as over these last few weeks."

"Conditions in Jerusalem have become intolerable," said Elam.

"We have learned of Antiochus's decrees from other refugees—and of the deaths of several who have chosen to obey God rather than evil."

Zedekiah stood still for a moment with his eyes closed and then spoke. "This Antiochus is the great horn of a terrible beast that has a mouth speaking arrogant things against the Most High. He makes war against the holy ones and prevails; he tries to change the sacred seasons and the law. But"—Zedekiah opened his eyes and looked squarely at Elam—"the Ancient of Days will come and give judgment for his holy ones. Kingship and power and the greatness of the kingdoms of the world shall be given to the holy people of the Most High; their kingdom shall be an everlasting kingdom."

A younger man in Elam's company asked, "When? How long must we wait for God to help?"

Zedekiah turned to look at him. "Not long. For a short span, this Antiochus makes sacrifices and offerings to cease and leaves God's sanctuary desolate, but God has decreed already the end that shall come upon the desolator."

Elam could see immediately why Zedekiah's preaching in Anathoth had made such an impression and why so many had been eager to spread his word to the pious even in Jerusalem.

"God is recreating his holy people in the wilderness—and not just a people, but as also in the wilderness after Sinai, an army. Already the angelic prince of Israel goes forth into battle against the princes of the nations, and God will call us to fall into his battle lines as well."

Zedekiah smiled at the young man, turned his gaze forward, and began to walk again. "But the Sabbath is almost upon us, and tonight you all must rest, be refreshed, and seek the Lord. There is shelter for you just ahead."

The squad of soldiers followed Ariston through the streets to the district northwest of the Temple. He was not as squeamish as other Jews such as Meir, his old companion from gymnasium days, about what it took to get ahead in Menelaus's Jerusalem. Pork was as good as any other meat. The Sabbath was just another day to work—or to play at the amusements he could afford because of Menelaus's patronage. He had indeed come a long way since his unenlightened boyhood.

This evening, the Sabbath was a good time for fishing.

As they turned into the third street heading west from the Temple, the squad leader signaled for half of his men to slip down into the alleyway beside the house that was their target. It would do no good to lose half their catch through a back door or window. Ariston crept halfway down the alley to a shuttered window and listened closely to the voices inside. Satisfied of the criminal activity therein, he signaled the squad leader at the head of the alleyway. Two soldiers carrying a portable ram broke down the front door and poured into the house, followed by the remaining half squad. They saw a dozen or more people— families—gathered in the living area around a table with lighted candles. A few started from their seated position and began to run toward the door, but an old man in the circle called out to them.

"Don't run from the post God assigned you. We knew this time would come. By paying the price for obedience we will remind all Jews of its value."

The soldiers surrounded them and called for reinforcements from the alley.

Ariston walked up to the squad leader and pointed to the old man. "That one's Eleazar."

Two soldiers lifted the old man from the ground and shackled his wrists behind his back. "Lord Menelaus was most emphatic that we should find you tonight."

The soldiers began to shackle the others as well.

"Take half of the prisoners back to the Akra with you," the squad leader instructed his soldiers, "then return for the rest. You three, stay here with me to keep them secured."

"I'll go back to the Akra," Ariston volunteered. "Perhaps I can still help another of the squads. Lord Menelaus wants as many of these lawbreakers rounded up as possible, to be ready for the king's arrival."

"Lawbreakers?" Eleazar scoffed. "Better to be accused of being a lawbreaker in front of Menelaus and his court than in front of God and his!"

"You'll think differently, old man, when the king arrives." Ariston looked around the room at the prisoners. "But don't worry—King Antiochus and Lord Menelaus are merciful. You'll all be given the chance to repent of your stubbornness." He turned back to Eleazar. "And ample incentive to do so, I expect."

7

The sun's circle had sunk entirely below the horizon, leaving the barren hillsides a murky gray. The movement of the fifty men making their way south through the ravines and wadis would have been barely perceptible in the daylight. Gray themselves in the dusk, they appeared as no more than a mist moving through the cracks in the mountains.

Mattathias held up his hand, signaling the company to stop and sit. Over the crest of this hill was an open plain, perhaps one-and-a-half kilometers across, leading to the village of Elasa. After a few hours, when it was fully night, they would cross over. The men remained quiet, some closing their eyes, trying to slow their adrenaline-infused pulse and find a little rest before their swords, sickles, axes, or hammers drew their first blood. Simon sat with his father, Judah, and Avaran, reviewing one last time the information he had gathered from his visit to the village two days before.

It was just two nights before the new moon, and the clouds were cooperating to dim even the light of the stars. When Mattathias was satisfied that most of Elasa's occupants would be sleeping, he roused his men and led them across the plain toward the short wall of the village. Two men, the last on the rotation of ladder detail, leaned the makeshift ladder against the wall. Judah climbed to the top and peered over cautiously. Satisfied that they had chosen their point of entry well, he signaled to Avaran and two other men to follow as he jumped to the ground. The four men moved through the shadows until they approached the village gate. The two brothers came up behind the two Syrian soldiers on duty. Judah cupped his hand over one's mouth and slit his throat with a knife. Avaran merely snapped the neck of his mark. The other two revolutionaries quickly opened the gate while the brothers guarded their backs.

Mattathias and the main force spilled into the village. Their first target was the barracks that housed the small Syrian garrison of twenty soldiers. They had the superior force by far, but still moved with stealth to preserve the element of surprise as long as possible. Mattathias would far rather achieve his objectives without a fight and preserve the lives of all his men. Ten revolutionaries fell upon the four soldiers on watch while the rest streamed into the garrison and killed the remaining soldiers on their cots. They took the weapons from the corpses and found another dozen swords and assorted daggers and helmets in the closet that served for an armory.

The men regrouped in front of the garrison. Simon led forty of them through the village, sending them in groups of five to break into particular houses. Each group emerged with a baby boy in his hands followed by screaming parents and frightened siblings. They brought the babies to a table that Judah had dragged out from the garrison and laid each one in turn before Mattathias. The older priest pulled out a flint knife from his belt and sterilized it in a fire.

"These are children of the covenant," he roared above the din of the growing assembly of parents and other villagers. "They belong to the God of Abraham. If you have not done your duty toward your God, I will." He inspected each baby. Those who had already been circumcised he ordered returned to their parents. Those who had not, he kept before him. Mattathias began to intone the customary benediction.

"Blessed are you, O Lord our God, King of the universe, who has made us holy by the giving of the law and commanded us concerning circumcision."

Judah held the first baby as Mattathias leaned over him with his knife. A villager approached the line of revolutionaries with his hands raised before him to show that he intended no harm. As they allowed him to pass, he began to speak the proper benediction as his baby cried out.

"Blessed are you, O Lord our God, King of the universe, who has made us holy by the giving of the law and commanded us to enroll him in the covenant of Abraham, our father."

Mattathias looked up at the child's father approvingly and handed the child to him. "You must have the courage to bring this child up in the way of God's commandments. Obedience to the covenant is our debt and duty to God, whether it costs us nothing or costs us everything."

Mattathias proceeded to circumcise the remaining babies. Some parents shouted out curses, two other fathers joined in the blessing. What mattered to the priest was that God would now look down upon this village and not see abomination.

Simon returned to the garrison with the last five men. These were dragging an older man.

"Are you going to circumcise him, too?" said Avaran, provoking laughter from the other freedom fighters.

Mattathias looked down at the figure who had been dropped at his feet. "You are an elder of Israel, entrusted with leading God's people. And where have you led them?"

He picked the nobleman off the ground by the back of his neck, drove him to the altar that had been erected in the courtyard in front of the garrison, and threw him down before it.

"'If anyone secretly entices you saying "Let us go worship other gods,"'" Mattathias recited for the whole village to hear, "'show them no pity or compassion and do not shield them. You will be sure to kill them.'"

"No, please," the elder begged. "I don't want any trouble. I left Jerusalem to return to my own estates to avoid all the trouble."

"You worshiped in front of this idol, at this altar, didn't you?"

"I had to. We had to. The soldiers came. There was no choice."

"There is always a choice." With these words, Mattathias thrust his sword through the man's bowels.

The gathered crowd fell completely silent.

"The Torah prescribes death for the village that embraces other gods," Mattathias said evenly, "but I sense that this is not the case here."

Almost at once, a group of villagers approached the altar. They stood to one side of it and, pushing and lifting with all their strength, threw the large horizontal stone to the ground. Others came up and knocked down the idols that had been erected in its vicinity. One man reached out his hand for the hammer carried by one of the revolutionaries, and then used it to smash the faces of the idols.

"Today Elasa has been cleansed of its defilements," Mattathias declared. "See to it that you walk in the ways of the Lord, turning neither to the right nor to the left, from this day on. Tomorrow evening begins a Sabbath. Observe it, and let it be a day of new beginnings for you. And remember," he added with a hint of menace, "the law also has its champions."

Mattathias signaled his company to move out. As they crossed through the gate, a villager called out: "You're just going to leave us here? What do you think will happen when this garrison fails to check in? What will the next group of soldiers do to us?"

"You can always tell them that we did this," Mattathias replied. "Or you can decide to do the same to them."

Memnon had been riding eastward from Jerusalem through barren mountains for almost two hours, a double column of one hundred soldiers maintaining a fast march behind him. The sun was now beating down on them in full strength. Their scout brought them at last to the squad of soldiers that had sent for reinforcements earlier that morning. Memnon rode up to the squad leader, who snapped to attention and saluted the commander.

"At ease, Captain. What's the situation?"

"We've continued scouting this area since sending our messenger earlier this morning. We've identified a system of a dozen or so caves in this mountain range. There may be several hundred refugees from Jerusalem living inside."

"The revolutionaries who fled?"

"It's probable that there are some present in the mix, sir, but we have also observed families—women and children—present."

Memnon rode forward toward the mountain range before him. It would not be easy to take these caves by force.

"Come down from there and return with us to Jerusalem!" he shouted out. "Do as the king commands, and you can live in peace!"

"You have taken Jerusalem, our holiest place," a voice called back, echoing down the cliff face. "Leave us these caves and this desert, so we can worship our God here at least!"

"These caves also belong to the king, and his commands will be obeyed here as they are in the rest of Judea," Memnon retorted. "Come down, and obey the lord of this land!"

"We *do* obey the Lord of this land," came the reply, "and we will not break his laws."

Memnon cursed under his breath, rode back to his soldiers, and dismounted. "Unload the catapults and position them over against those largest caves. We're going to have to do this the hard way."

He walked to the circle of squad leaders within his own cohort and began pointing to areas on the mountain. "Attacking from below is suicide, since they have the high ground and, I imagine, an unlimited number of rocks to throw down on our heads. So lead your squads up that ridge and enter the caves from above, there, and there. We'll provide cover fire from the catapults until you're in position."

Within half an hour the first soldiers had reached their positions and begun to hammer iron spikes into the limestone ridge. More followed, taking their positions and securing their ropes similarly. The catapults continued firing at the mouths of caves, a few lucky stones flying squarely in, brief screams testifying to their effects. Memnon signaled the last volley. In the briefest of silences that followed, he heard the sound of chanting rolling down the cliff face.

The first wave of soldiers rappelled down into their assigned caves and took up positions expecting immediate resistance. Successive waves followed until several dozen soldiers had entered each of the three largest caves in the cliff. No rocks were thrown, no angry or desperate revolutionaries assaulted them. The soldiers only found scores of people on their knees, singing tunes that seemed, to those who had been stationed in Judea for some time, reminiscent of what they had heard in Jerusalem's Temple years ago.

The soldiers moved toward the people gathered in the rear of the cave, their swords drawn. The men had positioned themselves closer to the caves' entrances to shield their families from the bombardment with their own bodies. Now they turned to face the soldiers, their families still behind them. One of them, Joram ben Levi, rose to stand in front of his wife and two children, who had escaped Jerusalem to meet him here. She continued singing and buried her children's heads in her bosom. The soldiers hesitated, first because they were still expecting that at some point they had to be met with violent resistance, then because they were perplexed about what to do to an enemy that did not lift up a sword or spear. One of the squad leaders stepped forward and plunged his sword up under Joram's rib cage and into his chest, restoring clarity of purpose for the rest of his troops. Within the space of a few minutes, the singing had stopped.

Antiochus entered Jerusalem preceded by two hundred soldiers and followed by two hundred more. He rode into the city in a carriage as a safeguard against dissidents' projectiles—he did not plan on taking any chances with the local population where his personal safety was concerned. He disembarked only when he arrived at the Akra and his troops had taken up positions throughout the square, on the platform of the Temple, and on the parapets of the fortress itself.

Menelaus emerged from the Akra. "You are most welcome in your city, Highness."

"This is not a social visit, Menelaus," Antiochus said, brushing away Menelaus's greeting like an unpleasant odor. "I am here to do what you could not."

"We have been making good progress in rooting out the recalcitrant, Majesty. If you had given us just a little more time . . ."

"I did not travel these past four days to be regaled with excuses. Have you done as I ordered?"

"Yes, Highness. More than fifty lawbreakers have been arrested and are being kept under guard in the Akra. Initial interrogations have given us leads on several dozen more. They will be rounded up before the night is over."

"I want to begin by mid-morning, after a good night's sleep."

"I thought we might set up in the Temple itself."

"Interesting," mused Antiochus. "Let's have a look."

Menelaus led Antiochus, accompanied by his personal bodyguard of twenty, up the ramps and stairways into the Temple courts. The place was surprisingly empty, save for a few devotees at the shrines in the outer courtyard.

"I want this place filled tomorrow, Menelaus," Antiochus said. "Call a special assembly to join in sacrifices to the gods and to feast on the meat in their honor."

He walked across the courtyard and through the inner courts to the area of the great altar itself with its three shrines to the highest god as known by the Greeks, the Syrians, and the local population.

"We'll set up here," Antiochus said, "beside the altar."

His eyes ranged over the marble tables, the pillars with their hooks for suspending the sacrificial animals, the braziers filled with fire ready to be employed for any ritual.

"The place comes almost pre-equipped for our purposes," he observed grimly.

Antiochus waved to the captain of his bodyguard, who immediately left the premises to organize the detail that would take the instruments they had brought for the occasion into the Temple and set them up.

"Your prisoners will obey and worship, or they will die. Gather the residents tomorrow morning, Menelaus. I want everyone who might still resist your decrees to be here to witness the penalty for such rebellion."

The squad leader drew back the bolts on the wooden door and pulled it open. A stench of sweat, urine, and excrement billowed out into the hallway. Binyamin fought not to gag. Inside, Jews sat crowded together, covering the floor from one wall to the other. A large stone jar sat in the corner, no doubt serving as the latrine. Soldiers pushed him, Ari, and Miryam into the converted storeroom and slammed the door shut behind them. The air was thick and stifling. The only source of light was a small square opening near the ceiling where a single stone had been removed. Legs retracted here and there throughout the room, and just enough space appeared for them to sit and wait.

Binyamin surveyed the faces in the room, willing his eyes to adjust to the dimness and his lungs to accept the foul air. Against the wall he saw the face of one of his neighbors. One eye was swollen shut and the cheeks were lacerated and bruised. Binyamin looked closer to see that his left hand cradled a mass of blood-soaked rags where his right hand had once been.

"Shaul? Is that you?"

"Binyamin, Miryam," Shaul answered with his eye closed. "Forgive me. It's my fault you're here. They wanted names . . . I tried not to give in, but I . . . I . . ."

"Hush now, Shaul," Miryam said reassuringly. "Your wounds are proof of your courage—and your friendship."

"Binyamin? You, and Miryam, too?"

Binyamin immediately recognized the voice of Eleazar and turned toward it.

"Master Eleazar. We had heard that you were taken but had no means to visit you."

"Well," he replied with a half-hearted smile, "now we can visit."

"Ari's with us as well."

"Ari? Last I heard you were in Modein with Mattathias."

"I came back when I heard what was happening in the city. I was afraid for Mother."

"You're a good son," Eleazar acknowledged. "But I should have preferred to have remembered you fighting for God's cause alongside Mattathias and Judah."

"I'm not afraid to fight for God's cause here alongside you and Binyamin."

"I don't doubt it, little lion."

"Is Hannah here with you?" Miryam inquired.

"My wife—" Eleazar struggled to suppress the feelings that choked out his words. "She's dead, God rest her soul. She was already sick when we were taken. She didn't last three days here." He regained his composure and nodded to himself. "Better, really."

They fell silent for a few moments, to honor her memory and Eleazar's loss.

Binyamin spoke. "Antiochus has arrived in the city."

"It won't be long, then," Eleazar said.

"What do they want from us?" asked a voice from another corner in the room.

"They want to make examples of us," Eleazar answered. "I say, we let them." Eleazar sat himself up straighter against the wall on which he had been leaning. "Brothers and sisters," he began, "we have been brought here to give testimony to our nation and to our relationship with the one God. What we do tomorrow in the face of whatever happens to us, that will be the witness we bear. For myself, I hope that my witness will be like that of the three young men who were Daniel's companions in exile in Babylon.

"Nebuchadnezzar was a powerful and arrogant king, like this Antiochus. He, too, thought himself a god, able to sail on land and march on water, able to order people to forget the gods their people had known for generations. One day he had the idea to erect a great golden statue on the plain of Dura, and he issued his decree that whenever the trumpets and pipes should raise their clamor, all people were to stop what they were doing, fall down, and worship the golden idol. If they did not, they would be thrown alive into the fire of a great furnace.

"Well, the trumpets and pipes made their clamor, and people dropped to the ground left and right, fearing the king and his furnace more than their own gods—all except Hananiah, Mishael, and Azariah. They knew the living God, our God. And they knew that they owed God greater reverence and obedience than any human king. So when they were brought before the king and threatened personally by him with the choice of worshiping the golden idol or dying in the flames, they said: 'If it pleases our God whom we serve to deliver us from the furnace and out of your hand, let him deliver us. But if not, understand that we will not serve your gods and we will not worship the golden statue that you have set up.' And so they were thrown into the fire."

Eleazar looked around at the faces of the faithful huddled together around him in the prison, trying to pour his own strength through his eyes into theirs.

"That is the witness I pray that I will be able to give tomorrow. I want to tell Antiochus, Menelaus, and anyone else who is there to watch that our God and our way of life are worth dying for, and I am praying for the strength to do so."

He looked to the ground for a moment and smirked as he thought to himself about the end of their story.

"Now, I should also like to find that an angel will come and cause the flames to bend around this old body rather than ravage and consume it. But I think that I should not expect that to happen. You see, we are surrounded by all kinds of abominations here—here, in God's most Holy City and in God's most holy Temple. For how many years has God's law, God's covenant been abused in this place? How many insults has God borne from the people he chose from among every other? We have not been taken into exile or seen our city leveled to the ground, like Daniel and his companions. Our punishment is still ahead of us.

"So I am not praying that God will send his angel to deliver me from dying tomorrow. I am praying that God will accept my death and whatever precedes it as an offering on behalf of our people. I pray that the reverence I hope to show God tomorrow will be received by him as restitution for the assaults on his honor by our nation, so that, perhaps, he will become merciful toward us again and restore us to our former security, governed by his laws."

His lips formed a smile of resignation as he looked into their faces once again. "What other atonement offering can we make in Jerusalem?"

8

Meir and Tavitha followed the crowd up the ramps and into the Temple. The shrines in the outer court were bustling with activity, and the courtyard was filled with Jerusalem's residents. As they looked around the space, they could see that the cohorts from the Akra were also present in full force. Smoke was already billowing over the wall of the inner courts, signaling that the sacrifices to Zeus Olympios, Baal Shamen, and the God of Israel were already well under way. Meir was in no rush to enter that space. He came into the outer courtyard only reluctantly, afraid to disobey the summons that all Jerusalem's residents should come together to celebrate the city's unity and recovery after the recent uprisings.

They bumped into Telamon, who was making his way toward the inner court.

"Morning, Hilaron, Tavitha," he said, acknowledging them both. "Quite the festival. I can't remember when the Temple has been this alive."

"Yes, it seems everyone obeyed the command to show up," replied Meir, reminding his friend of the underlying cause for the good attendance. "Where's the king?"

"In the innermost courtyard. He's going to try to rehabilitate some rebels that Menelaus rounded up."

Meir's heart skipped a beat. Tavitha noticed immediately that something was wrong. She took his hand and squeezed it, peering into his eyes with an inquiring look.

"They're not rebels, Telamon," he said after a moment. "They're just Jews who want to be able to observe their religion the way they used to—in the manner that Antiochus's father and brother before him allowed."

"Well, Hilaron, whatever they are, I wouldn't want to be one of them right now. I saw Antiochus's soldiers setting up last night. Pretty nasty equipment."

Hilaron slowed his pace.

"Go on ahead, Telamon."

"All right, but you better hurry. It should be quite a show!" It was obvious that Telamon regretted the words as soon as they escaped his lips. He often forgot that Meir was himself a Jew. He shook his head apologetically and continued to make his way into the inner courts.

"We don't have to go in there, Meir," Tavitha said soothingly.

"I know some of the people in there," he replied slowly. "Eleazar was arrested over a week ago, together with everyone that gathered in his house for the Sabbath." His voice trailed off. "He'll be in there. I know it."

Meir thought about all the evenings Eleazar and Hannah had spent at their home, and his family at theirs, both before his father's death and all the more after. How much they cared after his family during those first few difficult years. "I have to go in," he said.

Tavitha squeezed his hand again as if to help brace him for the journey, and they walked across the rest of the outer court, through the middle court, and up the stairway to the inner court. As they neared the top of the stairway, they could see that the place was crowded with worshipers and spectators. Priests stood atop the altar, tending to their rites while attendants were preparing the meat for distribution to the crowd. Soldiers lined the entire perimeter of the courtyard. In front of the steps leading into the sanctuary itself, Antiochus's soldiers had erected a platform on which the king, Menelaus, and their closest friends and advisors sat in portable but elegant chairs. Tables were spread in front of the platform, and servants walked among the dignitaries, offering them food from their trays of meats, bread, and fruit.

It was hard to see much else from behind the crowd of people standing at the top landing of the stairway. Meir began to push his way through, Tavitha following in his wake. After they had passed through about three meters of spectators, they could see the whole of the inner courtyard. Unfamiliar furniture had been brought into the place. A wooden rectangular frame stood in the empty space between the altar and the tables formerly used for butchering the sacred animals. A heavier wooden table, set horizontally, was not far away. Meir began to make out the details of gears and axles on the second. It began to dawn on him what these furnishings would be used for. He began to search the courtyard more anxiously, noting the tools spread out on one of the marble tables near the two frames. They were neither the tools used for construction nor for sacrificial rituals. Flames leaped over the rims of the familiar braziers, licking the bases of the unfamiliar iron implements that had been placed in them.

"Oh, Meir!" Tavitha exclaimed as she gripped his upper arm.

Meir looked at her, then looked off in the direction of her gaze. There, to the right of the instruments, was a squad of soldiers surrounding a group of prisoners. The captives were shackled and had been forced to their knees, so it was easy to overlook them. Now, however, Meir could see the faces of at least one-third of the prisoners. His knees buckled beneath him as he recognized his mother and his brothers.

"Any preferences, Menelaus, as to where to begin?"

Menelaus surveyed the group as if thinking about Antiochus's question, but he had made up his own mind days before.

"That old man toward the front of the group," he said, pointing to Eleazar. "He's been a thorn in my side from the start and has become a leader of popular resistance. Get him to turn, and the rest will follow more easily."

Antiochus rose from his chair and pointed to Eleazar. A soldier grabbed the person to Eleazar's right, and Antiochus shook his head and wagged his finger toward his own right. The two soldiers descended upon the old man together, grabbed him by his upper arms, and hauled him forward to stand in the middle of the courtyard.

Antiochus took a few steps toward him while an attendant carried a platter piled high with cooked meat and held it in front of Eleazar.

"We have sacrificed the prescribed animals to the gods who watch over Antioch-at-Jerusalem," Antiochus began, addressing all the prisoners together, "and we invite you to join your fellow residents in sharing in this meal as a sign of your willingness to live in peace and solidarity with them."

He walked toward Eleazar, each step deliberate.

"Take a mouthful of this meat, and all is forgiven. We will start over together with a clean slate."

Eleazar did not even glance at the platter and continued to avoid eye contact with the king.

"I don't want to hurt you, old man. Really, I'm more embarrassed for you than angry. You've lived so long, but in all that time you've never examined your native superstitions, so as to be free to make wise choices."

He took out the dagger he wore on his belt, stabbed a piece of the meat sitting on the platter, and held it up between Eleazar's face and his own.

"This meat seems to me to be as good as any other," he continued as he made a show of examining the pork. He waved it in front of his own face and inhaled deeply. "It smells as inviting as any other, and perhaps better than most."

He took a bite and chewed it thoughtfully. "It's delicious, really. It will sustain me as well as any other meat. I frankly don't see the problem here."

Antiochus dropped the remainder of the piece back on the platter and returned his gaze to Eleazar. "Why refuse this gift, from all of nature's great bounty? Isn't it an insult against nature—an act of injustice, really—to despise her gifts as you do?"

Eleazar looked away from the king with a glimmer of impatience in his eyes, as if he just wished Antiochus would get on with it.

"Or do you object to the fact that the meat comes from an animal sacrificed on that altar? You know, no one would have a problem with your special devotion to your tribal god if you didn't also provoke everyone around you by claiming that their gods—whose claim on your neighbors' devotion is just as strong as your own god's on yours—don't exist." Antiochus leaned closer to Eleazar's ear. "That's not very generous minded of you, and highly insulting to the rest of us."

Antiochus walked past Eleazar and addressed everyone gathered in the court. "And for the good of this city and my empire, it all stops today!"

Many of the spectators broke into applause for their king at this final statement, while Antiochus looked at the captain of his guard and jerked his head in Eleazar's direction. The king returned to his chair as two soldiers dragged Eleazar to an upright wooden frame. They pulled off his tunic and his linen loincloth, leaving him completely exposed. Some of the people, even those gathered on the dais with Menelaus, momentarily averted their eyes out of shame. The soldiers proceeded to shackle his wrists to the top of the frame and his ankles to the bottom corners. Then they went over to the table where their instruments were arrayed and picked up a pair of leather whips. One stood behind the old man and cracked the whip against his back, leaving a single laceration that began immediately to run with blood. The other soldier took his position in front of Eleazar and did the same across his stomach. The captain stood off to one side, shouting at him.

"Tell us you'll eat the meat, and we'll stop."

Eleazar made every effort to keep himself from shouting out in pain as the soldiers continued to take turns, each new blow of the whip now spattering the blood from previous blows onto the pavement below him.

"Agree to eat, old man," the captain urged. "This can end any time you choose."

"No!" Eleazar screamed, as much to declare himself as to give himself an opportunity to cry out.

The soldiers continued until Eleazar collapsed under the blows. Antiochus held up his hand for them to stop. The captain reached for a bucket of water and dashed it against Eleazar's face. His head jerked upright as the water ran crimson off his body onto the pavement.

"There, old man," Antiochus said as he rose and approached him a second time. "Feels good when it stops, doesn't it? We don't have to continue. Your wounds are still treatable. Oh, yes, there will be scars, but no permanent damage. Have pity on yourself. Eat the pork, and this will all go away."

Eleazar's eyes failed to focus, and his body trembled from pain and shock.

Antiochus grasped Eleazar's hair and lifted his head toward the sanctuary.

"They say your god is merciful and compassionate. Surely he'll forgive you, if you go against his commands under such compulsion as this?"

Eleazar could tolerate no more.

"What arrogance!" he spat through labored breaths, startling Antiochus with his sudden force. "You think you're more compelling than God? The God we've known and worshiped for a thousand years? You think you're more compelling than my own conscience? After living my entire life in line with the wisdom of God's law, I'm not about to throw that all away by polluting myself now just because you don't understand it!" He looked away from the king back to the sanctuary. "God will receive me pure, and my ancestors will welcome me. You may bully ungodly people to go along with you, but you won't bully me!"

"Unbelievable," Antiochus said in a mixture of surprise and rage as he walked back toward his chair and signaled to the captain to move on to more extreme procedures.

The pair of soldiers went to the nearest brazier and pulled out two flaming torches. Alcimus jumped off his chair and knelt on one knee before the king's path.

"Highness, please wait. Your anger is deserved, but consider—we're just hearing the ravings of an old man who's clearly lost his wits. Please give me leave to try to talk some sense into him before you go any further."

Antiochus held up his hand, stopping the forward advance of the soldiers, and nodded curtly to Alcimus.

The priest rose and walked up to Eleazar. "Eleazar, please. You don't need to die like this. Say you've been hasty; ask the king for an hour to consider his arguments. In the meanwhile, I'll have someone scare up some cooked lamb and I'll bring it to you myself. We'll pretend it's the pork. You can avoid polluting yourself and live at the same time. Antiochus doesn't care what you eat. All he needs is a public sign of your acquiescence."

Alcimus looked directly at Eleazar, his eyes pleading along with this voice. "Think of the people around you," he continued. "If you keep on in your stubbornness, your example may only serve to make them throw away their lives as well. Think of the pain you can save them."

Eleazar's eyes widened in understanding. "I am thinking of them, Alcimus. I'm not going to play the role of a coward just to live a year or two longer—and that at the cost of encouraging them to eat defiling food because I prove to them that God's covenant is not worth dying for."

Alcimus opened his mouth to object.

"Don't waste another breath," Eleazar said. "And you, tyrant," he spat out to Antiochus, "let's get on with it."

Alcimus backed away in disbelief as the soldiers approached. One touched the torch to Eleazar's back, causing the blood flowing from the lacerations to sizzle and his skin to char. His body went rigid from the sudden onset of pain, and he screamed out to God. The soldier withdrew his torch and the captain shouted into his face, but Eleazar did not seem to hear him. Both soldiers were now holding their torches against or under parts of his body, sending wisps of black smoke into the air, a new odor of burning flesh filling the Temple court and competing with the lingering odor of the morning sacrifices to the gods. Eleazar, however, kept his gaze fixed on the sanctuary. In that moment, he was aware of nothing so powerfully as the presence of God with him in that place. He channeled all that might have gone into screams of agony into the chanting of psalms at the top of his lungs.

Hear my prayer, Lord; let my cry reach you!
Don't hide your face from me in my distress,
My life passes away like smoke,
My bones burn like a furnace . . .

The soldiers finally withdrew their torches from his blackened flesh, leaving Eleazar gasping heavily and trembling violently.

"God," he hissed through shallow, gasping breaths, "you know that I could have saved my life, but that I chose to die for your covenant. Please let my obedience count on behalf of your nation. Let my punishment be enough for their disobedience. Restore your people, restore your covenant, and drive the ungodly from the land!"

A wave of convulsions wracked his body, then a perfect stillness as he bowed his head and hung with all his weight from his hands. The stillness permeated the entire Temple court as the onlookers watched in silence, some waiting to see if Eleazar was truly dead, others stunned by his courage and commitment.

The king shook his head and broke the silence with a single word. "Delusional!"

He rose from his chair and addressed the gathered crowd. "I think we've seen enough madness for one day," he declared. "We'll reconvene to offer sacrifice again tomorrow morning, and invite the remainder of our reluctant subjects to join us in a spirit of unity."

The two soldiers moved toward Eleazar's body and began to unshackle his burned limbs.

"Leave him there," Antiochus ordered. "It will help the others think about what awaits them."

Meir knocked on his apartment door, the volume and rapidity betraying his agitation. The latch slid back, and the door swung inward.

"You've been gone for hours," Tavitha said, her tone full of concern for her husband. "Did you find any help for your family?"

"Timarchos was able to get me into Menelaus's palace, but Menelaus kept me waiting for three hours while he finished entertaining the king and his friends. When he finally deigned to see me, he was a stone."

Meir sat down on a mat and leaned against the wall, feeling at last the exhaustion of his own anxiety. "Timarchos tried to negotiate some kind of deal, but Menelaus wouldn't budge. No special favors, least of all for someone like me, who was once a client of one of Jason's closest friends."

Tavitha sat down beside him and took his hand in her own. "What will you do?"

Meir remained silent. It would be impossible to convince his family to eat the unclean meat—and wrong for him to try. If Menelaus refused to help, who could?

"I could try to get in to see Antiochus. He might grant a favor."

"How would you get to him, if not through Menelaus?"

Meir had no answer, and at the moment no idea.

"I need to go see my family. Let them know that I'm trying to help them. Take them some food . . ." His voice trailed off in despair over his impotence to do anything more to help them than take them some dinner.

"Why can't they just eat the meat and save themselves?"

Meir was surprised by the question, but quickly realized it was the same question that Antiochus and so many others would be asking.

"Would you, if Menelaus had decided to try to force all our Gentile residents to renounce their gods, or declare the superiority of our God to yours?"

Tavitha's silence was an admission of an answer.

"That's the difference, Tavitha. They wouldn't be who they are without God and our covenant with him. They couldn't betray our God for the sake of escaping any more than they could betray each other to do so without becoming something else, something unrecognizable."

Meir rose up and walked into the kitchen. He emerged with a bag bulging with foods and a wineskin.

"This will all take some time," Meir explained.

"Do you want me to come with you?"

He reached up to brush a strand of hair back from her face and touched her cheek gently. "More than anything," he replied, "but I think I need to do tonight's work on my own." His hand moved to the back of her neck and drew her lips to his own while her arms found their way around his back and held him close.

"Whatever happens tonight and tomorrow," she said, "remember that I love you."

"Whatever happens," he replied with a warm smile, "remember that I love you, too."

Meir stepped out across the threshold, and Tavitha closed the door behind him. He lingered there for a moment, gripped by a sudden reluctance to leave, as if he might not find his way back. Staying was not an option, however, so he shook off the feeling and headed into the evening. In fifteen minutes he had entered the Temple and crossed the outer court. As the day's schedule of sacrifices had been completed, a guard stopped him at the threshold of the middle court.

"What is your business here?"

"I'm here to see my family. They're inside."

"Too bad for them," the guard replied. "Let me see what you're carrying."

The guard rifled through the bag to make sure there were no weapons that could be used to deprive the king of his plans either through the suicide of the prisoners or attacks on the guards.

"And on your person?"

"Nothing," Meir replied as the guard patted him down.

"All right, you can go in. And try to talk some sense into them—that's my advice," the guard called after him.

Meir ascended the staircase into the inner court. Guards stood in groups around the fires in the braziers, warming pieces of meat from the day's sacrifices skewered on their swords and daggers, laughing over soldiers' tales. Others remained more vigilant around the prisoners, still herded together right of center in the open court. Meir made his way toward them.

"Mother?"

Miryam turned around and smiled. "Meir! I was hoping to see you tonight." She raised a shackled hand and Meir helped her onto her feet. She lifted her arms so that Meir could slip in under her chain for a warm embrace.

"I . . . I brought you some food," he stammered, opening the bag and producing a loaf of bread and some fruit and cheese.

"A last meal, Brother?" Binyamin observed.

"No!" Meir objected. "I'm not giving up on you. I spent all afternoon trying to see Menelaus, but he's not willing to help. There's still a chance. If I can just get in to see Antiochus, he might at least allow me to take you out of Jerusalem, even out of Judea, anywhere he would designate. It would be exile, but it would be better."

Binyamin and Ari looked at each other and then at their mother.

"Don't trouble yourself, Meir," Binyamin said at last. "Why should we escape when so many of our brothers and sisters here face death for the sake of the covenant?"

"This is where God stationed us," Ari added. "This is where we'll take our stand."

"Take your stand?" Meir asked incredulously. "This is where Antiochus will cut you to pieces."

"But he won't turn us," Ari replied, "and so he won't beat us."

"And then, maybe he'll see that he can't fight the nation's commitment to the covenant, and he'll stop what he's doing here," Binyamin added. "Lives will be saved."

"At the very least, we'll tell him and everyone else that Israel's covenant with the one God is worth dying for."

Meir could not suppress the tears that began to fill and overflow his eyes.

"I want you to live!"

"I want for us to live also," Miryam said. "I want to see my grandchildren. I want to see Ari married and settled down. I want to see all of you live long and happy lives. But tomorrow we may have to choose between what we want and what is God's due. And how could we live after tomorrow, if tomorrow we betray all that we are by betraying God?"

Meir embraced his mother again and sobbed on her shoulder.

"There, there, Meir," she said soothingly. "Hush now."

She drew him back down with her into a seated position on the floor and continued cradling him in her arms until he had regained his composure. He sat upright again and looked at the corpse of Eleazar for a few silent moments.

"Jason never wanted any of this," he said at last, not taking his gaze from the body.

"Jason made all of this possible," Binyamin replied as gently as he could manage. "This is the result of his arrogance, thinking that he knew better than Honiah—and better than God—how God's land should be governed."

Meir simply nodded. It was true.

Ari pulled off a piece of the loaf of bread and started to eat. He noticed Binyamin staring at him, and he broke off another piece and offered it to Miryam. Binyamin smiled and reached for a piece of the loaf himself. They ate for a while in silence, savoring the taste of the bread, taking nothing for granted this night.

"Remember what Passover was like when we were all together?" Ari asked. "I always loved the feeling of Passover and hearing the stories of Moses leading us out of Egypt."

"I remember one Passover in particular when Father lifted the cover from the dish that was supposed to contain the boiled egg and there was nothing there," Binyamin chimed in.

Miryam worked to recollect the event, then looked at Ari and let out a short laugh.

"What?" asked Ari.

"You were just four," Miryam said, "and you had gotten into the eggs before dinner and eaten them all without telling anyone." Meir smiled to remember as well. "And of course it was also a Sabbath, so there was no chance to buy any more, so we just had to pretend there was an egg there."

Ari smiled and nodded in acknowledgment.

Binyamin looked slyly in Meir's direction. "Then there was the time when Meir was five years old and Father had read to him the story of Adam and Eve."

"Oh, not this again," Meir objected.

"And I catch a glimpse of Meir walking out into the street stark naked, so I run after him to stop him, and he says, 'But Abba said that when God made us, we were naked and unashamed.'"

"Yes, very funny, Binyamin," Meir muttered beneath the laughter.

Binyamin grew more serious.

"There were also moments of great pride: when you and Ari came of age and became sons of the covenant, reading from the Book of the Covenant for the first time in the assembly; when you became a better metalworker than I would ever be; even when you won those stupid Greek games."

Meir's eyes began to tear again as he looked up at Binyamin.

"Oh yes, I hated the fact that such things had been introduced into God's city, but how could a part of me not be proud that my little brother bested all those Greeks and Syrians at their own games."

Binyamin fell silent again as he reflected further.

"And while it's . . . difficult for me to accept the fact that you married a Gentile, getting Tavitha out of the sex trade promoted by our own 'nobility' was an absolute good."

Meir nodded as he fought back his tears.

"I've tried to walk a tightrope between the covenant and the Greek way of life," he admitted. "If I didn't fall off, Binyamin, it's because of your influence."

Binyamin smiled. He extended his hand to Meir, and they clasped each other's forearms. Miryam beamed.

"Well, one prayer answered at least," she said.

They sat silently together for a few moments, allowing years of conflict to drain away and living fully in the moment of homecoming.

"I wish Abba were here," Ari said.

"I wish we weren't," replied Binyamin.

A few seconds later, they broke out together in nervous laughter.

"We've enjoyed many good things," Miryam said. "Remember that it was all because of God, who gave us life. It's right to use our lives now to defend God's law."

She poured all her effort into fighting back the sorrow threatening to engulf her. "Tomorrow will be a difficult day. But on the other side of tomorrow lies eternity. Keep your hearts fixed on that harbor during tomorrow's storms. We'll sit together again there, and your father will be with us, and Abraham, Isaac, and Jacob will welcome us, and God will wipe tomorrow's tears from our eyes."

Miryam reached out, and her three sons moved into her embrace. They stayed there for what seemed an eternity, reliving a lifetime of her love for them, drinking in all the love that she yet had for them for the decades ahead.

They finally released one another.

"You should go, Meir," Binyamin said.

"Take Tavitha and get out of the city," Ari added. "Find Mattathias and Judah. You could help them."

Meir nodded to his brothers. "I'll stay a little longer."

An hour after first light, the sound of soldiers' boots upon the limestone pavement began to rouse the prisoners. None had slept well or much, but by the fourth watch most had sufficiently succumbed to exhaustion to doze. Miryam had not slept at all but had cradled Ari's head in her lap as he rested. Binyamin awoke surprised to find Meir still there, leaning his back against his mother's, his head on her shoulder.

The soldiers unshackled Eleazar's corpse and threw it upon the great fire on the altar to dispose of it. Priests began to appear to prepare for their morning sacrifice to the three faces of the God of the Temple. Three of them began to have words with the soldiers about their use of the sacred fire but were dismissed with profanity.

The prisoners quickly lost interest in the activity around them, and began to use these early morning hours for prayer. They recited psalms under their breath, confessed their sins, prayed for deliverance. If one became too loud, a nearby soldier would strike him or her with the butt of his spear. They paid scant attention to the crowd beginning to gather, the arrival of the king, or the offering of the sacrifice under the direction of Menelaus himself, who had become quite adept in the rites of all three deities. The descent of the captain of the guard and his two torturers seemed to push the prisoners more fervently into their prayers, as though they hoped somehow to escape into those supplications.

The two soldiers surveyed the herd of prisoners, waiting for Antiochus to make the selection. Binyamin watched their actions for a moment and thought about his companions, some of whom were weaker than others. He rose to his feet and stared directly at Antiochus. The soldiers turned and looked to the king.

"What audacity!" Antiochus said just loud enough for the men closest to him to hear. He gestured impatiently to his soldiers, as if it should have been obvious to them what to do.

Meir jumped to his feet and began to move toward Antiochus to make a last, desperate plea.

"Meir!" Binyamin's voice stopped him in his tracks. "It's all right, Meir. My heart is ready." Binyamin raised a shackled hand and placed it firmly and lovingly on his brother's shoulder before the soldiers dragged Binyamin forward.

The captain approached him, followed by the attendant with a plate of fresh meat from the morning sacrifice.

"Will you eat in solidarity with your fellow residents and in obedience to the king's commands?"

"I will eat what is proper for servants of the living God," Binyamin replied, "and in obedience to the One."

Antiochus rose from his chair and took a few steps toward Binyamin. "Don't rave with the same madness as that old man did yesterday. You saw where it got him in the end. There's no honor in being tortured to death out of some sad devotion to a backward way of life—the way of life of a conquered people."

"I believe the same things as that noble and gentle old man," Binyamin said emphatically. "Should I show cowardice in the face of what he endured so bravely for the sake of God?"

Antiochus shook his head slightly from side to side in disbelief and gestured for the soldiers to let the man have it his way.

As they stripped Binyamin and shackled him to the wooden frame, the king leaned over to Menelaus and asked: "Who's that young man in the Greek tunic? He wasn't there yesterday."

Menelaus raised an eyebrow and looked sideways at Timarchos. "That, I believe, is Hilaron, Majesty. A client of Timarchos."

Timarchos blushed and looked away.

"Well what on earth is he doing there?"

"I believe that's his family he's with. That's his brother you're flogging right now."

"Oh," the king replied. "Unfortunate."

The captain continued to shout out the invitation to eat the meat and end the pain, but Binyamin did not pay any attention. He focused instead on reciting a psalm, his inflection rising in conjunction with the striking of the lashes against his flesh. The captain finally turned around to face the king, his look communicating what was also obvious to Antiochus. *We're not getting anywhere with this.*

Antiochus held up his hand for the soldiers to stop. He strode across the courtyard and stood in front of Binyamin, watching him as he panted, hanging from his wrists because he was no longer able to stand.

"Is that your mother over there, trying to look strong, but bending over in pain anyway?" Antiochus asked. "Can you imagine how much she's suffering for you right now? Mothers feel everything that happens to their children. And you're really going to make her watch more of this? Have some pity on her. Don't put her through any more of this."

Antiochus lifted Binyamin's head by the hair, dripping with sweat, and tilted it toward the group of prisoners. "You have a duty to live and to take care of her into her old age."

"Your first duty is to God, Binyamin, who gave you to me," Miryam shouted.

Antiochus stood upright suddenly as if splashed with cold water. He stared at Miryam with disbelief.

"I have . . . a duty to be the person . . . that my mother and father raised me to be," Binyamin said between gasps. "I'm not going to put them to shame by giving in to you."

As Antiochus continued to gaze at Miryam, the surprise in his eyes turned to hostile accusation, as if to suggest that what would follow was more her fault than his own.

The two soldiers walked over to the wooden table and rotated and locked it into a vertical position. Unshackling Binyamin, they dragged him over to it and fastened strong ropes around his wrists and iron clamps over his ankles, securing them at the base. One walked over to the marble table holding their equipment and grabbed two meter-long iron bars, tossing one to his comrade. Working together, they inserted the bars into rectangular holes carved into one of the axles and began to turn it, repositioning the bars in a new hole every quarter turn. A metal catch kept the axle from turning in the opposite direction.

The first few turns went quickly and easily, as the slack was taken up. Then Binyamin's limbs went rigid and his wrists moved upward noticeably. The soldiers strained harder on their next turn, while Binyamin's back arched and his eyes and mouth opened wide in shock from the pain of the tension upon all his joints at once.

Meir and Ari stood close to their mother and put their arms around her waist and shoulders, supporting her as they felt her legs give way. Her body lurched forward from the waist in response to a convulsion in her belly, where she felt Binyamin's pain.

The captain approached him again, confident that the point had now been made. "Agree to eat, and we'll release you."

Binyamin turned his head momentarily to look at him, his eyes still wide, gasping for each breath. Then he turned away to look at one of the flaming braziers with the irons sticking out of its mouth. How it resembled his father's old furnace in the metalworking shop.

The captain waited for another moment for some response. When none came, he signaled to the soldiers to give the wheel another quarter-turn, and then another. But Binyamin was no longer present in the Temple court. He was sitting as a boy with his father, watching him work, listening to him tell the stories of their people.

"And why do you think Cain killed Abel, Binyamin?"

"Because God was pleased with the way Abel had worshiped him, but not with the way that Cain worshiped," he heard himself responding in the voice of an eight-year-old boy.

"And this story keeps repeating itself throughout the history of our people. Those who don't know God, and who don't know how to worship the living God, have always attacked those who do."

Binyamin suddenly found himself back in the Temple court, the captain standing before him with an empty bucket. He could scarcely take sips of air despite the convulsing of his diaphragm for more.

"Life and death are right in front of you. Which one do you want?"

"Life!"

The captain gave the signal for the soldiers to stop turning the axles.

"The life," Binyamin gasped, "that God . . . gives . . . to the faithful!"

The captain looked at him for a moment in disbelief, then turned once more to the king, who simply waved his hand impatiently. The captain commanded the soldiers to continue. One more turn, and Binyamin could no longer breathe. The last thing he heard was the sound of his vertebrae separating from one another. One final turn, and the ligaments and cartilage in his shoulders, elbows, and knees, already disjointed several turns ago, began to snap, the courageous soul that held them together having departed.

Yoshe ben Yoezer walked ahead of two dozen men toward the ridge before them. They had spent the better part of the night moving through the desert and its rocky hills and were glad to see greener land with its promise of water and, if they were fortunate, help. They did not notice the scouts watching them until they had reached the foot of the ridge.

"Who are you?"

Adrenaline shot into Yoshe's blood as he whirled around toward the sound of the voice and drew his sword, ready to defend himself and what was left of his people.

The scout revealed himself with his palms raised to show that he intended no harm.

"It's all right," he said. "See? I'm a Jew like you, and you're clearly not friends of the apostates and their armies, so you are welcome here."

"I am Yoshe ben Yoezer," he replied wearily, "and this is, as far as I can tell, what's left of the *Hasidim*."

The scout's face fell as he surveyed the few dozen in the company.

"Come with me," he said. "I'll take you to Zedekiah."

The scout led the company over the ridge and down into the ravine nourished by the Wadi Qilt. Yoshe and his people rushed to kneel beside the stream, drinking from cupped hands. After a few handfuls, Yoshe straightened his back, his closed eyes showing his gratitude to God for having survived. When they had refreshed themselves, the scout instructed them to continue west along the stream while he ran ahead. The band arrived at the edges of the camp and began to notice people gathering fruits and nuts from the plants that grew within the ravine, while others sat at the mouths of caves. They had not walked another hundred meters before they saw a white-robed figure approaching them.

"Yoshe ben Yoezer," said the man. "Blessed be God for preserving your life."

"Zedekiah?"

He remembered the young man of twenty from the Temple. The face before him was worn and gaunt, aged at least twenty years rather than the expected ten. The eyes, however, were unmistakable—the eyes of one who saw the unseen.

"I had prayed for your success in the city, but it was not yet God's time. His wrath was still heavily against our nation for its faithlessness."

"It had better be God's time soon, or else there will be none left of the faithful!" Yoshe declared.

"What befell your company in the desert after your flight from Jerusalem?"

"We hid in caves," Yoshe began. "I had left with these men to look for food. We went toward Tekoa to raid the estates of apostates there. It took us longer than I had expected, and we had to spend the Sabbath not far from the village. When we returned to the caves, we found hundreds of my comrades dead, their wives and children slaughtered beside them. None had put up a fight. They must have been attacked on the Sabbath, and they chose to die rather than violate the day of rest. There were too many to bury, and Syrian patrols were still in the area. So we went into hiding further into the western desert."

Zedekiah raised his eyes to heaven and shut them. "The time is drawing close. The blood of God's faithful ones cries out to him from city and countryside. God must surely avenge their deaths."

"We are hoping to find Mattathias and join up with him. I had hoped that our path would bring us to your camp so that we could leave these few wounded survivors we retrieved in your care while we searched further east for him."

Zedekiah continued to direct his attention heavenward and seemed for a moment not to have heard Yoshe. Then his eyes snapped open, and he looked directly at him. "It is time for all of us to seek him out together."

Zedekiah turned around abruptly and began to walk west toward the heart of his camp. Yoshe found himself trailing after and calling out. "Do you know where he is?"

Zedekiah answered without turning around. "We learned of his activities in Elasa and other villages west of here. I sent my scouts to look for signs, and they believe he and his men went off to the north of those villages."

"Hopefully the Syrians didn't see those same signs."

Zedekiah stopped suddenly and turned to face Yoshe. "God keeps their eyes from seeing what he does not wish them to see. In ten years, no Syrian soldier has ever found *us*."

The priest turned west again but seemed unable to proceed, as if overcome by the momentum of the trajectory upon which God had set him. He fell to his knees. Yoshe stepped forward quickly intending to help him, but stopped when he saw Zedekiah raise his hands and face to heaven.

"God, you have been just in all your actions. You have brought upon us all the curses that you swore to bring upon the unfaithful. Your words have all proven true. Calamity has come upon Jerusalem such as the world has never seen before."

He bowed himself low and seemed to grip the very ground with his outstretched arms as the people near him left off their tasks and fell upon their knees around him.

"Today we have no priest, no burnt offering, no sacrifice, no place to make an offering before you and to find mercy. But let our sorrow and humility be accepted by you as if it were accompanied by many burnt offerings of rams and bulls! May our sacrifice be thus in your sight today, and turn your anger away from your people. Let your face shine once again toward your desolated sanctuary."

"Amen, and amen," said the people around him. Yoshe found himself joining his voice with theirs.

Zedekiah rose and addressed the people around him. "Today let us prepare to leave our place of refuge and join in a holy war. God is raising up a deliverer and an army to accomplish his good purposes." He turned to the scout who had brought him to Yoshe. "Take eleven men with you and carry out a search to the northwest." Zedekiah's eyes pierced the scout with their intensity. "Find Mattathias!"

It had taken Tavitha the better part of an hour to push her way through the crowd that had gathered in what had formerly been the Women's Court and to make her way up the staircase into the inner court. She could deduce from Meir's failure to return home that he had never found a way to get to Antiochus to plead on his family's behalf, and she knew he would be here with them now. As she neared the top of the stairs, it became increasingly difficult for her to force her way through people who were trying to defend their own proximity to the events taking place in the courtyard beyond. She heard a man scream and the gasp that ran through the crowd at the sickening snapping of ligaments and joints that ended his contest. At this, Tavitha drew in a sharp breath in shock at the Jew's fate—and at her king's cruelty.

"This isn't going well," Antiochus observed.

"You see the kind of stubbornness that we've had to deal with here," Menelaus replied, hoping to win the king's sympathy rather than censure.

"I've seen stubbornness many times before, Menelaus. This is well beyond that." Antiochus seemed to be looking for the right label for what he was witnessing.

He began to question the wisdom of coming to Jerusalem and felt a tremor of doubt about proceeding. *What if the whole day goes like this? What will that end up proving?*

"Perhaps you would favor another adjournment, Majesty?" Alcimus suggested, trying to hide his own desire for an end to the spectacle.

Antiochus thought about it for a moment. But as he viewed the group of prisoners, anger at their resistance welled up and washed away more prudent considerations.

"I am not going to retreat before a bunch of rebellious Jews," he declared as he signaled for the captain to select another contestant. *Retreat? Strange choice of words.* Egypt was still very much on his mind, he decided.

As the captain surveyed the prisoners, Ariyeh burned into him with his glare. The Syrian noticed the challenge and scoffed. He signaled to the soldiers to bring that one forward. Antiochus rubbed his hands up and down over his face and rolled his neck around in a few circles to work out the tension before rising from his chair and crossing the distance to the middle of the court.

"And what is your name?" Antiochus half-surprised himself with the question, realizing that he was beginning to take this all quite personally.

"Ariyeh," the youth said defiantly. "It means 'God's lion.'"

"No doubt it does," the king said. "A soldier's name. Perhaps a revolutionary's name?"

"Let me have a sword for a fair fight here, and I'll show you."

"Such spirit!" Antiochus exclaimed. "Unfortunately for you, fair fights can only happen between equals. I am your king, and you are a disobedient subject. Hardly the cast for a fair fight."

Antiochus looked at the young man for a moment and said, "But we really don't have to fight at all. There isn't some script that we have to follow, as if this is a drama, and we certainly don't have to play out a tragedy. Forget that all this," he said, waving vaguely at the instruments, "is even here—none of it has to apply. As much power as I have to punish the disobedient, so much power do I have to shower favor upon those who show themselves loyal to me."

He took a few steps closer to Ariyeh.

"What are you, seventeen? Eighteen maybe? Your prime is still ahead of you, and decades of life after that. Enjoy your youth to the full by adopting our way of life. Leave these provincial prejudices behind, and I'll take you under my own wing. We'll have you trained in the gymnasium, enrolled in the registry of citizens. Eventually, when you're ready, I will see to it that you have a place of honor in my government, either here or abroad—whatever pleases you . . . and your family. What do you say?"

"I may be younger than my brother," he said, gesturing to the body that still dangled awkwardly from the rack, "but I'm not less committed to God. And I'd rather prove worthy of God's favor than of yours."

Antiochus flushed with anger. "Then I'll give you your chance."

He whirled around to return to the platform while the soldiers stripped Ariyeh and shackled him to the frame. They began to pick up their whips when Antiochus shouted:

"No! Let 'God's lion' feel the claws of my lions."

The soldiers returned to the table and donned two pairs of iron gloves fitted with curved knives on each of the fingers. One held up his glove in front of Ari's face while the other walked behind him and placed his fingertips on Ari's shoulders. The soldier in front made a fist with his iron gauntlet, and the other scraped down Ari's back to the waist. He cried out in a piteous wail as the soldier left ten long lacerations a centimeter deep. Miryam lurched instinctively forward, but Meir held on to her and tried to steady her.

Ari managed to stop his screaming and hung from his wrists, gasping for air.

The captain approached him and waved his hand in front of Ari's glassy-eyed expression, trying to get him to focus. "Take a mouthful of this meat and live. Go home with your mother. Let her bind your wounds. You'll have your life back in a month."

The captain took a piece of the meat in his right hand and Ari's lower jaw in his left, stuffing a bit of the pork into his mouth. Ari finally realized what was happening to him and he jerked to attention, spitting the meat onto the floor in front of the captain's boots. The captain shrugged and took a few steps back.

The two soldiers began to drag their gloves across Ari's body once again. This time, he channeled his wailing into an impassioned cantillation: *"Sh'ma, Yisrael, Adonai Elohenu, Adonai echad!"*

Fueled by agony and devotion in equal parts, the song rose above the din in the outer court and called everyone to attention like the melody of the Sirens. The soldiers continued to tear into his flesh, but he continued to wail this single chant, now above an eerie silence.

One of the soldiers looked to his captain, who responded with a curt nod. The soldier held his fingers rigidly straight and plunged the knives up beneath Ari's rib cage, piercing and draining his heart. The silence continued in the inner court, a silence that Antiochus was sure signaled admiration more than horror among the spectators.

Timarchos noticed Meir now moving toward the bodies of his brothers. As he was not a prisoner, there were no shackles or bonds to restrain his movement.

"Hilaron, what are you doing down there?" Timarchos shouted out. "Come back up here where you belong."

This drew Antiochus's attention. *Of course—the young man who won the games here so many years ago.*

Meir seemed not to hear Timarchos calling to him as he stared at the blood-drenched body of his younger brother, but eventually he managed to respond. "No, Timarchos, I'm quite certain that I belong here."

Tavitha broke through the last lines of people to the row of guards that had been stationed to ensure crowd control. She looked between the two guards facing her to see Meir standing in the midst of the courtyard's horrors. Realizing his intent, she tried to scream out to him, to beg him to think of her and leave while he could, but no sound escaped her mouth.

In that instant, she was overwhelmed by the awareness of a presence she had never encountered before in that space or anywhere. It was the One whom Ari had proclaimed in his death-song, who had come in response to the deaths of his faithful ones. Dread flooded her soul, dread on account of the horror of the defilement of his Holy Places with the sacrifices offered to gods that were not gods, dread on account of standing where, she knew now instinctively, she had no place as an idolater herself. She drew back a step in fear, but remained fixed in her gaze on Meir as he bore witness to all, to her.

Meir turned away from the bodies of his brothers and looked incredulously at Antiochus.

"What did I ever see in what you and your way of life had to offer? I can't even remember now."

He looked again toward Ari. "How could you do this to men made of the same flesh and blood as yourself? How could you order such savagery? You were supposed to bring enlightened culture. Instead you brought barbarity such as this city has never seen—even under Nebuchadnezzar."

"I realize this day has been difficult for you, Hilaron," Antiochus said, "but have a care for your tongue. You're not the first to have had to leave family behind to embrace a better way of life—though I grant that few have had to witness what you have."

"All they wanted was to obey our ancestral God and hold on to the traditions that have been handed down to us for centuries upon centuries. Those traditions made them just, brave, and virtuous in every way."

He turned again to Antiochus. "You should have honored such people, not brutalized them!"

"It's hard for you to accept, young man, but they were rebellious and disobedient. No one defies a king's decrees with impunity, and the rest of your people needed to see that."

Antiochus tried with some effort to modulate his tone. "Time will heal these memories. You've had a promising start to life here, and I will make sure that your circumstances improve. I remember you, you know. You're a gifted young man, and now I feel some measure of responsibility for you. Come back with me to Antioch. I'll find an appropriate place for you in my government. A change of scenery, new responsibilities and their rewards to take your mind off things here—you'll see. All will be well for you."

"I don't believe you've tried the pork," Menelaus interrupted.

Antiochus looked quizzically at the priest.

"I don't believe you've tried governing your own sisters and brothers with compassion and modesty," Meir shot back. "Menelaus," he said to Antiochus, "has destroyed the peace of Jerusalem. You were mistaken to get behind him and his insane policies."

"In all his years of moving among us," Menelaus continued, "I've never observed him eat anything that was prohibited by the old laws."

"Is this true, Hilaron?"

"Yes, it's true. I never read anything in Plato or Aristotle that suggested I had to violate my own nation's sacred heritage in order to be a virtuous and accomplished person by Greek standards. I did read, however, about tyrants trying to force virtuous people to act against their consciences."

"I'm willing to allow you some latitude here under the circumstances, Hilaron, but don't forget yourself."

"My name is Meir, and I've forgotten myself too long. I have no wish to go with you to Antioch or anywhere else. I would rather die alongside my brothers. That would be a greater honor than anything you could offer. And may God accept my repentance on behalf of our nation and be reconciled to us quickly."

A tense silence hung in the courtyard.

"So be it," Antiochus decreed.

Twenty soldiers marched in formation behind their captain and his lieutenant westward on the road to Beth Horon. Commander Memnon, who had succeeded to the command of the garrison in Jerusalem after Apollonios's departure and Sarpedon's murder, had ordered such patrol activity intensified in the area between Beth-Horon and Bethel in the wake of furtive attacks on settlements in that area. To the captain, this was all an exercise in futility. Patrols were conducted during the day; every attack in the past weeks had occurred during the night. Nevertheless, it gave the local supporters of Menelaus and his regime in this area the impression that their government was taking steps to ensure their safety, and that was the main goal.

The captain continued to look lazily toward the hills on either side of the road as he trotted forward until movement a hundred meters ahead of him on the road caught his eye. A man appeared to be alternately dragging and stopping to strike a second person. The captain and his lieutenant dug their heels into their horses' sides and sped ahead to intervene, leaving their cohort behind to catch up on foot. They quickly closed the distance, jumped off their mounts, and pulled the first person off the second. The victim was revealed to be a young woman. Even beneath the dirt and tears that stained her face, the captain could see she was uncommonly beautiful.

The captain turned to the man, who was evidently twenty or more years her senior, and buried his fist in his stomach.

"No, don't hurt him!" she cried out. "He's my father!"

"Your father?" the captain asked incredulously. "He looked like he was trying to kill you."

"I loved a Syrian man, a soldier like yourself," she explained. "My father brought me here to do as the Torah requires. I'm grateful to you for saving my life. Take me away from here," she pleaded, "but let him live."

He smiled down at her and offered his hand to help her up. She returned his smile with a new sparkle in her eyes and reached upward with her left hand. He allowed himself to continue to gaze into her eyes as he took her hand and lifted her up, not noticing the dagger she had drawn from a fold in her garment until she plunged it beneath his leather armor deep into his thigh, opening his femoral artery.

The older man pulled out a dagger from his own cloak. The lieutenant was still staring at his captain, grasping his thigh and bleeding out on the sandy road, when Mattathias plunged the blade into his throat, twisted it, and withdrew it again. The lieutenant's eyes grew wide with shock as he grasped at the hole, his gasping breaths making the blood bubble as it poured out of the wound.

The foot soldiers broke into a sprint to run to their fallen commander's aid. By the time they noticed the four dozen men bearing down upon them from the north and south slopes flanking the road, it was impossible for them to fall into a defensible formation or to escape. Judah, Johanan, and their men quickly dispatched the leaderless cohort, landing most of their blows to their exposed limbs and throats.

Mattathias lifted Johanan's wife from the ground, gently brushed the dust from her face, and ran his hand over her disheveled hair.

"You, too, are a brave warrior, my daughter," he said proudly.

He strode back down the road toward Judah. The men had already begun stripping the leather armor and helmets from the fallen soldiers, carefully removing areas of excessive blood with cloths dampened with water from their flasks.

"Find some armor for yourselves and make sure it's a good fit," Mattathias ordered. "We need to look like proper soldiers. And somebody round up those two horses."

Eupolemus was walking down the northern slope.

"Find yourself some armor, Senator," Mattathias said. "The lieutenant was about your size."

Judah walked with Eupolemus to the corpse, spared the senator the unpleasantness of taking off and cleaning the armor himself, and helped him strap it on properly.

"Perhaps once you try this on you'll want to start going on raids with us," Judah prodded good-naturedly.

"We all have our contributions to make to this cause, Judah," Eupolemus replied, clearly uneasy about doing what he was called upon to do on this day. "I'll leave the manic warfare to you."

Mattathias and Johanan assembled twenty of the men for whom there was no armor. They tied a rope around the left wrist of each one, and then another around the right wrist. Judah came up to a few of them and made some superficial lacerations on their cheeks and arms.

"Sorry, but you all did draw the short straws."

"All right, then," Mattathias shouted. "Let's form up!"

The twenty men in armor took their places in two columns with a dozen of their "prisoners" marching in a single row between them. The latter marched holding their wrists crossed in front of them, completing the appearance of being bound. The remaining eight prisoners held with both hands onto two ropes trailing from the two horses, also giving the impression of being securely tied. The soldiers for whom there was no further role in the unfolding drama remained behind, carrying the corpses out of sight of the road, depositing them just over the top of the north ridge.

Within an hour, Mattathias and his cohort emerged from the ravine-protected road into the open approach to Upper Beth Horon. It took some time for them to grow comfortable marching out in plain view, but as the farmers whom they passed paid no attention to them—or looked sympathetically at their prisoners—they began to trust their disguise and Eupolemus's idea. "Sort of a local adaptation of the Trojan Horse," he had tried to explain to freedom fighters who had never read Homer.

They came within thirty meters of the city's gate, which was open but heavily guarded—another consequence of the heightened security.

"Thank the gods!" shouted a sentry in mock acclaim. "The roads are safe again thanks to our patrols from Jerusalem! It's during the night that we need you," he chided, "not broad daylight!"

"And we don't need your gibes by day or night," Eupolemus answered in

Greek, trying to sound as gruff as he could. "The commander tells us to go, and we go. Does he ask us for our advice about when or where? And a good thing for you, since we were able to catch this lot planning mischief from a camp not three kilometers east of here. So now you can stand there happily scratching yourself all day in safety."

"All right, all right. What watchword did the commander give you?"

"'Your mother is a wildcat in bed,'" Eupolemus continued in perfect Greek. "Now get your girls here out of our way. Some of my men are hurt."

The sentry responded in kind, but followed it with a hearty laugh and yelled an order to the men standing below, who parted before Mattathias and his cohort as they entered the city.

"Where's your commander?" Eupolemus asked from inside the gate. "We need to billet these prisoners and have our wounded attended to."

"Wait here for him." The sentry nodded to one of the guards at the gate, who ran along the base of the wall and up a flight of stairs to the south entrance of the garrison's headquarters, a kind of miniature of the Akra in Jerusalem. Within minutes a more decorated officer emerged from the north side followed by a dozen soldiers.

"Welcome to Beth Horon," he said curtly. "I'll take possession of your prisoners here. Your wounded can go to our camp surgeon inside the garrison there."

Mattathias's cohort began to break ranks slightly to position themselves more effectively as the commander's soldiers began grabbing the prisoners by their upper arms and leading them toward the garrison.

"Now!" shouted Mattathias.

The "prisoners" drew their daggers from folds in their robes while Mattathias and his soldiers unsheathed their swords. All began to strike down their nearest targets. The captain of the watch drew his sword and shouted orders mixed with obscenities to the guards by the gate, who were, however, already set upon by Judah and his men stationed toward the rear of the file. Civilians scattered from the area and a handful of soldiers came running down the main street, though there were few comrades left alive for them to help by the time they arrived. One cut deep into Mattathias's thigh as he was turned to engage another soldier attacking from his horse's opposite flank, but Eupolemus brought his own sword down upon the Syrian's forearm, detaching it from his body before he could land a second blow on their leader. Mattathias pressed his hand down hard against the wound and charged toward the garrison, his men following close behind. They ran inside, dispatching the few soldiers who were left and searching for the armory. When they found the weapons cache, they slung as many shields and scabbarded swords over their shoulders as they could carry and tucked knives and other weapons into their belts.

Mattathias remained outside on his horse, shouting to the people of the city.

"Who is loyal to the covenant and to God? Who will fight on the Lord's side? Come with us!"

Mattathias's men emerged from the garrison and began to throw down into the street the weapons they would not be able to carry back with them to their camp in the hills beyond Gophna. The Jewish residents began to return to the site of the skirmish.

"Israel!" Mattathias continued. "The Gentiles have made war on the covenant; the wicked among us have made a covenant with the uncircumcised and sold themselves to do evil. Rise up, and you will see God's deliverance!"

First one man, then another, then another stepped forward and, not taking their eyes off Mattathias as if drawing their very will to move from his zeal, reached down to pick up a sword.

Miryam staggered forward from the herd of prisoners into the middle of the courtyard. She stood silently, looking at what remained of her three sons. She moved hesitantly toward Ari, reaching up with her shackled hands to caress his face. Her fingers made contact with his cheek and, all at once, she collapsed to the ground and released the wail that had been building within her since the first strike of the lash fell upon Binyamin, the cry she had stifled so long in order to be strong for them.

"I don't suppose there's much point trying to get you to eat some of the meat," Antiochus said. "As if you'd much care to live now anyway."

He watched her as she knelt in a heap in the midst of her sons' bodies.

"You could have saved them, you know," he chided.

Miryam drew in a sharp breath and seemed to regain her composure. "I did," she replied quietly, as if in a dream.

He dismissed her with a wave of his hand. "Go. You've suffered enough."

Miryam gathered her strength and rose to her feet. She lifted her head, her eyes piercing Antiochus. "No, Your Highness," she said with defiance. "You've suffered enough—enough defeats for one visit, at least. First an old man, then my beautiful boys. It would be even more embarrassing for you to be bested now by a woman."

Antiochus's eyes narrowed as he tilted back his head in anger at the challenge. "I'll attribute that to your grief speaking. Get out of here before I change my mind."

"So I, a frail woman, can make you change your mind, when you've been unable to make any of these men change theirs? You are as weak as you are wicked."

As the two soldiers who had killed her sons moved in on her, anticipating Antiochus's order, she rounded upon them with a ferocity and a fury that stopped them dead in their tracks.

"You—more animal than human, ripping at my sons like the beasts you are! You will not lay your filthy paws on me."

She turned and ran across the courtyard and up the ramp to the top of the great altar. The soldiers recovered themselves and ran after her but stopped at the bottom of the ramp as she positioned herself by the fire.

"I've bested you three times already today, Highness," she spat. "Three times you tore out my heart and my bowels, but not once did I cry out. Not once did I do anything that might have weakened my boys' resolve. Now they live with God, and you will never come near them to touch them again."

Miryam turned away from Antiochus and looked across the flames. On the other side, she saw Meir and Ariyeh standing on either side of Binyamin, his arms around their shoulders. Behind them she saw Zerah, smiling at her with pride at how his sons had turned out under her nurture. She did not notice the soldiers creeping up slowly behind her, but they did not matter anymore. She stepped forward to embrace her family with open arms.

The soldiers watched in amazement as she walked away from them straight into the fire. Immediately her clothes and hair burst into flame. She took another two full steps before collapsing in the center of the great altar. The pair of guards turned down the ramp to the courtyard. The captain looked to the king for his selection of the next prisoner, but Antiochus was still watching the flames above the altar.

The captain walked over to the group of prisoners and began to look for someone showing signs of weakness. Seeing the captain surveying the lot, one man stood up, looking defiantly at the captain. He began to sing. "Sh'ma, Yisrael, Adonai Elohenu, Adonai echad."

Before he had finished, another began to sing and stood up as well. A man with only one hand rose to join them as they repeated the chant, then an older woman. Within a minute, the entire group was on their feet, singing at the tops of their voices.

"That's what the young man was screaming," Antiochus observed. "What does it mean?"

"Majesty," Alcimus explained, "it is from the book of the covenant. *'Listen, Israel: The Lord is our God; the Lord alone.'*"

"Damn!" Antiochus exclaimed as he closed his eyes and shook his head.

The captain looked at the king for instructions. Antiochus waved his hand horizontally.

"Kill them all!" he shouted in exasperation above the chorus of prisoners. "Just kill them and be done with it!"

The captain signaled to the squad surrounding the prisoners. Drawing their swords, they began plunging them into the prisoners, who never stopped singing their creed to object or even to scream. When their voices had been silenced, Antiochus rose from his chair and walked into the courtyard, inspecting the bodies. In his mind, he had seen most if not all of these Jews alive and integrated again into the population of the city—perhaps a handful of fanatics, but not every last one. Then he realized that he still heard their song. He listened more closely.

"Sh'ma Yisrael, Adonai Elohenu, Adonai echad."

The sound was coming from several different directions—the outer court, the lower city to the south. *So it has not been silenced, after all.*

Menelaus rose from his place upon the dais. "Thus shall all who resist the king's decrees be punished!"

He had meant it to sound like an impressive declaration, signaling their adjournment, but to Antiochus's ears, the words rang embarrassingly hollow.

9

Johanan ran to the lean-to where Mattathias lay resting, surrounded by his other sons.

"Father," he said softly.

"Hm?" grunted Mattathias as he opened his eyes and took a second to focus. "What is it, Johanan?"

"A group of men are approaching from the west. There's a long trail of them, I'd guess over a hundred."

"Soldiers?" Mattathias asked, propping himself up into a seated position.

"They appear to be our countrymen. Some of them are dressed all in white."

Mattathias smiled through his discomfort. "They might be our countrymen indeed. Send out a scout to be sure; tell the men to be ready just in case the Syrians are trying our trick."

"Already done, Father."

Mattathias smiled in approval, allowed himself to recline once more, closed his eyes, and nodded off. He was jolted awake again by his son's voice and opened his eyes to see a gaunt man, dressed all in white, his tanned, sundried face peering at him as he knelt beside his mat.

"Zedekiah?"

"Yes, Mattathias. I am sorry to find you in distress."

Zedekiah placed a hand ever so gently on the blood-stained cloths wrapped around Mattathias's thigh. He became absent for a moment and appeared to pray, then opened his eyes again somewhat more sadly.

Mattathias looked at the man kneeling next to Zedekiah.

"Yoshe! I'm so glad to see you alive!"

"I made it, Mattathias," he replied soberly, "but so many good men and women didn't. Joram—"

"I know," Mattathias broke in. "Other survivors have found their way here." He reached out his hand and clasped Yoshe's arm. "God spared you. He spared you for us. You bear no blame."

Yoshe nodded his appreciation, though his face betrayed his uncertainty as to his guilt for outliving so many who had followed him, trusted him.

Zedekiah looked thoughtful. "God honors your piety in regard to the holiness of the Sabbath, Yoshe, and your fallen friends now shine with his reflected glory in the heavens. But if we persist in this, the enemy will surely stamp us out."

He looked up as if pronouncing the decree he heard the Lord speaking in his ear. "Let us not attack on the Sabbath, but if we are shamelessly attacked on our holy day we must defend ourselves to preserve God's army."

Jonathan watched Zedekiah keenly. *This man could be of great use.*

Zedekiah turned his attention back to Mattathias with a suddenly rekindled fervor.

"And God is raising a holy army, Mattathias," he said. "Look—I have brought the division that God has gathered around me. More will come from the city that has suffered abominable things, *abominable* things. God has shown me."

Zedekiah sat more erect and addressed himself also to Mattathias's sons.

"You are the family," he pronounced, "through whom God is giving deliverance to Israel."

A chill ran through Jonathan's body, and he could sense that it had run also through everyone that stood within earshot of their strange guest. He looked at the freedom fighters standing suddenly more erect, their chins slightly higher, their eyes instantly more confident. *Of great use indeed.*

Yoshe rose, walked over to Judah, and led him a few paces away from Mattathias. "What happened?"

"A sword blow during our attack on Beth Horon," Judah explained. "The cut was deep, and he lost a great deal of blood before we could cauterize the wound. Beginning this morning, a fever took hold."

"Will he be all right?"

"Am I a soldier? How many wounds like this do you think I've seen?" Judah took a breath, then proceeded more calmly. "I don't know. Helah, a woman from Modein, has been packing the wound with herbs and brewing something for the fever. We can only wait and pray."

Yoshe nodded sympathetically and placed his hand on Judah's shoulder. "They don't come tougher than your father," he said reassuringly. "He'll pull through."

Jonathan appeared beside Judah, leading Johanan and Simon behind him.

"Zedekiah," he said simply. "Grandson of the brother of Simon the Just, cousin of Honiah." He paused. "Next in line as rightful high priest?"

Judah, Yoshe, and the others looked at him quizzically, as if waiting for the punch line.

"Bind his cause more firmly to our own?" he added, his tone seasoned with a slight impatience for his brother's lack of political instinct.

Johanan was the first to begin to nod in agreement.

Jonathan and his brothers returned to their father's lean-to.

"Father, Zedekiah has pronounced our family to be entrusted with a great calling from God, but he, too, comes from a family with a great calling. Ought we not to commit to him, as he has committed himself to us?"

Mattathias processed what his son was saying, then smiled and nodded.

"Brother Zedekiah, scion of the house of Simon the Just," Jonathan began, "when God has allowed us to take vengeance on the usurper Menelaus, that priest of abominations, you will take your place as high priest in Jerusalem. We will restore God's Temple and God's order with a pious Zadokite from the house of Honiah."

"As it pleases the One," Zedekiah responded, certain that it would.

Antiochus had retired abruptly from the Temple to the guest wing in the high priestly palace and did not emerge again until the next afternoon. Menelaus had been growing increasingly anxious with each passing hour, wondering how Antiochus was processing what he had witnessed in the Temple. He had decided to conduct all business that day from his office in the palace so that he could be informed quickly when the king entered the public spaces again. He found the king in the main atrium, speaking with Memnon.

"Have my two cohorts ready to leave for Antioch at first light. We'll take the seacoast route."

"Good afternoon, Highness," Menelaus said as he bowed deeply. "I did not anticipate that you would have been so worn out from having made such a marvelous example of those pig-headed, disobedient Jews yesterday."

His remark drew a look of disdain from Antiochus for his appointee's lack of perception. "An example indeed," the king replied. "I have given them a chance to show the rest of your people how to die for their sacred laws. Yesterday was no victory, Menelaus," he sneered. "*We* were beaten out there, not those dead Judeans."

Antiochus released a deep breath to regain his composure. "This was the birth of revolution," he continued. "If they're willing to die like that here with no hope of escape, what kind of bravery do you suppose they will show when they meet you in the field with swords and spears in their hands?"

Menelaus moved more directly into damage-control mode. "After yesterday's spectacle, Majesty, who would dare resist your decrees?"

Antiochus could not decide if Menelaus was really that stupid or just thought his king was. "An old man, three brothers, and a woman dared to resist yesterday for everyone to see. There's really nothing that I can do to a human being that is worse than what I did yesterday, and still they resisted without a second thought."

Antiochus closed his eyes as if remembering something new. "And they're your decrees, Menelaus, not mine. This was *your* strategy for eliminating resistance in Jerusalem, and it has failed miserably. How could you have underestimated your own people's attachment to their traditions so completely? You all but forced my hand here, and the results have been a political disaster."

An officer entered the atrium and stood at attention near Antiochus, waiting to be acknowledged.

"Yes, what is it?"

"Majesty, there are reports of rebel activity to the north of Jerusalem. There was an attack on a patrol on the road to Beth Horon yesterday. Shortly afterward, the garrison at Upper Beth Horon was destroyed. This all followed close on the heels of a nighttime attack on Elasa and its neighboring villages, with our soldiers and local supporters there slaughtered."

Antiochus wheeled on Menelaus.

"This is what I'm talking about! My possession of Judea has become decidedly less secure under your administration—if it deserves to be called 'administration'—than under Jason, who seemed to know your people far better."

He turned back to the officer. "We'll need to nip this in the bud. Recall Apollonios with as large a force as he can spare from Samaria. Have him bring his force to Jerusalem as a base of operations for fortifying our outlying garrisons and rooting out the trouble in the north."

"Yes, Majesty," the officer said with a sharp nod before striding off to carry out his orders.

"Every drachm I spend on this is coming out of your purse, Menelaus."

"Of course, Highness. With Apollonios's help, we will quickly restore stability to this region."

"See that you do," Antiochus said as he moved back toward the guest wing. "If matters continue to deteriorate, I will hold you personally responsible."

Antiochus stopped and turned to face Menelaus once again to drive his point home. "You've seen how determined I can be."

The day after Zedekiah's arrival at Mattathias's camp in the hills north of Gophna, the scouts reported a large number of men, women, and children moving toward them from the south. Judah took a dozen men to investigate firsthand.

"As Zedekiah predicted," Jonathan said to Yoshe as Judah escorted the refugees into the camp.

"This is Asher ben Moshe," Judah said.

"Asher!" Yoshe declared as he stepped forward to clasp the priest's forearm. "I am glad to see you well."

"Well enough, Yoshe, compared to many in my company who have been hiding in the hills outside Jerusalem for weeks without provisions or a plan. I shouldn't doubt that many more refugees will be coming in the days ahead."

"How is it in Jerusalem?" Judah inquired.

Asher's eyes betrayed the sorrow of a man who had seen the unthinkable. "Antiochus and his false priest have ravaged the faithful. I have never seen such cruelty—nor such courage."

The people in the camp, many of whom had left relations and friends in the city, began to gather in greater numbers around the newcomers. Asher paused to collect himself and looked straight into Judah's eyes.

"I watched Eleazar, a pillar for the faithful, and the family of Zerah torn to pieces and burned to the bones in the heart of the Temple. But they remained loyal to God to the end. No soldier on a battlefield ever endured so much. Dozens more were slaughtered before the tyrant was through."

Judah's heart jumped to his throat at the mention of the victims. "The family of Zerah? All of them?"

"Three brothers and Zerah's widow," Asher confirmed.

Judah closed his eyes in grief at their fate, especially to think of Ari dying in such a way. He remembered the story of the three young men in Nebuchadnezzar's furnace, reciting a part of it as an epitaph. "'They disobeyed the king's command and yielded up their bodies rather than serve and worship any god except their own God.'"

"The men who are with me are also willing to yield up their bodies in God's service," Asher said, his eyes confirming his determination, "but will do so on the battlefield under your command."

Judah nodded soberly. "God is raising up a holy army," he said almost to himself, remembering Zedekiah's words.

Boaz was too far away from the center of things to hear Asher's report, but he was also more interested at the moment in the presence of a particular woman among the refugees toward the edge of the group. When she perceived him moving closer to her, she turned her face away.

"I know this woman," Boaz said. "She's a Syrian. Are you here to spy on us?"

A number of men from the camp moved threateningly toward her. Eupolemus moved quickly to the spot and held up his hands toward the freedom fighters to prevent any precipitous action.

"Who are you?" he asked.

"I am the wife—no, I am the widow of Meir ben Zerah. I watched Antiochus have Syrians butcher him along with his brothers and their mother. My mother."

She stood her ground bravely in the midst of the freedom fighters who had encircled her.

"What I was, I can't be any longer. I want to join myself to my husband's people."

Ari's death song and the chant taken up by the victims in the Temple had continued to play in her head during the two days of her journey from the city. *"Adonai Elohenu, Adonai echad!"* she declared, as if adding her voice to theirs.

Shoshanna stepped through the circle of men and put her hand on Tavitha's arm. "She is my sister," she said. Shoshanna looked at Tavitha. "Binyamin?"

Tavitha shook her head sadly from side to side as Shoshanna's eyes and lips closed tightly in grief. Now Tavitha put her hand on her sister's arm to comfort her, and Shoshanna led her away from the crowd toward the makeshift tent that had been her home since she had fled Modein along with her parents.

Avaran jogged up to Judah as he escorted Asher and his entourage to an area where they could begin to set up their camp as best they could.

"Judah, you'd better come with me. It's Father."

Johanan, Simon, and Jonathan were already sitting beside their father's mat, with Yoshe and Eupolemus standing just behind them. Judah looked inquiringly at Helah, who sat behind Mattathias, dipping a cloth in water and holding it to his forehead. She simply shook her head.

"Arrogance!" Mattathias said suddenly, as if shouting at something that had happened in a dream. "Contempt for God! Everywhere . . . Powerful . . ." His voice trailed off.

Judah and Avaran took their place beside their brothers.

Mattathias moaned slightly as he struggled toward consciousness. He opened his eyes and became aware of familiar presences around him. "I'm dying," he said. "I wish it had been sooner. I've seen too much already."

"No, Father," Jonathan objected. "You have to fight."

"No," he replied. "*You* have to fight. You have to *win!*"

He gathered his strength and pushed himself up on his left arm as best he could. Simon shifted his body over, never leaving his sitting position, so that Mattathias could lean against his folded legs.

"Johanan," he said, reaching out his right hand.

His eldest son clasped it. "Here, Father."

"You are my firstborn, and you will be the head over our family, but Judah shall lead our fighters into battle. He will be your general."

Mattathias released Johanan's hand and took each of his sons' hands in turn. "May God make you all strong for the years ahead. Pay back the Gentiles in full for what they did to God's city and God's people. Drive the ungodly from the land. Restore the covenant."

He sank back into Simon's lap, and Simon lowered him gently back down onto his mat. He continued to speak, but his words became softer and slurred. Occasionally a phrase from a psalm came through clearly enough.

Judah placed the back of his hand on his father's cheek. It felt like a smooth stone hot from the midday sun. He then cupped his father's cheek lovingly in his palm.

"Rest, Father. The battle belongs to God."

Judah and his brothers spent the following day in mourning for their father after laying his body in a small cave and covering the entrance with rocks. When circumstances allowed, they agreed that they would move his bones to their family tomb in Modein.

Toward the evening, a pair of scouts rode into the camp from the north and told them of Syrian troop movements in Samaria. Apollonios had amassed an army of at least two thousand men and had already begun the journey southward. Judah reasoned that their goal would be to reach Jerusalem to put a stranglehold on the city and the villages around it while searching out the rebels' camps. They could not allow the army to reach Jerusalem, so now they sat perched just over the north and south ridges of the Wadi Haramiah, a narrow east-west ravine through which Apollonios's great army could pass no more than four abreast. Their clothes were still damp from the dew that had settled on them during the night as they took their positions and waited for the enemy to break camp and continue their march.

Judah considered the "army" that God had raised so far. He had mobilized perhaps five hundred men from the camp the previous night, mostly farmers, artisans, people who had never been trained to fight, let alone ever won a battle. He had stationed twenty experienced fighters with each group of a hundred new recruits. Some of the men to the rear would have to wait for the men to the front to kill enemy soldiers before they would even have swords to use themselves. They would learn soon enough if God would indeed fight for them.

A single scout ran along the south side of the crest of the southern ravine toward Judah, out of sight from the ravine below. "They're coming, Judah. Not two kilometers behind me."

Judah sent the scout further east to alert Avaran, who was charged with putting the stopper in the bottleneck. He continued to watch to the west as the column of soldiers began to appear, flowing like a rivulet into the ravine. The stream spilled past Judah's position and continued its eastward flow toward Avaran's. The soldiers marched as Judah had imagined, four abreast, each row keeping about two meters distant from the row in front of it. Over two hundred soldiers had passed by his position before he saw his target—two men on horse-back, riding side-by-side. Judah peered over the top of the ravine, still hidden from view from below by a rocky outcropping, and signaled to Yoshe on the crest across from him. When the men on horseback were at the center of the trap, Judah sprang it.

Judah led over a hundred fighters down the southern slope into the ravine while Yoshe led a similar number down the northern slope. Apollonios tried to call his men into a defensive position around him, but they were spread too thinly along the length of the ravine. Judah and Yoshe smashed into their battle line, their two hundred fighters quickly dispatching the hundred or so soldiers in that stretch. Apollonios's horse reared in the commotion and threw its rider to the ground. Hanan planted his sword squarely through his chest. Apollonios's lieutenant managed to land a few blows before he, too, was dragged from his horse and killed.

As soon as the sounds of battle reached him, Avaran led his men into the ravine east of the confused army and began to crush the head of the serpent, working his way back toward Judah and Yoshe through the thin ranks of Syrians. The soldiers retreated toward each other, limiting their ability either to swing or to dodge blows. Others continued to advance from the west, pushing the embattled ranks closer together. Finally Simeon and Johanan led their companies down into the ravine half a kilometer west of Judah and Yoshe. Again, the thin line of soldiers, now leaderless and confused, was quickly cut down.

"Keep the upper ground!" Judah and Yoshe yelled as their companies continued to spill east- and westward over the surviving column of soldiers, consuming them like fire burning through paper.

Syrians began to flee westward by the dozen, but with no leader to help them regroup they were easily slaughtered from the rear as Simeon and Johanan gave pursuit. Finally Judah signaled for a ram's horn to sound, and the freedom fighters broke off their pursuit, yelling and breaking out in psalms of victory. They gathered in the ravine and began the task of stripping the fallen Syrian soldiers of their armor and weapons. Among the carnage, they counted only fifty of their own dead alongside more than a thousand of the enemy.

"We cannot afford to lose so many in each encounter," Judah observed soberly.

"We lost this many today, but not next time," Yoshe assured him. "Today most of our fighters had neither armor, nor weapons, nor training. That will never be true again."

Yoshe placed his hand confidently on Judah's shoulder. "Now encourage your men. The Lord has given us a great victory today!"

Judah nodded in agreement. As he walked along the ravine, he began to be cheered by the spirits of his fighters. He clasped hands with many, complimenting them by name for their courage, clapping them on their backs as they bent over to equip themselves with the armor of the enemy. He came at last to the body of Apollonios. He took the general's sword from his hand and examined it. *No blood. He didn't get off a single blow.* Judah felt its balance and examined its edges as Zedekiah walked toward him from the crest of the southern slope.

"God's anger has once again turned to mercy, Judah," he said. "God is reconciled to his people."

Judah thought of Ari and his family, of Eleazar, and of the many others who had sacrificed their lives on the altar of covenant loyalty. Perhaps such acts of extreme devotion tipped the scales that had been so weighted down with the nation's affronts to God. Whatever the case, Judah was certain that this victory was theirs as much as it was his—and, if so, then it was indeed God's.

"Not to us, Lord, not to us," he began to chant, "but to you belongs the honor, because of your unfailing love and your faithfulness."

His soldiers momentarily stopped what they were doing, then took up the psalm as they continued gathering resources from the fallen.

"Why should the nations be allowed to say, 'Where's their God now?'"

Judah began to walk with Zedekiah back up the southern slope. "Antiochus will send more soldiers," he said.

"So will God," Zedekiah replied simply. "You will always have enough men with you to fight, and few enough with you never to doubt that God is winning your battles."

Judah raised an eyebrow and nodded to acknowledge the aptness of Zedekiah's comment, sheathing Apollonius's sword in his own belt.

"God will smash the Gentiles who have colonized our land as one smashes a clay pot. And you," Zedekiah said, stopping to look squarely into Judah's eyes, "you will be the hammer in God's hand."

ACKNOWLEDGMENTS

I moved toward telling this story through a series of academic books and projects on the Apocrypha in general and on 4 Maccabees, one of the few ancient literary sources for this story, in particular. I am deeply grateful, therefore, to the directors and editors of Kregel Publications for allowing me the opportunity to make this ancient story come alive in the form of my first historical novel. Jim Weaver originally embraced the project with enthusiasm; Dennis Hillman inherited it and continued to give it his full support; and Steve Barclift shepherded the project with a gentle and kind hand. Dawn Anderson holds a special lien on my gratitude for her astute editing and wise counsel.

The Jewish sage ben Sira wrote that the work of the scribe—in many ways the ancient equivalent of the tenured professor—"depends on the opportunity of leisure" to study, reflect, and create (Sir 38:24). While "much study" is also its own form of wearisome labor (Eccl. 12:12), it does depend upon the great freedom that an academic appointment affords for research and writing. It is my pleasure and duty, therefore, in this as in my many more academic books, to express my deep appreciation to the trustees, administration, and faculty colleagues of Ashland Theological Seminary who have now supported and encouraged me in this ministry of writing for two decades (1995–2015).

LIST·OF·CHARACTERS

Names of people known from the ancient sources appear in **boldface**.

Agathon, a close friend and supporter of Jason.

Alcimus, born Eliakim, a moderate priest.

Amnon ben Imlah, a priest loyal to the covenant.

Antigonos, commander of the mercenary armies of Hyrcanus ben Joseph.

Antiochus III Megas ("the Great"), king of Seleucid Empire from 222–187 BCE, father of Seleucus IV and Antiochus IV.

Antiochus IV Epiphanes, king of Seleucid Empire from 175-164 BCE, son of Antiochus III and younger brother of Seleucus IV.

Apelles, a tutor in the gymnasium in Jerusalem.

Apollodoros, citizen of Antioch, friend of Philostratos, potential investor in Jason's Jerusalem.

Apollonios, a senior military advisor and general in Antiochus IV's court.

Ariston, a Jewish resident of Jerusalem and comrade of Meir from the gymnasium.

Ariyeh, "Ari" to his friends, the youngest son of Zerah and Miryam and brother of Binyamin and Meir.

Asher ben Moshe, a priest loyal to the covenant.

Avaran ben Mattathias, fourth son of Mattathias (more commonly known as Eliezer in the historical sources).

Bacchides, a general under Antiochus IV.

Binyamin, the eldest son of Zerah and Miryam, older brother of Meir and Ariyeh.

Boaz, a neighborhood friend of Ari and fellow revolutionary.

Castor, a slave, steward of Jason's household.

Dionysios, a citizen of Antioch, friend of Philostratos, potential investor in Jason's Jerusalem.

Elam ben Jacob, a conservative member of the Jerusalem senate.

Eleazar, an older priest and scribe, devoted to the covenant.

Eliashiv ben Joab, husband of Helah and father of Shoshanna, resident of Modein.

Epaphroditos, protégé of Philostratos.

Ephraim, leader of a desert sect, the "sons of Enoch."

Eupolemus ben Johanan, a member of the Jewish senate, loyal to the covenant.

Hanan, a Levite and Temple guard loyal to the covenant.

Hannah, Eleazar's wife.

Helah, wife of Eliashiv ben Joab and mother of Shoshanna, resident of Modein.

Heliodoros, minister of finance first to Seleucus IV, then to Antiochus IV.

Heracleitos, citizen of Antioch, friend of Philostratos, potential investor in Jason's Jerusalem.

Herakleon, minister of foreign affairs in Antiochus IV's court.

Honi, the nickname of **Honiah IV**, son of the high priest Honiah III.

Honiah III, a Zadokite priest, the older son of the high priest Simon II (see Sirach 50:1-21) and high priest after him.

Hyrcanus ben Yoseph ben Tobiah, the youngest son of Joseph, alienated from his brothers due to his own political ambitions and maneuvering.

Jason, born Yeshua, a Zadokite priest, the younger son of the high priest Simon II (see Sirach 50:1–21), supplanter of his older brother, Honiah III, and high priest himself from 175–172 BCE.

Johanan ben Mattathias, oldest son of Mattathias.

Jonathan ben Mattathias, youngest son of Mattathias.

Joram ben Levi, a conservative Levite and a leader of the revolutionary movement.

Judah ben Mattathias, third son of Mattathias and eventual leader of the Maccabean Revolt.

Mattathias ben Johanan, a pious priest from Modein and father of the five brothers who become the leaders of the Maccabean Revolt.

Meir (or Hilaron), the middle son of Zerah and Miryam, younger brother of Binyamin and older brother of Ariyeh.

Memnon, commander of a Syrian cohort stationed in Jerusalem.

Menelaus, born Menachem ben Iddo, supplanter of Jason, high priest from 172–163 BCE.

Menes, a slave, steward of Agathon's household.

Miryam, widow of Zerah and mother of Binyamin, Meir, and Ariyeh.

Nicanor, a general under Antiochus IV.

Niobe, a slave, Jason's personal attendant.

Parosh, a Levite and Temple guard loyal to the covenant.

Philip, temporarily the commander of the Akra under Menelaus.

Philodemos, minister of internal security in Antiochus IV's court.

Philon, a Jewish citizen of Antioch, friend of Philostratos, potential investor in Jason's Jerusalem.

Philostratos, minister of education and culture in Antiochus IV's court, principal of the gymnasium in Antioch.

Pompilius Laenas, a Roman senator and envoy, a friend of Antiochus IV.

Ptolemy VI Philometor, king of Ptolemaic Empire, based in Egypt, from 180–145 BCE.

Rivkeh, wife of Honiah III.

Salmon ben Azariah, a priest loyal to the covenant.

Sarpedon, commander of a Syrian cohort stationed in Jerusalem.

Seleucus IV Philopator, king of Seleucid Empire from 187–175 BCE, son of Antiochus III and older brother of Antiochus IV.

Seraiah ben Joseph ben Tobiah, an older son of Joseph, heir of the bulk of his father's fortunes and estates.

Shoshanna, wife of Binyamin and daughter of Eliashiv and Helah of Modein.

Simon ben Mattathias, second son of Mattathias.

Simon ben Iddo, brother of Menelaus, an advisor in Antiochus IV's court.

Tavitha (professionally known as Persephone), an orphaned daughter of Syrian immigrants to Jerusalem.

Telamon, a Syrian resident of Jerusalem and comrade of Meir from the gymnasium.

Timarchos ben Yoab, a priest, a friend and supporter of Menelaus.

Yair, a neighborhood friend of Ari and fellow revolutionary.

Yehoshua ben Sira, a scribe and teacher in Jerusalem bent on nurturing loyalty to the covenant, active from about 200–175 BCE.

Yoseph ben Tobiah, the former chief deputy over Judea under the Ptolemies and arguably the richest man in Palestine.

Yoshe ben Yoezer, a priest and leader of the revolutionary Hasidim, also uncle to Alcimus.

Zedekiah, a Zadokite priest, grand-nephew of the high priest Simon II and close
  relative of Honiah and Jason.

Zenon, a Greek, the director of the gymnasium in Jerusalem.

ABOUT·THE·AUTHOR

David deSilva became fascinated by the Apocrypha growing up in the Episcopal Church, where he occasionally heard "Old Testament" lessons read from books that were not in his Bible. So at the age of fourteen, he checked a copy of the Apocrypha out of the church library and began to read it. Decades later, his interest in this literature and the period that spawned it is undiminished. David is ordained an elder in the Florida Conference of the United Methodist Church and serves as Trustees' Distinguished Professor of New Testament and Greek at Ashland Theological Seminary in Ashland, Ohio. He is the author of several introductory books on the Apocrypha, the New Testament, and the Greco-Roman environment; commentaries on 4 Maccabees, Galatians, Hebrews, and Jude; and specialized studies on Hebrews and Revelation. He participated in the revision of the Apocrypha for the English Standard Version and oversaw the translation of the Apocrypha for the Common English Bible. He resides in Punta Gorda, Florida, with his wife, Donna Jean, and his three sons—to whom, when they were much younger, he would tell the tales of Tobit, Judith, and the Maccabean heroes at bedtime.